P9-DEP-510

THE
MAN
WHO
LOVED
Mata Hari

Other Novels by Dan Sherman

THE MOLE
RIDDLE
SWANN
KING JAGUAR
DYNASTY OF SPIES
THE WHITE MANDARIN
THE PRINCE OF BERLIN

THE
MAN
WHO
LOVED

Mata Hari

by
DAN SHERMAN

DONALD I. FINE, INC.
New York

Copyright © 1985 by Dan Sherman

All rights reserved, including the right of reproduction in whole or in part in any form.
Published in the United States of America by Donald I. Fine, Inc. and in Canada by Fitzhenry
& Whiteside, Ltd.

Library of Congress Catalogue Card Number: 85-70276

ISBN: 0-917657-27-6
Manufactured in the United States of America
10 9 8 7 6 5 4 3 2 1

This book is printed on acid free paper. The paper in this book meets the guidelines for
permanence and durability of the Committee on Production Guidelines for Book Longevity of the
Council on Library Resources.

For Lorry and Charlotte

*If I did not tell you everything before, it
is only because I felt somewhat ashamed.*

. . . Mata Hari

PART I

The Early Years

Prologue

THOSE in search of the site where Mata Hari died are usually directed to the court-yard at Vincennes outside of Paris. Do not be deceived. The actual place of execution lies two miles south of the courtyard on what is now a parking lot. There is no monument, and the stake to which she was loosely tied has been removed. There are, however, several eyewitness accounts, and from these it is possible to reconstruct her final hour.

She died on the morning of October 15, 1917. The temperature was thirty-five degrees Fahrenheit, the landscape obscured by a river fog. When convening officers entered her cell she was reported to have cried, "But this is *impossible.*" Although there is no record of a reply, it is easy enough to imagine the numbed silence. . . .

She is permitted twenty minutes to prepare herself, but after a lifetime of flamboyant excess she can only sit on the cot while a guard selects her clothing. She will wear a pearl-gray dress, a straw hat and veil, blue coat, black gloves. (Her jewelry has been confiscated earlier.)

Descending the staircase to a waiting car, she holds the hand of a young nun, a Sister Leonide from one of the local convents. Journalists and spectators line the corridor between the compound and the prison gates. No one is certain who has alerted them.

The motorcade departs at half past five. The temperature has dropped another degree and the fog has still not lifted. En route, a Reverend Arboux from Saint-Lazare reads passages from the Bible until overcome with nausea. Except for an occasional delivery van the boulevards are deserted.

The field must have been an arbitrary choice. Locally known as the Polygone, it is generally used for cavalry maneuvers. The ground is uneven, tufted with high grass and clumps of thistles. The perimeter is ringed with trees, mostly beech and poplars.

Assuming that the fog is not too thick, she will probably see the soldiers as soon as the motorcade penetrates the wood. They are Zouaves, survivors of a regiment that was butchered at Verdun. All her life she has been attracted to men in uniform, and now there are twelve, waiting in two rows of six.

The motorcade stops at the rim of trees. Farther afield two ranks have been assembled from a cavalry unit, still another from the infantry. The journalists have also come, but for once they keep their distance, lingering under the poplars, speaking softly among themselves until she steps out of the car.

Now everyone performs as if the ritual has been rehearsed. Sister Leonide accompanies the prisoner to the stake, then withdraws. Reverend Arboux and four officers move slowly to the right. The sentence is read, and although Mata Hari refuses the blindfold, she accepts the last glass of rum (roughly the same portion allotted to soldiers before battle).

Traditionally, only one member of a firing squad is actually issued a bullet; the others are given blanks. On this day, however, all the cartridges are live.

She remains unmoving until the officer raises his sword, then shuts her eyes.

Prologue

There is a photograph of the execution. Obviously taken only minutes before the shots were fired, she appears as a dark silhouette against the surrounding vegetation. Also visible are the expressionless faces of soldiers, a few spectators, and a handful of journalists who would eventually become obsessed with the woman.

Over the months that followed, dozens of those who had known Mata Hari were contacted and interviewed by European journalists: former lovers, friends from the theater, servants, and casual acquaintances. Yet despite an intensive search, the one man who supposedly knew her better than all of them continued to remain a mystery. His name was Nicholas Gray and this, more or less, is his story. As, of course, it is hers.

About twenty-five years after the execution a rumor began to circulate that a particularly key participant in the Mata Hari affair was living in the monastery at Montserrat, a truly remarkable place. Founded by Benedictine Monks in the eighth century, it stands three thousand feet above the river Llobregat outside of Barcelona. Traditionally held to be the site of the Holy Grail, it is also, one would think, a rather perfect setting to meet the only man said to have loved Mata Hari till the end.

He has been described as a gaunt figure with white hair and pale eyes. Although he never took monastic vows, apparently he lived as if he had. His room was a low rectangular cell adjacent to the outer court. The furniture was crude. He was an accomplished painter; visitors often found him sitting at an easel by the window or wandering along the plateau with a sketchbook. It was said that he never tired of the landscape.

Gray first met Mata Hari in 1905, and then carried her photograph for years. A fairly well-known publicity shot, it shows her half naked, with studded breastplates and an Indian diadem. There are dozens of hothouse orchids at her feet, potted palms along the edge of the stage.

Of course he insisted that she was very beautiful, with particularly captivating eyes. Then, too, he maintained that she possessed a certain dark charm, a certain sensual innocence that always left men enchanted.

He said that he liked her best in the odd hours . . . exhausted in her dressing room, lounging backstage with friends. He said that they often discussed literature that she had never read, and art that she did not understand. He also said that she lied compulsively, never paid her debts, and slept with almost everyone. But that she was not a spy.

Gray's account of Mata Hari's death had an intensity that always left visitors unsettled. He claimed that there had never been a genuine investigation, only a scheme. He claimed that there had been no attempt to establish the truth, only a shoddy myth. Witnesses were silenced while the trial continued grinding on with an awful inevitability, and in the end they did not execute her for a crime—they murdered her for their own reasons.

Chapter One

HE first saw her in a photograph, a thin girl astride a bicycle. One hand rested on a bare thigh, the other seemed poised above her breasts. Her hair and eyes were very dark, the lips slightly parted. All this had been in the spring of 1904, in a Paris that we shall always remember.

The photograph had been taken by a Russian friend, a pale youth named Vadime de Massloff. Like Gray, he had originally entered this city the year before, after failing to meet expectations at Oxford. By winter they were living across a narrow courtyard from one another, and often meeting for drinks in the evenings. Although a gifted photographer, de Massloff often found himself photographing nudes to pay the rent . . . hence this obviously suggestive portrait of the young Mata Hari.

In retrospect these days would always come back to Gray in terms of specific impressions: a subdued conversation in a cheap cafe, the skyline in blue light, the feel of a cane in a gloved hand. It had been a cold year, with a premature frost in October. Then came March with hard rain, then at long last April.

According to de Massloff, she first appeared in the last week of April, on a clear day filled with the scent of new blossoms. He had just returned from a midmorning break to find her seated on a low settee in the corner of his studio. She wore a black dress, brown shoes, and a beige coat.

There were theatrical props along the far wall, and at first he had her pose beside an Oriental vase. Next he had her kneel on a cushion with her arms laced across her breasts, her nipples faintly high-lighted with rouge. Finally he had her stand beside that bicycle, simply gazing into the camera.

When it was over she quickly put on her clothes, collected her money, and left by a side door. Although she had actually posed for seven photographs, only the one with the bicycle survived the darkroom.

The photograph lay on a sagging table in de Massloff's room. Gray had pulled it from a stack of twenty and tossed the others to the floorboards. Rain had been falling since five o'clock, and although they had both been drinking steadily they had not succeeded in getting drunk.

Gray's first impressions were casual, almost superficial. He might have been talking to himself. "I like this one. Who is she?"

De Massloff had been half dozing in a rattan chair, idly picking loose plaster from the wall. He generally never discussed his nudes. "Who?"

"The girl with the bicycle. Who is she?"

De Massloff shrugged. "Just a girl, Nicky."

"But I like her."

De Massloff slowly turned his head. The Mata Hari photograph had actually been one of a series, all involving bicycles. They even-tually ended up with a pornographer in Liverpool. "The composi-tion isn't right," he finally said.

"Really? I wouldn't have noticed."

"And there's no contrast."

"Yes, but she has marvelous eyes, don't you think?"

The Early Years

Regardless of what would be finally said about the painter's introduction to Margaretha Zelle, that first cool evening remained
uneventful. Gray and de Massloff dined near the *quais* among parties
of restless young people like themselves. They chatted briefly with
another Russian immigrant, then shared a bucket of oysters. Later,
as a testament to these simple evenings, Gray would leave several
charcoal sketches of sawdust restaurants, several watercolors of
blue lightening on the rooftops. Toward midnight they moved
on past the river to a languid terrace near the Tuileries. But here
there were only the friends of friends, and Gray's tribute to them
never seemed quite defined: dark profiles of women in lamplight,
gentlemen with only the shadows of smiles. Indeed, it wasn't
until the appearance of Zelle that he even came to understand
this world.

"You don't happen to recall her name, do you?"

"Whose name, Nicky?"

"That bicycle girl."

"I think it was Maggie."

"Live in the area?"

"Honestly, Nicky, how can I possibly—"

"Because I think I'd like to paint her, you see. I just want to paint
her."

They said nothing more about her that night, and quite possibly
she might have been forgotten, along with all the other intriguing
strangers that Gray had seen since entering this city: young dancers
from the Moulin Rouge, flower girls in the Bois de Boulogne, faces
in the windows of passing trains. But two days later, while cleaning
out a drawer, de Massloff actually found her name among a list of
available models. Jotting it down on a slip of paper torn from a
magazine, he waited for Gray until the late afternoon.

"Still interested in that bicycle girl?"

Gray nodded. "I suppose, yes."

"Well her name is Zelle. Margaretha Zelle."

"Got an address?"

"Of course," and just as casually, dropped the paper into Gray's
open hand.

We know little about her first days in Paris beyond the fact that she lived rather badly in a boarding house near the railway station. Also, she had no friends with money, and her family sent her nothing.

It was a Friday when Gray met her, an unseasonably warm Friday with a southern wind raising a white dust everywhere. Gray presented his card at the door, then found himself in a shabby room below the staircase. A few minutes later Zelle appeared in a pale blue dress with a ribbon in her hair. She was taller than he had expected, and oddly shy when he explained that he wanted her to pose for him.

"Under what circumstances?" she asked.

"In my studio."

She glanced at his hands. "Alone?"

"Well, yes."

"I'm afraid that's out of the question."

"But I—"

"I'm terribly sorry."

He would always remember the wind, an odd wind, perhaps even an African wind. Shutters were banging all over the neighborhood. People seemed confused. For a while he remained fixed at the window, watching bits of paper whirling below. Then he moved back to the easel and a botched landscape of poplars.

He worked quickly, almost desperately, unable to smear the paint on fast enough. He found that he couldn't seem to stop even when the darker tones began to spread too far, the green too thick.

Until the knock at the door.

He opened it without thinking. She was standing in the half-light, wearing that same pale dress, her hair still tied in a ribbon. He stepped back to let her enter, but apparently she did not intend to stay.

She said only, "I've changed my mind about posing. When shall I start?"

He glanced back at a waiting canvas. "How about tomorrow? Say, eight o'clock?"

She looked up, questioning. "Eight?"

"I'll need the light."

"Very well, but then it's thirty francs, not twenty."

Afterward it seemed that he could not keep from thinking about her, trying to recall the sound of her voice, the way she brushed her hair from her eyes. Toward dusk he left his studio and wandered again, moving with the evening crowds along the boulevard Saint-Germain. The air was moist and cool, particularly among the chestnut trees where in later dreams she would always be waiting for him.

She was very beautiful seated in a rectangle of sunlight, head cocked a little to one side. Even immediately after undressing she hadn't lost that sense of composure. She had simply walked across the room and sat down—obviously certain that he would be compelled to watch.

He worked slowly, carefully, because none of the old tricks applied. Her arms weren't any girl's arms, and the eyes were nearly impossible. He worked with charcoal because this first vision demanded something soft and vague. He hardly spoke, because he could not think of anything amusing to say. During breaks she put on a bathrobe, and he watched her smoke on the balcony. When it was over he watched her from the window, moving between the brickwork.

Soon he simply found himself waiting for her footsteps on the staircase. She always appeared a little late, but never seemed to realize it. If he kept her through the lunch hour she always expected a sandwich. If there was wind in the streets she would waste another twenty minutes brushing her hair. If she talked, she only talked about herself. But when she finally emerged naked again to kneel in that patch of light, he had to admit that she was worth every inconvenience.

"I wonder if you could lift your head a little," he would tell her.

"Like this?"

"Yes, thank you," as her presence suddenly filled the room.

By the end of the week he had completed six preliminary sketches, although none was entirely satisfactory. Something continued to elude him, something in the angle of her shoulders, the slope of her back, those eyes. He sketched her again in the afternoon, then once more by gaslight in the evening. He experimented with crayon and a dozen shades of ink . . . until he finally caught himself simply gazing at her photograph, wondering if it was even possible to sketch this girl without having slept with her first.

De Massloff sensed the change immediately, first in the trailing conversations, then in the drawings themselves. It was late. He and Gray had returned from dinner to open a bottle of brandy in Gray's room. The Zelle drawings were propped against a wall opposite a wooden chair.

"So this is what you've been doing with that bicycle girl."

The painter grunted. "They're not finished."

"But they're good, Nicky. They're very good." He stepped back to the window and turned up the gas jet. "In fact I'd say that they're your best yet."

Gray shrugged and poured a second glass of brandy. "She's a difficult subject."

"Yes, but you've handled her wonderfully. I particularly like what you've done with the eyes."

"The eyes are shit," and he poured a third glass.

They drank in silence for a while—Gray with a cigarette, staring at the roofs and an indigo sky, de Massloff still gazing at the drawings.

"Do you know something?" de Massloff finally said. "I think that you're getting quite serious about this girl."

Gray looked up above the rim of his glass. "Mmmm?"

"I said that I think you're getting serious about this little bicycle girl of yours."

"I don't know what you mean."

"Ah, but it's right here in the drawings. I can *see* it."

Gray laid the glass down. "I don't know what you're talking about."

De Massloff smiled. "Yes you do."

He slept badly that night, then woke at dawn to the sound of thunder and hard rain. He spent a long time cleaning brushes and priming a canvas, then settled into a chair by the window to wait. As the appointed hour of her arrival came and went, he began to eye what was left of the brandy. And yes, de Massloff had been right, it was getting serious.

But at some point just before the rain stopped he heard her climbing the staircase again. She entered with a black umbrella. The cold had brought out the color in her cheeks, but her eyes were about the same.

"I thought you weren't coming," he heard himself babble.

"Why? Because of a little rain? I love the rain."

He gave her coffee fortified with brandy, then used the last of the coal on a wood fire. When she finally emerged naked again, he pretended to study an earlier sketch while following her movements in a cracked oval mirror. He had always loved these nonchalant moments between undressing and the formal pose. He loved the way she walked on the balls of her feet, the way she ran her fingers through her hair.

He worked methodically with only the simplest lines. He worked with the shadows, because if you understood the shadows, the form would take care of itself. He used only what he knew best and ignored everything else. He just tried to paint the girl . . . until she began to come alive on the canvas—this mysteriously beautiful girl from nowhere.

It left him exhausted, resting in a chair with a glass of cheap wine. She had slipped into her dressing gown and lit a cigarette, but for the first time in days he ignored her.

"Is it finished?"

He nodded. "Nearly."

"May I look at it?"

He nodded again, then shut his eyes and heard her whisper, "But it's really me!"

He took a deep breath. "I'm glad you like it."

"No, Nicky, I love it. It's beautiful, truly beautiful."

She moved back to the wall, and although he still hadn't looked at her, he knew that she was watching. "You should have told me," she said quietly.

"Told you?"

"That you could paint like that."

She laid the cigarette aside, swept back her hair. It was raining again. "If you want to paint another I could come back tomorrow."

He shook his head. "No, not tomorrow."

"Why not?"

But before he could answer she knelt down beside him and took his hand. "Because I really want you to paint me again, Nicky. I *really* do."

He could not quite avoid her eyes or the lingering scent of her hair. The first kiss was tentative. Then she moved to the bed without speaking, and there were no other sounds from the neighboring rooms . . . only the hiss of rain.

He moved to her slowly, consciously trying to ingrain an image of her waiting for him on an unmade bed. After the second kiss she lay very still while he gently ran his hand across her belly, her smooth thighs, her hips. After a third kiss she arched slightly, lifting her breasts to him . . .

And later, years later, when they would all say that she had been a remarkably adroit lover, Gray would still remember this relatively shy girl barely stirring when he touched her again.

Like a vision slightly out of focus, there is something elusive about Gray's early portraits of Mata Hari, something that defies definition. De Massloff has said that in the beginning the painter really knew very little about her, and perhaps this is what we see: an exceptionally beautiful girl who might have come from anywhere.

It was half past eight in the evening when de Massloff finally found his friend again—slumped in a chair by the window watching the yellow fog. There were still glasses on the table, blankets on the floor . . . but the portrait now stood in the corner, propped against the wall.

"Well, it's absolutely marvelous, Nicky. You have succeeded in making her look like an angel."

Gray reached for a cigarette—one more exhausted gesture. "She's a sweet girl, Vadime."

"Of course."

"And I like her."

"Not surprising."

"And I definitely intend to see her again."

The fog seemed vaguely yellow now, suspended above pools of rainwater. There were sounds of passing wagons below and the cry of an itinerant vendor.

"Well, at least tell me if you enjoyed it." De Massloff smiled.

"Enjoyed what?"

"Your afternoon with the bicycle girl. I mean, is she in fact amusing?"

"Shut up, Vadime."

"Oh, Nicky, I'm merely—"

"I said shut up."

He drank through what was left of that night, and hardly moved from the window.

He met her again in the Tuileries. He wore a pale morning coat and dark flannels. Her clothing was slightly less suitable. They walked for an hour, lingering under the ivy, while a carriage continued to circle on the gravel. She told him that her favorite flower was the orchid, although she also favored lilacs and Parma violets.

She became silent along the banks of a willow pond, clutching his arm like the child he would never forget. Further along the damp path she stopped to kiss him on the neck.

"I really shouldn't be keeping you from your work," she told him.

He smiled. "It doesn't matter now."

"But it does, Nicky. If you don't keep painting, how do you expect to become immortal?"

It was not quite midnight when they returned to his studio. Another fog had risen. She leaned against the cold plaster as he slipped the dress past her shoulders. She shut her eyes when she kneeled to remove her stockings. When he drew her to the bed she pressed his hand against her breast. When he momentarily left her for a cigarette, she called out his name.

De Massloff sat in his room in the darkness with a bottle of cognac and a cheap cigar. He had extinguished the lights an hour ago, and had remained all but unmoving ever since. Earlier, when he had realized that he would not be dining with his friend tonight, he had wandered into the outer streets looking for a prostitute. He had only found a bar, then returned to his room to become this uneasy figure in the darkness.

Margaretha Zelle . . . could he believe her? She talked about a previous marriage but never said who her husband had been. She also talked about children but never showed a photograph, and although she claimed that she had traveled extensively throughout the Far East, she actually knew little or nothing of the culture except a few Indonesian dance steps and the words Mata Hari—Eye of the Dawn.

Chapter Two

IN her fantasy she had been born on the coast of Malabar, in the holy city of Jaffnapatam. Her father had been called Assirvadam, the Blessing of God. Her mother had been a ministrant of the temple. Her world extended no further than the cloistered gardens and moss-encrusted stone, while beyond lay a jungle humped in silence. At fourteen she had danced for the Elders, naked under the torchlight, deep within Siva's recess. At night she was chained to a wall and whipped.

Finally one evening among the suspended vines her eyes met the eyes of a young English officer. Although neither spoke, something clearly passed between them, an impossible union in the lucid stillness. He came to her again in the dead of night and carried her off to a snow-capped mountain retreat high above the caravan routes.

In the spring a son was born, with his father's fair hair and his mother's elusive gaze. For three years they lived in unbroken contentment until a jealous servant poisoned the child with venom drawn from a cobra. Then lying down with a broken heart, her husband also died, which finally left Mata Hari in a twilight world, moving from city to city.

Like other stories she would later tell, this one had a grain of truth. As the wife of a garrison commander in Java, she had indeed spent time in the East. As a mother in Sumatra, she really had lost a child at the hands of a malicious servant. Finally, she actually had seen the temple dancers, but only briefly and from a distance.

She generally talked about her past in terms of fragmented images, usually at night after having had too much to drink. As she spoke—either slumped in a chair or reclining on the bed—Gray would sit with his sketchbook hoping to catch her passing expressions. Although she told so many lies to so many men, she told him the truth.

She said that she had been born in the city of Leeuwarden in Holland's northern province of Friesland. Her father's name was Adam Zelle, and he had owned a haberdashery on the Kelders. She had three brothers, two younger than herself, one older. They often visited papa's shop on Saturdays.

After her mother's death and the failure of her father's business she had found herself living with an uncle in the town of Sneek, where she had briefly studied to become a kindergarten teacher until an instructor attempted to seduce her behind a gashouse. From Sneek she moved to Amsterdam to live with a friend of her father's. She would often read at night, and walk the canals in the mornings.

At seventeen she met a Dutch military officer on home leave from the East Indies. His name was Rudolph MacLeod, whom she described as a harsh man with a bald head and a sweeping moustache. On their first meeting they discussed the tropics. On their second they talked about marriage.

The ceremony was simple, with barely a dozen guests waiting on the steps of the city hall. They spent their honeymoon in Wiesbaden, and nine months later a child was born, a son. Although she had originally hoped to call the boy Jan, her husband insisted that they name him Norman after his uncle, a retired general.

Four months after the birth of their son, MacLeod received his papers recalling him to Java. They sailed from Amsterdam on the first day of May. The weather remained variable until well past the North Atlantic . . . There were overtones of a dream to her descriptions of Java, a certain sense of time slowing down and finally stopping altogether . . .

While describing those first illusory months, she tended to fix on small objects in Gray's room: a bottle of brandy on the windowsill, a burning cigarette, the gently billowing curtains. Then pausing midsentence, she would reach for a glass on the table.

"Do you believe in ghosts, Nicky?"

He shrugged, watching her eyes. "I doubt I've ever thought much about it."

"Well, Java is filled with ghosts, and I believe they have the power to influence people . . ."

At first she and MacLeod lived in a bungalow outside of Ambarawa, south of Semarang, on the north coast of Java. It was a mean place, dark doorways and feeble lantern light. A breeze through surrounding bamboo sounded to her like someone sighing, and the birds like frantic children.

One evening, after accusing Margaretha of flirting with a coffee broker, MacLeod tied her to a bedpost and lashed her with a riding crop. She said that she would never forget the expression on his face or the shadow on the wall.

Their second child was born in May, a daughter. MacLeod called her Jeanne-Louise, after an aunt who had always hated Margaretha. A few months later they moved again, this time to Malang, and here too it seemed that the hills were filled with discontented spirits.

A nursemaid was hired to help with the children, an unusually tall girl from a backwater village to the south. One evening the girl was caught with a stolen pig, and MacLeod gave her fifty lashes with his belt. Less than a week later he and Margaretha returned from a cocktail party to find that the door of their home had been left ajar, while shutters banged madly in the wind. There were odors of kerosene and vomit, then a distorted vision of her children on the nursery floor.

There was a bird, she told Gray, that supposedly sang whenever a child was to die. She never heard the bird. The physician found her in the garden and told her that he had managed to flush her daughter's intestines of the poison. She did not have to ask about her son, because it was in the doctor's eyes and the way he kept fumbling with a watch chain . . .

By now it was dawn, and she lay on the bed with her arm across her eyes. Faint light was breaking from the rooftops, leaving the chimneys in black relief against the sky.

"I had the plague," she said.

"The plague?"

"Typhus. After my son died I had typhus. They sent me to a coffee plantation to recuperate. It was beautiful, but also very lonely. One night I took a long walk. The road was dark and the jungle around me was very thick. But somehow I knew that I had to go down this road—a red road, red clay, you know? So I kept walking, and the farther I went the stronger this feeling became—something important was waiting for me, something that would change my life."

She paused, reaching for a glass of brandy on the nightstand, while Gray lit a cigarette.

"There was a village at the end of the road," she continued. "It was one of those very dirty places filled with mud. But that night there was a festival and all the people had gathered in a circle. Of course I was afraid to join them at first, but I *had* to see what was in the center of that circle. Many of the people were staring at me, but I didn't care."

She paused again, rising on an elbow, and he briefly caught a glimpse of an intensity he had never seen before. "Have you ever had a vision, Nicky?"

He shook his head. "I don't think so."

"Well, I had a vision that night—of dancers. It's difficult to explain really, but it was like watching a dream. I didn't understand everything, but I *felt* it. I felt it very strongly, and it changed me. Two days later, when I saw my husband, I told him that I was

28

leaving . . . which I'd say he took pretty well, considering."

She lay back down, and Gray moved to the window. "Where is he now?"

"Amsterdam, I think."

"And your daughter?"

"Also Amsterdam, but naturally I will bring her here just as soon as I've become a famous dancer in the oriental tradition." She did not smile when she said this.

It was the first time he had ever heard her mention it. A mid-August dawn, she on the mattress, he at the window, and then from nowhere: *just as soon as I've become a famous dancer in the oriental tradition.*

She said nothing more about it the next day, or the day after, or the day after that. And even later in October, when she actually began to rehearse for her Paris debut, there did not seem to be much one could say. She was to dance on the fourth of February in the salon of a Mme. Kireesky. Her sponsor was the director of a riding academy. Vadime de Massloff would take the photographs, Gray was to help with the background sets. The evening was to be billed as a selection of "authentic" oriental dances by the incomparable Mata Hari—"Eye of the Dawn."

Chapter Three

THERE is a photograph of her first performance, probably taken by de Massloff. She appears in studded breastplates and a low sarong descending to her hips. An Indian diadem curls above her hair, knotted along the shoulders. She seems to be tearing a veil away, while a young attendant kneels at her feet. Suspended from a balcony are chains of hothouse orchids and clusters of her Parma violets. Torchlight tends to deepen the mystery, while a four-armed Siva emerges floodlit from behind.

In a second photograph, taken at the later reception, she appears in a sumptuous gown with an oversleeve of white brocade. To her left stands the industrialist M. Guimet, dark and powerful against the damask. In profile to her right stands a thin young man who vaguely reminds one of Jean Cocteau, and finally there is also Gray.

His own memories of this night would never be as precise as the photographs. After drinking too much in her dressing room, he withdrew to a garden filled with ivy and terracotta urns. Long after they had all described her as marvelous, he would clearly remember her naked, slightly trembling on the marble, waiting for the applause. . . .

Six truly happy weeks followed that first performance, six weeks when he had her all to himself. They celebrated her reviews in a basement cafe near the university, and at first she had been quite modest. She claimed that her audience had only loved her because she had taken off her clothes, and then they had only wanted her because they could not have her.

He felt closest to her in the casual moments: dozing by the window on a cold day, kneeling on a bed to brush her hair. He usually worked in the early mornings, doing sketches of her sleeping in a tangle of sheets. In the late afternoons they would walk to the river, to a special place where the currents were particularly deep and inviting. In the fall there would also be chestnuts here, but by that time she would be gone, leaving him with his drawings and a pocketwatch . . .

"Darling, I have a surprise for you," she said.

"Surprise?"

"A gift."

It was a Sunday and still early. He had fallen asleep the night before after three or four glasses of rum. She laid a tiny box on the mattress and told him to open it. Inside he found the watch, thin gold and engraved: *Forever.*

"It's beautiful, Margaretha."

"Yes, but now you'll have to think of me whenever you want to know the time."

Except that six months later the mainspring broke. Never mind. He would think of her in all those timeless moments.

In a way it seemed that every day had been a little timeless through that March and early April. She danced twice more before the month had ended, first at the home of a shipping magnate, then again at the Trocadéro. On both occasions Gray met her later in a courtyard, when she smelled of cigarettes and cheap perfume. As always after dancing she was desperately hungry for simple food: sausages and beer, hard cheese and potatoes. Then too, after taking off her clothes for strangers, she always wanted him to watch her undress.

Eventually, as a consequence of her growing notoriety, even Gray had a minor victory: that first desperate portrait of her sold for seven hundred francs. The work had been hanging in a window of a Montmartre gallery for more than a month when suddenly a buyer appeared out of nowhere on an otherwise empty afternoon . . .

"Nicky," she called. "Nicky, come here. I want you to meet someone."

It was a Friday and a relatively modest affair at the home of an American patron. He and Margaretha had arrived a little late. As usual, he gravitated to a corner with a cigarette and a glass of dry sherry. While across the room Margaretha had been clinging to the arm of a lanky French officer.

"Look who I've found, Nicky. The gentleman who bought your portrait of me . . . Colonel Rolland Michard!"

He was a sleek figure with silver hair and narrow chiseled features. He nodded slightly as Gray approached, then turned back to Margaretha. "So, this is your young painter."

"Yes, my painter."

"Well, I very much like your work, Mr. Gray."

"Thank you."

"Also I like your model."

"Yes."

"But unfortunately not for sale too, correct?"

Followed by a burst of laughter.

It was late when he brought her back to his studio, nearly dawn again. By this time the walls were covered with drawings of her: seated, reclining, pensive, asleep. None, however, seemed as deeply revealing as that portrait that the colonel had purchased.

"You didn't like him, did you?" she said.

"Who?"

"Michard."

He shrugged. "I don't know, he bought my painting, didn't he?"

They were lying together on the bed, but not touching. It appeared that the day would be cold—possible rain, definite fog.

"He told me that he liked you," she said suddenly.

"How nice."

"Yes, he said that he's always been fond of the English."

"Lovely."

She turned, running her fingers through his hair, tracing his lips with her nails. "Don't be jealous, Nicky. I could never love someone like the colonel."

"But you intend to see him again, right?"

She pulled at a loose thread on her nightgown. "I don't know. He asked me to lunch."

"Did you accept?"

"I can't remember."

But she was gone in the morning, leaving telltale signs everywhere: lipstick on a glass, a camisole dangling from a chair, torn stockings. He made himself a cup of coffee and drank it by the window. Fog had settled in the courtyard below, pouring over the rooftops, obscuring the ranks of chimneys. He picked up a novel she had been reading, a vapid romance of obsession in the tropics. He turned and reached for a cigarette, then caught a glimpse of her profile in pencil.

You've changed.

He descended to the courtyard, climbed the crumbling staircase to de Massloff's room. The photographer was hunched at a sagging bench, carefully dismantling a camera. There were dozens of photographs scattered on the floorboards—seated nudes, reclining nudes, pensive nudes.

"Care for a drink?"

De Massloff continued staring through an oval lens. "Where's Zelle?"

"Out."

"I'll get my coat."

They found a cafe in the shadow of a hotel filled with refugees and prostitutes. They ordered rum because of the cold. They ate because there was nothing else to do.

"She's left you, hasn't she?" de Massloff said.

"Of course not."

"Then what's wrong?"

"Nothing." But after another hollow pause, "Who's Rolland Michard?"

De Massloff smiled. "Dear boy, everyone has heard of Rolland Michard, playboy of the General Staff."

"Fine. And beyond that?"

De Massloff smiled again, tracing his jaw with a finger, a slightly devious gesture. "Son of a ruined countess. Loves war, loves women, especially loves women. Also fancies himself as something of a patron and moves in all the appropriate circles."

"Married?"

"Good God no."

Gray poured a second glass of rum. "He's having lunch with Zelle."

"So? He takes a lot of women to lunch. Maxim's, a table is always reserved."

"He's also the one who bought my portrait of her."

De Massloff looked sternly at him. "You know, Nicky, jealousy can be very boring."

They parted at dusk, the restless hour when the streets were filled with clerks and typists moving to the Métro. For several blocks Gray simply followed these crowds, only half conscious that he had no place to go but home, nothing else to do but wait for her.

She returned just after eight in the evening. He was sitting at the easel, staring at a still life. He had lined the empty bottles on the sill beside a pear and a slice of bread. Closer, he realized that she still smelled faintly of the colonel's cigar. Still closer, she kept avoiding his eyes.

"So how was it?"

She sighed, a bit too dramatically, he thought.

"Tiresome."

"Where did he take you?"

She hesitated as if she couldn't remember. "Maxim's."

"Well, at least the food must have been good."

"I suppose," but in a tone of voice she had obviously picked up at the salons.

"What did you talk about?"

She stepped to the mirror, unpinning her hair. "War. The poor man is convinced that there's going to be a war with the Germans."

He took a deep breath. "Must have been fascinating."

He watched her for a while, drawing back the curtains, frowning at the fog that still drifted in from the river. She took off her ring, a worthless piece she had picked up in Java. He loved her hands.

"Anyway," she finally sighed, "I'm tired. Yes, very tired."

But when he looked again she was seated at the mirror, vigorously brushing her hair.

"Margaretha?"

"Yes, darling," not breaking the stride of her brush.

"Margaretha, did you sleep with him?"

"Oh really, Nicky."

"Did you?"

"Nicky, why would I possibly want—"

"Did you sleep with him?"

"Yes," as her hair continued to spread out under the brush.

Yes. There was sitll a little Burgundy on a sideboard, still a clean glass on the table. The first drink tasted like turpentine, the second like nothing. "Why?"

When she shrugged her hair fell across her eyes. "I don't know. I just don't know."

"It's the money, isn't it? You're in love with his stinking money."

She was watching him in the mirror again, eyes like water under static clouds. "You just don't understand, Nicky. You don't understand."

"Understand what?"

"Me . . . *Me.*"

Of course, she was gone in the morning, leaving still more telltale

35

signs of the restless night: loose strands of hair, a broken cup, an empty bottle of gin. He wasted at least three or four hours brooding on the balcony, smoking. Then moving down to the streets again, he spent what was left of that burnt-out day staring at the works of all those artists who had managed to stay away from their models.

She became a rumor in this city after that, the sort of woman one saw only from a distance, extending her hand to a waiting footman, stepping from a carriage in the evening. Naturally passing gentlemen always paused to watch; just as naturally she pretended not to notice.

He only saw her once through those first dead weeks of summer: a fleeting glimpse in a crowd, still exceptionally beautiful in black organdy and a trailing cape. He followed until she met a servant in a doorway, a stiff figure undoubtedly employed by that colonel.

His routine during these days was to give up trying to paint by eleven o'clock in the morning, then successfully drink through the afternoon. In July he spent nine days in the south with de Massloff, then returned to his room to begin, gradually, to paint again.

By August he must have started half a dozen portraits of her, although none seemed particularly inspired. The eyes still remained impossible, the face still slightly out of focus. Occasionally she would appear for a moment in a waking dream, but he could not seem to retain the image. And then she was back . . .

It was a Tuesday, a blue September evening. She knocked softly, as though frightened of what she would find. Then hesitating in the door: "Hello, Nicky. How are you?"

As if it wasn't obvious from the shambles of his room.

"What do you want, Margaretha?"

She ignored him, moving to the easel and another unfinished portrait. "Is that supposed to be me?"

"It's an experiment."

She frowned, toying with a bracelet that her colonel must have bought her. "Well, don't experiment with me."

He kicked away a heap of dirty clothing, found the previous night's bottle, and started to pour her a drink.

"No, Nicky, I can only stay a moment. In fact I merely came to give you this." She dropped a white card on the table.

He looked at it. "An invitation?"

"To dine with the colonel and me."

"Why?"

"Because he wants to talk to you."

"What about?"

"Oh, darling, don't be so primitive. I'm doing you a favor. The colonel is a very influential man, he can do marvelous things for your career. Besides, there's no reason in the world why the two of you shouldn't be friends."

When she was gone he went to the window and inched back the curtain for a last look. It was an automatic gesture, as close to fear as a free-fall from the balcony . . . or as his eventual response to the colonel's invitation.

The colonel's apartment was on the boulevard Saint-Germain, a fashionable gray-stone in ivy. Past the wrought-iron gates were rows of clipped trees and a circle of white gravel. Two waiting servants stood at the gates, a third attended to the carriage.

It was half past nine when Gray arrived: he glanced at a cheap watch he had purchased to replace the watch she had given him. She greeted him at the foot of the steps, as did the scent of her perfume —clearly expensive. Inside were flesh-colored walls, a vase of dried violets, and groves of enormous furniture.

"I thought perhaps you and the colonel might have a drink together before dinner," she told him. ". . . I thought perhaps that would be best . . ."

He lit a cigarette, an exotic blend he had snatched from the drawing-room table. "Where is he?"

"Upstairs in his library."

The corridor was dark with only faint light from beneath the last door. He paused before knocking, then heard a languid voice telling him to enter. In mottled shadows the colonel was hardly more than a shadow himself poised by an open window.

"Drink?"

"Thank you."

He filled two glasses from a small decanter on the rosewood, a rare cognac. "I generally reserve this for myself."

A real gentleman. And altogether French. "Yes, it's very good."

"Margaretha prefers champagne, but a soldier only drinks champagne when there's nothing else."

He got up from his chair and swept aside the drapes. "Do you enjoy the darkness, Mr. Gray?"

Gray shrugged, waiting for his cigarette ash to ruin the rug. "Sometimes."

"Well, I've always loved the darkness," and now as a silhouette against the panes, he seemed much taller than before, the hair a richer silver.

They sat in silence for a moment, the colonel's magnificent silence, with the colonel's magnificent cognac that he usually kept for himself. "Tell me, Mr. Gray. Were you surprised to receive my invitation?"

"Surprised?"

"Or did you think this was Margaretha's idea?"

He cocked his head with an equivocal smile. What he thought was that he shouldn't have come.

"Because it wasn't Margaretha's idea. It was mine."

"Oh."

"You see, although I don't regret winning her affection, I would hate to think that you dislike me. Particularly in view of your future."

"My future?"

"As an artist. A painter. Now, I have always been a great lover of the arts, and have always regarded it as an honor to help a budding talent. Which is precisely why I've asked you here tonight. You see, I would like you to paint me."

Gray helped himself to the next glass. "You want me to do your portrait?"

"Yes. Perhaps seated like this. In uniform. And should it turn out all right, I'll certainly make a point of passing on your name to friends."

Gray laid down the glass in case it suddenly shattered in his hand. "I don't do commissioned work, colonel."

"Not even for two thousand francs?"

"I'm sorry."

"What about for Margaretha?"

"Margaretha?"

"Well, inasmuch as you still seem to want her, perhaps I might be persuaded to let you have her back, for a night . . . Now what do you say to my portrait?"

Although he must have said something, he would remember nothing except the man's face somehow filling the entire room. While out among the white forms of trees he also must have been ill, because in the morning he was still filled with the stench of it.

So perhaps this is how we should remember her? One more pretentious dancer in costume jewelry and a low sarong to reveal her hips and slender thighs . . . her failing: frivolity, not a devious scheme . . . her passion: men, not money.

After yet another performance at the home of the Rothschilds, she was seen at the better salons trailing a scarf and too much perfume. And after her association with Colonel Rolland Michard of the French General Staff, she was always seen dining on the better terraces.

Chapter Four

GRAY first saw the stranger from a distance: a blackened figure against the bricks, a shadow of a dangling umbrella. This had been on a Monday, the first week in October. It was a time of fine sunsets, and Gray often sketched the nightscape of roofs and chimney pots from his balcony. Then from nowhere came this stranger, watching for a quarter of an hour, and then withdrawing.

He saw the stranger next on a Wednesday, a damp morning filled with the scent of coal and drying streets. There, among the pools of rainwater the man was hardly more than a brief reflection: a homburg and dark flannel. And again Gray saw him, or thought he saw him, along the boulevard Saint-Germain—a solitary gentleman in an overcoat.

The stranger was like any apparition in a foreign city: a passing curiosity, a momentary thought. Meanwhile, life continued much as it had before. Gray painted through the better hours, chatted with friends in the slack time. His sketches indicated that by the fall of 1906 he was already obsessed with the expressionist spirit. The colors were muted, the details subservient to the mood, and he was obviously fascinated by, say, the subtle despair of a half-deserted street.

It was still quite early when the stranger finally emerged. Traces of a pre-dawn mist were still suspended above the drains. The milk wagons had not yet completed their rounds. Gray had gotten up into the cold, drunk another cup of foul coffee, then moved out with his sketchbook into the narrow slums along the rue de Bierre. As one more unknown artist, no one ever bothered him.

Then he heard the voice from behind: "I say, that's rather interesting. Mind if I take a closer look?"

He turned, but since the light was still low between the tenements he only saw another blackened outline: a homburg and overcoat.

"Yes, that's most impressive. Tell me, have you been studying long?"

Gray mumbled something about a year, two years.

"Well, I think your work is remarkable."

He gave the stranger a watery smile. "Thank you."

"It reminds me of, oh I don't know, certain things I've seen in Berlin."

"Berlin?"

"Yes, the new modernists." He sat down and offered Gray a cigarette—English and expensive. "You know, I think I've seen you working around here before."

Gray shrugged. "It's possible."

"But I had no idea that your work was so . . . so mature. You never studied in Germany, did you?"

"No."

"Then it was Oxford, right?"

"Yes."

"I thought so. But in the end I suppose Paris is really *the* place to be, isn't it?"

"So they say."

Leaning a little closer, Gray could finally see the face, the pencil moustache, the thin lips. He might have been a clerk on holiday, or

41

any lonely Englishman in Paris, except that the eyes seemed too eager, too probing.

"Tell me, would it be terribly forward of me if I asked to purchase one of your works? I'll give you a very decent price for it."

"How much?"

"Well, whatever you think it's worth."

So he tore the thing out of his sketchbook and handed it over. "Here. Keep it."

"You mean as a gift? But I couldn't."

"I want you to have it."

"Well, then at least let me take you to lunch."

He said his name was Anthony Craven and Paris was a holiday, the first in years. He worked in a London bank, he said, and lived with his mother in Chelsea. Beyond that he talked about art, while Gray simply nodded and responded to questions. No, he was not familiar with the young Spanish moderns. Yes, he was very fond of Goya.

At Craven's request they returned to Gray's studio for a broader view of the artist's work. Then, while Gray laid out all those botched landscapes, Craven kept up a litany of praise: "Oh that's truly lovely . . . oh yes, that's wonderful . . ." Until he finally found his way to the darkest corner of the room and a charcoal sketch of Zelle. "And I do fancy this one *very* much."

"Mmm?"

"This girl." He pulled it off the wall to examine it by the light. "Yes, she is magnificent."

Gray shrugged. He had never intended to display Margaretha. "She's just an early model."

"Yes, but she's stunning. I say, do you possibly think—"

"No, that one isn't for sale."

After that it seemed that Craven was always turning up, always buying drinks, always suggesting dinner. Gray at first assumed only that the man was a lonely soul, a little confounded by life, a little enamored of the romance of an artist's existence in Paris. On Saturday they toured the local galleries, on Monday they walked the Louvre.

Then came Friday with a piano recital in the evening. Once again Craven suggested dinner, and again Gray could not seem to find a way out. So they wandered into a back-street restaurant, a forgotten place between a seaman's hostel and the river. The waitress was a quite lovely-looking girl with rich blonde hair, but even when ordering dinner Craven kept an eye on the door. There were other signs: Craven requested a table at the rear, then sat with his back to the wall.

"Funny thing happened to me the other day," he began. "I ran into that model of yours."

Gray had been picking at a chicken's thigh, hardly listening. "What model?"

"Oh you know, the girl in your portrait."

He realized that his hand was shaking and put it out flat on the table. "You saw her?"

"At a benefit for the Russian fund. She danced. And was actually quite good."

Gray lit a cigarette, fumbling with the match. "If you like that sort of thing."

"Oh but I do." Craven smiled. "Although I can't say much for her escort."

"Huh?"

"French chap. Military. A Colonel Rolland Michard."

Gray said nothing. *I'm the eye of the dawn,* she had once told him. *I'll always come back.*

"But then I don't suppose I have to tell *you* about Michard, do I?"

Another cigarette while the first was still burning—"What makes you say that?"

"Well the little cad took her away from you, didn't he?"

"Did he?"

"So they say. Outbid you, as it were. Which I imagine must have been rather frustrating."

For a moment Gray only looked at the man, vaguely conscious that he had stained his cuff, and felt a chill. "Who are you?"

"Who am I? Let me put it like this. I don't actually work for a bank, and I'm not altogether certain that Rolland Michard is a loyal French officer."

They walked after that, ending up at the river once again. A fog moved in, distorting the clang of a distant bell and the echo of a passing barge.

"You've been lying to me all along, haven't you," Gray finally said. "Lying and stringing me along."

"Oh, I don't know, Nicky. I do admire your work."

Closer to the water there were odors of tar and debris, the drifting carcass of a gull. "We would like you to do a job, Nicky. One job. We don't expect it will take much time, and it should be fairly satisfying, particularly in view of the fact that Rolland Michard is a pig."

Gray took a deep breath. "My God, you're some sort of a spy, aren't you. A bloody special agent . . ."

"It goes like this," Craven said, not responding directly. "As an extravagant bachelor and figure in society, Michard found himself short of funds. Rather than cutting back expenses, including a string of beautiful women, he sold himself to the highest bidder. Which unhappily seems to have been the Germans. The particulars are that we think he's controlled by a man named Spangler, and we think he's been passing them both French and Whitehall secrets."

Gray reached for the railing, feeling something sticky. Chocolate? "I don't see how any of this—"

"He's lonely, really. Lots of women, but never any genuine friends. People don't quite take him seriously, you see. No one listens to him. And he's very fond of artists."

"But he doesn't even like me—"

"Oh, we can fix that."

It seemed that the fog had become a solid wall, advancing up the river with a steady wind. "I wouldn't be asking if it wasn't vital, Nicky. If it wasn't extremely vital."

"What would I have to do?"

"Be a friend to him, become part of his circle."

"What about Zelle?"

"Well, she's your reward at the end, isn't she? Assuming you play your cards correctly."

Another passing barge sounded like someone moaning, and the gulls across the wharf might have been children crying.

"You must admit that it makes it all very simple, doesn't it?" Craven said at last. "I mean, I love England. You love Zelle. And consequently we both hate Rolland Michard. So how about it? Do you want her back?"

"But I wouldn't even know where to begin."

"We'll teach you."

A fish broke the water less than twenty feet away . . . Zelle had always believed that jumping fish were good luck.

"Besides, you love your country too, don't you? That is, apart from this dancer, you do also love England as well?"

Gray looked at him, said only, "Why didn't you come out with it from the start?"

"Because we had to be certain."

"Certain of what?"

"That you were capable, trustworthy."

"And am I?"

"Oh, I think so."

There is an overriding sense of romance to the early chronicles of Her Majesty's Secret Service, a sense of lost adventure and fascinating intrigue. The pages are filled with the exploits of young English amateurs, and although their methods may have been simplistic, their eventual success was said to have been magnificent . . . now and again.

Technically the service that enlisted Gray in that fall of 1905 had only been born a few months earlier. Its director was the legendary Mansfield Cummings. Generally known to the public as "C," he would eventually become an almost mythic figure within the secret world, establishing a tradition that would last more than thirty years. Agents were gentlemen, because only gentlemen could be trusted. Professionals were avoided, because the motives of a professional were said to be impure. Artists were of interest, because they could create an entirely new personality.

Given the times, Gray's early experience was fairly typical of a young man rather haphazardly recruited by the service. He was trained near Melun in a half-timbered estate that might well have been an English country home. A stone wall enclosed a formal garden of circular hedgerows. Inside, there were high-beamed rooms filled with mock-Tudor furniture and mullioned glass. The odors were distinctly English: boiled meat, tobacco, and dust.

Gray would spend six days under Craven's supervision. Training was mostly informal, with long conversations in the garden, or evening discussions over glasses of port.

"You must never attempt to strain a relationship," Craven told him. "Always go for the natural approach."

"Like the approach you took with me?"

A Cheshire smile. "With you it was different, Nicky. You were a friend."

The first day was spent discussing the larger political scope, including the decline of Russia as a potent military presence in Europe, and the alliance between England and France. Strategists tended to think in terms of counterbalance, and as the strongest nation on the continent, Germany could be held in check only through a Paris–London link. Although a formal military alliance between the British and French would not become a popular notion until the following year, tentative plans had been laid the previous summer. In the beginning these discussions centered on the assumption that a German attack would consist of a wide flanking sweep through Belgium. In response the British proposed an independent thrust along the Baltic coast, ninety miles from Berlin. Through June and July a tentative summary was even committed to paper and shared with the French General Staff . . . which, Craven suggested, was how Rolland Michard managed to get hold of the plan and pass it on to Germany.

"We believe he was recruited about nine months ago," Craven said. "Since then he's been methodically handing the Germans everything."

"But if you're so certain that he's guilty, then why hasn't he been removed?"

"Because we're after bigger game."

"What bigger game?"

"You'll find out soon enough."

In the evenings they played memory games. Various objects were placed in a room, small objects: saltshakers, china figurines, tin soldiers, a notebook, a keychain. Gray would be invited into the room, and while engaged in a meaningless conversation he was to note as many of the objects as possible. In the beginning he was not particularly successful.

Next he was given only a passing glimpse of the room, eventually just a brief reflection in the mirror.

"You must never assume a cover, you must live it. You must react to situations as you would normally react. You must let them accept you gradually."

"What about the dancer?"

"It's all the same."

There were subtler games, involving the knack of directing a conversation to a critical topic, or phrasing a question so as to appear disinterested in the answer. "A gentleman has spent a weekend abroad," he was told. "You are to find out where and with whom . . . but casually, as if you were merely asking the time of day."

On the third morning a nameless instructor appeared with two Webley revolvers and an 8-mm St. Etienne. Targets were tacked against bales of wet newspapers. The bullets were laid in a dish. At first he was told just to hold the empty gun, feel the weight of it, toy with the breech. The Webley broke from the top, automatically ejecting the spent shells. The St. Etienne featured a loading gate that swung to the rear. After he practiced aiming for a while they gave him the cartridges in two handfulls of six.

He fired slowly, timidly, sighting along the barrel with both eyes open just as they had told him. The recoil was much worse than he had expected, and the noise was deafening. Still worse, he couldn't hit anything, except perhaps a recurring vision of the colonel.

When it was over Gray stood at the far end of the garden, a

neglected corner of weeds and ivy. "Was all that really necessary?"

"Everything is necessary," Craven said.

"Yes, but what's the point?" His ears were still ringing, hands still trembling.

"It builds confidence."

They walked in the evening, Craven gently leading Gray by the arm. It seemed that the man was always touching an arm or a shoulder, as if to strengthen the bond. Past a rusting gate lay a paddock, a windblown stretch. There were two wicker chairs beneath an oak, and Gray suddenly imagined that the chairs had always been waiting for him, suspended in time.

"I suppose I might as well tell you about the last twist of the knife," Craven said. "The German."

"What German?"

"The one who controls Michard."

The field around them also seemed static, slowly filling with red leaves.

"You see, Michard is really only a means to an end," Craven continued. "The real target is the German I mentioned earlier. Spangler, Rudolph Heinrich Spangler. He originally surfaced in London about two years ago. He seems to run his agents on the move. And he's a killer, which is something you musn't forget."

"How will I recognize him?"

"You won't, another key point. He may appear as anyone: a postal clerk, a servant, young, old, anyone. He speaks both French and English flawlessly and he's highly adaptable—the worst sort of illusionist."

Later that evening they chatted again, Craven talking abstractly about loyalty and England. Gray supposed that time was running out. He was right. As a parting word Craven left Gray with one insinuating image of the colonel and the dancer. Although Gray knew that the reference had been consciously manipulative, he still couldn't seem to get the image out of his mind—the colonel placing a hand on her breast, a cigar clenched between his teeth.

The last day was tranquil, ending with a long walk to a vale above the tributaries. There were poplars here and open pastures cut with cart tracks. In tune with the landscape, the tone of Craven's speech was also languid, a few inspirational words for an eager young Englishman, with a score to settle.

Of course there were case notes, and of course Craven immediately brought them to Mansfield Cummings in London. This meeting took place in the last week of October. There was a sort of backstairs intimacy to every meeting with Mansfield Cummings. He generally received colleagues in a cramped Richmond flat with a view of a garden lane under ivy. He tended to serve only dry sherry, or jasmine tea and biscuits. He often fiddled with small objects while speaking: a penknife, a cigarette case, an ornamental dagger.

Typically his first questions concerned the German. He said, "I want to know what that monster eats. I want to know where he keeps his money."

But Craven could only describe the man as a ghost or a vampire, depending upon one's point of view.

They also discussed the painter, and Craven characterized him as a reasonably bright young man with serviceable flair for the game. Then they discussed Michard, whom Craven called a bore.

After a second round of drinks the conversation became informal, and Craven made a first passing reference to the dancer improbably named Mata Hari. "She does a sort of oriental display," he said. "Then she takes off her clothing."

In Cummings's personal notes, about four handwritten pages filled with references to the Kaiser and crude drawings of German soldiers, the name Mata Hari appears only once, misspelled, but otherwise unmistakable.

Chapter Five

MONDAY was cold, with a premature frost turning the dawn streets to ice. Gray left his studio in the usual way, then walked for an hour until he was certain that no one was following. Just beyond the market square Craven was waiting in a room above a vacant brewery. The walls were brown, stained from broken water pipes.

"You're going to start with a letter to Michard," Craven said. "You're going to apologize for your behavior the other night. You're going to tell him that you had too much to drink. You're also going to tell him that you've changed your mind about his portrait. You'd be honored if he'd consent to pose for you . . . but you want to paint him in his library. That's critical. He's got to let you into his world."

Gray had moved to the window. The light was bad—one sputtering gas jet. He drew the curtains back and a long strip of rotten muslin came off in his hand. "What makes you think this will work?"

"Because Michard is vain, and quite foolish."

There seemed to be someone watching from a doorway below, a figure in a sailor's coat. Gray couldn't see the face, only the glowing tip of a cigarette. *London has sent us a few lads for tactical support,* Craven had said earlier. *But you'll never see them.*

"What happens after he . . . takes the bait?" Gray asked.

"Then you'll probably have a filthy glass of cognac in his filthy little library."

"What do I do about Zelle?"

"Stay away from her. As far as Michard is concerned the woman is your friend, nothing more. You might even hint that you've found someone else—a proper English girl."

Despite popular notions of adventurous gentlemen in a black-tie world, the early twentieth century game was not all that different from the game today. Agents approached their targets with a polite succession of quiet steps. The artistry was subtle, a discreet manipulation of unwitting people . . .

After six hanging days Gray received a reply from Michard. Then, as predicted, he returned to that library for a glass of excellent cognac. Against his role as the contrite young painter, the colonel played the forgiving patron. They even discussed Michard's portrait, including the esthetic advantage of a seated pose. "You must paint me as you see me," Michard said. At this point Gray hardly knew what he saw: Suave traitor? Vain fool? Poor bastard?

Just as Gray was preparing to leave, Margaretha appeared. "I'm so glad that you and Rolland are friends again," she whispered in Gray's ear. But instead of a kiss, she merely extended her hand.

Two days later he began the preliminary sketches. Arriving just after nine o'clock in the morning, he found Michard already posing in uniform, a riding crop in his hand, an open book of poetry on his knee.

As counterpoint to the first few sittings with Michard were the furtive meetings with Craven. Usually Gray met him after dark, either in that dismal room above the brewery or else in some equally remote corner of the city . . .

"Has he told you about his bloody horses yet?"

"No."

"Has he asked you out to his wretched château?"

"No."

"But he keeps offering you drinks, right? Is friendly?"

"Yes."

"Then keep it up. You're doing fine."

Gray usually saw Zelle only in passing: lounging in Michard's garden with late morning coffee and oranges, emerging from bedrooms. It seemed these were transitional days, a sort of still-point between her life as a dancer and her life as a mistress. Although she had rented a suite of rooms on the rue de Balzac, she still spent most nights with Michard. Their bed was enormous.

Gray found himself alone with her only once. It was an exceptionally clear Tuesday morning. He had arrived at Michard's home at the usual hour but a servant informed him that the colonel had been called away on a military matter. As Gray was moving back along the path, he saw her: blue between white branches.

"He's not here," she called out.

"I know."

"He's gone to see some general."

She moved a little closer, twirling a strangled orchid. Her eyes seemed darker than usual. Her face was very pale.

"I like what you've been doing up there," she said.

"What?"

"Your drawings of Rolland. I like them."

Then suddenly tossing the orchid away, "But tell me the truth, darling. Why are you *really* painting his portrait?"

He grinned, leaning forward as if to kiss her: "Money, darling."

The next time he saw her she all but ignored him, clinging to the colonel's arm, laughing at some private joke. Descending the steps to the garden again, he actually saw them embracing. She had always had a special way of throwing herself into the arms of men.

"He's asked me to dine with them," Gray said. "I gather it's going to be a small affair."

Craven laid a bottle of gin on the table. "When?"

"Saturday."

Since the first morning in this room, someone had made a few small improvements. The torn curtains had been replaced. A camp stove had been laid on cinder blocks.

"Who's going to be there?" Craven asked suddenly. "On Saturday."

"Some general."

"Foch?"

"I don't know his name."

Through a slit in the curtains Gray saw only a narrow vision of the street with blue pools of moonlight on the cobbles, silver reflections on standing water. She had always loved nights like this, he thought. But not here, not in a room like this.

"You've got to keep listening to him," Craven said. "No one ever really listens to him, so you must be the exception. And ask questions. Let him know that you truly value his opinion on all matters."

Gray turned from the window. He badly wanted to get out of this room. "Look, I've got to go now."

Sometimes, after a session in the library, Michard would ask Gray to stay on for coffee in the garden. Here the light seemed almost translucent, green through laced tunnels of ivy. Beyond the spikes of a wrought-iron fence there were often children on a lawn, and women in white like swans.

In these late October mornings, conversation tended to remain subdued. For the most part Michard would talk about his childhood, recalling early memories of winters in Zurich and summers along some forgotten Baltic shore. Once he even produced a photograph of himself as a husky boy against a limitless European plain.

Another time he talked about Zelle. He called her his Circe, his ultimate temptation. He described her as a spoiled child, but also very much a woman. He said that as a Frenchman he had always been attracted to beauty, but as a soldier he had always been fascinated by destruction. No wonder his obsession with Zelle.

On a rainy Friday the conversation finally centered on politics. At first Michard's observations were academic. He discussed the Prussian victory at Sedan and said the French had still not recovered psychologically. Next he talked about the Kaiser's commitment to a naval program, and suggested that the British must also come to terms with German aggression. He talked vaguely about his own future, but mostly Gray held the visual image—Michard against the window, glaring at thrashing leaves.

"Let me tell you a little story," Craven said. "About three years ago Michard fell in love with an actress. Beautiful girl, very expensive. She took him for nearly fifteen thousand francs—birth of a spy."

By now the room actually seemed hospitable, with a cot, a wash basin, and a few books. It was still cold, however.

"He wants me to help him select a birthday gift for Zelle," Gray said.

"Excellent," Craven smiled.

"And he's asked me to lunch on Sunday—just the two of us."

"Really? What's the occasion?"

Gray glanced up to the ceiling. An imperfection in the plaster looked a little like a naked girl. "Margaretha will be out, and I imagine that he simply doesn't want to spend the day alone."

"So he asked you over for veal and pickled cucumbers. How bloody charming."

There were night sounds again, cries of whores and the garbled voices of drunks. Yet for days now every distant sound had slightly haunting overtones, like the fragments of conversations overheard in cheap hotels.

"It seems that the French are also playing with us now," Craven said abruptly. "A certain Ladoux from the Fourth Bureau. Know him?"

"No."

"Well, he's done a rather nice job of filling in the larger view. For example, we're now quite convinced that Spangler is after our naval strategy, and as a General Staff adjutant Michard has probably been in a position to supply him with a good deal of it."

Gray pressed his hand to his head. A fever? A chill? "He's never mentioned the navy except in passing."

"Perhaps not, but he's thinking about it. I can assure you of that."

Gray moved to the chair, slumped down, and shut his eyes. Another symptom of the secret life: always exhausted, never able to sleep.

"It won't go on much longer, Nicky," Craven said. "You see, he's close. He's very close. I can feel it."

Gray looked up. "What the hell are you talking about?"

"The German. Rudolph Spangler. He's close. I can feel it in my bones."

There were social affairs through November, suppers at Michard's apartment, evenings on the boulevards. As the colonel's artistic discovery, Gray nearly always received an invitation. These tended to be forced affairs, filled with near-hysterical laughter and rambling loud dialogue. On one occasion Margaretha danced half naked on cold grass while fifty spectators watched from the lawn chairs. Another time the guests were transported to the prison yard at Saint-Lazare in order to witness the execution of a strangler. Then, as all the contrivances, all the elegant perfection against a sordid life fell away, Gray also found himself drinking too much.

There were also drawings from these nights: quick sketches on the backs of menus, exaggerated portraits in a small notebook. Gray would usually record these impressions during the slack moments between conversations and cocktails, between an introduction and a parting kiss. Most were flawed, many were eventually burned, but there was one pencil sketch that was neither destroyed nor forgotten: the profile of an elegant stranger who appeared very suddenly one Saturday evening at the theater.

His name, he said, was Diderot, and the encounter was accidental. Gray had accompanied the colonel and Margaretha to a production of *Lear*. At some point between the cloakroom and the lobby, the colonel was greeted by a gentleman on the staircase. Although this momentarily surprised the colonel, it soon became obvious that he and the stranger were long-standing friends. There were references to summers in the south, arrangements with a foreign bank. When Margaretha was introduced, the stranger bent to kiss her hand. Then, turning to Gray, he alluded to the portrait, "which Rolland assures me is nothing less than brilliant."

Gray smiled.

"But not too brilliant, I hope."

"Excuse me?"

"Otherwise we may lose sight of the original."

The man's laughter was melodious, head tipped back, lips revealing perfect teeth, slender hands holding a pair of gloves. The perfect picture of amused elegance.

It was the name—Diderot—that attracted Craven's attention. He and Gray met along the piers in the shadow of an arch. At the mention of the name, Craven was immediately intrigued, asking Gray to describe the man, to recount the conversation in detail.

Exhausted, and having drunk too much, Gray offered his drawing. "He was sitting in the gallery below the colonel's box. I had the profile for about an hour."

"And you didn't see him later?"

"No."

"Albert Diderot," Craven said. "I seem to recall that he first appeared in Spain. A ship's manifest had him as a local merchant, but our people were quite certain that he had come right out of Berlin. You did say he was alone, didn't you?"

"Yes, he was alone."

"Well, then, he very well could be our man."

"Our man?"

"Spangler. Look, there's going to be a rather high-level conference next week between some of our people and some of theirs. Now obviously Spangler knows about it, and he's come to prime Michard."

Gray turned his back on the wind to light a cigarette. When he looked again nothing seemed real, not the glowing streetlamps, not the water, not even the slabs of concrete.

"That's why it's particularly critical now," Craven went on. "Michard won't actually be attending the conference, but I intend to make sure he gets enough so that we can pull in Spangler. That's why you've got to stay close. I'll need everything now, every irregularity, every change. Do you understand?"

Gray shut his eyes and nodded—one time more for Zelle.

There was a sense toward the end that meaningless events were at last falling into a pattern. With the advent of cold weather the colonel tended to spend his free time at home with novels that he never finished, conversations that led nowhere. With the arrival of the British staff and the commencement of strategic talks, Gray also noted another change in the colonel's behavior: a greater need for company, particularly Zelle's.

"Rolland's terribly upset about the Kaiser," she confided. "He fears for all of us . . ."

Yet from the stillness of his room above the brewery, Craven saw an entirely different obsession.

"We've fixed it so that your lovely colonel has access to the minutes—or at least a reasonable selection. We've also let him see a few Admiralty briefs, so it should only be a matter of time now . . ."

But there were no references to strangers from abroad, no indications of a clandestine meeting. Except that one evening, after a modest meal with Michard, Gray was casually invited to spend a week in the country.

It was a beautiful night with soft rain. Following supper Michard had asked Gray to step into the sitting room. The curtains were drawn. The lamplight was low, two yellow cones on the ceiling. Gray had picked up a candlestick, admiring the face of a girl cut into the silver. Michard had laid out two glasses on the occasional table, but there did not seem to be anything except champagne.

Then suddenly he said, "Tell me, Nicky. Do you shoot?"

The question caught Gray by surprise. "No, not really."

"Then I shall have the honor of teaching you."

"Teaching me?"

"Yes. Come with us to Fontainebleau and I shall teach you to shoot."

When Gray found Craven waiting in that room again there were bits of paper scattered everywhere: handwritten notes on the floor, diagrams of border installations, photographs of Michard's country château. And for Gray, an extremely dry sherry.

Somehow this last morning felt like the first, as if winter had suddenly receded, leaving a glistening spring. The light was clear and white with oyster tones in the narrow lanes. Lost colors seemed to be returning to the trees. Damp roofs were faintly steaming.

"I understand that it's really quite beautiful," Craven said.

"I suppose."

"I mean the forest at Fontainebleau. I think you'll like it. And Michard's place is nicely situated with a marvelous view of the countryside."

Gray let the curtain fall. "How do you know that Spangler will show?"

"Because it's a perfect situation for him. He likes to meet his agents in remote places. He thinks it safer."

"And is it?"

Craven smiled, nearly reaching out and touching Gray's shoulder again. "You mustn't worry, Nicky. If Michard suspected anything he would have never asked you along. As it is, you're to be part of

58

his cover: a country holiday with mistress and artist friend."

There was a map torn from a guidebook. Craven laid it out on the table, securing the ends with coffee cups and a cigarette case. "We've rented a farmhouse here," he said. "We'll also have an observation post here. But you'll still have to be our eyes as far as Michard is concerned. Understand?"

"How does it happen? I mean, when Spangler meets an agent, what's the usual sequence?"

"It's all arranged in advance. Spangler slips into the area unobtrusively, often in disguise. There's a brief exchange of safety signals, then the rendezvous. All in all it takes about six hours."

"What do I look for?"

"The little things. Ostensibly Michard will spend his time enjoying the pleasures of country life, but sooner or later he's going to slip away alone. That'll be your signal."

"And then?"

"There's a path from the château to the farmhouse—here. It's about a twenty-minute hike over the vale. When Michard makes his move, all you've got to do is trot on over and give us the word. My people will do the rest."

Then there was the revolver. Gray had gone back to the chair, and Craven laid it gently on the table: black and enormous, the cartridges almost the size of a man's thumb. "I can't really imagine that you'll need this, but . . ."

Gray looked at the thing, couldn't seem to move his hand to touch it. "You know, Michard told me that he has this dream about dying like a hero," he said.

Craven shrugged. "So I've heard. I told you he was vain and foolish."

There was also a letter, sixteen encoded pages from Craven to Mansfield Cummings. Typical of Craven's approach to the game, the letter was filled with wry humor and dangerous optimism. There were several snide remarks concerning Spangler and Michard, several complimentary notes regarding Gray. Responding to an earlier suggestion that the French be enlisted for tactical support, Craven wrote that it was almost insulting to assume that a few good English lads were incapable of capturing two foreign spies.

Chapter Six

THE Fontainebleau estate, then as now, was a pastoral place. There were distant chains of low hills rising from the river, shallow dingles, and deep woods. Proust would later write of this country, recalling memories of tadpole-haunted streams; and although somewhat subdued by winter, Gray, too, clearly found the landscape enchanting, capturing it in watercolor . . .

He arrived in the early afternoon. Michard sent a carriage to meet him at the station. A gathering storm never materialized, and there were late-blooming roses in the garden. Earlier Margaretha had also collected a spray of hawthorns and a few surviving chrysanthemums for the parlor.

The first evening was somber. Following plates of cold pheasant Gray shared a bottle of port with Michard. Margaretha remained in the background, leafing through a magazine by firelight. What with the wine and his persistent exhaustion, it seemed that every sentence was a little dislocated. While Michard kept talking about a

phantom stag he had seen in the forest, Margaretha hummed caba-
ret songs.

There was one telling moment, a brief conversation with Zelle. It
came as Gray was moving up the staircase to his bedroom. There
were several moments of silence; then suddenly she followed him
and took hold of his arm.

"I'm glad you came," she whispered. "Especially for Rolland's
sake."

He gave her a strained smile. "I'm glad too."

"But you should know that Rolland hasn't been himself. He
hasn't been sleeping, and he hardly eats."

"Perhaps he's just tired—"

"No. It's more than that. Which is why I'm glad you're here
. . . so you can help him."

He tried to pull his arm away but she still wouldn't let go. "Me?"

"Well, he's fond of you, isn't he? I mean he's really very fond of
you."

A little later Gray heard them talking through the walls. Michard
seemed to be complaining about a bad dream, while Zelle offered
the sort of affection that any man would have killed for.

From the start, Gray supposed
that this was what he had always wanted—a conflict reduced to the
utter simplicity of three people in an isolated country home. After
shutting his bedroom door he remained awake for hours, toying
with the revolver, senselessly spinning the chamber until he was
certain that the pretense was over. This had nothing to do with
England. This was personal. This, damn it, was for Zelle.

He found her in the morning on the terrace. It was a warm day,
a reminder of July in early December. There was coffee in a blue pot,
pastries, and Italian grapes. Since Michard seemed in better spirits,
Zelle was happy. She laughed at everything.

After breakfast she insisted that Gray accompany her into the
forest. They chose one of the narrow paths between the ferns and
the riverbed. There were long shafts of bottle-green light, a budding

grove of larkspur. Along a deer track she took his hand, brief contact that left a lingering impression for hours.

But like a blow repeatedly falling on the same bruise, the night was filled with reminders that she was still the colonel's woman. "Pour this old soldier another glass of wine," he would tell her, and then, turning to Gray: "Look at her eyes, Nicky. Doesn't she have marvelous eyes?"

In the morning there was fog, a low fog, like water between the pines. Half a mile from his rented farmhouse Craven was waiting on a fallen log—the the very model of an adaptable British spy. He wore country tweeds and carried a walking stick. He had also brought a flask of brandy.

"No problem slipping away?"

Gray shrugged. "They're still asleep."

"What about the cook?"

"Asleep."

At first there were only forest sounds here: running water and the cries of unseen birds. Then there were footsteps on the sodden leaves and voices from the deeper wood.

"Your people?" Gray asked, suddenly uneasy.

Craven nodded. "Poor lads have been at it night and day. But they're still keen, very keen for this one."

"I think I saw them earlier, from the gate through the trees."

"Yes, well naturally we've—"

"And if I saw them, you can be damn sure that Michard has seen them."

Side by side on a fallen log, they began to pass the brandy: Craven pretending to drink, Gray hung over from the night before.

"Incidentally, we think we've located their meeting place. A little hunting lodge just south of the estate. It's also possible that Spangler is already on his way. Nothing definite, but do keep your eyes open, eh?"

"How do you think he'll come?"

"As something humble, I should imagine. A farmer perhaps, maybe a tinker."

"On horseback?"

"Possibly."

"Armed?"

Craven laid his hand on Gray's knee. "It's not as if we haven't played this game before, Nicky. Both my lads have had quite a bit of experience."

Gray looked at him. "Michard has a shotgun. And he bloody well knows how to use it."

There was rain in the afternoon and a cold wind from the north. While Margaretha slept, Gray played a game of chess with Michard. But between the wind and ticking clocks he could not seem to concentrate. Then, too, Michard was a fanatic about the game.

"You must learn to employ your rooks, Nicky. The rook is vital."

"Yes, I suppose you're right."

"And you rely too heavily on the queen. The queen is not the only solution, you know."

Toward dusk they played a second game, but pinned between the colonel's knights and flanking bishops Gray lost again. "Primarily because you lack the warrior's vision," Michard told him. "Which is to say, you lack the necessary aggression."

Evening came with a deeper chill and random bursts of lightning. After sherry and cold salmon it seemed that every hour lasted for a small eternity. There was Zelle slowly turning the pages of her magazine, Michard cleaning his shotgun. Finally, out of desperation, Gray even agreed to play a last game of chess, another dreadful slaughter.

"You musn't keep letting Rolland win," Margaretha told him. "He becomes intolerable if he always wins." But what ultimately seemed intolerable was her face in the lamplight, her dolphin's smile.

Dawn brought a windless cold, with snow gathering like ash. After waking to the sound of wagon wheels below, Gray found the colonel chatting with a boy in the courtyard. Moments later Michard entered the scullery with a freshly shot rabbit, apparently a gift from a neighbor.

"For our supper this evening," he said.

Gray glanced at the carcass dangling from a gloved hand. "Looks lovely."

"And tomorrow I will teach you how to shoot them for yourself."

"Can't wait."

Noon brought new flurries of snow, muffling sounds all through the house. After nibbling on a few bits of cheese, Michard retired to his bedroom, leaving Gray and Margaretha to an afternoon of small-talk and more sherry. But eventually becoming concerned about her soldier, she moved upstairs to check on him. When she returned all she said was, "He's tired. Very tired."

There was a full moon at night that left the landscape glowing with suggestions of ghost shapes. After another meager supper the colonel sat with a novel. For long periods of time he hardly moved his hand to turn the page. Then, suddenly rising from his chair, he announced that he was going to bed.

But who could sleep on a night like this?

For a long time after entering his room Gray had remained very still on his bed, one hand locked around the post, the other dangling free. Then, hearing a footfall in the corridor, he had dramatically told himself, "This is it, this is the end." But what had sounded like Michard must have been only the settling timber.

Flowered counterpane and blue embroidered coverlet, the Trinity on the nightstand, the water jug, the glass bell-clock . . . a quarter to four in the morning. He shifted his gaze past the curtains: a polar landscape with no depth and no shadows. He ran his hand across his forehead: cold-perspiration. He shut his eyes for one last vision of Michard: also motionless on the bed, also staring at the trees.

This was the only logical ending, he supposed. Waiting with the man in a darkened house, hearts beating together, each caught in the same obsession. We could have been friends, Gray suddenly thought, but knew it wasn't true. Well, we could at least have lived in peace—also not true.

He watched the fingers of his left hand move, and wondered if Michard's hand was also moving. He heard the shudder of branches in the wind, and wondered if it was actually the sound of a softly closing door. Then came the footstep on the landing, then definitely footsteps on the staircase.

He felt calm, actually quite relieved. Rolland Michard was a traitor, and everything was suddenly very simple. He slipped off the bed to a chair, vaguely wondering what the signal had been, what little tick-tack from a child's game had told Michard that this was the night. *For our supper this evening . . .*

He heard the gentle tread of bootheels below, the click of another shutting door. He waited a moment, then parted the curtain. At first he saw nothing, and thought, It's all a bloody joke. But then, between the stark rows of trees—Michard. He wore black in contrast to the snow. He carried that shotgun in the crook of his arm.

There were penny candles in a drawer, a box of matches on the nightstand. Gray stuffed them into the pocket of his coat: *So this is how you catch a spy.* There was a hurricane lamp on the bureau, one of the classic British models. He checked the wick. *So this is how you saved England.* Finally, there was also that revolver, oddly lighter than he remembered, somehow more comfortable in the hand. *No, this is how you saved Zelle.*

Downstairs the rooms were filled with shifting moonlight, while outside snow still reflected a pale glow to the sky. Gray opened the door, stepped onto the gravel. There were tracks between the hawthorns, imprints of the colonel's handmade boots. Still farther it looked as if Michard had paused before veering off into the forest. Then there was nothing except a clean path of virgin snow to the rise above the vale—to Craven's rented farmhouse below.

The farmhouse lay in shadows between the pines, hardly more than a low timber cottage with loose shingles and a crumbling porch. There were lights in two windows but no sound could be heard. The silence was like a presence, a heartbeat in a vacuum. Gray began the descent. The snow was soft, muffling the sound of his footsteps. The wind had momentarily died.

Then he heard the shots: two distinct and clipped, a third and fourth like a cannon reverberating out of the farmhouse, then a fifth, oddly hollow.

For a long time he remained very still, kneeling between clumps of frosted willows. A bird, obviously disturbed by the shots, kept crying from the pines. He laid the lantern aside and withdrew the revolver. *I can't imagine that you'll be needing this but . . .*

He started forward again, half crouching along a furrow. There were deer tracks across the snowbound field, and pools of ice. At twenty yards he paused again, waiting for the sound of Craven's voice . . . or a last shot from the window above. But there was nothing except that door.

It was slightly ajar, waiting for the slightest nudge. He pressed it open with the palm of his hand, then stepped back against the timber siding. Light came from an upstairs room, but the entrance was dark.

He entered, feeling his way along the rough plaster. It was a large room with looming shapes of furniture, a cold stove, and the outline of a staircase rising to a landing. There were sounds of a ticking clock, dripping water. Then, with the wind from an open window gently lifting a curtain, he finally saw Craven.

He was seated in the corner, half lost in shadows. One hand casually dangled from the arm of a chair, the other lay across his knee. There were fragments of a shattered glass at his feet, and something definitely wrong with his eyes—one literally bulging out of the socket, the other staring into the middle distance.

"Hydraulic pressure," Michard said softly. "A physical reaction to the impact."

Gray turned slowly, to the landing above. Michard was a silhouette against the light from an oil lamp, the shotgun resting on his hip.

"You killed him . . ." Not able to believe it . . . "You actually killed him."

"Not just that one, Nicholas. I killed them all . . . all your damned English spycatchers."

The scream that came out of Gray filled the whole room as he swung the revolver around, firing blindly.

Michard stepped aside, leveling his shotgun again. The first blast shattered the banister. The second narrowly missed as Gray threw himself back through a blackened doorway.

He took stock. It was a still life. The room was a windowless scullery with brick walls and a stone floor. There were tins of preserves on the shelves, smoked meat, and a wheel of cheese. There was also something in the corner, a shape without form ending in another bloody torso.

"You can't escape from there, Nicholas. Your only exit is in my line of fire."

There were bloodstains on the far wall, and Gray realized that Michard must have taken them all by surprise—three dead. He slipped off his coat and sagged to the floor. Four shots left. He let his head sag back to the bricks—one way out, Michard's line of fire. He shut his eyes. Nothing came.

"Nicholas, this is pointless . . . Nicholas, do you hear me?"

He picked up the revolver, peering out past the scullery door. Michard had become an indistinct figure among the shadows. He brought the revolver up, bracing the barrel against his elbow—brush to canvas.

But before he could pull the trigger Michard had brought the shotgun around. The impact tore away the the doorjamb as Gray rolled back.

"Nicholas, if you don't come out I will be forced to come down and get you. Do you hear me? I'm coming down . . ."

There were traces of blood from flying glass, the taste of copper from fear. He lowered himself to the floor, leaning out for another glimpse—still nothing except looming shapes of furniture and shadows.

"Nicholas, your position is hopeless. Do you hear me?"

He heard, but suddenly wasn't entirely certain he agreed. Because although he may have lacked the soldier's insight, at least he had the artist's perspective of shadows. Even the critics had noted that shadows were his forte, and these were particularly enticing, what with the long rectangles in blue, suspended ovals in brown, black spheres along the staircase where Michard was crouching, waiting.

Gray hesitated, the last pause before the final touch, the signature before one could call the work finished. *Hey, colonel . . . what do you think of my portrait now?* As he reached back clutching his coat, hurling it through the scullery door.

Michard's response with both barrels left Gray momentarily dazed, stunned by an aftershock and more flying plaster. But even a colonel from the General Staff couldn't reload fast enough. Gray fired twice, first low into the wainscot, then higher into Michard's stomach, leaving him against the wall . . . for a seated pose.

Gray rose out of the scullery now, moving slowly forward. Michard remained very still, eyes also fixed on the middle distance. There was blood, a lot of it, but he did not seem particularly troubled.

"So, Nicholas. You've finally become a warrior. Congratulations."

Gray picked up the shotgun and tossed it away. Without taking his eyes off Michard, he eased into a chair, the revolver still steady. "I want to know why you did it."

Michard half smiled. "Because I'm a soldier . . . a bad soldier, perhaps, but still . . . By the way, I hate Germany, always have. Hate the English too . . . maybe even more . . . goddamn superior—"

"Where's Spangler?"

Michard shrugged. "He got my warning. He's far away—"

"Your warning?"

"That business with the rabbit . . ."

There were sounds of shutters banging in the wind. Michard's face was pale, beaded with perspiration. "Tell me something," he finally managed to get out. "What did they tell you about me? That I was the supreme traitor of the French people, the snake of the century . . . ?"

"They said you did it for the money."

"Ah yes, the money . . . money for champagne, for little gifts . . . for all my beautiful women . . . But I did enjoy them, I honestly enjoyed them all . . . Only problem was I couldn't afford them, not on a colonel's salary . . ." He was paler now. "You did it for Margaretha, didn't you, Nicky? They told you to spy on me for God and country but in fact you did it for Margaretha."

Gray nodded, staring at him. "Yes, I did it for Margaretha."

"Everything for Margaretha?"

"Yes."

Michard glanced at the walls, the door, his shotgun on the floor. "All this just to get her back?"

"Yes."

"You'll never get her back, not after the world I've shown her."

Then nothing, not the wind, not the snow . . . nothing but the ticking clock.

"You know, even Spangler said she was an extremely expensive woman, Nicky. One brief encounter and he saw that she was very expensive. Not that he wasn't also impressed, perhaps even intrigued . . . But face it, Nicky, I've turned her into something that will always remain beyond your grasp . . . too expensive, too much for the likes of you . . ."

Then neither spoke, fifteen seconds, twenty seconds—a long time. Gray turned away from him, not wanting to hear, or believe. When he looked again, Michard was no longer breathing, and his mouth was cracked in an empty smile.

Gray left the revolver on the floor, his coat in the scullery; he left everything where it lay and moved out into the snow. It was not yet sunrise, but the pines were glowing faintly with a false dawn. It was possible, he thought, that Margaretha had heard the shots, but muffled by the snow he did not think it was likely. Besides, she had always slept soundly, with long unbroken dreams. Like the dreams of the innocent . . .

70

Chapter Seven

NOVEMBER remained uncertain, somewhere between freezing and thawing. After a brief winter's spring there were even transitory blossoms on the hedgerows. Then came the hard rain, smashing it all back into the gravel.

There were two inquiries following the death of Rolland Michard. The first, a whitewash, conducted by the French and obviously intended to preserve the reputation of the military, concluded that the death had been a suicide, with an earlier diagnosis of cancer of the stomach. The colonel's last act, appropriately directed at the site of the malignancy, had simply been a logical alternative to a long and painful illness.

The second inquiry, conducted from London and not intended for public consumption, focused on Craven's failure to capture Rudolph Spangler. A sixty-two page brief found Craven remiss on two accounts: as operational director he had underestimated Michard, and by failing to enlist the French he had weakened his defensive capability.

Through the course of these investigations Gray was only contacted once, on a Monday evening by a trim little man from the Foreign Office. They met in a cheap beer house not far from where it all began. After a few halting exchanges, Gray was presented with a four-figure check and quietly told to forget. Michard was mentioned only in passing. Zelle was not mentioned at all.

But her name did appear in one critical paragraph: *Is it not possible that a separate line may have also existed between the effort from Berlin and the aforementioned dancer? Please advise.*

The question was posed by a Cummings subordinate, one of the armchair investigators, a Martin Southerland of later involvement. Although not immediately addressed, a handwritten transcription of the document was committed to the ministry vaults, where it bided its time in the darkness.

What of Margaretha's perception of these events? Apart from a few lingering questions, she eventually came to accept Michard's death precisely as explained: stricken with a terminal illness, the man bravely and privately took his own life. As evidence of this, Gray would point to a revealing afternoon with Zelle in her apartment on the rue de Balzac.

It was the first chilled week in December. Arriving unannounced, Gray found her composed on a low divan amid newspaper clippings and neglected correspondence. She wore black with only a shadow of mascara—to emphasize her melancholy? There were photographs of Michard on the mantle, and an odor from scented candles on the windowsill.

They drank claret to the strains of Chopin on the gramophone. She told him that her colonel had favored the Preludes, especially on languid afternoons. Then reaching for Gray's hand, she broke down in tears. "Oh, I know that he wouldn't have wanted me to cry, but I can't help it. Nicky, I simply can't help it."

A little later she talked about Michard's restless spirit, and a certain apparition that had come to her the night before . . . "It was a feeling, really. A feeling that he came back to let me know that

I mustn't be sad for him, that right to the end he had a rich and happy life with a proud soldier's death. Which was why he never told us that he was ill, you see. He didn't want anything to spoil the last days."

And then she talked about herself. Michard had always appreciated her dancing, she said, and if only for his memory she had to continue. Also, it seemed that a certain impresario had recently expressed an interest in her career, and there were firm possibilities for an early spring engagement in Spain.

As he was leaving she allowed him a brief platonic kiss. "Thank you so much for coming," she told him. "I'm so glad you came." But when he tried to hold her gaze, she simply smiled and looked away.

So it seemed Michard may have been right . . . she was someone beyond his grasp. An irony there: having established himself as a friend in order to destroy her lover, it seemed he would always remain a friend, just a friend.

He saw her intermittently through what was left of that December, generally in the company of men he did not know, men he did not want to know. Once, after a performance at the home of some shipping magnate, he even saw her on the arm of another military officer, a major of good family, obvious means.

Then on a Thursday he met her for dinner on the rue de Lille. She arrived late, still a little breathless from an earlier appointment with the impresario Gabriel Astruc. She talked about her upcoming performance in Madrid and a tentative appearance with the Ballet Russe in Monte Carlo. She talked to her friend about her men . . . Jules Cambon of the French Foreign Office, Giacomo Puccini, Jules Massenet, some nameless count, some probably fictional prince. Friend Nicky had to sit there and hear it all. Had to. Couldn't help it.

It was a Friday when things came to a head, a supposedly educational afternoon in the Louvre. She had asked him to "reveal" the moderns to her, presumably so that she could discuss them in polite society. He met her in a hired cab that he could not afford and spent more than seven hours dragging her through the galleries.

To her credit she tended to like the better stuff: Renoir's lillies, Monet's laurels, Seurat's poplars in translucent light. True, Goya left her a little cold, but she must have seen something in van Gogh because afterward she was unusually pensive.

They dined on chilled salmon and asparagus. An earlier rain had left the air invigorating, so they walked from the restaurant to her apartment. It was still early, a prolonged winter's evening . . . he casually invited himself upstairs.

Since his last visit she had filled her sittingroom with things he had never seen before: oriental masks, frayed tapestries, a hideous bronze Buddha. The photographs of Michard, however, were gone.

She offered him a cup of cocoa, but he asked for cognac. She slipped off her shawl, he laid his coat across the arm of the chair. After a moment of silence he wandered to the far wall and a curious sketch of a dancer at the feet of an Arab.

"You?"

She brushed aside a wisp of stray hair. "Yes, that's me. But I didn't actually pose like that. He made it up."

"Who's the artist?"

"A friend. Don't you like it?"

"No, not much."

He crossed the room, sweeping back the drapes: black clouds in an indigo sky, long vistas of rose trees in the headlights of passing automobiles.

"Did I tell you that they may want me to appear in Vienna next year?"

There was a lamp on the table, a black spider of a thing. He switched it off. "Vienna?"

"Well, of course, it's only tentative. But don't you think I'd adore Vienna?"

"I don't know. I've never been there."

"Really? Well, then you must come along. Yes, Nicky, you really must come along with me . . . and explore."

He faced her from a velveteen armchair, finished his cognac, and poured another. She told him that he shouldn't drink so much. Then he finally reached for her hand. "Margaretha, I really think we've got to talk."

"About what, Nicky?"

"About us."

She pulled her hand away and turned to the window. She was biting her lower lip.

"Margaretha, I know that I can't give you everything that Rolland gave you—"

"Nicky, please. We can't go back to the way it was."

"Why not?"

"Because it's different now."

"What's different?"

"Everything. You're different. I'm different. We've changed."

She got up and approached the window. There were dried flowers in a vase on the sill—last year's bloom. She absently tore off a petal. It crumbled to nothing.

"Margaretha . . . you don't seem to understand."

"I don't understand what, Nicky?"

"Everywhere I look I see your damn eyes."

For an awful moment he thought she was going to scream, to smash that vase against the wall. But then he saw her face was tracked with tears.

"You're the one who doesn't understand," she said.

"Me?"

"Oh, Nicky, don't you know that I'd only hurt you, that sooner or later I wouldn't be able to stop myself from hurting you? Don't you know that by *now?*"

He shook his head. "I don't care—"

"But you'd care if it happened. The moment it happened you'd care."

Later, walking along the Montmartre, he must have seen a dozen women as beautiful as Zelle. But in the end there was no end, because she still remained the only one.

He thought about her too much during the days that followed. He thought about Craven, and wished he had had a chance to say he was sorry. He thought about Michard, what he had said.

As December faded to January he found himself returning to the semblance of the life he had led before. He painted through the mornings and early afternoons, then rested and met de Massloff for a drink in the evenings. At one point he even engaged another model, a thin girl with a boyish figure and cropped blond hair. After a modest exhibition of watercolors he spent fifteen days wandering through Italy, compiling a notebook of impressions, moving from one cheap hotel to another.

From a week in Venice there were several wry portraits of children along the canals and comical sketches of young men fishing in the shallows of Chioggia. In Rome he was fascinated with the architecture. In Florence he met a young Englishwoman traveling with an aunt, but it came to nothing.

On his return to Paris he found that nothing much had really changed except that perhaps the memory of Zelle was a little less insistent. He followed her career through the newspapers now, and through gossip at those cafes where they had known her. It was said that her performance in Madrid had been an enormous success, and that from Madrid she had moved on to Monte Carlo, where she had appeared in *Le Roi de Lahore* with Geraldine Farrar and the incomparable Zambelli. A photograph later published in the local press showed her smiling from the deck of a yacht. He received a postcard from Nice with a photograph of gulls on a boardwalk and a barely legible message: *Still wishing you the best!* Anything for a friend.

Defined only by these blurred photographs, these stray notes and newspaper clippings, she no longer seemed quite real. Rather she had become what he suspected she must have always wanted to become—a dream without a focal point, everyman's woman. While the Spanish kept comparing her to Isadora Duncan, the Italians found her virtually incomparable. While some Russian duke was apparently asking for her hand in marriage, the prince of Monaco was rumored to have asked her to stay at his summer villa. Accounts of her past remained obscure. Accounts of her love life tended to vary depending on her mood, or the mood of the reporter.

And if only it could have ended here, between the harmless lies and the drab truth, then perhaps she would have been remembered as just another trivial entertainer from those riotous years before the Great War. But toward the end of January came the sort of incident that would ultimately shatter all the dreams, a signpost to the black year that no one would ever forget. . . .

It began on a minor note with an announcement in the newspaper concerning the liquidation of property from the estate of Rolland Michard. Presumably the auction had been authorized by convening solicitors in order to cover outstanding debts. Interested parties were encouraged to arrive early.

Gray supposed that it was curiosity as much as anything else that finally drove him to the auction house that day, an odd desire for one last look at the colonel's scattered life. He arrived late, well after the bidding had ended. The floor was nearly deserted. All that remained were a few odds and ends that no one seemed to want.

He entered cautiously, still not certain what he was looking for. Merchandise that had been sold lay in an adjoining warehouse, each item tagged for shipment. There were long columns of dusty light from a rank of windows above, mounds of furniture under dustcloths, brass lamps, candlesticks, and porcelain figurines. Finally there was only one path forward, one clean line to that first crucial portrait of Zelle.

The painting had been propped against a teachest like any piece of worthless junk. *But it's really me!* He ran his hand along the frame —rather the worse for wear. He stepped back to examine those half-forgotten brush strokes. *You should have told me that you could paint like that.* He picked it up.

"I'm sorry, monsieur, but that painting has been sold."

He turned to face a woman in a blue smock with a canvas ledger. "Sold?"

"Yes, monsieur. All these items have been sold."

"To whom?"

"Monsieur?"

"Who bought the painting?"

She frowned. "I believe that it was purchased through an intermediary on behalf of a foreign collector."

"Yes, but what's his name? Can't you just tell me his name?"

She sighed, obviously exasperated. "I must consult the record." Then, confirming what somehow he already suspected: "Spangler. Rudolph Heinrich Spangler."

Beyond this there were only hints and rumors. In Berlin she was said to have lived with a lieutenant from the Westphalian Hussars, but there was no indication that Spangler approached her, no indication that anything lay beneath the facade: receiving lovers in a rented château, naked under a cotton frock, a limousine waiting beneath rustling poplars. Her letters during that season abroad were also quite innocent, with references to places she had never seen and men who would never really love her.

PART II

The Middle Years

Chapter Eight

SHE usually received her lover in the evenings, often waiting at the window with Chopin played on the gramophone. From here lay a long view of the Nachodstrasse below a silhouette of the Berlin skyline. Apart from these encounters her stay in this city was fairly subdued. She tended to live nocturnally, appearing at unorthodox hours, strolling through the cold roses of deserted parks.

Her lover was a wealthy Junker named Kierpert. They had originally met in Madrid, a chance arrangement across a dinnertable. Although married to a Hungarian beauty, he would always be remembered as Margaretha's splendid lieutenant from this summer of 1907: displaying her along the Friedrichstrasse, escorting her to the Imperial Army maneuvers in Silesia. On occasion they were even seen in cabarets and music halls with friends from the theater. But mostly this was a private affair, conducted after dark in Margaretha's room.

He would usually arrive at half past eight on Monday and Thursday evenings. He would enter without knocking. In deference to his fantasy Margaretha wore something reminiscent of the East: a blue kimono slipping from her shoulder, trailing silk loosely pinned at the waist.

The first kiss was a promise and a tease, her tongue sliding between his lips and then withdrawing. After champagne or cocktails on the balcony, she would put another record on the gramophone. He favored the slow seduction, lounging on cushions in the lamplight. He liked her reclining dark and passive while he traced the outline of her breasts, the smooth plain of her belly. In response she would shut her eyes, faintly shuddering, like the wingbeat of a gull asleep in the air. Sometimes an hour would pass before he undressed her completely.

Although he was technically the master of the house, the bedroom had always been her province. There were mirrors in scalloped frames along the far wall, and she did love watching him slip off his uniform, then appraising the hard angles of his hips, the white saber scar along his collar bone, the barely perceptible change in his eyes when he stretched her out on the bed.

He would come to her slowly while she lay still, clutching the sheets or the cool brass. He would enter her gently, whispering in German while she responded in English or Dutch. On occasion he called her his captive, clenching his teeth and pinning her wrists together . . . then again he was often very tender, almost afraid.

Afterward they would lie together in the darkness with sounds of the avenue below: ranks of chestnut trees in the wind, a passing van, students at midnight. Between casual remarks and muttered endearments they tended to focus on simple pleasures. His cigarettes were tailor-made, imported from Ankara. Her robe was like a second skin, green with a pattern of lilies.

"You possess me," he would tell her. "Even when we're apart I feel myself possessed."

"But it's only an illusion, darling. Love is only illusion."

"An illusion? A deceptive enticing illusion?"

"Exactly."

Then pressing his hand to her breast or turning her face to the light: "But this is no illusion, Margaretha. This is real."

The Middle Years

Unless otherwise engaged he would usually stay until dawn, dozing beside her or toying with her hair. His hands were long and muscular, and she loved watching them slide across her skin.

Before leaving he would always kiss her at the door, encircling her waist and forcing her lips apart. And, of course, she always left her robe undone, falling away as she arched back so that her nipples were faintly bruised against his uniform—a real soldier's kiss.

There were usually one or two introspective moments after he had gone, slowly running her fingers through her hair, drifting back to the dressing-table mirror. In a way she had chosen this apartment for its mirrors, stratigically placed to keep her in touch with her body. Sometimes she would spend as much as an hour examining the tracks of her lovers' fingers, retracing a slight discoloration from a satisfying night; and although she would soon become concerned about her age, the initial theme of these middle years still revolved around youth and beauty . . .

These were her halcyon days— solitary mornings in the Tiergarten, blue evenings along the Land-wehr Canal. Apart from Kierpert she had only a few casual friends: poets and musicians from the Romanische Cafe, one or two women from the neighborhood. The composer Jules Massenet met her briefly here in order to discuss a collaborative ballet, as did a choreographer named Chassieux. There was, however, no sign of Rudolph Spangler, regardless of later accusations.

She said she had come to Berlin to rehearse for a midwinter debut in Vienna. A parlor had been converted to a studio, a pianist had been engaged in the late afternoon. In a photograph, presumably taken by Kierpert, she appears in a gossamer veil. Her fingers are laced high above her head. Her arms and legs are dark in contrast to silver bangles.

In all she would spend four weeks dancing in Vienna, competing for attention with Maud Allen and Isadora Duncan. Newspapers described her as slender and tall, with the flexible grace of an animal. Heated debates arose concerning the question of nudity on stage. Her leisure time was mainly spent with Kierpert, and like others who would find themselves in tow with her, his public role was almost subservient. He was often seen waiting in the wings or fetching champagne while she talked with adoring fans. She knew how to please, and to inflame. One went along or one didn't.

Inevitably there were quarrels, mostly over the dozens of young men who appeared after every performance. The pattern would be a dull exchange in a cluttered suite of the Bristol Hotel, clothing flung over furniture, plates of congealing hors d'oeuvres on a trolley.

"Perhaps you should tell me about him," Kierpert would begin.

"Tell you about whom, darling?" Without turning from a window or laying down her hairbrush.

"That little Pole."

"Which Pole is that?"

"The one you were talking to all evening ˙ . . talking to, while ignoring me."

"But, darling, he wasn't anyone of importance. Really he wasn't."

"But you made him feel important, Margaretha. That's the trouble. You make them *all* feel important." Then pouring a drink or lighting a cigarette and sagging to a chair: "I will not tolerate this anymore, Margaretha. I simply will not tolerate this."

She never attempted to respond, not against his guttural vowels and hard consonants. Instead she would merely wait, biding her time until she lay down beside him with still more whispered endearments: "I love you, I need you," and the rest of it.

The curtain on her last performance in Vienna came down in mid-January 1907. After briefly passing through Paris again, she and her lieutenent went south to Marseilles, boarding the North German Lloyd steamer *Schleswig* for Alexandria. It was a cold day, a Wednesday with rain. Two competing fanfare orchestras played the "Marseillaise" and "Santa Lucia." Zelle remained in her cabin, dashing off postcards to influential friends, and a short note to Nicholas Gray, revealing virtually nothing.

Egypt was another fantasy, captured with watery snapshots of Zelle posing in the shadow of the pyramids and lounging beneath mosquito netting. Some residents of the European community would later remember her as a blithe spirit astride a camel, moving out across the dunes. She was also seen on occasion in the native quarters, attempting to talk with the women. No one was precisely certain what she wanted.

From Egypt they moved back through Athens to Rome, Zurich, and finally Berlin. There she returned to her studio, working with enthusiasm on a dance she would entitle "The Rose." Kierpert continued to see her, mostly on Mondays and Thursdays. Yet while his gifts grew increasingly extravagant—jewelry, furs, a Fabergé egg —these were no longer days of romantic intensity. He merely continued to arrive by carriage in the evening, and to leave on foot at dawn. And if everyone told her that at last she was famous and free, in fact she believed herself trapped, desperately waiting for still another man to take her far far away.

She met him on a Friday, on a white morning in the Tiergarten. He appeared out of the mist in dove-gray flannels and an overcoat. She heard him before she saw him: uneven footsteps on the gravel, the syncopated tap of a walking stick. Then suddenly on the lane ahead—a young British gentleman.

He did not seem to be a particularly striking figure: a stuffed bear of a man with button eyes. His clothing, however, was clearly expensive, and she rather liked his formal walk. There was also the scent of cologne, a scent she had noted before but couldn't quite recall.

He approached casually while she rested her elbows on the railing, looking out across daffodils and hyacinths. She waited until he came up beside her, then spoke softly without really thinking: "I've seen you before, haven't I?"

He nodded, now also resting his elbows on the railing. "Yes, I expect you have."

"Here?"

"Yes."

"Then you've been following me." And she smiled, but only slightly.

"Yes, I suppose I have. Although it's not what it seems."

She smiled again for the enigmatic pose. "They say nothing ever is."

They began to walk, slowly drifting to a circle of chestnut trees and an iron bench on the lawn.

"The fact of the matter is that I saw you dance. In Vienna."

"Oh, really?" As if no one had ever approached her like this before.

"You were sensational, truly smashing."

"Thank you," said in her coolest, most professional voice.

"So it was a coincidence, really. I mean first seeing you dance in Vienna, and then spotting you here." He laughed to cover the silence. "Then, of course, I just had to know whether or not it was really you."

She paused, holding his gaze for another suggestive moment. "Well, it's me."

"Yes," he grinned. "It *is* you."

They settled onto the cold bench, his hands resting on his walking stick, hers demurely folded in her lap. The mist appeared to be receding, leaving everything marginally brighter.

"My name is Dunbar, Charles Dunbar," and he produced a card from his waistcoat to prove it, a tastefully delicate card with a London address.

"And what brings you to Berlin, Mr. Dunbar?" she said softly, consciously trying out the name.

"Business. Family business."

"Nothing too dreary, I hope."

He gave her a wistful smile. "Investments."

All around them it seemed that the gardens were awakening with voices of pensioners and children. The earlier magic hour had passed, and the city was once more respectable.

"I don't suppose I might see you again . . ."

She caught a glimpse of his button eyes, his plump hairless hands. "Well, that depends upon what you have in mind."

"Dinner?"

She smiled again, toying with the fringe of her dress. "Dinner is awfully serious, don't you think?"

"Then how about lunch?"

She bit her lower lip. "Well, actually I'm more or less involved at the moment."

"Involved?"

"With a man."

"Oh, I see."

"But perhaps if you were to give me the name of your hotel, then possibly—"

"The Esplanade."

As with other intriguing men in her life, her first response to this brief encounter was merely a harmless fantasy: she and Charles Dunbar sculling on some provincial river, he in white flannels and a boater, she in mauve crinoline. Following wine and chicken in aspic they would return to his mock-Tudor cottage—she and her fine Englishman with his handsome foreign investments.

Apart from these solitary daydreams her thoughts were mainly idle reflections. She wondered how it would feel to be loved by a nice inconspicuous youth. She wondered what it would be like to spend a night in the Esplanade. Once, she even found herself lingering in the Tiergarten, hoping to see him again—not that she would have known what to tell him, not with Herr Kierpert still paying the bills.

It was a Tuesday when Kierpert came again, a typically drab Berlin Tuesday. He arrived in the late afternoon smelling of beer and his wife's perfume. The sky by now was cloudless and steel blue. Their voices were once again flat and expressionless.

"Are you feeling well?" she asked. "You look tired." In fact he looked half dead, with dark circles around his eyes and a gray pallor.

"It's my nerves. My nerves are bad."

"Well, you know what they recommend for that—cocoa. I shall make you some nice hot cocoa."

He grunted, waving her off with his hand. "Just get me a brandy, Margaretha. A big one."

She gave it to him in a smudged glass without looking, then settled to the floor at his feet. On better afternoons they had been able to sit like this for hours while Kierpert drank himself into oblivion.

"I received a letter today," she said casually. "From my agent."

He gave her a look that she had seen before: *Your personal affairs hardly interest me.*

"There's talk of an engagement."

He mumbled some reply but obviously couldn't have cared less.

"In fact I think they want me to dance in Madrid again," which wasn't altogether true, but she rather liked the sound of it: *They want me in Madrid again.*

"Madrid is a cesspool."

"Yes, but there's still the money to consider."

"What money? You don't need money. I give you money."

On another afternoon, in another mood, she would not have even bothered to respond. His notions of women and life had always been impossible to counter. Yet today she couldn't seem to conjure up that demure and passive dancer for him. She couldn't even pretend. "Just the same, darling, I think I'll give it a try. Yes, I think I'll definitely give it a try."

"Get me another drink, Margaretha."

"I don't think you understand, darling."

"Of course I understand. Now get me another drink."

"I'd be leaving on the fifteenth."

"The drink, Margaretha. I want another drink."

"Difficult to say how long I'd be gone."

He reached for her shoulder, absently running his finger along her collarbone. Then suddenly grabbing her hair, he twisted her head back. "The drink, Margaretha? Get me the *drink.*"

"You're *hurting* me."

"The drink."

She crossed the room without speaking. The decanter had been left on the mantle, but her hands were shaking so badly that she had to move it to the table in order to avoid a mess. Then returning to his chair, she couldn't seem to raise her eyes . . . until she faced him, motionless, the glass of brandy in her left hand.

"Now give it to me, Margaretha. *Give* it to me."

She must have waited two or three seconds before tossing the stuff in his face. For another second or two neither moved. Finally Kierpert rose, slapping her across the face. She reeled back, screaming at him as he slapped her again, full force, back-handed. The third blow left her sobbing on her knees, her robe parted to the thigh, a trace of blood in the corner of her mouth.

"A drink, Margaretha." His voice was firm but soft: the soldier addressing an errant child. "Fetch me a drink."

When she did not respond he grabbed her hair again, drawing her face up to his. "A drink."

His eyes were blue, flecked with gold, and they held her for an instant before she shot back, "Go to hell. Go straight to hell."

She saw his eyes narrow slightly. Then another stinging blow left her breathless, staring at a border of stylized birds woven into the edge of the rug.

He closed on her slowly, slipping his hand under her robe and tearing it off in long strips. When her arms reflexively moved to her breasts, he pinned her wrists together, forcing her head to the floor. For a moment they both remained still, breathing hard, rhythmically.

There were mirrors on an opposite wall, and an almost ludicrous vision of herself as a trussed-up chicken. Kierpert lowered his trousers and dropped to his knees behind her. His eyes were glazed, and she couldn't help wincing as he slipped between her legs, prodding, exploring. Then he was on her like a furious ghost, driving deep inside.

When he had finished he left her on the floor, trembling slightly but not uttering a sound.

He dressed in the shadows, watching her, also not speaking. A quick impression of his profile in the glass left her with only a momentary thought: *how German* . . . Then, without warning he spoke; flat, emotionless, as if nothing had happened. "I won't be able to see you on Friday. I have previous commitments."

She reached for the bedspread in a half-hearted attempt to cover herself, "Get out."

"If, however, you should need me—"

"Get *out* of here."

For a long time after he had gone she scarcely moved. Although it was still early, the neighborhood was silent—just another ordinary Tuesday afternoon stuck in time. Then, by degrees she returned to ordinary pursuits: washing her hair, running a bath, turning down the bed. Sounds of distant traffic made her sad, so she placed another record on the gramophone.

There was a bruise on her left cheek, bruises on her wrists. She didn't worry about them. Only a man would be concerned with such temporary imperfection. Men . . . so vain, so foolish.

Dreams covered moods like this, dreams of a daughter that she hardly knew, and a house in a country she had never seen. They would live as only independent women could live, drying their hair in a garden filled with ragged grass and hibiscus trumpets, chatting over tea and biscuits. Men would remain peripheral entities: delivering letters, chopping wood, killing each other off. Artists of consequence would visit on Sundays. And if, on occasion, these simple pleasures were not enough, one could always turn to an innocuous soul like that young Charles Dunbar at the Esplanade Hotel.

She went to him on Sunday, a little after the visiting hour. There was a full moon above the factory roofs, a warm breeze bringing odors of damp brick and coal. Beyond a residential neighborhood, the cafes were filled with students from the local academy, speaking softly over tankards of beer. As an unescorted woman in black, she suspected they were discussing her —but she didn't care. Still farther along the Kantstrasse she passed the sort of common prostitutes who were forever underestimating their power over men, regardless of whether they met them in a beer hall or a suite at the Esplanade.

She entered the lobby at half past eight, passing a note to a bellboy. Someone emerging from a reading room tried to catch her eye, but she ignored him. The lounge was appointed with potted palms and a vase of sulphur roses. She never doubted for a moment that her Englishman would come.

She saw him first on the staircase, looking somewhat bewildered in a dinner jacket, with a shy smile and child's eyes. In the lamplight he looked a little shorter than she remembered, his hair a little thinner. But closer she realized that nothing had changed, and although he took her hand he didn't have the confidence to kiss it.

"I was afraid that you had already returned to London," she told him.

A shy grin. "Well, as you can see . . ."

"Yes, as I can see." She turned so that the light would not accentuate the bruise on her cheek. "And now perhaps we'll have some time together."

He wet his lips, glancing back to the staircase. "But I thought you were—"

"No longer."

They wandered out to a formal garden of junipers and sculptured hedgerows. She slipped her arm through his, casually brushing his thigh with her wrist. Then along a mossy path she broke away, calling, "Don't you simply adore the fragrance, Mr. Dunbar? Don't you simply adore it?"

He finally caught up with her under a trailing wisteria. It was dark here, and the odors were basic: wet soil, leaf mould, and her perfume.

"I don't suppose you'd care to dine with me?" he said, almost in a whisper, although they were alone.

She smiled, but looked away as if distracted by the flowering hydrangea. "Tonight?"

"If you're available, that is."

"Where?"

"Wherever you like?"

She stepped closer, almost touching him again. "Someplace extravagant?"

They dined on a terrace above the Tiergarten lanes, not far from where she had originally seen him. He ordered brill in white butter sauce and a small flotilla of lobsters. They talked about England, and about simple existence in the countryside with horses, vast lawns, and croquet. In response to another reference concerning capital investments abroad, she ran a forefinger along his wrist—back and forth, back and forth.

They spent the remainder of that evening walking, strolling along the more obscure lanes between stunted pines and the banks of a pond. Against the reverberation of crickets, conversation seemed pointless, so they sat side by side on a bench—her hand lightly pressed on his again. Seeing that his values were still clearly traditional, she eventually left him with only a glancing kiss, her lips momentarily brushing his under those fantastic elms.

She met him next on a Tuesday, arriving on foot in a simple skirt and blouse. They spent the first hour in the National Gallery, then moved out to the gardens, then into a coffee house to escape the rain. Conversation remained trivial, with anecdotes from Dunbar's childhood and memories from summers along the coast; and through it all Zelle would laugh and smile, reach and withdraw, like an angler deftly playing a trout in cold water . . .

She brought him to her room about midnight, after a great deal of champagne. She sat him in a chair with a glass of mineral water, then slipped into a simple frock. A veil tossed over a lampshade turned the room to a deeper blue. A scented candle on the mantle cut the smell of damp.

He had mentioned that he wasn't feeling well, but she ignored it and led him to the bed. She slipped off his shoes, his tie, his waistcoat, and his shirt, and told him to lie down. His body was soft and pale, like a child's. His chest was smooth, almost hairless. Although the air was fairly cool through an open window, he had already begun to perspire.

She played with him, seated in a chair beside the bed. She let her finger drift across his thighs in lazy circles, then lower, gently caressing with the tip of one finger, then only with the nail. He responded with a long sigh, rolling back his eyes and rising to meet her touch. She replied with a half nod and a knowing smile.

When the play was over she had still not undressed, still had not spoken. His body was wet with perspiration, the heartbeat a visible shudder. An earlier wind had died, leaving only the warm torpor of this night on the cusp of summer.

"I should go," he said. "It's late."

She shook her head and moved to the dressing table. "No, it's not late."

There were bottles of perfume on the table, and she picked one up at random—an expensive but unsubtle German scent.

She was still examining the label when he softly called her name, "Margaretha, let me take you back to London."

She smiled, fully aware of his imploring eyes in the mirror. "London?"

"We'll have a smashing time, I promise."

She put down the perfume, crossed the room and gently kissed him on the forehead. "But I don't want to go to London."

"Why not?"

"Because I don't believe they'll like me there."

"But of course they will."

She ran a knuckle across his shoulder, then lower to the nipple. "Besides, the spring is so lovely in Paris."

He sat up, wrapping himself in a sheet and frowning. "Paris? But my parents are expecting me in London."

She took his head in her hands, pressing his face to her breasts. "Then it seems that your parents will be disappointed, won't they?"

They left Berlin on an afternoon train the second Tuesday in May. Four scribbled pages to Herr Kierpert explained nothing and said everything. An outstanding bill of three thousand marks was discreetly settled by Dunbar. Buried in her luggage were two porcelain figurines for Jules Cambon and a tiny Rembrandt etching for Gray.

There was also a letter to a woman that Zelle had befriended earlier that year, an occasional singer and mistress of an officer. Margaretha's message to her was essentially a note on a familiar theme; all men are basically the same, she wrote, with the same obsessions, the same demands and insecurities. A beautiful woman need only cater to their fantasies in order to get whatever she wants. There were also references to old jokes concerning desire as a weapon and love as a means to an end—all notions they would later dredge up to destroy her.

Chapter Nine

GRAY'S first impressions of Dunbar were informally recorded one evening in pencil along the Champs Élysées. Like other sketches from the period, the portrait of Dunbar seems slightly exaggerated, perhaps even a little comical. The man had showed up with Zelle in the doorway of the Chinese Pavillion, and his seated pose is framed by interlocking dragons enameled on a screen. Zelle is shown leaning on his shoulder with adoring still-brook eyes.

Given the setting, the portrait seems to be an obvious enough statement. Here, Gray seems to be saying, is a pleasant but somewhat naive young man entertaining extravagant friends. His clothing is fashionably conformist with a modest pinstripe and a tight-budded rose in the left lapel. The smile is faintly bemused.

Beyond what is evident in the work, Gray's initial feelings for the man were equivocal, possibly clouded by alcohol, definitely clouded by jealousy. Dunbar, he would later say, was like a lot of fellows one met in English public schools: simple, affable, too concerned with what others thought. Indeed, Dunbar's first conversation with Gray concerned Oxford and various dons they had known. Apparently Dunbar had been something of a figure on campus, remembered for his lavish dinner parties. He had also run successfully for the better clubs, the Carlton in his freshman year, then the Grid and the Union.

Yet with Zelle in Paris the man was shy and solicitous. He was generally content to let her hang on his arm and whisper in his ear. On occasion he would even let her speak for him, smiling while she was saying such things as, "Oh, but Charles drinks champagne at all hours," or "Charles doesn't care for the Germans one bit." For his own part Gray knew better than to interrupt while Mata Hari was displaying a new lover.

It was a warm night, and after supper Margaretha insisted that they take a walk. After an hour on the boulevard she led them to a terrace for still more champagne and light conversation. When she excused herself for the powder room, Gray for the first time found himself alone with Dunbar. It was obviously a calculated move, possibly even prearranged.

"Margaretha tells me that you were her first Parisian friend," Dunbar began.

"Yes," Gray said, "I suppose I was."

"And wasn't there also a photographer? A Russian chap?"

"De Massloff."

"That's right, Vadime de Massloff. I understand that she was very fond of him as well. A bit of a character, but fun."

"Yes, fun."

A waiter appeared with champagne and plates of oysters on a bed of ice. The view through the laurels was also reminiscent of earlier days, with ranks of cabs along the curbstones and wandering violinists.

"I imagine it really must have been something . . ."

"Hmm?"

"That first spring in Paris," Dunbar said.

"Yes, it was something."

"And you still find it stimulating? The city, I mean."

Gray lit a cigarette, inhaling. "I suppose."

"But surely you must miss England occasionally. I know I would."

Gray shrugged with the thought that they might have been in England now, whispering in the darkness of some wretched boys' dormitory, exchanging secrets and bits of chocolate. "No, I can't say that I miss England now."

"Well, then I suppose I envy you. I mean, to have made such a clean break of it all. Don't think I'd have the courage, really."

Then give it a week, Gray could have told him. Give it a month, give it another few nights with Zelle.

She returned with an orchid that she must have snatched from a vacant table. She wouldn't touch the oysters but accepted more champagne. It was late, and the parties were dispersing along the garden paths. Exhausted waiters were chatting among themselves.

"You like him, don't you?" she told Gray after Dunbar had been dismissed to secure a cab. "I mean, within limits you *do* like him, don't you?"

He mumbled a civil lie. "Of course."

"Then it's settled! I'm appointing you his guardian."

He looked at her. "Guardian?"

"Well, you're both English, aren't you? Besides, he's filthy rich, which should make it fun for all three of us."

So it began—with all the old obsessions, the unreasoning desire, the hunger. By the second evening their roles had been established: Gray as the quiet observer and confidant, Dunbar as the perfect fool, Zelle as herself. They dined with obscure friends along the river, then sauntered through the botanical gardens. Margaretha at times made jokes at Dunbar's expense. He did, they said, seem to invite them. Dunbar pretended not to notice.

Toward that midnight they moved on to a table at Maxim's,

where Gray found himself reliving a drama he must have witnessed a dozen times before: Zelle in a circle of admiring friends, clinging to the arm of a lover who would finally pay the bill. The stories were the same, mostly creative anecdotes of her adventures abroad. Then came the obligatory goodnight kiss, followed by the long walk through damp streets to his room.

His studio had hardly changed since those first days with her. There were still those furtive sketches on the wall, still her letters in a drawer. Then again there were moments when it almost seemed she had never left, moments when he almost felt her watching from behind the oval mirror.

Ordinarily, after a night on the town Gray would spend an hour on the balcony with a beer and a sketch pad. After this particular evening, however, he wanted absolute solitude. He wanted the windows shut, the door locked. He wanted the light from only one small lamp.

He slipped her photograph out of the drawer and laid it on the drawing table. Although he had several photographs, he nearly always returned to the original: that compelling portrait of a naked girl astride a bicycle. He would study the face, jogging old memories and feelings. He was careful not to look at it too often, out of fear of exhausting the impact. Or building it to intolerable levels.

It was almost dawn when he finally put the photograph aside. Pigeons clustered on neighboring roofs. The air outside was heavy and still. Hot winds from the south were due at any time. Now and again he thought he also heard the distant whine of trains, each one calling him away from her. He knew he should have left her long ago, collected his things and left without warning—forwarding address unknown. On arriving in London he could have looked up one or two old friends with connections to respectable galleries. Then, over the course of five or ten years—five or ten years of normalcy —she would have become just another memory of long limbs in a twisted bedsheet.

But it was useless, all useless; knowing that whenever she called he would come. He would come on the odd nights as an escort. He would come as a friend to amuse her lovers. He would come uninvited as the eternal voyeur, silently watching from a corner table as she wasted her time with the ones like Charles Dunbar.

                                          It was now the dead heat of summer, windless and stagnant. Zelle had been spending her days in rehearsal for another autumn tour, and consequently Dunbar had a lot of time to kill, some of which he would spend with Gray over afternoon drinks.

They usually met in one of the more atmospheric cafes along the Left Bank. Dunbar always arrived early, always overdressed. On the first afternoon they discussed Oxford, where Dunbar explained that he had fared badly his freshman year, failing to do himself justice on Ovid's *Metamorphoses*. Gray, who couldn't seem to recall a thing about the place except a vague impression of shuttered lanes and the bells of Christ Church, found himself muttering whatever seemed appropriate.

From Oxford they moved on to art and politics, discussing both without real conviction. Next came the theater, then at last they came around to Zelle.

"You know she's awfully fond of you," Dunbar said. "In quite a marvelous way."

"She seems fond of you too," Gray said, "in quite an obvious way."

"Yes, but I sometimes wonder if yours isn't the safer route—emotionally speaking, that is."

Gray looked at him. They had ordered wine as a prelude to champagne, but after several glasses he still remained too conscious of everything.

"It's not that I'm complaining," Dunbar went on. "It's just that I don't always know where she stands, if you get my point."

"Oh I think so." Gray smiled, wondering if the waiter could possibly bring him a brandy, and in a hurry.

"Then, too, there's the question of patience," Dunbar added. "I mean she can be infuriating, can't she?"

She can be infuriating, can't she? It was the first time that Gray had ever heard the man express dissatisfaction with Zelle, the first tiny crack in the glass. Yet not reading what probably should have been obvious, he thought nothing of it at the time.

Following that afternoon by the river, there were five days of relative calm. Dunbar spent the time leisurely, touring the Louvre and the Luxembourg Gardens. In the evenings he and Zelle either dined alone on the Champs Élysées or with friends in the artists' cafes. Although Gray eventually joined them on a number of occasions, he would specifically recall only the first . . .

It was a torpid night, the city might have been fixed beneath a bell jar. What had looked like fog turned out to be industrial fumes, and the back streets were mostly deserted. On Zelle's suggestion they dined in one of the Russian cafes where friends from the neighborhood tended to gather. The food was only mediocre, but there were always violinists in the gallery.

From the start there was something discordant about that night. Even before the cocktails had arrived, Dunbar was sent on some menial errand, only to be rewarded with a deprecating smile. Next there were comments concerning his clothing and his hopelessly English perspective. Nor was she pleased with his choice of wine.

It became a pattern, a repeated blow on the same bruise. Dunbar would offer some innocent opinion, and Zelle would casually tear him apart. As the evening wore on and the silence grew increasingly oppressive, it seemed that even the waiters became uneasy, hesitating in the wings with another bottle for that famous scandalous dancer.

It was midnight when her party finally deteriorated. Dunbar had been sent to find a taxi, while Zelle retired to a balcony. From here there was a broad view of the river across the rooftops, and mounting rain clouds on the horizon.

Gray approached slowly without speaking. Zelle did not turn around. Her hair hung freely at her shoulders; and although her eyes were still clear, he sensed the exhaustion in her voice.

"I can't imagine any place as beautiful as this," she told him.

He stepped a little closer until their hands were nearly touching on the railing. "But then you've never seen England, have you?"

She tossed back her head. "Oh, so that's it. You've come on behalf of Charles."

"You did appoint me his guardian."

"That was a temporary measure. He's on his own now."

"But hardly succeeding."

"What's that supposed to mean?"

He glanced away, shoving his hands in his pockets. Three stories below another lost soul seemed to be searching for a cab.

"Do you love him at all, Margaretha?"

"Really, Nicky."

"Do you?"

"Of course."

"Then why do you treat him like some bloody poodle?"

He expected a burst of sardonic laughter, but instead she merely wet her lips, suddenly like that child again. Her voice was also very soft. "He's all right, Nicky. Honestly he is. It's just that . . . well, sometimes things get out of hand."

"Then send him back to England. Cut him loose and send him home."

She smiled. "You sound like a priest, a jealous priest. And they're the worst kind, fanatic with unseen motives."

"Send him home, Margaretha."

"But I love him, really I do—"

"No, you don't."

He had her to himself only once more that night—a few parting words in a courtyard stinking from ruptured sewers. Dunbar had been told to wait in the carriage. It was very quiet.

"Don't talk about Charles," she said. "There's no need."

She had placed her hand on his shoulder, an absent gesture.

"Margaretha—"

"No, listen. Charles and I have an understanding, so you see it's really all right. I mean it's all quite harmless. Nicky, don't look at me that way. I'm telling you the truth—it's harmless."

And no doubt she even believed it.

A week passed before he saw her again, and from these days are four drawings of her seated in a cane chair. Her dress is black, and her hair, drawn tightly back, gives her face an unaccustomed degree of severity. The eyes are fixed on the naked form of a boy at her feet. There is no sense of affection; and her hand, reaching for the boy's leg, seems to be a foreign object . . .

Yet when he finally saw her again his private vision almost seemed absurd; she actually appeared quite pretty in a simple and innocent way. Her hair was loosely tied with a ribbon, her eyes were accented with only a hint of shadow. Nor was the conversation even remotely sinister—merely a discussion concerning her forthcoming tour.

She said that she would be performing for at least seven weeks, including eight nights in Vienna. She said that the money was by no means grand but one could always use the exposure. Finally she mentioned that Dunbar would be accompanying her to help with the practical arrangements. Gray said, with less emotion than he felt, that Dunbar, a practical fellow, ought to be a real help, what with his firm grasp of numbers.

It was about eight o'clock when they separated, and what had opened as a wretched day ended rather beautifully. The sky was pink and cloudless with a white moon above the apartment blocks. The crowds were gradually thinning except along the tram stops. Yet, to have a final impression of this evening, Gray briefly paused at the edge of the square for a last glimpse of her. She was standing at the curbstone to receive an arriving cab. Dunbar was apparently leaning from inside; and although her eyes were unreadable, the smile was familiar enough.

They left on a Monday, a clear day under a white sky. The leaves had still not turned but there was a distinct sense of summer's end. Although Gray did not actually see them off at the station, he was able to envision the event clearly enough: while Dunbar supervised the porters, Zelle waved exuberantly from the step.

As always, the first week was the worst, and Gray spent it either working furiously or sitting with friends in crowded cafes. Yet even a thousand miles away one could never really forget her, for in those days when her fame was still at its peak there were constantly reminders in the newspapers. The initial reviews reached Paris in October, and it seemed the critics also loved her.

But what finally left the most lasting impression was a letter, not from Zelle but from Dunbar. It arrived mid-October on an otherwise ordinary day. Gray had spent the morning sketching fishermen below Pont Neuf, then returning to his room in the afternoon, he found the thing tacked to his door: six carefully handwritten pages from the Bristol Hotel in Vienna.

In effect Dunbar had sent two letters, one between the lines of the other. Vienna was chilly, he began, but the setting could not have been more beautiful with a hundred red trees along the Ringstrasse and the continual strains of the waltz. There was also, of course, the Danube and stimulating evenings in the common. The nights, however, were tiresome and one could not escape the Jews.

There were two brief paragraphs concerning Zelle's bohemian friends, then a long and ambivalent description of her first performance. "Like all Austrians," he wrote, "the Viennese can be exceedingly possessive, particularly when consumed with a popular entertainer . . ." He further noted that the local aristocracy was a bore. After all, it was not English.

From these idle reflections it seemed that Dunbar's message took a cryptic turn, with vague complaints about Zelle's schedule, her relationship with others, and an even vaguer recognition of his own obsession. Apparently he had been reading Freud, and there was something about cyclical disturbances that held him like a magnet.

In contrast to all this, however, his closing remarks were cheerful and reserved. An acquaintance of Margaretha's had invited them to the country, where he hoped to shoot stag but would settle for pheasant. Zelle was looking forward to riding, and naturally she sent her regards . . .

It was four in the afternoon when Gray put down the letter. Four o'clock, the dazed hour. Zelle probably would have been napping, while Dunbar brooded in an adjoining room. The light would have been blue or steel-blue, her clothing flung all over the place.

It was obvious from the closing remarks that Dunbar expected a reply, but even if one had known what to write, another five or six pages on Zelle seemed pointless. One could never hope to explain her, analyze or dismiss her. She was much too complex to define, and advice from another man was irrelevant.

"But I never quite know when she's joking and when she's serious," Dunbar had said. Then you probably never will, Gray could have told him. For ultimately she came from another world, an odd place that one entered through a low door in a wall. Everything was slightly out of focus, and the roads all led in circles. Time was also a little warped so that a single night could feel like a thousand years.

More than six weeks passed without further word from Dunbar, and from these days are a number of what seem to be simple drawings suggesting a return to basics. He worked with honest light and austere shapes. He spent a long time dissecting a wicker chair. He had also become intrigued with the neighborhood cats, and eventually adopted a stray called Bolero. The animal still survives in a watercolor from the fall of 1908.

Away from the easel, life had also lost its complex dimensions, suggesting his first eighteen months in this city. He spent evenings with Vadime de Massloff, and occasionally rode the omnibus in search of new perspectives. Eventually there were even periods (particularly toward the end of October) when it seemed that he had actually survived the worst of it—as far as Zelle was concerned, he had actually managed to survive. His life, laid out before him in momentary glimpses, still seemed reasonably bright. He tended to envision himself in some quaint London suburb working with oils and concentrating on landscapes. His neighbors, simple but kind people, would see him as a mild eccentric who had almost lived the life that everyone dreamed about . . . and if certain young women found him attractive he might finally consent to paint them too.

These then were the visions that consoled him through that autumn, the rainy-day thoughts that kept him from fixating on Zelle.

At one point he even went so far as to inquire about outlying property in Berkshire, then spent an afternoon with *The Times.* But in the end, of course, there was to be no escape, not in England, not in France, no real escape . . .

It was a Friday when Dunbar's telegram arrived, one of the first cold days of the year. The sky was gray, the gutters filled with frost, and suddenly from nowhere: *Arriving eight o'clock, gare Saint-Lazare.*

Had Gray followed his instincts, he might have torn the message up, bolted the door, and drawn the curtains. But instead he simply waited, seated by a window with the first hard drink he'd had in days. Then around dusk he went down to the streets. It only took a moment to find a vacant cab.

The station was cold with damp air from the rafters. Voices seemed remote against the rattle of incoming trains. It was half past the hour when Dunbar appeared: one more figure in the steam. He was alone, badly dressed in expensive clothing, searching, as always, for his luggage.

Night had turned even colder with a chilled rain. There was also a north wind, driving pedestrians from the streets. Because Dunbar had not booked a hotel room, Gray had no alternative but to bring the man home. It was cold here too, but neither seemed to notice.

Their first moments together were strained with long silences and unanswered questions. Gray had poured two glasses of cheap sherry while Dunbar studied the more recent drawings on the wall. He seemed particularly interested in three portraits of Zelle: sitting, reclining, and fixed at still another mirror.

"These are new, aren't they?" he said.

Gray nodded. His voice was cautious. "Yes, those are fairly new."

"Well, I definitely like them. In fact should you ever want to sell them—"

"What happened, Charles?"

"Hmm?"

"What happened with Margaretha?"

Dunbar shrugged. "Nothing. A lot." His eyes settled on another portrait, an early nude in crayon. "And I like *this* very much indeed."

"You've seen it before."

"Have I? Well, I can't say that I remember. And I would have remembered, because it's really quite stunning."

"What happened, Charles?"

He shrugged again. "I'll tell you some rainy day."

"It's raining now."

They sat in an alcove facing the rooftops again. Gray had set the bottle of sherry on the floor, and as the rain died the familiar night sounds returned: pigeons stirring under the eaves, the cries of cats. Then it began, a slow monologue of Dunbar's first week abroad with Margaretha.

They had arrived in Monte Carlo on a Wednesday, he said. Zelle had been disappointed that no one of importance had met them at the station. There had also been difficulties with her luggage, and the Grand Hotel had been unable to provide a suite. In the evening they dined with some odious Hungarian and two shadowy characters that Zelle had met in the casino.

There was a change, Dunbar explained, a gradual change in Zelle the moment she reached Monte Carlo. Presumably she was there to discuss her role as Cleopatra in a production of *Antar*. There had also been some talk about a series of private performances at three thousand francs a night. For the most part, however, she spent her time with gentlemen she met at random, often around the tables. Dunbar was rarely asked to join the party, and the excuse was always the same: these were influential men with a real capability to help an artist. They were not, however, entirely free from personal fantasies, which meant that they wanted to see her alone.

There were definite stages to the decline, Dunbar said, the emotional, physical, spiritual decline. In the beginning, so he claimed, he had been understanding, tolerant of Zelle's evenings away. There were "lovely botanical gardens" not far from the hotel, and he eventually came to enjoy a solitary hour in the late afternoon among the vegetation. He also used the time to read: Ruskin, Dickens, Freud. But ultimately, he confessed, jealousy was a tangible thing, and there were also bad dreams and bad nights waiting for the sound of her key in the lock.

The Middle Years

It went from bad to worse, with a recurring vision of her slipping off her clothing in an unfamiliar room. Talk of it always ended unpleasantly. Once she even accused him of intentionally trying to ruin her career, and there were two nights when she did not return until dawn.

Of course he considered leaving, slipping away in the morning while she slept. Eventually he even found himself studying the train schedules and composing farewell notes. He rather thought that something brief and cavalier would have been best: *Darling, by the time you have read this I'll have reached the Coast . . . adieu.* However, he never got further than packing a bag. (In this, Gray thought wryly, they were not so different.)

In time Dunbar came to see that her behavior followed a pattern, a cyclical pattern of cruelty and affection from which there was no escape. Following Monte Carlo they moved on to Sofia, Budapest, and Prague. The weather remained irregular, and Zelle became increasingly moody. Although there were still occasions when she genuinely tried to please him, more and more it seemed that their relationship had taken a bad turn. There were distinctly sadistic overtones to the nights, and twice she actually struck him with her hairbrush. She had "grown rather fond of ordering me about," he said.

There was an epilogue to Dunbar's story, but at first he seemed too tired to tell it. Since the rain had stopped, he had returned to the window, moodily describing a few last impressions. He said that although she continued to live nocturnally, she honestly loved the mornings. He said that more than once he had found her on a balcony just after dawn. "I also seem to recall that she specifically enjoyed a certain garden in Sofia," he added, "and of course the Danube was very beautiful, although I can't imagine why they say it's blue."

Through all this Gray had sat watching from the wicker chair. Earlier he had asked if Dunbar was hungry but had gotten no reply. Now again: "If you're hungry . . . if you want something to eat?"

"No, not hungry, not cold. Just tired."

There was whisky in a cupboard, half a bottle that hadn't been touched for years. Gray poured another two glasses without asking, then said, "I can fix you a bed on the divan."

Again Dunbar declined. "Not tired, not in that sense . . ." Then, turning away from the window: "You know, the funny part is that I didn't actually leave her. Not even at the end. *She* left *me*. Simply ran off with another man. Which is always, I suppose, the story."

Across the room, still watching, Gray had put the glasses down. He wanted air but it was too cold to open a window.

"It happened in Vienna," Dunbar said suddenly. "The second time around after Prague. Things had been rather comfortable for a while, then one evening she turned up with this captain. A German she called Rudy, which I gather was also the name of her first husband, wasn't it?"

Gray nodded. "Yes, her husband's name was Rudy."

"Well, at first I thought nothing of him. I mean, it wasn't as if he'd been the first. But then it began to dawn on me that this was different. This one was for keeps." He shifted his gaze from an early crayon to another flawed sketch in charcoal. "I say, is that also new?"

Gray mumbled something. His throat was suddenly dry, breath a little short. "Did you ever meet him?"

"Hmm?"

"The German. Did you ever meet him?"

Dunbar couldn't seem to take his eyes off that charcoal. "Had dinner with them both. Not many laughs, though. Margaretha had a headache, you see. And this Rudy didn't drink, or at least didn't show it. I seem to recall that he talked about horses . . . Then, in the morning, they were gone. All gone. Care to see her goodbye note?"

Gray did not answer, did not set down his glass now that the whisky was gone . . . all gone, like Zelle . . . "What was he like?"

Dunbar turned. "You mean the German?"

"Yes, what was he like?"

"I don't know . . . quiet."

"Did he speak English?"

"Yes."

108

"And French?"

"Yes."

"Flawlessly? Both English and French flawlessly?"

"Nicholas, I'm not sure—"

"Flawlessly?"

Dunbar took a step back, then another. "Yes, now that you mention it, I suppose he did. But I'm afraid that I—"

"And was his last name Spangler? Rudolph Spangler?"

"Yes, but how—"

"Because I knew him. Knew of him . . . from a long time ago."

The night never returned to normal, and if nothing else they would ever forget the storm. It seemed to break from above the rain, directly over the city. By dawn the back streets were littered with debris, the smaller gardens a ruin.

It was very close to winter the day that Dunbar finally returned to England. There were icicles suspended from the water pumps, the breath of waiting horses in the air. The station was also very cold, which seemed to inhibit conversation.

They spoke calmly now about Zelle while waiting for departure in a coffee house above the crowds. Dunbar in particular seemed comforted by certain theories of the day concerning hysterical women. "Read Freud," he said. "Read anyone. The woman is a classic case. Venus with Medusan tendencies." Their parting words were mumbled goodbyes on the platform.

After Dunbar had gone Gray spent at least another hour at a table with a beer, watching the locomotives. Then at last he joined a disembarking crowd in search of something else to drink. On returning to his room he busied himself with small tasks . . . washing a few plates, tossing out empty bottles, then tearing those portraits of Zelle off the wall and putting them in a drawer with all her other bloody relics . . . including that sketch of Spangler.

It was late when he extinguished the lamps, much too late for anything except a few last random thoughts: Spangler was back, just as one day Dunbar would probably be back, just as finally the others would come back, some that she wouldn't even remember. They would come when she least expected it, demanding retribution or worse; and even if it were possible to shoot them all, their ghosts would still come, just as the ghost of Michard kept coming back to him now and again on balmy nights.

Chapter Ten

*L*IKE others from the forma-
tive years of German intelligence, Rudolph Spangler
would always remain an elusive figure. Whole decades of his life
have never been accounted for, and even his name is suspect. Because he habitually changed his appearance, the few existent photographs are unreliable.

Of his early years all that is known for certain is that he was born
to a family of modest means somewhere north of Bremen. His
father was an unsuccessful merchant, and probably an alcoholic.
His mother was consumptive. He entered the military at a young
age, and seems to have distinguished himself in one of the German
colonial wars. Although there is no indication of where or when he
was initiated into the secret world, it is quite possible that he was
one of the last surviving protégés of the remarkable Wilhelm
Stieber, Bismarck's prince of foxes.

Despite humble origins he was an urbane and well-read man. He
was also, according to Mata Hari, a decidedly handsome man. His

111

hair was fair. His eyes were gray-blue. He was slender but muscular and stood about six feet tall. Although his rank was unknown he generally wore the uniform of a Bavarian cavalry officer, and was said to have been an accomplished horseman and hunter with appropriate rights on all the better estates.

This was undoubtedly the Rudolph Spangler who captivated Mata Hari during that Viennese winter of 1908: an engaging soldier with obvious means and taste. Although she would never recall having met him before (in his earlier incarnation as the Swiss financier, Diderot), she would always insist that there had been a subconscious recognition, as if they had been lovers in a previous life.

Their initial meeting, as Dunbar had described it: One evening while attending an embassy soirée, Margaretha sensed the gaze of a man across the room. Turning, her eyes met those of a solitary German officer. He held two glasses of champagne in one hand, the stems between his fingers. In response to her casual smile he merely extended his arm and nodded. Moments later they adjourned to a terrace where conversation remained polite but suggestive. Still later they danced to selections of popular waltzes including "The Blue Danube."

From the start there were unusual undertones to the relationship, an odd sense of compulsion and blind desire. Following their first evening together she met him for lunch in an obscure provincial cafe. They dined on blood sausage and pumpernickel. There were no other patrons. Although he said nothing particularly revealing about himself, she would tell others that even discussing the weather with him somehow seemed meaningful. He tended to speak slowly, with a soft, melodic voice. She also liked the way he handled small objects or lit a cigarette, always with calm and deliberate movements.

They spent their second afternoon together in a half-deserted coffeehouse with a view of leafless trees and wet cobbles. Once again nothing of real importance was discussed, but she enjoyed the sound of his voice and his measured response to her questions: no, he had never seen her dance; yes, he had been to Paris once, but a long time ago . . .

Next there was the unavoidable dinner with Charles, during which Spangler clearly established himself as predominant. And there were drinks on the Ringstrasse, leading to the inevitable proposal: "Since you are returning to Paris anyway, why not travel with me to Geneva, where I have a small matter to attend to? I know a certain place there which I think you will find very beautiful."

She had reservations, Dunbar not the least of them. Then, too, there were practical considerations involving appointments with agents and further commitments abroad. But nothing really seemed to matter in the wake of his smile, and the suggestive, "I think you will find Geneva very beautiful."

They left on a Monday, shortly after dawn. Her farewell letter to Dunbar took hours to compose, but ultimately communicated nothing. Beyond Vienna the landscape was very still and beautiful, with an early snow between the dingles. She slept for an hour, without the intrusion of a dream.

On arriving in Geneva he took her to a small inn nestled among the pines on the edge of the lake. There was a long view of the quays and irregular hills. Her room was charming with sturdy pine furniture, like something from a sailor's retreat. In the afternoon a wind rose, muffling sounds from below. In the evening she dozed to the tick of a clock, then wept for a while without knowing why.

It was late when he finally came to her. She was still half asleep on the bed. The lights were low, and for a moment he looked almost spectral in white flannels and pale-gray silk. He knelt beside the bed to unfasten her dress, stepped back when she was finally naked, watching but still not speaking. His eyes also seemed remote. His arms hung at his side.

"You really don't know who I am, do you?" he said at last. "You really don't know."

She tried to smile to break the tension, but all that came out was, "Who you are?"

"Yes. Who I am."

He turned away and lit a cigarette, but she realized that he was still watching from an oval mirror above the dressing table. He had removed only his waistcoat. There was a slight smile on his thin lips.

"Of course there is always the possibility that you're lying, but somehow I don't think so."

She shifted her naked thighs, conscious of his gaze as a tangible force. "Rudolph, I really—"

"Yes, Rudolph. But beyond that you actually don't know, do you?"

"Rudy, please . . ."

"Oh, don't be afraid. Even if you're lying, I wouldn't hurt you."

Then, extinguishing his cigarette, he slowly crossed the room and undressed. His body was hard and white in the moonlight, below his ribs was a scar that resembled a crescent moon. He whispered again, bending to kiss her: "No, you really don't know, do you? He laid his hand on her breast, and for several seconds neither seemed able to move. Then he was on her like a white scarf, briefly suspended before falling.

The stillness returned the moment he withdrew from her, as if it might have crept into the room from under the door, a force in its own right. He poured her a glass of sherry and laid it on the table beside the bed, but at first she hadn't the strength to touch it. Then too, she didn't want to wash away the taste of him.

"Why did you ask if I knew who you were?"

He smiled. "Call it a soldier's preoccupation."

Her hand slid across the bed, moving to that scar. Somehow it seemed more prominent now. She touched it, curiously, as a child might touch a dead thing. "And *how* did you get this?"

He smiled again, lighting another cigarette. "War."

"Yes, but *how?*"

"I was stupid, I think. Yes, I was stupid."

"Was it from a bullet?"

"I don't know, I can't remember."

She shut her eyes and kissed it, then kissed it again. "Well, if I had been your nurse, you certainly would have remembered."

He smiled, lifting her head to the light. "Yes, Margaretha. Yes, I think you would have been a very good woman in a war."

The tempo of the first day continued. In the mornings they walked for a mile past the quay. In the afternoons they usually rested quietly, sitting together on a balcony. Conversations remained dry and superficial. He never again asked if she knew who he really was.

The tone of the nights also never changed. He would usually enter her room just after ten o'clock. Occasionally he brought champagne, more often sherry. He took the first glass in a chair by the window, watching from the shadows while she undressed. Then laying down the glass and extinguishing his cigarette, he would move to the edge of the bed. Although he was always very gentle with her, it was clear to her from his eyes, his manner, that only absolute submission was acceptable.

He never told her that he loved her, but now and again she tended to sense a unique devotion. "You are definitely a woman to die for," he said. "Or definitely a woman to kill for." As for her own sense of devotion, she supposed that these were spellbound weeks, as involving as any dream. She loved watching him from a distance as he moved across the dunes with a gray fedora and a stick he had picked up at random. She also loved to watch him sleeping, with his uniform draped across a chair.

They only quarreled once, toward the fogbound evening of the last day. He had left her in the afternoon, meeting a carriage and then going into the city. When he returned she was waiting by the window on a velveteen sofa. She had finished his bottle of sherry, which left her tired and slightly ill. She was also finally tired of the stillness and the predictable church bells.

"So. Was your day a success?"

He smiled but didn't respond.

"Because mine was a dismal failure."

He had entered with an attaché case, an elegant one that she had never seen before. He laid it on the table beside her and withdrew a flask of brandy. "I'm exhausted, Margaretha. Don't play games with me now."

"Not playing games, darling. It's just that I think I have a right to know where you went."

He tossed back a mouthful of brandy. "I met someone."

"What sort of someone? A juggler? A clown?"

"An associate."

"And what did you discuss with this associate?"

"Business."

"What sort of business?"

He took another mouthful of brandy and settled into the chair. She continued to watch him until he shut his eyes, then idly reached for the attaché case and opened it. It was heavier than she expected, with dozens of handwritten pages and what looked like a sheaf of blueprints. There was also a pistol, a woman's pistol with a pearl grip.

"What do we have here?" she said playfully, spinning the chamber, fumbling with the hammer.

Spangler opened his eyes. "Put it back."

She bit her lower lip, aiming for an empty glass on the window-sill. "Is it loaded?"

"Put it back, Margaretha."

She swung it around, aiming for her own reflection in the mirror. "But surely just one shot wouldn't hurt anything, would it? *Would it?*"

Eyes registering no emotion, he got up from the chair very quickly, crossing the room like a cat. She tried to escape but he caught her wrist, twisting it back until the pistol dropped.

"Don't ever do that again, Margaretha. Do you understand, never again."

She almost left him that night, almost called for someone to collect her bags while he slept in the adjoining room, but finally it seemed that one minor quarrel hardly warranted such a drastic measure, particularly inasmuch as their relationship had reached such an interesting stage . . . which simply meant that she wanted him. Beyond everything else at the moment, she wanted him.

The affair ended as it had begun, on a casual note. Spangler told her that he was needed in Berlin,

116

then handed her a one-way ticket back to Paris. There was also a promise to meet in the spring, and a last formal dinner on an enclosed terrace facing the lake. Conversation remained trivial, for the most part with Spangler describing a childhood in Bavaria that he had never experienced. His one or two questions about the earlier men in her life were not pressing, and there was still no mention of Rolland Michard.

This then, according to Zelle, was the sum total of her eight-day interlude with Spangler: a chance meeting in Vienna followed by a fairly uneventful week in Geneva. Apart from disappearing without warning and insisting that he sit with his back to a wall when dining in public, she would always maintain that he behaved like any respectable soldier. She would also insist that he had been an exceptionally skilled lover—which, oddly enough, finally convinced interrogators that she must have been lying in her teeth.

Chapter Eleven

S HE returned to Paris toward the end of November, leaving us with only scattered impressions: a photograph from a day at Longchamps, an exaggerated interview in the *Daily Mail,* and a letter to Nicholas Gray inviting him to visit her at the Ritz. There were also one or two newspaper articles linking her romantically to a certain Polish count, but in fact these were relatively solitary days.

She tended to live for herself now, answering neglected correspondence, spending long mornings in bed with popular fiction. On Tuesday afternoons she employed the services of a young masseuse. On Fridays she consulted an astrologer. She also—against the advice of her attorneys—attempted to contact her daughter, writing more than a dozen letters to Rudolph John MacLeod before receiving a curt and discouraging reply.

It might be said that these days were marked by a new maturity, perhaps even a degree of regret. For a time she worked with some enthusiasm on a series of dances thematically based on the *Thousand*

and One Nights. Then, apparently without quite knowing why she abandoned the project, sending a young pianist back to the conservatory where she had found him. With no alternative project to fill her evenings she often took to walking into neighborhoods she scarcely knew—always alone, always avoiding the eyes of men. Occasionally she wandered as far as the kosher butcheries near the rue de Blanc-Manteau or the catacombs below Saint-Jacques. Then again there were nights when she simply walked in circles.

Her letter to Gray came from a night such as this, a sleepless night with nothing beyond the silence except the rattle of primitive plumbing. Earlier, she had planned a quiet evening with *The Brothers Karamazov* or Swedenborg's *Apocalypse Revealed,* but finally it seemed that she simply and desperately just wanted a friend.

Her letter to Gray was handwritten in green ink, the stationery embossed with a black border. The tone was light and informal. The closing was typical: *Eternally, M.* Although completed well in time for the morning post, she actually had the letter delivered by hand . . . then spent at least two days waiting for a reply that never came.

In fact Gray did respond to Mata Hari's letter, spending more than an hour on his balcony composing a short but tender note. He never sent it; and for two distracted days he remained indoors frantically working with pastels until he hardly even thought about her. For company he had his cat. For solace he had a bottle of gin, left over from that night he had heard about Spangler.

At the end of those two days he attended an exhibition of moderns at one of the smaller galleries, then drifted at random through the Latin Quarter until he found a suitable girl. Her name was Julie Réage, and she too eventually survived in three or four watercolors.

End of an obsession with Zelle . . . or so it seemed that week in mid-December. For the most part Gray also lived mainly for himself, once more returning to an insular world of still lifes and nightscapes. He grew particularly intrigued with a vision of hoarfrost on the windowpane. He spent hours attempting to duplicate candlelight. Eventually he even spent an evening with a very pretty red-haired child from Bouville. But he did not sleep with her . . . and although it was late when he finally returned, Margaretha was still waiting patiently.

He saw her first through a half-open door, dozing in yellow lamplight. Her hair, like a shadow, fell across her face. Her hands looked very small and pale. A few of his later drypoints were scattered at her feet. The cat was asleep in her lap. For a moment he actually considered slipping away, finding a cab, and going off. In the end he sat down on the window box and reached for another cigarette. After what must have been a minute, but felt like an hour, she opened her eyes.

"Hello, Nicky. How are you?"

"What do you want, Margaretha?"

She smiled. "Nothing really." Then reaching for the dangling cat's paw: "And what's *his* name?"

Gray took a deep breath: "Cat."

"As in stray cat?"

"I suppose."

"Well, I don't like it. I think you should have named him Socrates. Or maybe John-Phillip."

It was cold, so he brought her a brandy, while keeping the gin for himself. Her coat was new but torn at the sleeve, and from the condition of her shoes he guessed that she must have walked miles.

"I like what you've been doing," she said at last. "Particularly those winter scenes. They remind me of—oh, I don't know—Christmas."

When all the while he'd been trying to paint death. "Look, do you want something to eat?"

She shrugged. "What have you got?"

He moved into what served as his kitchen and began to rummage through the cupboards. He found nothing except a few tins of meat, cheese, and a rotting biscuit.

"I suppose we could always go out, maybe try the Baretta," he said. "Or some other place."

"Why didn't you answer my letter, Nicky? Two weeks and you didn't answer. So why?"

He sat down again, fishing for another cigarette. "I've been busy."

"Or else talking to Charlie Dunbar, yes?"

He glanced at the far wall, where the lamplight had thrown their shadows: to his mind hers like a thin child's, his like a sick ape's. He lit the cigarette and realized that his hand was shaking. He wanted that drink but couldn't seem to locate another clean glass.

Finally, as calmly as possible: "Who's Rudolph Spangler?"

She smirked. "So you did speak with Charles, didn't you?"

"Who is he?"

"A friend."

"What sort of friend?"

"A new friend."

"A rich friend?"

She shook her head with an exaggerated sigh. "Christ, Nicky. You didn't expect me to spend my life with Charles, did you?" Then, toying with the cat's paw again: "Anyway, he got what he wanted."

He watched her in silence as she ran her hand along the cat's spine. "How long were you with him?"

"Humm?"

"Spangler. How long were you with him?"

She shrugged. "A week."

"How was it?"

"Fine. He took me to Geneva. Ever seen Geneva?"

There were footsteps on the staircase below, possibly a drunk neighbor, or else that ghost of Michard again. "How did you meet him?"

"At a party."

"What was he like?"

"Casanova. Now for Christsakes leave it alone, Nicky. I couldn't take it with Charles anymore so I ran. Now is that such a sin?"

"Are you going to see him again?"

"Charles? How should I know?"

"I *meant* Spangler."

She lumped up her mouth for an irritated frown. "I don't know, maybe."

"When?"

"I don't *know*."

He got up from the window and drifted to the easel, where a number of brushes lay soaking in turpentine. He heard her talking softly to the cat and thought, She still doesn't know. He caught another glimpse of her face in the lamplight and supposed that nothing had really changed. He wondered what would happen if he kissed her.

"You know, I've always wanted a cat," she said. "Ever since I was little. But I seem to recall that papa wouldn't let me have one."

He stepped to her side, hoping to catch a glimpse of her eyes. "I thought you said that papa gave you everything."

"I lied."

He filled her glass with more brandy, which she drank in silence, a silence that seemed to be drawing them closer again. In the background were distant bells tolling midnight, the last song from the corner cafe.

"I don't know if we'll ever find a place to eat now," he said.

She smiled. "I wanted to see you, Nicky. That's honestly the only reason that I came. I just wanted to see you again."

"And then what? Then it's back to Dunbar, or back to Spangler, or back to—"

"Please don't, not now. I'm lost again. Can't you see that? I'm really lost this time." Then clutching his arm and pulling him closer, "And you're the only one who can find me."

He kissed her, saw that she was crying and kissed her again. At first she responded like a child, oddly shy and mumbling something about the cat. Then he felt her lips parting, her heart actually beating next to his.

She undressed in the darkness, then stepped into the light from the window, and he saw that she was smiling. He ran his hand along that still perfect curve of her back. It wasn't raining, but the wind through loose shingles sounded a lot like running water.

And of course, there were two or three minutes when he wanted to stop her, wanted to tell her to leave him alone. But then it passed, and he only regretted not having changed the bedsheets.

The Middle Years

She stayed fourteen days, from the week before Christmas through the first of the year. Paris was cold with an early storm, but they rarely left his room. The mornings were particularly beautiful, the windows glazed with white frost. Dawn, however, came slowly, struggling with the wind.

As for specific memories, they would always remember Christmas Eve. Gray had been raised Church of England while Zelle had more or less abandoned a structured faith years ago, but just the same they decided to attend the midnight mass at Saint-Bernard. Although less extravagant than Notre Dame's, the services had always been very beautiful here, and from that night are two impressions in pencil of local children kneeling to receive the Sacrament.

They celebrated simply, with meat pie, stewed apples, and vanilla cream, on a low table. Nor were the gifts extravagant, mainly just trinkets purchased in neighborhood shops. Zelle, however, did receive an unusually haunting lithograph of that forest at Fontainebleau.

After supper they undressed in silence, then lay down together on thick rugs by the stove. For a long time he simply held her in his arms, consciously trying to form memories that he knew might have to last for years. He studied her breasts very carefully, the dark nipples, that dolphin's mouth, those still-brook eyes. He asked her questions, concentrating on the sound of her voice, which was mostly dry but clear. From time to time he found excuses to leave her so that he could study her body from different angles.

As for Zelle, she too remained fairly quiet, oddly conscious of future memories: a vision of him seated at his easel, a slow response to a simple question, the faint smell of turpentine, burnt matches and pomander. She also loved the way he handled a palette knife, or bent under the lamplight to sharpen a pencil. But the drawings themselves were still a little unfathomable, like a glacier.

The succeeding days were also cold, but mostly it was a windless cold and they often walked in the evenings. They tended to avoid familiar cafes or the loitering crowds on the boulevards. They also tended to avoid discussing the future.

Finally they did not leave his room at all, so that the last three nights felt like a single night. They lived on food delivered by a boy: dried fruit, pickled cabbage, meat pie, and beer. They rarely slept before dawn. They played chess in silence but without really concentrating. They kept the lights low.

The last day was Sunday. By nine in the evening her bags had been packed, her coat laid out on the bed. A train ticket stood propped against a jar on the mantle—first class to Cannes, where she was to perform on behalf of some merchant from Antwerp. Another storm lay on the horizon to the east. Earlier, they had seen it above the skyline as a solid wall of clouds. And now there was the wind again.

For a while Gray toyed with the idea of asking her to stay . . . begging her . . . demanding . . . But there seemed to be no point. "It's only for a week," she had told him. "One silly little week, and if you really want to, then come along," she told him. "Come along, and we can languish by the seashore together."

At least he knew better than that.

Following a supper of cold cuts and beer, they sat side by side on the low divan. She wore her oriental robe embroidered with white chrysanthemums. He wore what he always wore. After a long silence he asked if she wanted a glass of sherry. Her reply was strangely formal, her voice disconnected and flat: no, she wanted nothing more to drink. Sometime later he asked if she cared to take a walk to the river or the municipal gardens. Then, although her response was the same, he realized that she was crying.

It went on for a long time: the silence like a taut wire, clouds churning somewhere above Versailles, the two of them still frozen while her eyes filled with tears. Then, very softly: "You know, I do wish I could love only you, Nicky. I really do."

She left in the half light just after dawn. Rather than him seeing her off at the station, they parted in the courtyard below. There was still a feeble snow blown like ash. After the carriage arrived, they stood on the step while the driver loaded her luggage. Although she continued clinging to his arm, he knew that she was already gone.

"I meant to tell you," he said. "That is, I think it would be a good idea if you took a moment and wrote to Dunbar."

She nodded, but her eyes were a thousand miles away. "Yes. Yes, I suppose you're right."

"I know it would mean a lot to him."

"Yes, of course."

"And naturally if you get the chance I'd also appreciate . . ."

She smiled, lightly running her fingers along the corner of his mouth. "Don't be serious, Nicky, not now. Anyway, I'll be back in a week."

"Yes, a week."

"Or two."

Followed by a parting kiss and, whispered from the carriage door, something about taking care of that cat.

It took him a long time to exorcise her from his room, a long time before he stopped finding small reminders hidden under the furniture or tucked away in drawers. It was also, of course, a long time before he heard from her again . . . at least five or six months.

By then she was living in the village of Esvres, south of Tours. Her lover was an amiable stockbroker by the name of Xavier Rousseau. She had met him at a musical soirée, then had more or less installed herself in a château he had rented from some local comtesse. Although married and still actively employed in Paris, he saw her at least once a week.

It was a scenic journey from Paris to Esvres, a slow route through the Touraine and across the Loire River. Eventually Gray came to know it quite well; usually leaving on a Monday or Tuesday to return before her lover arrived on Thursday or Friday. The arrangement was serviceable. While Rousseau paid the bills and kept her occupied on weekends, Gray filled up the slack time.

They rode horses—there is a photograph of her mounted on her favorite: a magnificent stallion called Raja. They played chess or Mah-Jongg, and she always lost for failing to concentrate. They spent quiet afternoons under the trees or in a whitewashed rotunda . . . and they also made love.

At the end of the year she returned to Paris to live where she would always be remembered: 11, rue Windsor in the heart of Neuilly-sur-Seine. Here she lived for herself again, entertaining friends in the garden and dancing to Chopin on the gramophone. Although Gray only slept with her irregularly, he never managed to stay away for very long.

This was as it always was with Zelle, he would later explain. You lived your life around her, not with her. You gave her what she wanted, not what she needed. You came when she called, and left when she became tired. You played by her rules, or you didn't play at all.

Except Spangler. Although she still occasionally talked about him, he never attempted to contact her, which didn't seem to concern her one way or another. Dunbar, on the other hand, was another story. More than once she admitted feeling badly about the way she had treated him, and eventually considered asking him to visit. In the end, she never got around to writing—not a card, not a note, nothing.

Chapter Twelve

HER home at 11, rue Windsor still stands, a lovely half-timbered cottage behind moss-encrusted walls. Past the courtyard's double gate lies the garden, virtually unchanged, with white gravel paths intersecting the lawn. The trees, too, still stand, mostly beech and poplar. There are two large rooms on the ground floor, one with an open fireplace. There is a view from the bedroom of a neighboring villa and the narrow lanes beyond.

For many years the surrounding lanes were dark and shuttered with branches. There is still the smell of leaf mold and grass, but some say that the newer estates have ruined the deeper solitude. In particular, there was once a patch of open ground on a rise not far from the house, an empty field of high weeds where sometimes one could catch a glimpse of Zelle.

Dunbar came here, watching for three or four hours one night from the window of a hired motorcar. From his vantage point there must have been a fairly clear view of her home, perhaps even a view of the path to the gate. Then, assuming he had left the road and walked to the rise, he may have also glimpsed a portion of the garden where she often received lovers on warm summer nights.

And what would he have seen? Given that he had been watching on a Friday or a Saturday, he may well have seen her descend the steps to meet Xavier Rousseau. Quite likely she would have been wearing white, a faintly diaphanous frock or a thin silk kimono. Her hair would have been full and loose at the shoulders. Her feet would have been bare. Had he continued watching for awhile, he might have also seen her on the balcony, briefly suspended in Rousseau's arms before slipping to her knees.

Dunbar's Parisian adventure lasted only eight days. Originally he had entered the city on behalf of his father's textile concern and had not intended to see Zelle at all. Indeed, he had even chosen a remote hotel where no one of consequence stayed. Yet given certain memories, certain feelings on familiar streets, he eventually found himself watching from that field with a pair of Swiss binoculars. Later, he would also admit to having purchased her a gift—a rather cheap scarf. And although he did not venture to say what might have occurred had he found her alone . . . he had definitely been drinking hard for days.

In the main these were difficult days for Dunbar. His life had no real purpose. Most of his friends were merely acquaintances. His women were generally whores. On returning to London from those eight days in Paris, he more or less picked up where he had left off. He walked in the afternoons. He drank to excess in the evenings. On occasion he attended the theater or the cocktail parties of friends. His rooms were comfortable but not extravagant. He lived alone.

He kept Zelle's photographs, about a dozen of them, wedged between the pages of a book. He kept her last note locked in a drawer. Like Gray before him, he continued to follow her career through the newspapers, although as everyone knew, the newspapers were hardly reliable. If there were moments when he missed her very badly, there were also moments when he hated her.

The Middle Years

It was a casual conversation with a stranger that ushered him into the next phase of his life, a seemingly chance encounter with a friend of a friend from university. It was a Friday, the end of September. He had entered his club at the usual hour and soon found himself drinking with a young man named John Allenby. About an hour later an associate of Allenby's joined them, a slender, fair-haired man named Martin Southerland.

Initially the conversation was harmless, a quiet chat about Oxford and the fate of absent friends. Then, with no clear transition, the discussion turned to politics, specifically the German threat, and in response to a question Dunbar found himself describing his stay in Vienna and his brief encounter with Spangler. (Much later he would definitely remember that Southerland had become silent the moment Spangler's name was mentioned.) Then there were questions, some of them quite pointed. Did Dunbar happen to recall what Spangler was doing in Vienna? Did he recall where the man had been staying. He was also asked the name of Spangler's regiment, and what Spangler had looked like.

Dunbar's life never really returned to normal after that evening in Manchester Square. Odd things kept happening. On the following Tuesday Dunbar discovered that an inquiry had been made regarding his financial standing. Next it seemed that someone had been tampering with his mail, particularly letters from abroad. Finally, on a warm Sunday afternoon, he distinctly sensed that someone had followed him from Saint James's to the National Gallery. Twice he caught the reflection of a nondescript man in a shop window, then thought he saw him watching from the edge of a crowd: a gentleman, judging by the clothing, definitely not the police.

In all probability none of these events would have added up to much had Dunbar never seen Southerland again. As it happened, however, only ten days passed before he found the man waiting at his club—once more sipping dry champagne, once more extraordinarily friendly. And curious.

They dined on chops and a decent claret, finished with sherbet and a marvelous brandy. Although nothing of obvious importance was said, without Allenby's presence the conversation somehow seemed more meaningful, intimate. They talked about their respective families and childhoods, about their respective notions of duty, and of honor. They talked about England and a tangible naval threat to the nation.

It was a matter of sacrifice, Southerland said. Was the twentieth century Englishman still willing to make a fifteenth century sacrifice, such as was made at Agincourt. Of course the question was rhetorical and Dunbar was not expected to answer. But the essential theme was clear: how far should a young man go in the service of his nation?

It was a balmy night, with a scent of damp lawns and summer roses. For a time the two men seemed to walk aimlessly, first along the Serpentine, then gradually deeper into the hedgerows. They spoke softly, sometimes with a dormitory whisper of youth. They occasionally poked at the ivy and kicked discarded bottles. Time seemed suspended with select reminders of childhood: the Round Pond in moonlight, clumps of seeding thistles and foxglove, a night bird in the shrubbery. There were even allusions to a child's dream of a secret society with a cloistered den somewhere in Richmond.

"Technically we're under the Admiralty," Southerland began. "But naturally our jurisdiction extends beyond all that . . . which is why we're interested in your chap."

"My chap?"

"Rudolph Spangler."

They had reached the broad lawns where Dunbar had once imagined escorting Zelle, perhaps in the rain with a black umbrella.

"He's been in the picture a long time," Southerland went on. "Mostly on the continent, and against the Frogs. You're the first one, though, who's actually dined with him. And lived to tell about it."

"But I don't know much," Dunbar said. "I mean, it was really just a social occasion. Anyway, Margaretha isn't a politically minded woman."

"No?"

"She likes soldiers, that's all. Likes the uniform. I suppose you could call it a fixation of sorts."

Southerland jammed his hands in his pockets, smiling, or possibly sneering. "Just the same I'd like you to talk to my people."

"And tell them what?"

"What you told me . . . about Spangler and that dancer."

"When?"

"Whenever you like."

They began to walk again, moving slowly side by side. There was music from somewhere, a waltz reminiscent of that last night in Vienna. There were also beds of tangled roses and a certain kind of pale violet that Zelle had always loved . . .

"Did I mention that I saw her photograph?" Southerland said suddenly.

"Her photograph?" He was recalling that she had also loved orchids, the rarest hothouse variety.

"In the Sunday papers. And I must admit that she really is quite beautiful."

Dunbar shrugged, also jamming his hands in his pockets. "The photographs can be deceptive. She's not at all the same in person."

"Still, she must know how to use her looks. After all, she spent eight days with Spangler, eight very cozy days by the lake in Geneva."

Dunbar turned to him. "What are you talking about?"

"After she left you . . . eight days in Geneva. The innkeeper remembered them very well. Seems they particularly favored strolling at dawn."

There were no sounds except their heels on the gravel. The wind had died, leaving everything motionless: clumps of hollyhock, white ivy, and tulips—all dead still.

"Look, I can understand if you have certain personal considerations," Southerland said. "I mean, I do know how a woman can affect one's sense of proportion—"

"No, it's not like that at all."

"Then I can tell them? I can tell them you'll do it? Meet with them?"

Dunbar took a deep breath. "When?"

"How about tomorrow? Say, ten o'clock?"

"Yes, I suppose ten is all right."

"There's no need to worry, old boy. They're really very decent people, as you'll see . . ."

In the morning there were torn parts of her photographs all over his room, also pieces of broken bottles and traces of blood.

There were romantic, seductive overtones to Dunbar's first brush with the secret world. In the beginning, of course, he did not meet with Mansfield Cummings, but with an entertaining subordinate named Furnival-Jones. Talks began informally in one of the Richmond house anterooms, then continued in a shuttered library, a curious room with high, coffered ceilings and Chippendale fretwork. The light was low through green shades. There were etchings of naval encounters on the wall.

Dunbar found himself recounting not only his evening with Spangler, but also his affair with Zelle. He was asked how he had met the woman, how she had responded to his initial approach, and how she had later received him alone in her room. Next there were questions concerning Spangler's mannerisms. How, for example, had he held his knife and fork? How quickly had he responded to direct questions? Had his voice been varied or fairly constant. Finally there were questions relating to Margaretha's basic attitude toward men, and specifically how she would respond if the German were to contact her again.

It was close to four in the afternoon when the interview ended. Southerland appeared with a bottle of sherry. The curtains were drawn back to expose a view of blackened roofs and chimney pots. There was also a quality to the light that Dunbar would not forget: an illusion of brickwork slowly decaying as the day began to fade.

Although there were still questions at this point, the tone was more congenial. Yes, Dunbar admitted, there were branches of his family in Germany . . . but really only withering extremities. No, he had never subscribed to the Anglo-German fellowship, but yes he occasionally enjoyed a good lager. In response to a question about his plans for the future, he replied only that he hoped to do what was best . . . while still maintaining "a degree of decency and sobriety." Naturally it got a laugh.

It was about seven when the party finally adjourned. The twilight was as beautiful as any of the season. There were long shadows across the boulevards, salmon tones along the river. The sky was also faintly pink against white unraveling clouds. Although there appeared to have been no formal arrangement, it seemed that Southerland had been chosen to close the day. First he accompanied Dunbar to the courtyard, then walked with him arm in arm across Saint James's, where docile crowds were waiting for the trams.

"I dare say you made quite an impression," Southerland told him. "Definitely quite an impression."

Dunbar glanced away as if hardly surprised, or hardly interested. "I can only hope that I was of some small help."

"Oh definitely. That is, it's always a matter of bits and pieces, bits and pieces adding to a greater whole."

"And when it's complete?"

Southerland shrugged. "Well, that's the game, isn't it? Intelligence."

They had reached a narrow towpath and a glimpse of floating debris in the water: driftwood, paper, cigarette butts.

"I don't suppose I can ask how long you've been doing this?" Dunbar said.

"Four years."

"And specifically you—?"

"Coordinate."

Past the bridge lay rows of shops, and Southerland paused a moment gazing at all the muddled junk. "Your father was military, wasn't he?"

"Grandfather."

"Still, it's the same thing."

"I'm sorry?"

"The calling. The need to serve." Then turning from the window, his hand on Dunbar's shoulder, "Look, Charles, I'm not suggesting anything in particular, but these people do pay badly enough to assure you decent company."

Traditionally there has never been a specific path that young men have followed into the British Secret Service. Rather, those possessing the right sensibilities have usually been recruited on a haphazard basis, generally by tutors and dons at Oxford or Cambridge. Although somewhat more direct, Dunbar's entrance was no less casual, with idle conversations in Knightsbridge. And when it was done, he would finally tell others that one was not so much accepted by the service as absorbed by it.

At first, his duties were parochial and dull. He read a great deal: selected articles from the German press, embassy dispatches from Vienna and Berlin. He helped with tedious paperwork. He manned the telephone. Yet in spite of the boredom these were good days. There were six young men attached to the overt research department, two of them vaguely familiar from Oxford. Their offices were on the second floor of a cramped, sooty annex. The furniture was crude and the cold inescapable. Nevertheless, Dunbar came to love these rooms. He loved the odor of damp paper and plaster. He loved the tread of footsteps along dowdy corridors. He loved the deeper sense of secrecy and shelter. He loved Martin Southerland, and, for a change, he loved himself.

There was a chophouse not far from the Richmond annex, a red brick cavern where Southerland and Dunbar often met for dinner. Eventually Dunbar would look back on these evenings as instructive, his first introduction to the technique of handling spies.

For the most part Southerland tended to speak theoretically. Fear, he would say, turned men into children, and to that extend an agent was a child: clinging love and sudden hatred, unreasoning desire and uncomplicated greed. Agents also tended to be impulsive, he said, but usually responded to a firm hand.

Only once were there specific references to real people and real situations. It was an otherwise prosaic Thursday on the eve of the second Balkan war. There was a yellow fog, and no relief from the damp.

At first Southerland talked about the Germans, specifically Walter Nicolai and his formidable Third Department. He called them

134

strivers, meticulous strivers with a generous budget for almost seven hundred foreign agents. "They're also killers," he added. "Even on neutral ground they're killers."

From the broad view he moved to the refined vision of secret warfare, and described a shadow-game of feints and counter-feints. He said that there were at least two hundred German spies between Scotland and Cornwall, monitoring everything from troop movements to the price of beef. Undoubtedly there were even one or two in Whitehall . . . although you couldn't hope to roll them up from the bottom, not with existing resources. So one had to concentrate on the masters, those who recruited and serviced the networks. Those like Rudolph Spangler.

There were perhaps three hours between the first glass of dry sherry and this reference to Spangler. Only a handful of patrons still remained, and the waiters were growing impatient.

"In a sense," Southerland said, "I'm not at all sure one can ever come to terms with the likes of Spangler—not psychologically at any rate, and probably not intellectually. Did I mention that he shot a Pole last year? In cold blood? In the back of the poor bastard's neck?"

Dunbar nodded. "Yes, I believe I heard something to that effect."

"Not that we're certain it was Spangler, which has also been part of the problem. No one seems to know anything about the man . . . except that he likes Geneva."

Dunbar had been pouring another glass of brandy. "Geneva?"

"That episode with your dancer."

"Oh."

Next Southerland asked if Dunbar had read the latest appreciation on Spangler: an eighty-eight page monstrosity with a supplementary index. "Which, I might add, is still another part of the problem. We study the man. We write about him. We catalogue and file him until he's larger than life. Naturally no one wants to underestimate the enemy, but this is ridiculous."

"Still, he does seem to have a way about him." Dunbar sighed. "That is, he does seem to inspire something."

"Blood and money. And possibly a stinking respect among the

research pools. Incidentally, your chum Allenby was partly responsible for those eighty-eight pages."

"So I've heard." Dunbar smiled.

"Not that he's stupid, mind you."

"Of course not."

"But where does it end? Where does it lead us? I mean, that's ultimately the point. Where do all these papers concerning old Rudy lead us . . . except back to the very fundamental question?"

"Which is?"

"How does one cut Rudolph Spangler down to size? Look, anyone can be burned, Charles. It's simply a matter of timing and technique. And we do know that Spangler has at least one obvious weakness, don't we?"

Dunbar shrugged, waiting for the reference to Zelle. "Yes, I suppose we do."

"Also, the man's a fanatic, and that sort almost always makes mistakes sooner or later . . ."

Given such evenings with Southerland, and days with the others in the Richmond annex, it seems possible to believe that Dunbar was diverted from thoughts of Zelle. There is, after all, something almost sexual about the secret world, something captivating. Perhaps it is the odd mixture of terror and secrecy. Perhaps it is the power of the secrets themselves. Whatever, Dunbar would maintain that Zelle was not really a factor in his life then, that she was merely a figure from a dream, a dream in which he either saw her coming back to him or else saw her slowly crushed like a swallow's egg.

Her name came up only once more that first year, a casual reference over a dinner table in Knightsbridge. Apparently someone had seen her perform abroad, while someone else had read about her in the newspapers. She was described as a remarkably alluring woman, but certainly not a lady. Dunbar kept silent and waited for the topic of discussion to change.

Yet regardless of how long one waited, she could never be entirely dismissed; and although she might lie dormant for years, there would always come a day when one had no choice but to deal with her.

That day came in the spring—a gray Thursday in April, 1913. Dunbar had arrived at the annex early and found Southerland waiting for him on the staircase. They went down to the garden, a dismal place, little more than a ragged strip of lawn and a few strangled shrubs.

There was no preamble. "It's about that woman," Southerland said. "I'm afraid she turned up again with Spangler."

They sat on a bench beneath the trellis. There was a view of red bricks and little else. There were sounds of typewriters from the window above.

"Of course nothing has been confirmed," Southerland added, "but I don't think we can ignore the signs. Apparently it happened in Madrid about eight days ago. It seems that she's been performing there, and Spangler approached her in the lobby of the Ritz. They've been seen all over town ever since."

For the moment Dunbar couldn't understand why he felt nothing, like a block of wood or a lump of granite. Nothing.

"Naturally you'll be talking to the Director, but first I thought I'd explain a few things, unofficially."

"She won't play with us," Dunbar said at last. "Regardless of what the speculation is, she's not the type to play . . . at least not for money or anything like that."

"Oh, I think I'm aware of her limitations."

"The best we can do is watch."

"Precisely. She'll help us keep Spangler in the picture."

"And she won't be an easy target. Her life tends to be erratic. I mean, there are days when she never leaves bed."

The bench was also cold, like spears of frozen steel. The sun was a pale disk in the sky. It's as though I've always been here, Dunbar thought. As though I've always been sitting right here waiting for what I'm hearing right now.

"I've suggested to Cummings that you coordinate the overall surveillance, Charles. We've got plenty of people in the area to help, but I'd like you to run the show. I mean, you do *know* the woman, don't you? Know her moves, her habits, her bloody routine. Anyway, I personally think you'll do a damn good job."

"But to what end?"

"Well, if Rudy Spangler has fallen in love—" he spread a hand in a gesture of mock sympathy—"don't you think it would only be proper if we were to help him along?"

Dunbar glanced down to his feet. Conceivably, he thought, the reverse might also be the case. "How would I start?"

"Slowly, carefully. And see if you can't find out who's on the sidelines."

"I'm sorry?"

"Spangler's agents, the bread and butter of his western networks."

"What about my current duties?"

"Oh I think Allenby can clear your table."

"And my supervisor?"

"Well, you're working directly for the Fourth Floor now, aren't you?"

In the beginning Dunbar's file on Mata Hari consisted of only eighteen pages, distilled from field reports collected from resident agents in Madrid, and primarily concerned with the romantic side of her relationship with Spangler. There were notations regarding an evening along the Castellana, and select observations from the lobby of the Ritz. The file was housed in a single steel cabinet adjacent to the window. Individual entries were typed on onionskin. The subjects were tagged with green cards. Although cataloging would change as surveillance shifted from Madrid to Berlin, the picture remained the same: a unique vision of a woman supposedly in love with a killer . . . perhaps the only man who had ever been able to leave her.

He often worked nights because he welcomed the silence, and the solitude. He shared his work with no one, afraid that they would not understand. On occasion he actually spoke with an agent who had seen her in Paris or Madrid, but on the whole his vision was oblique, filtered through the eyes of others.

On entering his office the ritual was always the same. First he would adjust his reading lamp, an enormous brass contraption with a green shade. Then he would bolt the door, draw the curtains, unlock the cabinet, and lay down the first file. At this point it seemed that anything might happen.

Privately he tended to think of these files as dossiers, and gradually filled them with the stuff of any clandestine surveillance. There were observations of agents positioned in restaurants and theaters. There were notes collected from wastepaper baskets, and copies of intercepted letters. Later he would include fragments of conversations overheard with the aid of a pneumatic listening device through the walls of adjoining rooms.

But if the parts of his file were ultimately greater than the whole, to Dunbar the whole was something very special. Indeed, now and again on cool evenings it almost seemed as if the thing were alive —a breathing extension of the woman herself, right there with him in that room. It could be frightening.

Chapter Thirteen

D UNBAR'S files: little towers of brown or buff folders, bound with red ribbon and tagged with black adhesive tape. In all there must have been thousands of individual entries, some most intimate, some even obscene. Dunbar's notations are found along the margins of the field reports. The photographs are scattered throughout.

Although originally intended to chronicle the dancer's relationship with Spangler, the earlier entries actually predate their Madrid affair by several months. Actually, the first reports concerned her movements in October of 1913, a relatively quiet period. After appearing twice at La Scala in Milan (once as Venus in Marenco's *Bacchus and Gambrinus*) she had returned to a simple existence in Neuilly-sur-Seine. She kept a stable of horses, and was often seen riding in white or brown habit along the lanes of the Bois de Boulogne. She worked intermittently on three Javanese dances, and corresponded with Sergei Diaghilev concerning a performance with Nijinsky in Monte Carlo. She also slept with several men, including Nicholas Gray.

The Middle Years

Dunbar's files contained a copy of her farewell note to Gray: two dry pages written on the eve of her departure for Madrid. The tone of the note was apparently optimistic—after a long hiatus she was enthusiastic about performing again, particularly in Madrid, where she had always been loved. Of course there was no mention of Spangler at this point, since she could hardly have known he would be waiting.

According to Dunbar's files, Spangler approached her in Madrid, in the lobby of the Ritz, on the morning of her third day there. In fact it was night, about eight o'clock; and rather than in the lobby he met her on a patio. Nor was there anything close to a tearful reunion. He merely stepped out of the shadows and spoke her name. The newspaper under his arm carried her photograph on the cover. For a moment she hardly recognized him. His hair seemed lighter than she remembered, his complexion vaguely darker.

His approach, as before, was casual. "How are you, Margaretha?" First in German, then in English. "Yes, how are you?"

She shrugged, tearing at the leaf of a potted palm. "Surprised."

"But not unpleasantly, I hope?"

"No."

They moved to the edge of the patio and a view of taller palms in black relief against the sky. He hadn't yet touched her, but the fix of his eyes seemed tangible enough.

"How did you find me?"

He smiled, tossing the newspaper at her feet.

"Not too difficult."

"But what are you doing here?"

"This and that. Although at present I'm between engagements, so to speak."

The lawns below were white with dew. The half moon was also white.

"I missed you," he said suddenly.

She glanced away with a thin smile. "I'm sure."

He ran a knuckle across her cheek, then a finger along the jugular vein. "Look, Paris is impossible for me. Besides, they told me that you had found someone else. A stockbroker."

She smiled again, tearing off a dangling palm leaf. "Yes, a stockbroker. An extremely considerate stockbroker."

"And now?"

"Now I'm considering alternatives."

"Such as?"

"Such as myself."

There were birds among the surrounding leaves, and a stationary cat on the wall. From certain angles Spangler looked like a cat, a sleek Tom from the streets.

She ran her fingers through his hair. "It's different."

"Don't you like it?"

She shrugged. "And where's your uniform?"

"Good question."

She took his hand in order to examine a scar, a pale circle between the thumb and forefinger. "And how exactly did you get this?"

"Opening a bottle of champagne."

"For a woman?"

"For the wife of a general."

"Then where's your medal?"

"It wasn't actually considered hazardous duty. Have dinner with me tonight."

She shook her head. "I'm already engaged for this evening."

"With a man?"

"Maybe."

"Get rid of him."

They lapsed into silence while his eyes continued probing. Then, suddenly back to the heart of the matter: "Margaretha, I want to see you tonight. I very much want to."

She would have moved off again but his eyes still held her. "I told you, not tonight—"

"Yes, tonight," and he kissed her. And again, encircling her waist, molding her breast through the crinoline.

142

The Middle Years

Also according to Dunbar's files, Zelle remained unaware of the surveillance teams; and if Spangler knew he would not have discussed it with her. Again, not true . . . Dunbar was, after all, a lover and victim, and a tyro at the secret life . . .

Midnight, and they had been lying together for a long time. Earlier a chilled wind had risen, leaving her a little unsettled, particularly with the sound of rattling palms. Spangler had that effect on her, unsettling, not in control, which was part of the fascination.

"I'm thirsty," she told him.

There was flat champagne in a bucket of ice, vermouth on an occasional table. There were also untouched melon balls in a bowl and a string of pearls he had given her that afternoon.

The tap water tasted faintly like steel. She put the glass down and moved to the window. Shadows on the wall took on human forms. "Do you want something?"

He shook his head, holding out his hand from the bed. "Just you."

She smiled and moved to the window. His shadow on the opposite wall looked faintly like a bird's—a crane or a hawk? The tip of his cigarette might have been the glowing eye. But finally what caught her attention was the figure of someone in the plaza below . . . a boy or a thin man in black.

"Did you know that there's someone watching?"

He extinguished his cigarette, then lit another. "So you've noticed."

"Who is he?"

"Difficult to say."

"What does he want?"

"Me."

She let the curtain fall and looked at him. "You're in trouble, aren't you?"

He slipped out of bed and moved to her side. "Not really."

"Then why are they watching you?"

143

He dropped his cigarette in her water glass, then slid his hand inside her robe, one finger circling a nipple. "Because that's the *game.*"

She managed to slip away from him, crossing the room and kneeling on the divan. She felt him looking at her thighs, at her hardened nipple through the fabric of her gown. She shook her head, holding a cushion to her breasts. "I don't like it, Rudy. It frightens me."

He smiled that composed cat's smile of his. Don't be frightened. They watch us, we watch them . . . a game."

"Who sends them?"

"Difficult to say."

"Are they English?"

"Perhaps."

"French?"

"I think more likely English."

"So then it's political, isn't it?"

"Yes, you could say it's political."

"Well, I still don't like it. I don't."

He moved to her side again, but only to take her hand, to brush a stray lock of hair from her eyes. While she thought: I suppose this is my weakness, like a disease, and nothing will ever change it—

"Margaretha, I want you to listen to me very carefully."

As if his voice hadn't always hypnotized her.

"This has nothing to do with you, nothing to do with us. They're just playing children's games. Do you understand? They're just acting out a fantasy."

As if children didn't also play for keeps, as if fantasies didn't demand fulfillment.

Sometime after midnight he took her back down to the streets again—dream streets filled with blistered paint and twisted iron. She did not see the men watching from doorways and windows.

And it seems that Dunbar's account, along with the sinister parts, contained nothing of the genuine affection, nothing of his commitment, nothing of her need. Dunbar, after all, could not bear to find or report that.

Spangler waited until the second week before suggesting that she return with him to Berlin, saying, as if the idea had only recently occurred to him, "Live with me in Germany, at least until the summer."

It was late. His arms were laced around her naked waist. His head was resting on her belly. Since their first night together she had tended to see this affair as a dream . . . a disconnected adventure out of the mainstream of real life.

She ran a finger along his hip. "Oh God, what would I do in Berlin?"

"Dance. You can dance at the Winter Garden."

"They'd never hire me."

"But of course they will."

She slipped out of his arms, reaching for a dressing gown.

"But I don't know anyone in Berlin."

He smiled. "What does that matter? They'll know you."

"And I've got commitments in Paris."

"Postpone them."

She crossed the room, closing on an oblong mirror. Earlier she had left a slight bruise on his shoulder. Now she noticed traces of skin beneath her nails.

"Where would I live?"

"Wherever you like."

"Perhaps the Friedrichstrasse . . ." She picked up a hairbrush and slumped to a chair. He had also left her faintly bruised. "When would we leave?"

"Tomorrow, perhaps the day after."

"By train?"

"By sea."

"What if you can't get me an engagement at the Winter Garden?"

"Then you'll dance at the Metropole." He got out of bed and went to her, put his hands on her shoulders. "Margaretha, I want you with me."

She put down the hairbrush, resting her elbows on the dressing table. His reflection in the mirror seemed more captivating than her own. "I'll need to send for a few things in Paris. I couldn't possibly manage on what I've got."

He bent and kissed her gently on the neck.

"And I'll need a studio, a large studio."

"You shall have it."

"And a pianist. I must have a pianist."

He bent to kiss her again, whispered: "I shall hire you a complete orchestra if you so desire."

She would also speak of Berlin as a fantasy that somehow demanded fulfillment. Although they arrived by ship from Vigo, via Hamburg, she would maintain that she had entered the city through Rudolph Spangler's blue-gray eyes. She would talk about her reception at the docks, and the newspaper articles that followed.

And yes, she lived on the Friedrichstrasse, with a view of apple trees above a wall. And yes, she signed a contract to perform at the Metropole. But apart from everything else these were still mostly romantic days. He continued to lavish her with gifts, some expensive. She was also said to have cost him a small fortune in clothing, what with winter furs from Saint Petersburg, and there were gambling debts. Spangler's only concern, or so it seemed, was whether or not she was happy.

Was she?

There is a letter from that winter in Berlin: four more handwritten pages from Zelle to Nicholas Gray. Berlin, she wrote, was somber, with continual rain and dark skies. There was, though, music in the evenings all along the Tauentzienstrasse. "I often read in the afternoons . . . Shelley, Balzac and others you'll remember. We hope to go north in April, perhaps as far as the Baltic."

Next there were a few brief paragraphs concerning her professional success, and another passing reference to Spangler. Perhaps between the lines he might have sensed a trace of dissatisfaction, but it was subtle. Then, almost as an afterthought, she invited Gray to visit her in Berlin. There was no indication of sexual desire, nothing even faintly suggestive. Merely, it seemed that she wanted a friend, someone to talk to while Spangler was engaged. Someone to keep her company through the bad time. Surely he understood. After all, he always had.

Chapter Fourteen

INTERCEPTED on a Thursday, Zelle's letter to Nicholas Gray reached Dunbar by the following Wednesday. It was a glorious day, with a scent of new blossoms in the air: larkspur and crocus, daffodils from Saint James's and the lesser greens. There may also have been a sense of spring in the corridors, what with idle chatter and the windows ajar. The fourth floor, however, remained sealed, particularly in light of Zelle's letter.

It was about ten o'clock when the letter arrived, nearly noon when the Fourth Floor finished with it. Then, predictably, Southerland appeared, quietly asking Dunbar to step out to the garden. New grass had emerged with the rain and the black trees were sprouting buds, while the leaves seemed swollen with moisture.

"Overall the Director was pleased," Southerland began. "Overall everyone was pleased. The question, however, is what does one do with it? Very well, so Rudy is making a rare ass of himself . . . but what does one do about it?"

Dunbar began poking at sodden leaves with a stick he'd found on the path. "Did anyone read my attachment?"

"Oh yes, they read it."

"And?"

"And how well do you know Nicholas Gray?"

They began to walk.

"Placing an agent," Southerland said, "that's the great trick, and too often the fall. Did you know that Gray played with us before?"

"I heard something about it, yes."

"Eight years ago, and it ended in a bloody mess."

"Still, he's very fond of her. You mustn't forget that."

"Not forgetting, Charles, but again, where does it leave us? Yes, Gray makes sense, vis-à-vis Spangler, but in the end . . . well, you see my point. He did not work out well for us."

"Experience must count for something."

Southerland turned to him. "Eight years ago it counted for three deaths, not including Rolland Michard."

They had reached the heart of the garden and the shadow of a moss-bound oak. Mushrooms had shot up overnight.

Dunbar said, "Look, regardless of everything, you . . . we are going to need a man inside. I mean, watching from the wings is one thing, playing the scene is quite another."

"Oh, I couldn't agree more. And well put, Charles."

"And Gray was invited, wasn't he? I mean, Zelle does want him in Berlin . . . for whatever reason."

"So it seems."

"Then, really, what's the problem?"

They had left the path, moving cautiously over damp grass and clotted leaves.

"Tell me something," Southerland said. "How completely do you believe in it?"

"Believe in what?"

"Spangler. That he's actually throwing his career away for a woman like Mata Hari."

"Well, first of all I wouldn't quite put it like that."

"Then how would you put it?"

"Well, that the man's relationship with her is putting him in professional jeopardy . . . costing him a great deal of time and money, possibly causing some bad feeling in his department."

"And you're suggesting that we exploit the situation through the use of an agent—specifically Gray. Is that roughly the idea?"

"Roughly, yes."

"And how do you propose to recruit him? Gray, I mean. That is, assuming we approve, what exactly would you say to the painter?"

Dunbar hesitated a moment, because a beat of silence was also part of the form at such times. "I shall simply tell him that it concerns Mata Hari."

"And you think he'll respond, agree and so forth?"

"Yes. Yes, I do."

"Even after the Michard affair?"

"I told you, Martin, he's very fond of her."

"Obsessively fond?"

"Fond."

Then there was nothing but the wall and a staircase, odors of paraffin and coffee, sounds of those clattering typewriters again.

"I shall be seeing the Director at three," Southerland was saying, "although I don't imagine we'll have a firm answer much before this evening." Pausing at the foot of the staircase, his eyes on a drainpipe, he added, "It's not just sexual, is it?"

Dunbar had also fixed his eyes on the drainpipe—into which, it occured him, one could crawl. "I'm sorry?"

"Our dancer's—how shall I put it—allure? Surely it's more than just sexual. I mean, all these affairs, all these situations with various types of men. Surely . . ."

Dunbar shook his head without the trace of a smile. "I'm afraid I really wouldn't know."

Or care to remember?

Dunbar's transition from passive observer to active case officer took three and a half weeks. On paper his plan to place an agent next to Rudolph Spangler (and Zelle) was in tune with the standard operating procedure of the time: a slow play based upon sincerity and deceit. The operational budget was modest. The groundwork was intricate, and those involved in these planning stages tended to work impossible hours. As operational director, Dunbar virtually slept in his office.

These preparatory weeks came to be seen as Dunbar's rite of passage. Within the space of a month he had grown from a rather diffident amateur to a slow-burning professional. His memos and dispatches clearly indicated a new maturity, as did his capable handling of his juniors, particularly the younger women.

But if this was the public man, the private one was a very different creature. He slept very little. Even when the work load permitted he couldn't seem to sleep. So he walked at night, sometimes for hours, from Paddington to Charing Cross. He also drank and, inevitably, he thought about Zelle.

He tended to remember the occasional moments best: a kiss on a staircase in Dresden, cocktails on a roof in Budapest, and especially a conversation in Vienna not long after that dinner with Spangler . . .

The setting was one more steel-blue evening in one more cluttered suite. They had made love, but badly. They had tried to sleep, but couldn't. A porter had been called to bring them a drink, but no one had responded.

"You hate me tonight, don't you? she said.

"Of course not."

"Yes, you do. I can see it in your eyes."

"Don't be silly."

"Not that I blame you, but the least you could do is show it. Yell at me, hit me. Anything."

"Oh do shut up."

"We've underestimated each other, haven't we?"

"I don't know what you're talking about, Margaretha."

"Yes, I think that's been the problem all along. We've underestimated each other. We saw only what we wanted to see. We never looked past the skin . . ."

And her skin still figured in his waking dreams, dreams inspired by an undraped mannequin or a riding crop displayed in a window. By secretaries bent over typewriters, the nape of the neck exposed. He supposed it was still cold in Berlin, so that even a fingertip across the thigh might leave a line suggesting a welt.

But finally it seemed that the consummate dream was simply what one was doing anyway: spying.

He loved the idea of himself as the deft puppeteer manipulating half a dozen lives. He also loved the concept of Berlin as the stage, and the challenge of running an agent like Nicholas Gray—a reasonable man with a quiet obsession.

The recruitment of Nicholas Gray took place in Paris, in the second week in April. It was a bleak day, with rain in the air and a stiff wind from the Seine. Dunbar had wired from Calais, and Gray met him near the place Contrescarpe, where they drank a vicious absinthe and smoked cheap cigarettes. Later they walked among the numbed crowds, then along the waterfront to a charming bistro where they dined on scallops and listened to the strains of Chopin from the floor.

Dunbar would report that when it was over the actual recruitment could not have been easier. One almost had the feeling that Gray had been expecting just such an offer, he wrote. Indeed, one almost had the feeling that the man had been preparing himself for it . . . as though it were not only a logical but inevitable next step.

Chapter Fifteen

GRAY'S recollections of that night by the Seine were not exactly Dunbar's. Yes, it was cold, with a wind through tattered advertisements; and yes, they ate scallops while a dull pianist played nocturnes. But Gray would also tell us that Dunbar was an idiot with all the worst assumptions of the ruling class.

Still, there was more than a degree of truth to Dunbar's account: Gray had indeed expected just such a meeting with someone from London. He had expected it for more than a month, somehow sensing that Zelle was close again. And they did initially meet near the place Contrescarpe, where the absinthe was vicious and the cigarettes were cheap. And yes, it was a bleak night.

And Dunbar looked faintly like a toad. Gray saw him first from the cafe door. He sat with his back to the wall, presumably just as they had told him to sit. There was a newspaper spread out on the table: French, which he could barely read. Perhaps because waiters still tended to ignore him, the table was otherwise bare.

"I wasn't certain you would come," Dunbar began.

Gray shrugged. "Why shouldn't I come?"

"Oh, I don't know. Obvious reasons."

A waitress finally appeared, a rather plain girl.

"I wonder if you know what I'm doing here," Dunbar said. "Why I wanted to talk to you?"

"Your telegram gave me some indication."

"Then I suppose you've gathered that I'm with the firm now, the same firm you worked with on the Michard case. Been with them eighteen months. They're not a bad group at all."

Gray couldn't help smiling. "Firm? Is that what it's called? The Firm?"

"Your last experience wasn't typical, Nicholas. Not typical at all."

"I'm sure."

"What we want now is not at all the same sort of arrangement. Indeed, I expect it will only take about three days."

"Where?"

"Berlin."

"Piss off, Charlie."

The absinthe arrived: definitely foul stuff in glasses smudged with fingerprints. Dunbar drank it, however, so as not to appear foreign.

"She's living with Rudolph Spangler, in case you haven't guessed. She wrote you a letter. I can't say exactly how I obtained it, but I can show it to you if you'd like. The important thing is that she wants to see you. I mean, she really *wants* to see you."

"What about Spangler?"

"Ah, well, that's the whole point."

Then came the cigarettes, a rank Algerian blend that Dunbar also accepted for the sake of appearances.

"The problem is actually fairly simple," Dunbar said. "Spangler's involvement seems to have taken him close to the edge, but we don't know how close. She's costing him a great deal of money that he doesn't have, and she's rather got him into trouble with his superiors . . . who, incidentally, don't like her one bit. But the question is, how does one take advantage of it? How does one actually drive it home?"

Zelle, Gray thought, had always said that home was just a place you started from. "When would I go?" he asked.

"Soon. But honestly, Nicky, all we actually want you to do is to accept an invitation. That's the whole of it. Spend a few hours chatting with her, have a drink with Rudy. That's it. I swear that's all there is to it. In on a Friday, out by Monday. Honest to God."

Zelle had also once said that one must accept God as unknowable, or else altogether disappointing.

"Where will you be?"

"Embassy in Berlin. And we only want your impressions. Your assessment of Spangler's professional status, your observations about the nature of the relationship, the emotional state and so forth. I suppose I should also add that we're prepared to pay . . . pretty much whatever you want."

What he wanted was a breath of fresh air, and a view of something other than drunks at a zinc bar. So they left and started walking—just as Dunbar would say—they walked through the numbed crowds with the wind at their backs. For a long while they didn't speak, just continued walking along the concrete embankment, where sounds were more substantial than shapes in the darkness: a blown bottle across the pavement, a distant barge, a smoker's cough.

"Before you give me an answer one way or another I think there's a personal side to this story you should hear," Dunbar said at last. "A very personal side."

"What are you talking about?"

"Well, we can't ignore the fact that Margaretha is in danger, real danger. I mean, at best Spangler will keep her in his power until hell freezes over. At worst she'll become an expendable pawn in a very nasty game. Now I'm not suggesting that the department is concerned, but you and I have certain responsibilities to the woman, don't we? . . . Well, *don't we?*"

Nor was Dunbar's description of the aftermath particularly accurate, for although they ended up in some waterfront bistro, the place was hardly charming. Nor was the conversation especially involving. Dunbar merely talked about himself while Gray quietly drank himself sick. There was, however, one point that Dunbar got quite right. Gray's ultimate reason for accepting the job—compulsion born of obsession.

It began, as before, in an isolated country home a few miles out of the city. Gray arrived on an afternoon train and found Dunbar waiting for him at the station. Beneath the dusty poplars stood a dark chauffeur, a wiry, muscular boy with a pockmarked face and the dull eyes of a boxer. Dunbar introduced him as Sykes, and for some reason seemed proud of him.

They drove for about an hour before they reached the farmhouse. It lay in a shallow ravine. There were apple orchards on the rise, fallow land below. As they left the car a slamming door sent waves of blackbirds rising from the bracken. It was the first time Gray saw Sykes smile.

The farmhouse was small—upper and lower floors—with a thatched roof. The floor was bare stone, dry rot had attacked the walls, the furniture was deteriorating from insects and neglect. Gray's bedroom, though, was acceptable, with a long view of cypress groves and what may have been a ruined chapel. After about two hours Sykes appeared with tea, which they drank in the conservatory, another damp room that smelled of cats.

Southerland arrived at dusk. Gray first spotted him from a second-story window: a figure in a mackintosh, a tipped cane on the flagstones. They met on the staircase.

"I trust you have everything you need." He smiled.

"Yes, thank you."

"And your room?"

"The room is fine."

"Not too drafty. I mean, these old places—"

"It's fine."

"Well, should you want anything, anything at all."

"Thanks."

At which point the conversation more or less evaporated, and they were left staring at one another.

The formal briefing began that evening. A wing chair had been dragged in from the conservatory, an oil lamp from the hall. Sykes built a fire with stuffing from the sofa as tinder. The log smoldered, but didn't actually catch. Southerland led off the discussion, but said little that hadn't been said before. Spangler was close to ruin —accumulating debts, neglecting his duties, devoting himself to a woman his colleagues considered a slut.

Dunbar added that Spangler had also been seen drinking too much, something that was definitely not done in his circle. And meanwhile there were half a dozen wolves circling, just waiting to appropriate his networks.

"It's always been that way," Southerland said. "Nicolai likes to foster competition among the ranks. His Third Department is a snakepit. Still, don't underestimate Spangler."

As for Zelle, it seemed that she was living quietly in a roomy apartment above the park. Her evenings were full, but she seemed to be wasting her days: riding alone in the mornings, dancing a little in the afternoons. From time to time she had also been seen at the National Gallery, but always alone and usually among the Moderns.

You're to be our eyes, they gold Gray. Also possibly our messenger, but definitely our eyes. He was to pay particular attention to details. How *much* did Spangler drink on a given night? Did he seem *concerned* about money? About his work? Did he seem bitter about his colleagues? Did he ever seem afraid?

Much of this information, they said, would no doubt emerge through conversations with Zelle, and so Gray was to spend as much time as possible with her. "She's at least always been candid with *you*," Dunbar said, "so it's really just a matter of directing the conversation into the proper channels."

They stressed the importance of what he was about to do. They said that regardless of how insignificant the assignment seemed, it was actually the very bedrock of intelligence. They said that the good spy always depended on prosaic social intercourse, collecting small impressions until he had an understanding of the greater whole. They said that the smart spy did not steal; rather he befriended and then observed.

The Middle Years

It was almost midnight when they finally finished. Sykes had reappeared with a tray of brandy, then vanished again. The fire had died, and a wind had risen. Periodically there had been tinkling chimes from various clocks throughout the house, all inaccurate. Now, however, it was still.

"I suppose we should turn in," Dunbar said. "The first train leaves quite early."

Gray looked at him. "Train?"

"To Berlin."

Southerland added, "Yes, that's right, Nicky. It's actually on for tomorrow."

Gray shrugged. "Very well, tomorrow."

He went up the staircase without turning back. The corridor was lined with tapestries of biblical quotations and an old print of Chantilly. There was also a crucifix tacked to the door of his room, another above the bed . . . Zelle had said that Christ the redeemer was not nearly as interesting as Siva the destroyer. Was she just trying to be outrageous?

He bolted the door, snuffed out the candle, and lay down without undressing. There were footsteps in the corridor, Southerland or Dunbar. Then only the sounds of rodents in the walls. He got up and drew the curtains shut, lay back down, and closed his eyes. But it was no use . . . she was already too close.

The corridor was dark, although there was still a light below. As he descended the staircase he saw Southerland sitting in a wing chair. At the moment he might have been a wax effigy, draped in an overcoat, motionless in front of a chessboard, the ivory pieces only marginally paler than his hands.

"Can't sleep?"

Gray's reply was an equivocal shrug. He reached for the decanter of brandy. "Where's Dunbar?"

Southerland nodded toward the staircase and bedrooms. "Charles, it seems, is more fortunate than you and I tonight."

There were sounds of rodents here too, mice in the rafters or possibly rats. The odors were distinctly human: burnt meat, sour cabbage, perspiration.

"Actually," Southerland said, "I'm glad you came down. I wanted an opportunity to speak to you alone."

"What about?"

"Berlin." He picked up a rook, slowly turning it over in his hands. "The fact of the matter is we may require somewhat more than was previously mentioned."

Gray lit a cigarette, one of Dunbar's Russian blends he'd taken earlier. "Such as?"

"Oh, I don't know. Pinch a letter, maybe. Plant a notion, help young Charles negotiate Spangler's defection."

"You're serious?"

"Well, if Spangler really is burning his bridges in Berlin, then perhaps we ought to show him the route to London."

"And if he doesn't take it?"

Southerland smiled, though his eyes remained unchanged, fixed on a red knight hopelessly exposed to the rook. "Well, we shall cross *that* particular bridge when we come to it."

"What about Zelle?"

"What about her?"

"How does she figure in it?"

"Oh, I don't know. I thought I'd leave her to you."

Gray shook his head. "I can't control her. I don't know what Dunbar told you, but I can't control her."

Southerland seemed to be considering pawn to king's three. "I understand. Still, there is always something one can do."

There were chimes of an unreliable clock, then silence. Southerland seemed entranced with the red knight knocking at the queen's door. "It's a dream of mine, actually . . . to lead Herr Spangler by a rope through the streets of London." Then, renewing the attack with a bishop, "Did you know that Anthony Craven was a friend of mine?"

Gray shook his head.

"He was my sponsor, my tutor."

"I'm sorry."

"Not that I'm a vindictive man, but God knows I'd like to get Spangler." His hands clenched two fallen pawns. "Incidentally, you won't be alone out there. Sykes will be watching your back, and as you know, Charles and I shall be only an hour away. So you mustn't worry."

Gray reached for the brandy again. "What if Spangler plays dirty, as he's been known to?"

"I told you, Sykes will be there. He's actually an extremely capable young man."

"What if Spangler remembers me from that night with Michard?"

"Oh I don't think he'll make the connection. I mean, eight years . . ."

They did not say goodnight. Gray finished his brandy and moved back to the staircase. He had nearly reached the landing when Southerland quietly called out his name.

"Incidentally, you are doing it for the woman, aren't you?"

Gray turned and looked at him. "Does it matter?"

Southerland shrugged. "You know, Charles has the same fixation. It's manifested rather differently, but essentially the fixation is the same. I'm afraid I don't quite understand it myself . . . but then I've only seen her photographs."

Later that night he heard Southerland again, prowling through the corridors, perhaps looking for another insomniac to face across the chessboard? Toward dawn, however, it was quiet again, and Gray actually managed to dream about her.

They left in the morning under dark skies. En route to the station Dunbar discussed contact procedures, then retired to a waiting room to catch a later train. Gray would remember the journey for its orchards in varying shades of green, pepperpot turrets on the cliffs of the Rhine, open meadows. He would also recall it altogether in terms of Zelle—a slow return to the heart of the matter through a changing landscape and dying light. There were soldiers from Berlin, merchants from Paris, women returning from holidays. But really all other pieces had been swept from the board—so that in the end it might have been described as a solitary duel between two pawns, irresistibly moving into no-man's land.

Chapter Sixteen

NATURALLY there were Gray's drawings of Berlin, pen-and-ink sketches of forgotten skylines, nightscapes of since-ruined boulevards: Bendlerstrasse, Anhalterstrasse, the Unter den Linden. For the most part these drawings were only mediocre: listless experiments with angular shadows and odd perspectives. There were, however, two or three rather interesting portraits of soldiers, and a truly stunning profile of Zelle.

Although he had wired in advance, she had not met him at the station; and when they met she looked tired and drained from a three-day bout with the flu.

They drank cocoa in the bar of the Bristol Hotel, then walked at random through back streets and public gardens. They talked of nothing—regardless of what Dunbar would say later—that really mattered. She asked about mutual friends in Paris, he replied that apart from de Massloff he rarely saw anyone. He asked about her career, her response was vague. They discussed one or two painters she had met at a party. Spangler came up only once—just before she had to leave to meet him for a drink in Kempinski's.

"You don't approve, do you?" she said. "I can see it in your eyes."

His eyes were on the skyline, on the Kaiser's neo-Grecian monstrosities. "Approve of what?"

"Rudolph, this city, everything. You don't even think I should be here, do you?"

"I suppose not."

"But that's because you don't know Rudy, and you certainly don't know Berlin." She paused, pulling him to a stop with her arm linked through his. "Tell me something. What *really* made you come and see me?"

There were a dozen answers he'd rehearsed on the train, but suddenly, as though the whole of Germany were waiting, what came out was: "Actually, I'm not sure."

They continued to walk, not quite in step, puddles from an earlier rain like bits of a broken looking glass reflecting the trees above. A passing tram briefly drowned her voice, then he heard her laughing. "Paris isn't the only city, you know. Besides, Rudolph gives me everything . . . absolutely everything."

"Where does he get the money?" Since everyone wanted to know.

"Who cares? As long as he gives me everything."

"Ah, well, in that case I guess I should meet him." The least he could do, given his assignment.

"And you will . . . tomorrow for dinner."

Dunbar was going to be thrilled.

"Say about eight o'clock."

And in the meantime he could drink himself into oblivion. "Yes, eight will be fine."

"And, Nicky?"

"What?" Catching a glimpse of something in her eyes he hadn't seen for months.

"I'm terribly glad you came, really I am."

Right then he nearly told her: get away from here, it's dangerous, I'm a spy again. But in the end he simply left her standing on the cold street, the color back in her cheeks, her beauty once more absolute and indisputable.

There was a park not far from the Wilhelm Platz and adjacent to the British embassy. It was a walled park with deep foliage and dark chestnuts. There were also birds that he would always remember from this city: mallards and swans, sparrows and woodthrush. Like so much else, however, one always heard them but actually rarely saw them.

It was dusk when Dunbar and Southerland arrived, a bluish dusk and somehow warmer than the afternoon. Gray found them waiting on a stone bench beneath an oak. They were dressed alike in raincoats and homburgs: Tweedledum and Tweedledee, he thought.

"I see him tomorrow," Gray said. "She's invited me to bloody dinner."

Dunbar nodded with a slow smile. "That's very good, Nicky. That's very good indeed."

While Southerland remained typically cool, asking only: "So then she did accept you? Your presence here, she accepted it?"

Gray took a deep breath and sagged to the bench beside them. "Why shouldn't she accept it? She's not involved, so she has no reason to suspect *anything.*"

Dunbar withdrew a leather-bound notebook, very expensive and purchased for just such an occasion. The fountain pen was also clearly dear, a Mont Blanc with a gold nib. "I suppose you might as well tell us about it," he said. "In as much detail as possible."

Details: a frantic sparrow in the thickets, a ground fog in the hollows, the echo of horse hooves, and this absurd meeting on a cold bench.

"She likes the city," Gray said. "She seems to like Spangler . . ."

"Does she have any idea where he gets the money?"

Gray shook his head. "It's not exactly the sort of question she would ask."

"What about their schedule? How often does he see her?"

"I don't know. Maybe three or four times a week."

162

"And his health?"

"She's the one who's been ill."

"It's the small points that interest us now," Southerland said. "For example, how would you assess her emotional state?"

Gray shrugged, exhaling smoke from a cigarette—one of the awful local brands. "I've seen her better."

"And what do you suppose the problem is?" Southerland persisted.

"I don't know. Perhaps she's bored."

"Or frightened?" Dunbar suggested. "Frightened of Spangler, or what's happening to him?"

Southerland gently embellished. "Because naturally that would be a factor, Nicky. I mean, if she's genuinely concerned about him, then it could mean that he's in real trouble, that he's desperate enough to consider alternatives—"

"Look, you've got it wrong. She likes the man. He pays the bills. That's the whole of it."

"Ah, but what are those bills doing to him?" Dunbar grinned. "And what is he willing to do in order to pay them?"

For an awful moment it looked to him as if Southerland was going to touch him, to lay a hand on his shoulder or his knee. "We're not trying to imply that the woman is materially involved, Nicky, merely that she's a vital barometer, so to speak. Which is why you've got to pay attention to the little things, the tidbits that give us the larger picture. Now you *do* understand that, don't you?"

He left them where he had found them: planted side by side on the bench, Dunbar speaking softly, Southerland occasionally nodding. As he neared the park's edge Sykes appeared. His hands were jammed in the pockets of his sailor's coat. His restless eyes were fixed on something in the distance.

"All done?" His voice was vaguely unpleasant, thuggish.

"What do you want?"

Sykes grinned, his head cocked at an odd angle. "Just to take a look at your back."

"What?"

He pointed to the road ahead. "Watch your trail. Make sure the wolves haven't picked up your scent."

Gray turned, watching him. "Look, I don't know what the hell you're talking about."

Sykes took a step closer, a finger pointing to his eye. "Just keep walking down the road, eh?"

Nor was the remainder of that night any less disturbing, with voices through thin walls, footsteps in corridors, and the screech of passing trams. Berlin.

Eventually Dunbar would record that Gray spent most of the second day preparing himself for Spangler. He exercised to calm his nerves, Dunbar would write. He rested with music on the gramophone. He ate fish and drank nothing but tea and mineral water. He rehearsed his approach in front of a mirror.

None of this was true: all Dunbar's flourishes to make himself interesting.

Gray would mostly remember the fog. It rose at dawn, spilling over banks of the canals, gently colliding with a windborne mist. By noon the heart of the city was also fogbound, with an ascendant chill from the alleys and drains. The fog seemed appropriate, and welcome, obscuring and softening what he had no desire to confront.

There were some eight hours on that second day to waste before the evening, and Gray used them like a tourist. He tried a gallery filled with derivative etchings. He wandered into a church. He visited a national monument and watched children tossing pebbles in a fountain until a policeman appeared. He sat on a park bench with a flask of whisky. There were also moments when he found himself unreasonably hungry, and understood that it was nervous fear. And there were moments when he could not stop shivering from the cold, and knew that it was Zelle. As dusk began to fall he also found himself, willy-nilly, thinking about Spangler.

He took a long time to dress that evening: laying out his clothing in a kind of trance, half dozing in a bath with another whisky at his elbow, smoking three or four cigarettes while waiting for a taxi. He was, he reminded himself, doing this for Zelle.

He arrived at her apartment at quarter past eight. She met him at the door with a kiss, then led him into a sitting room. It was pretty much what he had expected: a careful approximation of a real home. There were timid etchings of snow-laden fields, a seascape and a copy of an early Raphael. There was also a clock on the mantle with suspended brass weights, and two imitative oriental prints.

"So what do you think, darling? Respectable enough?"

"Oh, very."

"And naturally I also have my studio."

Nor was Spangler any surprise: first appearing on the landing, then floating down the staircase to shake his hand. He wore a smoking jacket and a burgundy cravat, charcoal gray trousers and a silk shirt. His face was somewhat cleaner than Gray recalled, but the eyes were decidedly familiar.

"So, you are the painter that I've heard so much about."

"Nothing too compromising, I hope."

"Oh, no, Margaretha greatly admires your work."

Then there came the sherry, appropriately dry; then an amusing story about a trip Spangler had once made to Africa. The meal was of a piece: cold poached salmon, iced lettuce, potato soup, sherbet.

Yet there was at least one telling moment, one critical juncture in the evening. It came later after Zelle had retired to her bedroom— obviously another calculated gesture. Spangler had poured the brandy and laid a box of cigars on the table. The servants had been dismissed. The curtains had been drawn back to reveal still one more blue evening with only traces of that earlier fog.

"So you see," Spangler said, "Berlin, too, can be quite inspiring."

The moonlight only tended to accent the man's profile, turning the skin to porcelain.

"Yes, it's very nice."

"Oh, I know what they say. It's not nearly as charming as Paris . . . but still, I think, very interesting, no?" Then, sliding his hand on the window pane, examining a residue of dust, "Tell me, do you miss England much? I think I would . . . assuming that I were an Englishman."

They were both watching one another's eyes in the glass.

"I haven't been home in a long time," Gray said.

"Yes, but does one ever forget one's home?"

His fingers might have also been procelain, the nails like translucent pearls.

"No, I suppose one doesn't."

"Then, too, I remember England as so inviting. Yes, that's definitely the word. *Inviting.* In fact, I've often had the notion of living there myself . . . in the country."

"I think you would find it cold. And damp."

"Ah, but I like the cold. And the damp reminds me of the sea, which I also like." He stepped back from the window, toying with the sash. "Of course there are tangible obstacles. Margaretha, for example, would probably not like it. And there would always be the matter of earning a living. You see, I am not financially independent. Consequently I would need some sort of employment. Selling art, for example." A beat. "Or information. What do you think?"

"I think that I'm not the one you should ask, Herr Spangler." He should not, he reasoned, be too eager. Besides, it was a small outlet for the anger Spangler stirred up in him.

He left at about midnight with a closing view of his host and hostess smiling out of the porch light. The suburbs were dead, but there were lights in every tavern window along the Bismarckstrasse. Closer to the park there were prostitutes and loitering youths with shaved heads.

Beyond the park lay a block of apartment houses: iron-gray and severe, but stuck at intervals with concrete foliage and faces of dwarves. There were no signs of life except a piano playing from a basement window and a discarded doll on the stoop. But Sykes was waiting just inside the doorway, while Southerland and Dunbar were in a room at the top of the staircase.

A room that was long and low, possibly once a nursery or a

servant's quarters. The furniture was a table and three chairs. The walls were bare and yellowed. The light was so poor that at first Gray saw only Dunbar's motionless outline. In any case, it was Southerland who spoke first—quietly from the darkened corner.

"I'm afraid we have nothing to offer you except a chair."

Gray faced them from across the table. He spoke slowly but steadily, as if recounting a dream he had just awakened from. Dunbar took furious notes. There was an occasional question, an occasional point when Southerland asked him to clarify, but mostly it was a monologue.

The discussion did not begin until later. By then it was very still and dark. Gray had moved to the window, where he could see Sykes beneath the fire escape. Southerland had lit a cigarette, and Dunbar had laid his fountain pen down.

"He knows," Gray said. "You realize that, don't you? Spangler knows precisely why I've come."

"Yes," Southerland replied. "He's probably known from the start—"

"Then why the bloody hell didn't you tell me?"

"Because at the time we didn't know. Not for certain, in any case. You see, I think we've underestimated the man. But then, if he comes over . . ."

Dunbar smiled from across the room. "You've done very well, Nicky. You've done very well indeed."

There were strains from that piano again, a clumsy sonata. Gray finally said, "Christ, you really don't get it, do you?"

"What's that?" Dunbar asked. "What don't we get?"

"That Rudy is bloody lying through his teeth. I don't think he's planning to come over. I don't think he's even considering it. I'd say he's just testing us, sizing us up for the kill . . . and what you said about his relationship with Zelle is also rubbish. I'm not even certain he likes her."

Southerland had moved from the window to a chair, exchanged glances with Dunbar. "It's not that we discount your opinion, Nicky. It's merely that we rather see the signs a bit differently. Yes,

Spangler is undoubtedly playing with us. And yes, he probably saw more than he should have in Madrid. But there are other factors at work here, Nicky."

Dunbar was grinning from across the room. "Small factors, but vital just the same."

"Which means what?"

"Which means that you shouldn't concern yourself with the odd remark or even the probing question. I mean to say, the man is precisely where we want him . . . or will be very soon."

Gray had moved away from the window, leaving an imprint of his palm on the glass. He had also left his cigarette burning on the sill.

"Look, why don't you just tell me how you want it played."

Southerland nodded. "Very well. See if you can't insinuate without being precise. And try to find out what he wants from us."

"It won't work. He's going to move at his own pace. He's not going to let us push him."

"Oh, I don't think so. After all, he's very much aware of the rules in this sort of thing."

Rules? As in a game? And they, the spectators, seemed pleased with his play so far . . . But then, they did not actually have to participate.

He met Spangler the following evening, supposedly to establish an understanding while strolling through the Tiergarten pines. These were difficult times, Spangler told him. Politically difficult, financially difficult, possibly even spiritually difficult. Consequently one could not help, occasionally, imagining a new life . . . perhaps in one of those quaint London suburbs where a foreigner would go largely unnoticed.

"And what would one need to establish such a life?" Gray inquired.

"Oh, I don't know. Maybe twenty thousand pounds, and certain assurances concerning one's physical safety."

Over dinner with Zelle, Spangler may have dropped another

oblique reference to his possible future in London, but by this time Gray had drunk too much to play on. Enough was enough.

It was about ten o'clock when the evening ended, midnight when Gray returned to that narrow room where Southerland and Dunbar were waiting. Again Sykes had been stationed beneath the fire escape. When Gray had finished his account of the evening Southerland produced three reasonably clean glasses and a wretched bottle of port. Then came the questions, and Dunbar in particular seemed pleased with the answers. Gray was the only one desperate enough to actually drink the stuff.

On the staircase Dunbar said, "Of course, you couldn't have played it any better, but now I think it's time to take another step."

"What sort of step?"

There was a draft from the doorway and the smell of cleaning fluid.

"See if you can't get him really to lay his cards on the table."

"Why? They're all bloody jokers—"

"Oh, I don't think so. In fact, I want you to tell him that you have certain connections that might be willing to help, certain friends in London."

"What sort of friends?"

"No need to specify."

"He's going to want to know."

"Then he's going to have to wait."

There was a brief interlude before the next round with Spangler, another brief moment with Zelle. They met in her apartment on an evening when he had not expected to find her alone. Then, on her suggestion, they moved out to the streets. Earlier there had been a soft rain, a summer rain, and the scent of it was still in the air. Birds, mostly sparrows, had gathered under the eves. Of course they talked about Spangler, but only peripherally and in terms of themselves.

169

"You like him, don't you?" she said. "Despite it all you've rather come to like him, haven't you?"

Zelle . . . Zelle . . . still convincing yourself that things are the way you'd like them to be rather than as they are. One day, and the sooner the better, you'll have to stop that . . . He was very conscious of her touch, the pressure of her arm on his, the occasional brush of her shoulder. They had entered one of the more sedate neighborhoods, the sort of place that Zelle had always tended to distrust, perhaps because she felt its residents would disapprove of her. There were long rows of dripping oaks, stone nymphs among the ivy, plaster ducks, solid doors.

"And unless I'm very mistaken," she said, "Rudy is also rather fond of you."

"Is he?"

"Yes, and you really should take it as a compliment, because he doesn't like many people."

"No, I can't imagine that he does."

She slipped her arm from his, then turned to face him. "What's that supposed to mean?"

"Go home, Margaretha. Go back to Paris."

She smiled, reaching for his hand again. "Why?"

"Because he's not the sort of man that you're used to."

"But that's why I love him . . . need him."

"Possess him?"

"No, it's not like that at all."

"Then how is it?"

She shook her head. "He's wonderfully strong. He's the strongest man I've ever known. Maybe he's even stronger than you."

They circled another block in silence before pausing beneath the sodden trellis that framed the entrance to her apartment. There were times when her eyes had extraordinary depths, but now they seemed flat.

"It's not just jealousy, is it?" she said.

He laid his hand on her shoulder to draw her closer. "No."

"Then what?"

He bent and kissed her lightly on the lips. "Is he upstairs now?"

She glanced up to a light in the window above. "Yes, I think so."

"Then go away. Go away for a little while. Take another walk, visit a friend, anything."

"But why?"

"Just do it."

He waited until he could no longer see her, then moved up the narrow staircase to her apartment. He knocked only once before Spangler told him to enter. The hall was dark, but there was lamplight from the corner where someone had laid out two glasses and a bottle. There was also a modest fire in the grate, and a vacant chair opposite Spangler's.

At first Spangler said nothing . . . only that he had recently purchased a notable claret from a merchant in Dresden. Then, shifting his gaze to the empty hall, he asked about Zelle.

"She's taking another walk," Gray said.

"On your recommendation?"

"Yes."

"Ah, so the honeymoon is finally over."

Gray slipped into the vacant chair, and they faced one another: Spangler in another velveteen smoking jacket, Gray with another cheap cigarette.

"I must admit that I was somewhat disappointed that they sent you," Spangler said. "So predictable."

Gray dropped an ash on the floor. "I'm not authorized to negotiate."

"Of course not. You're merely the artist gathering his impressions. Tell me, what do you think of our young German modernists?"

"Very impressive."

"Really? I find them too oblique, but then I've always preferred the realists. Turner, for example, now there's a painter, yes?"

Gray just kept looking at him. "I'm supposed to find out what you want, and what you can give. I'm also to say that I have friends in London who may be willing to help."

Spangler allowed a small, precise smile. "Of course, friends. Where would we be without friends?"

"They would like to conclude the arrangements as soon as possible."

"And yet they send me a painter, and a cryptic painter at that. No, this really won't do. I want to meet *them*. I want to form my own impressions."

He got up from the chair, moved to the table and poured the notable claret.

"You know, I'm actually in a very precarious position, Mr. Gray. I am vulnerable from all sides. Margaretha has cost me an absolute fortune. My colleagues are waiting for a plausible excuse to destroy me, and now I am asked to put my life in the hands of a painter, an English painter from an abstract school." He put Gray's glass on the table beside the chair. "You know, if I may say so, I think a lesser man would have crumbled weeks ago."

There was a curio cabinet against the far wall, and Gray watched as he examined one of Zelle's porcelain dolls. Even Rudolph's small gestures are perfect, she had said, even the little insignificant things like lighting cigarettes, folding napkins, picking up small objects.

"These people I work with," Spangler said at last, "they can be vicious. If I were to betray them, I don't think they'd forgive me."

Gray thinking, and you're a bloody pussycat . . . but saying, "I'm sure my friends in London understand that, and I'm sure they're willing to make certain guarantees regarding your safety."

"Then let them come to my house and make them."

"And in exchange?"

"I shall show them a sample of what I can do for them. A written sample from my personal safe."

From the curio cabinet he had drifted to the window, lifted the curtain, and then let it fall again. And Rudolph never misses anything, Zelle had said. He's like a panther in the trees. He can even see in the darkness.

"These friends of yours," Spangler said suddenly. "I imagine that they're fairly confident at this point, aren't they?"

Gray shrugged.

"But you, on the other hand, you still don't quite trust me, do you? You're still concerned about my motives."

"Perhaps."

"Not that I blame you. Motives are so difficult to understand . . . particularly in terms of defection. For example, there are some men who will spend their whole lives in misery without ever contemplating the idea. Then again there are those who have been moved to acts of treason only because some senior officer was unkind to them. As for myself, I think they will eventually blame it on Margaretha. I think they will say that she showed me a life that I had never seen before, a life that I found irresistibly attractive . . . and, of course, they will be right."

"She's not part of the arrangement, Spangler."

"Oh, I know that. It's every man for himself where Mata Hari is concerned. Still, I think she will give me another six months, don't you? And even if she doesn't, I shall always have the money to buy another just like her."

She appeared just before Gray left, returning suddenly, almost mid-sentence. Spangler had moved to the end of the room. Gray had risen from his chair. There had been one or two words regarding time and location, and then they heard her at the door. She entered slowly, toying with a rose she must have picked from someone's garden. When she started to speak Spangler cut her off, explaining that Mr. Gray would not be joining them for dinner after all.

This time Gray met Dunbar in an enormous black limousine waiting in a cul-de-sac. A thin drizzle lay on the air, warm and shifting in clouds around the street lamps. Sykes sat at the steering wheel, Dunbar behind him with a newspaper. Their breath had fogged the glass so that from a distance Gray could imagine he saw a third figure. Slipping into the back, however, he saw that Southerland was absent.

"Under the circumstances John felt that his presence was redundant," Dunbar began. "I hope you don't find that too distressing."

He had changed. There was something new in his voice, a confident slur, and his gestures seemed more expansive.

"Where is he? Gray asked. "London?"

"Heavens, no. He's merely tidying up a few loose ends at the embassy. I'm sure he'll be back for the finale. Which is?"

"Tomorrow. Apparently he'll have something to show you tomorrow."

"Me?"

"He says he's tired of dealing with a go-between. He wants to meet my *friend.*"

Dunbar grinned. "And what exactly have you told him about this friend?"

"Nothing. But he's worried about safety and I think he'll want more than the twenty thousand quid."

"Nonetheless he's still willing, isn't he?"

Gray shrugged. "I suppose."

"I'll say it again, you've done exceedingly well, Nicky. We're all very pleased." Then, as the smile slowly faded: "Now, about tomorrow. What are the particulars?"

"There's a warehouse by the canal. We're supposed to meet him there a little before midnight."

"And he'll bring the sample?"

"Something from his safe. He didn't say what."

"And assuming all parties are satisfied?"

"He claims he'll be ready to leave within four days, but he didn't discuss any details."

A van passed, followed by a slow dray. Amid the clatter Dunbar whispered something to Sykes, who responded with a slight nod. His gloved hands were still tight on the wheel, his eyes still sweeping the street.

"I suppose I should ask you about Margaretha," Dunbar said at last.

Gray felt something rising from his chest: a trace of vomit, Rudy's notable claret. "What about her?"

"I'm merely wondering if there's anything you should tell me about her. Observations? Difficulties?"

"I think she probably knows something is happening, but she doesn't know what."

"And Spangler is comfortable with the arrangement? No unreasonable expectations?"

"I told you. Money seems the main thing."

"Well, at least that's a motive we can all understand. Which reminds me, we never actually settled on your fee, did we? Well, have no fear."

As Gray was leaving, Dunbar stepped out of the limousine with him. "You realize that we'll have to keep Spangler in quarantine for at least eight or nine months."

"Quarantine?"

"Far from the madding crowd, as it were. Not that we won't ensure his comfort, or pay him what he wants. But we certainly can't have him running about Knightsbridge, can we?"

"What are you saying?"

"Simply that regardless of what we may promise, he's not going to keep Margaretha. And even later I imagine we'll settle him in Canada—for his own safety. Well, don't look at me that way. Isn't it what you wanted? Spangler out of the picture. *Isn't it?*"

There were eight hours on the last day that Gray killed between dozing in his room and moving aimlessly through wet streets. He also spent some time in a tavern on the Kantstrasse, thinking mostly about Zelle.

He wondered what he would tell her when it was over. He wondered how she would respond. He also found himself dwelling on a few select impressions . . . an evening here, a morning there, dawn by the river in Paris, dusk by the canals in Berlin.

At dusk another fog rose, slipping in from the Spreewald, invading the suburbs. For a while Gray watched from a window with his third or fourth whisky, but he realized this was not the sort of fog one could capture on canvas. Nor could one capture the restless silence, nor the sky in dull blue, nor, especially, the conflicting emotions.

175

He took a long time to dress, eventually choosing a necktie that Zelle had given him years earlier. He left his hotel at about nine o'clock, got to Dunbar and Sykes at about ten. They were waiting in that limousine: Sykes rigid behind the wheel, Dunbar studying a road map in the rear. Again a word about Southerland's absence, again the clatter of passing vans and drays.

"I don't suppose we'll have any way of knowing whether or not he'll be armed," Dunbar said.

Gray cleared a circle in the misted glass but saw nothing except the dead street. "Oh, he'll be armed."

"But only for self-protection. Right?"

"I don't read minds."

There was a hip flask, exquisitely tooled in silver, between them on the seat. When Gray had climbed into the rear Dunbar had offered it to him, with what Gray considered a silly reference to the soldier's ration just before battle. He had refused the stuff; Dunbar had taken three or four swigs.

"You don't think he'll bring anyone with him, do you?" Dunbar said suddenly. "I mean, given the circumstances, surely he wouldn't go so far as to . . ."

Gray breathed through clenched teeth. "I should think it's a bit late to worry about that."

Sykes glanced back from the driver's seat to say that it was time.

They drove slowly, and as they did it occurred to Gray that Sykes had never actually been a chauffeur. He might have been a soldier, or a killer, but he was not at ease at the wheel. The back streets were unlit, and twice they had to stop and consult a map. As they neared the canals, the mist became a thick, gelatinous presence from the sewers.

The warehouse lay at the end of a blackened street between a factory and a loading dock. The walls were brick, black with soot. There were odors of fish and creosote. On Dunbar's instruction, Sykes eased the limousine to a stop about fifty yards from the warehouse doors. There was a moon but no

lights, and the only sounds were of a creaking barge and old newspapers in the breeze.

"You're certain this is the place?" Dunbar said. Gray nodded.

"Then you had better not keep him waiting."

Gray turned to look at him. "What's going on, Charles?"

Dunbar smiled, avoiding Gray's eyes. "It's simply a matter of
form. Southerland and I felt it would be best if you and Sykes went
in first and brought him out . . . in order to establish a precedent,
in order to show him who's in charge." Then, "Well, I can't see why
you'd possibly object."

"Go to hell."

As Gray and Sykes stepped out of the limousine, Sykes glanced
back once through the windshield to Dunbar, then quickly nodded
to Gray.

They walked slowly, keeping to the shadows. The warehouse
doors were slightly ajar but there were no lights inside. As they
moved closer, Gray caught a glimpse of Sykes moving beside him:
shoulders stiff, jaw rigid, one hand locked around the butt of a pistol
in the waistband of his trousers. His eyes were fixed on the door,
and his face was beaded with perspiration.

They paused just inside the door, peering into the darkness. There
were vague forms of packing crates, and ropes suspended from the
rafters. A row of windows above threw parallel shafts of light on
the brick, but otherwise it was dark.

Gray waited almost a minute before calling out Spangler's name,
his voice remote in the silence. He called again, heard only the
sounds of scurrying rats. Sykes withdrew the revolver and put it in
his coat pocket. Gray called a third time, and then, from the deeper
silence: "There's really no need to shout, Mr. Gray."

Spangler appeared by degrees, first as a shadow on the corrugated
iron, then as a silhouette. He wore a greatcoat and riding boots. His
arms hung at his sides, making sure his hands were visible. Stepping
into the shaft of light, he emerged with a quizzical smile. His eyes
were on Sykes, and Gray decided he must have seen the gun.

"I don't think I've had the pleasure," he said.

"That's not the man," Gray replied.

177

"Oh?"

"We thought it would be better if you spoke to him outside."

"Better? You mean safer, don't you? Really, Nicholas, this is hardly a way to start a relationship."

Gray took another step forward, his hands also clearly visible. "It's a small point, and I think we'll be more comfortable. He's got a motorcar."

"I think not. I think I'd actually prefer to speak here."

There were two or three disconnected moments when no one seemed to move . . . except Sykes, sensing something and slowly withdrawing the revolver. Gray saw only a hint of it: the hammer briefly snagging on the lining of the coat. He heard himself shout, *No.* And then Spangler calling out something to the rafters, where a figure with a rifle had begun to emerge from the blackness. He heard a third voice in German, saw a glint of polished brass. The first shot lifted Sykes into the air, the second tore away the back of his head.

Another disconnected moment or two before Gray stumbled back to the door, one or two more paralyzed seconds looking into Spangler's eyes. He became aware of the others: soldiers among the packing crates, an officer with a megaphone, Sykes twitching in death throes.

Gray ran, first mainly conscious of the voices behind him, then the wavering lights of Dunbar's limousine. He slipped and felt his knee against his chin and the pain as he bit his tongue. He was up again, running to the shrill peal of a whistle, to the clap of his heels on the cobbles. He heard a pistol shot, then his own voice screaming Dunbar's name.

He lowered his head, arms and legs pumping furiously but, as in any bad dream, he couldn't seem to close the distance, couldn't seem to keep the street from flowing like a river . . . as the limousine pulled away . . . accelerating erratically because the bastard was obviously unfamiliar with the gears.

After that he supposed that he was running for nothing, entranced by the rhythm of his feet, lost in the night sky. Even later when they caught him, he was still running running—lying in a puddle of rainwater.

Chapter Seventeen

THEY brought him to the compound at Doberitz, eight miles from the heart of the city. Although largely forgotten as a center of atrocities, there were actually more than three hundred political prisoners there in that summer of 1914. Most were confined in rows of barracks on a stretch of reclaimed marsh. Conditions were primitive. Above the marsh stood a thirteenth-century manor, a sprawling, gothic place where the formal interrogations were held, and there were also cells here, subterranean cubicles cut into the stone.

Gray, on arrival, saw very little: a strangled oak in the courtyard, a length of sooty wall, a staircase to the vaults, a windowless room, a cot and a bucket. He was abused with random blows to the groin, the stomach, the kidneys; and then was left alone. The room was cold and painfully small. The bedding was infested with vermin. Between long periods of silence there were echoes of a scream and the slow footsteps of guards.

They had taken his wristwatch, so measuring time was impossible.

179

For the most part he tried to keep his mind from it. He thought of his work, and imagined an ink-wash of the Brandenburg Gate. He thought about Paris and of his cat on the window box. He thought about Zelle, because at least the pain of that was real. And he thought about Dunbar, and fed on the hatred.

In the beginning, the fleas seemed to be the worst of it; at first they attacked his neck and wrists, then found their way under his clothes. But they came for him on the second day: two guards in uniform, a third watching from the dark staircase. They led him to a large empty room with bare floorboards and bare walls. There were three or four chairs in the corner, nothing else. One of the guards dragged a chair to the center of the room and told him to sit. His wrists and ankles were fastened with an electrical wire.

At least another hour passed before Spangler and a woman appeared. She was young and actually quite pretty with white-blonde hair drawn back in a bun. She wore a tweed skirt and jacket, thick spectacles, and some sort of medal. Spangler brought over a chair from the corner for her and put it against the wall just on the edge of Gray's vision. As she sat down he caught a glimpse of a stenographer's pad and a fountain pen in her hand. Spangler positioned the third chair directly in front of Gray's. Then he sat, like the girl, with his knees crossed and his hands in his lap.

"You don't look well, Nicholas. You don't look well at all."

Gray shut his eyes, with a quick vision of the room as if viewing it from the ceiling: three chairs on an empty floor, one perpendicular to the other two.

"There's also the matter of your mental health, a matter which becomes increasingly delicate the longer you stay here."

Gray opened his eyes and looked at him. "Why don't you just tell me what you want?"

"Your trust, then answers to some questions."

"Go to hell."

"Ah, but forgive the conceit—this is hell." He got up from his chair and moved to the far window. As he edged back the blinds Gray saw a shred of blue, possibly morning sky. "First let me say that your instincts were correct. I never intended to betray my country. Indeed, the entire affair was a trap from the start, a test of British procedure and capabilities, an attempt to arrest and compromise a ranking officer. Unfortunately, we were left with only you."

Turning his head slightly, Gray caught another glimpse of the girl. Her lips were slightly parted, her eyes seemed fixed on his swelling ankles and bare feet.

"You should also know that your people will not lift a finger to help you. They cannot even afford to admit that you were acting on their behalf. Your ridiculous Charles Dunbar has already left the country. So really, Nicky, you are in bad circumstances."

Gray shut his eyes again. "I ask you to notify the British embassy."

Spangler smiled. "You know, you don't owe them anything, Nicky. They involved you in a stupid charade, then literally abandoned you to the enemy."

"I'd like a glass of water."

"Think about it, Nicky. Had your brave Charles Dunbar only waited another few seconds you wouldn't even be here."

"And I should like my coat and shoes. I'm cold."

Voices from the courtyard drew Spangler to the window, where the light tended to accentuate his movements: his hand in his pocket extracting a handkerchief, his eyes slowly shifting back to Gray.

"You know, I had actually prepared my questions for someone closer to the bone. Dunbar, for example, or that other one . . . Southerland. I think, however, that you'll be able to accomodate me if you try."

He came back from the window, rested his palms on the back of the chair. "Listen to me, Nicholas. This isn't your game. You have no stake in it. What's more, the questions are primarily academic. Simply help me clean up a few points regarding the arrangements at Richmond, and you can go. That's really all I want, a few details about the training facilities and field procedures."

Silence.

"Nicholas, please . . . Nicholas?"

The boy must have been waiting just outside the door, because he appeared the moment Spangler left. Gray saw him first from the corner of his eye: very blond youth with smooth features and a delicate mouth. He came in without speaking, then went to the girl —half bent, whispering to her. They might have been brother and sister, or even lovers—definitely a sympathetic pair. Briefly, the boy even laid his hand on her shoulder.

There moments of silence as the boy took off his jacket and carefully folded it on the back of a chair. His skin was faintly mottled in the cold, vaguely pink against his undershirt. The girl could not seem to take her eyes off him.

Although the boy must have carried the cane into the room with him, Gray did not notice it until the girl began toying with it— examining the silver tip, running her fingers along the varnished surface, testing its slight resilience. When at last she seemed satisfied, she handed it to the boy and watched as he performed a similar ritual, lightly testing the thing on his thigh.

The boy removed his wristwatch and pressed it into the girl's hand. She adjusted her glasses, as if to watch a theatrical display. Once more the boy picked up the cane and assumed his position to the right of Gray's chair. The girl nodded, and Gray watched as the cane swung back, and exploded onto his shins.

He was still conscious when it was over; conscious of the boy lifting his trousers with the tip of the cane, conscious of the girl examining his blackened wrists. There were voices around him, passing spectral shapes, and another woman's heels on the floorboards. He heard Spangler's voice ordering someone to take him away. He heard himself cry out as his legs collapsed.

After they had brought him back to the cell, he lay unmoving in the darkness. The pain had become a solid entity, extending from his legs through his groin to the pit of his stomach. Aware of his thirst, he could not keep from swallowing, compulsively swallowing nothing. He began to wonder if his eyes hadn't somehow been damaged . . . or else how could he have seen Margaretha like a white light deep in the stone?

She came, just as he had always known she would come . . . a friend in the worst hour, entering his cell like blown silk. Her voice was clear and soft, her hands were very cool. Although she explained that she could only stay a minute, she finally spent the entire night. . . .

After two or three days of brackish water, bread, and some sort of rat broth, they brought him back to the empty room. The seating arrangement was the same: the girl with her stenographer's pad against the wall, Spangler opposite the prisoner's chair. Although they had left Gray's ankles and wrists free, there was something new in the corner, something like a low bench with leather manacles.

"I want you to know that I'm not happy with this arrangement," Spangler began. "I'm not at all happy with it."

The girl looked beatific in a beige summer skirt and blouse.

"Nor can there be any change until you cooperate with us. So, again, I'm asking you, Nicholas. I'm sincerely asking you."

. . . But just last night Zelle had said that Spangler's sincerity cut both ways, left festering wounds . . .

"Look, don't you realize that there's going to be a war soon? Everything points to it. Your people are in bed with the Russians. The French are in bed with both of you. And when it happens I won't be able to keep them from executing you." He got up, crossed the room and peered out the blinds again. "Anyway, you can't go on like this much longer. You look like hell."

. . . Which wasn't at all what Zelle had said last night, in spite of his bleeding shins, cracked lips and empty eyes . . .

"Damn it, Nicky, please listen to me. This lovely child sitting here and her boyfriend are not ordinary people. They're Hansel and Gretel gone mad. They'll tear you apart unless you start talking to me."

He couldn't help glancing at her, noting her brief smile, apparently reserved for her special victims. He shook his head, heard the words "I'm sorry" come from his mouth. And he was sorry . . . he had no desire to be torn apart . . .

"Nicky, just answer two small questions about the arrangements at Richmond and we shall call it a day—"

"I'm sorry."

Spangler knelt beside Gray's chair. "Anyway, Margaretha very much wants to see you. In fact she won't even speak to me until I let her see you . . . and that makes thing extremely difficult, as you can well imagine."

Once again the boy must have been waiting just outside the door. This time he entered with two uniformed guards—silent men with shaved heads. The guards escorted Gray to the low bench, then forced him to kneel facing the wall. When they had secured his wrists, they stepped back, watching with detachment until ordered to leave.

The boy came forward after Gray had been stripped to the waist. He moved slowly. The girl had backed away to the window, lifting the blind so that a shaft of light fell across Gray's back. The boy, however, ordered that the blind be lowered again. Then, an instant sooner than expected—like a razor blade across Gray's spine.

When it was over he couldn't walk; they had to drag him, and the impact of the stones on his shin left him barely conscious. He recognized the smell as they descended to the cellars. He felt the damp cold beyond the last door. He heard the sound of a snapping lock.

He again sensed Zelle's presence in the darkness . . . She must have entered through the bars, or even from below through a drain . . . her hand was again cool on his forehead, her hair like a shadow. She told him he mustn't try to speak or move, to lie still in her arms. After a while she told him things he'd waited years to hear her say . . . He could hardly believe it . . .

He began to answer their questions on the tenth day. He did not consciously surrender, there just came a point when he found himself talking. Spangler, the gentleman, never suggested that one man's submission was another's victory. Indeed, everyone behaved quite decently, so that finally only Zelle was disappointed . . . but then she had always disliked weakness . . .

With submission came new liberties and new comforts. They moved him from the windowless cell to a small barrack room with a bunk bed, a chair, and a desk. There was a view of the marsh and a crenelated wall. Birds, mostly crows, occasionally flew in and out of the foliage. He was sent to a doctor, a mild man who said he was outraged that the patient had been so badly mistreated. There were also decent meals and bathing facilities.

Initially the interrogations were still held in that whitewashed void of a room, with the girl recording in her stenographer's pad. Then, exuding good fellowship, Spangler took him out to the gardens, to oaks to connecting flagstones through the shrubbery, and farther afield to an overgrown tennis court and the remains of a summer cottage. Spangler did not begin asking questions until they had lost sight of the main estate.

The first memorable session began with a casual question about Gray's first experience with the service. They had been walking along a narrow path between high hedgerows. It was a warm day with the promise of moist, static heat. Spangler was a step ahead of Gray, poking at the vegetation with a stick— a heavy, varnished thing with a knotted handle. "Tell me about your initial experience," he said. "How did you feel when you were first approached by someone from the Service?"

"Annoyed."

"Because you resented the intrusion?"

"Because I disliked Charles Dunbar."

Spangler seemed to consider the answer for a moment, hesitating on the path, the stick in his right hand. Then he turned, swinging hard for the shins again. The blow caught Gray by surprise, leaving him breathless with pain as he crumbled to the ground.

"I'm not interested in your relationship with Dunbar. I want to hear about the first time, about the role you played in the death of Rolland Michard. You think I didn't know about it, Nicholas? You think I was fooled by your silly performance? I've known about it for years."

They spent the rest of that morning in the shade of the fallen summer house. Except for not seeming to care that Gray's shins had begun to bleed again, Spangler was relatively congenial, and did not press for answers. There were even refreshments: a plate of whitefish, black bread, and lemonade. Afterward they walked into the broad yellow fields, and as another demonstration of friendship, Spangler even left his stick behind.

There was a change during the next three days, small indications, like signals—clattering trains at night, rising dust from caravans on the roads, an obvious decrease in the number of guards, sounds of shellfire from an artillery range beyond the marsh.

Still, for Gray these were still largely uneventful days. He read from the three books allotted to him: the *Meditations* of Marcus Aurelius, the *Nibelungenlied, The Will to Power.* He walked—once a day for thirty minutes—in a circular garden court. He dozed to the drone of flies and stagnant heat. Although the guards had been ordered not to talk to prisoners, the young man who brought Gray's meal always had something to say about the heat or the miseries of military life. There was also talk, overheard in the corridor, of new executions at dawn.

Finally Spangler returned. As before, Gray met him in the garden, and they sat on the edge of a reflecting pool that had been drained to inhibit mosquitos. Instead of a stick Spangler now carried a riding crop. He was also armed with a pistol.

"I'm supposed to ask your opinion about the will of your countrymen to fight," he began. "You in turn are to base your answer on your knowledge of the British ruling class."

"What's the point?" Gray said wearily.

"The point is, they shot the archduke, which means that there's going to be a war."

Gray let his head fall back, exposing his face to the light. He tried to feel something and couldn't.

"It's primarily a matter of alliances. Once the first shot is fired, everyone must mobilize."

Gray let his eyes close, his elbows slowly collapse. "And who is the first to be shot here? Me?"

Spangler, of course, ignored it.

They walked along a gravel path lined with white bricks beyond which were dying elms against a white sky.

"The Russians are expected to mobilize next week," Spangler said. "Which naturally draws us in with the Austrians, which in turn will draw in the French. Meanwhile there's been a lot of excitement along the borders."

"Tell them that England will never fight," Gray said.

Spangler grinned. "This's why you're so fascinating, Nicholas. Even in total defeat you find small ways to defy me. But seriously now, what do you think?"

They had stopped, Spangler watching something beyond the elms, Gray sucking on a tooth knocked loose the first night.

"I think that if there is any justice you will all rot in hell."

"But how can you say that when you know as well as I that there isn't any justice, except the kind you make yourself. Anyway there's going to be a war, and you will be locked up until it's over . . . or until you die in the typhus pit with the rest of them."

They had reached a ruined tennis court where executions were sometimes held; beyond lay ditches where they dumped the bodies.

"You know, actually I think this war will be good for all of us. Burn away the fat, wipe the slate clean. Or do you think I'm being too grandiose."

"Too optimistic."

"Oh, that's clever, Nicky. That's very clever." Then, finally turning back to the main path, "By the way, Margaretha still keeps asking about you, still keeps insisting that I let her see you. I think she's even grown a bit frantic, and she has refused to sleep with me."

"Why don't you rape her?"

"Too easy, Nicky. Besides, I happen to like the woman. It's just that I find her terribly frustrating. In fact, I sometimes even find myself wondering which of us has really won this skirmish."

It seemed that the countryside was alive with signs of coming war: lines of men and equipment moving east in the afternoon, a continuous echo of distant trains and sounds from the marshaling yard. There were also gunshots at dawn from the tennis court; apparently the war had resolved all sorts of problems.

Gray seemed to have been forgotten, or at least overlooked. With Spangler obviously needed elsewhere, and real events building, no one seemed much concerned about an English abstract painter. Even the more belligerent guards couldn't seem to find a reason to beat him. So they fed him, let him walk in the circular garden, ignored him.

After the third day they moved him to the regular compound and a barracks filled with about fifty other prisoners. There were towers, and then the deathstrip. Two men died the day of Gray's arrival, apparently shot on the wall while trying to escape. Eventually it came out that they were suicides.

There were incidents of cruelty, enforced homosexuality, even occasional murder. Yet perhaps because Gray was foreign, and thus largely an enigma, he was generally left to himself. His only real acquaintance was a Polish Jew, said to be half mad and violent. He and Gray generally met in one of the tooling sheds, and chatted quietly about art.

There were varying opinions about the war within the compound at Doberitz. There were those pessimists (realists) who tended to see the war as a violent conclusion to modern civilization. The few survivors would be scarred for life, the fortunate would die early. Then there were the optimists, mostly Russians and Poles, who saw salvation in terms of a German defeat. And there were the ones like Gray, who hardly knew what to think . . . except that in the face of great misery there were the small things to cling to: hope, memories, impossible schemes.

Initially Gray, too, found himself thinking of escape—either buying his way into one of the rumored tunnels or slipping out beneath the dung wagon. He also thought of killing a guard: not to escape, but to reclaim a little of what they had taken from him—a residue of self-respect.

The Middle Years

What he did, to his surprise, was to survive, to merge with the routine, and as rumors of imminent war were confirmed by newspapers stolen from the guard's quarters, to try to manage the vision of the future: three years, five years, even another decade of his life consumed on account of, in pursuit of, Zelle.

Chapter Eighteen

THERE are conflicting stories concerning Margaretha's movements on the eve of the Great War. One account has her spending the night with a legendary German spymistress (homosexual overtones implied). Another has her sleeping with a mysterious Prussian baron, then slipping across the border to France. Most popularly, however, she is said to have dined with a certain Traugitt von Jagow from the secret metropolitan police. Supposedly she met the man at about eight o'clock in the Romanische Cafe, and by midnight she had sold another dozen British agents down the river.

In all probability the misunderstanding concerning von Jagow stems from Zelle's own admission: "Towards the end of July [actually July 31] I was dining with a chief of police." The French, no doubt assuming that she meant *the* chief of police, took the man for von Jagow—chief in Berlin since 1909 and largely remembered for the dictum: "Streets are for traffic, others keep off." In fact, Zelle actually dined with one Herr Griebel, a metropolitan section chief and casual friend from her first days in Berlin.

The Middle Years

Nor was the evening in any way compromising to the British intelligence effort. After weeks of despair and frustration she had come to the man in the hopes of securing Gray's release. Griebel, however, told her that he was powerless to intercede in matters of state security, and sent her back to Spangler.

It was about half past ten when she finally left Griebel, almost eleven before she found a vacant cab. There were mobs blocking traffic all along the arteries, and an overturned lorry on the Unter den Linden. Closer to the Reichstag, the crowds seemed somewhat more disciplined, assembling in ranks for *Deutschland über Alles.*

She suspected that Gray had tried to warn her about this side of Germany, or at least she had glimpsed it in his drawings of shaved heads and hard jaws. She should have seen it in Spangler's eyes, particularly after one of their more intense nights together. And his words: "If you are to understand the German mind, then you must understand our passion for logic." But what seemed to pass for logic was more an adherence to strict discipline. She had also learned to hate the food.

It was nearly midnight when she finally reached the Bendlerstrasse, long past this city's usual bedtime. Soldiers attached to the ministry were milling on the steps. Students from the academy had gathered in the forecourt. There were one or two faces that she recognized, but no one she could trust on a night like this. So she telephoned from below, then waited another hour before Rudy appeared.

They met in the garden court where Schlieffen had supposedly convinced the chancellor that Belgium could not remain neutral. There were still voices from the streets, but increasingly distant. Spangler entered from a service door, then descended the staircase without looking at her: "I told you never to come here," he said.

She didn't answer. The pretending was over.

"It's about Nicky. I want you to let him go."

He turned away, cupping his hands to light a cigarette. "Not now."

191

"I saw Griebel. I saw that idiot at your office. They told me everything, and now I want you to let him go."

"Margaretha, this is not something that one can—"

"Tomorrow, Rudy. I want you to let him go tomorrow."

He pressed his thumb and forefinger to his eyes—an intentionally exaggerated gesture. "And if I fail to do this, you will leave me?"

"I'm leaving you anyway, but you're still going to let him go. It's only *logical.*"

He was looking closely at her. "You know, I'm very fond of you, Margaretha. I really am."

"You used me, Rudolph. You used me from the very start."

"No, only since Madrid. And even then there were feelings, strong feelings."

"Then let him go. You don't need him. He can't possibly make a difference now, so let him go."

He drifted back to the staircase as a swell of voices rose from the Steinplatz again, thousands of them.

"Did I tell you that there's going to be a war, Margaretha? Very soon, perhaps even tonight."

He couldn't have looked leaner in the half light, like something cut from soap with a razor.

"Your war is a joke."

"I don't think you'll say that once it actually begins."

She followed him to the staircase, then sagged against the bricks. She couldn't recall the last time she'd eaten, the last time she'd actually touched a man. "I'm begging you now, all right? I'm down on my knees and begging."

She heard him breathing through his teeth, felt him run a finger across her lips. "Your abstract painter broke the law, Margaretha."

"To hell with your law."

"He also lied to you. He lied to you for years."

"Not about the things that matter."

He reached out to touch her again, but she turned her face away. Tears left him sexually aroused.

192

"I wonder," he said, "I wonder if you would show the same concern had I been the one arrested?"

She ran her sleeve across her mouth. "People like you never get arrested. Maybe shot, maybe stabbed, but never arrested."

He smiled. "Yes, I suppose you have a point."

Then rigid again, perhaps reminding himself that the war was less than a day away: "Very well, my darling, I shall see that your painter is released, assuming that's what you truly want."

She could have killed him. "Thank you."

"Although I would like to know what it is that you see in that man. I really would like to know."

"Perhaps I see myself."

Even through the predawn hours there were footsteps on the asphalt, still distant voices from the Steinplatz. She slept badly after mixing aspirin with bourbon, then woke up at daybreak to stuff her clothing into a trunk. There was a frenetic, disjointed quality to the next several hours with rumors of indiscriminate arrests, mob violence, and the execution of suspicious foreigners.

Gray finally appeared in the late afternoon like some half-familiar ghost. (Dunbar would maintain that British Intelligence had managed Gray's release from Doberitz through a complex arrangement with Prince Lichnowsky in London, and Whitehall would back up that claim, as would the Admiralty.) He had been released at about noon. It was uncomfortably warm and at first he was told nothing. Two young guards escorted him to a windowless van. There were clothes on the rear seat: trousers, jacket, cheap shoes, and a shirt.

They drove for about two hours, suggesting a trip to the countryside. But when the van finally stopped, Gray found himself on a shaded side street off the Wilhelmstrasse. One of the guards told him to get out of the van and shut the door. Twenty minutes later he found himself in the British embassy, where no one quite knew what to do with him.

There were then perhaps six hours between Gray's release and his reunion with Zelle. In that time he bathed, ate a reasonably good meal, and briefly chatted with a frantic military attaché. As evening approached, the embassy grew increasingly filled with distraught British citizens stranded without papers, spreading rumors about four British subjects who had been supposedly murdered in the Tiergarten, and about many others left beaten in the streets.

Yet for Gray there was only Zelle, who finally appeared in the embassy carriage yard, also like some half-remembered ghost.

She wore a pale-blue dress, last year's fashion and so obviously nothing Spangler had given her. Gray wore a raincoat borrowed from the military attaché. There was a moment's hesitation before she ran into his arms. Then she was on him, whispering his name and something else she should have said before. "Oh God, I'm sorry, Nicky. Oh God . . ."

She was shivering, so he draped the raincoat over her shoulders. He lit a cigarette, and she watched him remove a speck of tobacco from his lips. There seemed to be voices everywhere . . . hysterical Englishmen just over the wall, hundreds of Germans gathering in the streets.

She said, "I suppose we don't have much time."

"No, I'm afraid not."

"And there's so much I wanted to tell you, only now I can't remember half of it."

"It doesn't matter."

She was crying, so he drew her closer again and he wished there was someplace they could sit . . . a bench, a ledge, anywhere.

"Listen to me, Nicky. I talked to Rudolph, but there wasn't a deal or anything like that. He just let you go."

"For your sake?"

"Maybe."

"And now?"

"Now I leave."

Her lips were suddenly cool against his fingers. Her hair was soft against his chin. "You're a scandal," he whispered. "Everywhere you go, you're a scandal."

She smiled, her eyes half shut. "But why did you do it, Nicky? Why did you get involved with those—those people?"

"Not because I'm a great patriot. And you know the reason." He kissed her forehead.

"And now there's going to be a war?"

"Seems so."

"Then let's run away to India."

"Too hot."

"America?"

"Too far."

She slipped away, clutching the raincoat to her throat, staring past the wrought iron gate to a milling crowd beneath the trees. "Then I'm going home." She'd decided that earlier.

"Home?"

"To The Hague. To be with my daughter . . . Well, it's time, isn't it?"

"Yes, I suppose it is."

"And you? You'll be in London?"

"Yes . . ."

"Good. Then we're both ready."

He couldn't see her face, but he knew she was crying again, still staring at the crowd, still clutching the raincoat, but crying.

He glanced at the sky, the growing blue shadows around them. "Maybe you should go," he said. "I don't imagine that the streets will be safe for long."

She shrugged. "Oh, *that* doesn't matter. I'm Dutch, remember? They only care about the Russians and the English." Then faintly smirking, "Besides, everyone loves Mata Hari."

He took a step closer and laid his hand on her shoulder. "Margaretha, I think I should tell you—"

"No, don't. Let's just leave it like this. Let's just say that we'll write to one another and always be friends."

He put his other hand on her shoulder and turned her face to his. "Margaretha, I'm not altogether sure I can live without you."

Although she was smiling, her eyes began to fill with tears again. "Now look what you've done."

He watched her from the balcony until he couldn't see her anymore. Then he went back to the embassy and slept. Toward seven or eight that evening he was awakened by footsteps and loud, frantic voices.

The mobilization had begun.

PART III

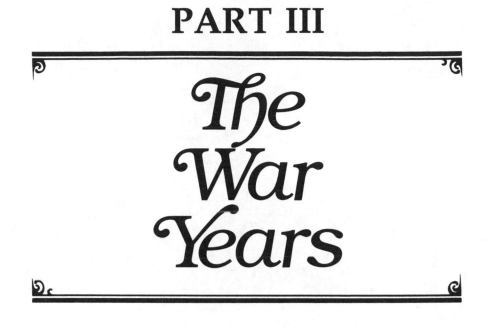

The War Years

Chapter Nineteen

HE returned to England on the ninth of August, leaving a continent in flames. London was warm, with a scent of cut grass, but the war was clearly very near. Soldiers filled nearly every public house, and the streets were littered with handbills and confetti. Along the Strand there were warning notices about spies.

He found a room in a modest hotel: no hot water, the cold running thin. He walked the first night, peering into dusty shop windows, conscious of just how long he'd been away. Toward dawn he met a prostitute, a sallow girl, with eyes like Zelle's. Which, of course, was nonsense. He shook his head, as if trying to exorcise her, and walked away.

The second day he met Southerland, in uniform, hair cropped close, in the hotel lobby. At first he let him do the talking, apologizing for what had happened in Berlin. ". . . And about the money, which I understand was part of the original agreement—"

"I don't want it."

"It's almost five thousand pounds, Nicky."

"Forget it."

From the lobby they went up to Gray's room for cigarettes and gin.

"I heard about what happened to you," Southerland said.

"What happened to me?"

"The punishment . . . Have you seen a doctor?"

"No need."

"I'm told it was pretty bad. Look, I can understand if you—"

"You can't understand." Then, reaching for a second glass of gin, "And where the bloody hell is Dunbar?"

It had become dark, and Southerland switched on the lamp. A fleet of trucks, a military caravan, was moving through the streets below. A handful of children cheered from a footbridge.

"I can give you the verdict, if you like?"

"The verdict?"

"Spangler led us down a very nasty alley. Charles was partly responsible. So was I. It could, however, have been worse."

"Tell that you your man Sykes."

"I was speaking tactically, Nicky. Of course, we all regret what happened to Sykes. Still, the fact remains that nothing of real consequence was compromised. That is, you were not in a position to tell them anything—"

"And Dunbar was?"

"Well . . . Yes."

Gray finished his gin, and returned to the window. The caravan had passed, the children had vanished, but the war had taken a step closer in this hotel room.

"Why weren't you there on the last night?"

Southerland began picking at an ancient doily, a bit of lace that fell apart in his hands. "I was engaged elsewhere."

"That's not an answer."

"All right. I had certain reservations."

"Meaning that you knew or at least suspected the whole affair was probably a set-up from the start, as even I did . . ."

"*Meaning* that I had certain reservations, but that there were also certain advantages to be gained. Look, if you want someone to blame, Nicky, then blame Spangler. After all, he's the enemy, not us."

Southerland got up from his chair, poured another glass of gin, and put it on the sill only inches from Gray's hand.

"There's a theory—not necessarily mine—but just the same a plausible theory that the woman might have been partly responsible."

Gray reached for the glass but couldn't seem to lift it. "Jesus, you people don't give up, do you?"

"Now, according to this theory, she was actually working for Spangler, and thus a great deal more involved than we'd thought. Consequently, when you initially made your approach—"

"Oh please shut up."

Southerland glanced at his wristwatch. Time, however, might have stopped, leaving everything static, suggestive: the flowered chintz, a porcelain bowl, cigarettes on the mantle—like the two men, waiting for the war.

"Have you thought about what you're going to do?" Southerland said at last.

Gray lit a cigarette and sagged to a chair. "Do?"

"Regarding the war. It's here, you know."

Each was staring at the other in a cracked, fish-eye mirror.

"No," Gray said, "I haven't thought about it."

"Because I'd like to make a proposal, Nicky. I'd like you to consider working with us. The Department," he added quickly. "I'm not talking about the field. I'm offering you a desk, a Fourth Floor desk in Richmond. What do you say?"

"I say leave me alone."

"Look, the war has changed the entire complexion of the game. I think you'll find it—"

"Go *away.*"

"This war, Nicky, will be far worse than you can imagine, far worse than anyone can imagine. They may tell you, join a decent regiment, stick a few Huns and we'll get you home by Christmas, but it won't be like that at all. It's going to be a bloodbath, a real bloodbath . . . I don't think you understand. I can keep you out of the trenches."

"No you can't. Now get the hell *out.*"

He drank through what remained of that night, first alone by the window, then in a public house of sawdust floors and broken chair seats. The war seemed to have grown a little closer. It might have been a subtle odor rising from the drains, or a slow influx of tepid air. For Gray, it was not the sort of thing you could paint.

Gray spent about six weeks in London before securing a commission with a "suitable" regiment. Then, as a fairly typical "public school officer" his early experiences were not unpleasant. The authority was somehow reassuring, and he liked his command—forty illiterate Welshmen from the Border counties. His chief concerns were largely physical: sore feet, exhaustion and diarrhea.

Training was hopelessly traditional. One learned regimental history, drill, musketry and Boer War field tactics. There was emphasis on procedure, on how to conduct oneself on formal occasions. Premature loss of one's colors was inexcusable. There was very little that would keep anyone alive.

Among the correspondence forwarded through Gray's bank was an encouraging word from Zelle. Although formally neutral, it seemed that her sentiments definitely lay with the Allies . . . particularly since the Huns had confiscated her luggage at the border. Every bit of clothing and all those lovely furs that Spangler had given her —all held at the border so that finally she had reached Holland with only the clothes on her back. A certain Baron Edouard van der Capellen—obviously a new friend and probably her Dutch lover— had suggested that she sue. Her solicitor, she reported, remained pessimistic. *C'est la guerre* . . .

After basic training Gray was given eight days of freedom to wander through London again. He frequented pubs, got drunk, and walked the streets. There were nights when he walked until dawn, as if blown by the wind. In a Lower Thames Street bar he met a young lance corporal recently back from Mons. They discussed ghosts and disturbing visions one saw under the Very lights. Next there was a girl, blonde, about thirty. She slipped out of nowhere along the riverfront to join him at the railing.

"So what are we doing here, soldier?"

He shrugged. "Thinking."

"Trying to remember or trying to forget?"

"Good question."

"Maybe I could help you make up your mind. What's your name?"

"Rudolph Spangler." He didn't smile when he said it.

He followed her back to a room in Soho with a penny notebook and a pencil stub. He sketched her on a chair by gaslight, then reclining on the unmade bed. Growing restless, she began to select her own pose: sliding a hand across her belly, caressing the nipple.

"Look, why did you pay if all you want to do is draw me?"

"Please."

"How about when you finish? Want to do it then?"

But having botched her portrait . . . it looked more like someone else . . . he certainly didn't deserve to sleep with her.

He left for France within the week, landing at Le Havre in the rain. The docks were fogbound and bone-cold. The roads were lined with children and prostitutes. Probably away from home for the first time in their lives, the ranks began to sing in the marshaling yard. Gray stayed in a corrugated shed, sipping whisky and tea with the officers. There were waiting trains at the terminal, but no order to board.

From Le Havre they eventually moved to a base camp at Harfleur, where they spent the days in a route march through the country-side. The nights were still cold with a steely rain, but the war remained distant—somewhere east of the railheads. Occasionally one heard rumors of fighting at the front, but the concerns were mostly local: fatigue, lice, the whims of commanding officers intent on absurd formality.

Gray spent his last evening in Harfleur with Vadime de Massloff, now Captain de Massloff with the 1st Russian Special Imperial Regiment. The meeting had been arranged through a friend of de Massloff, an intelligence officer with access to the personnel lists. Rain that left the village streets deserted drove them to a cafe, where they sipped champagne. The proprietor's daughter was lame but very pretty—another reminder of Paris.

"They want me to photograph Paris," de Massloff said. "Presumably to convince the rest of the world that it still exists."

"Then you haven't been to the front," Gray said.

"Good Lord, no. They've got me in propaganda. And you?"

"I think we're scheduled for Cambrin tomorrow."

"Ah, well, at least you'll miss the rush."

Inevitably there were reminders of Zelle, what with prostitutes on the boardwalk and a memorable song on the gramophone.

"You haven't seen her since Berlin, have you?" de Massloff asked.

Gray shook his head. "Just a letter."

"And?"

"And she's back in The Hague, with some baron."

"Well at least that simplifies things."

"Does it?"

De Massloff smiled, running his finger along the rim of his glass. "Want a bit of advice, my son? Forget about Zelle. Go to the front, kill a Hun and have yourself a marvelous time."

"Don't know if I'm quite up to that."

"Nonsense."

"You see, I'm afraid to get hurt. I've—"

"Oh Christ, Nicky, we're all afraid of that."

"Well, this is different, this is deep-down . . ."

"Then kill a whole platoon. That should cure you. And for God-sakes stop thinking about Zelle."

It took nearly twenty-four hours to reach the railhead at Béthune, then another day on foot to the lines. Beyond Saint Omer the war became obvious, with visible shellfire along the horizon, neglected fields and blasted trees. Past the Cambrin suburbs one could actually see the flares curving over the trenches.

There were four parallel trench systems here across eight hundred yards of lowland. The dugouts were crude, always in need of repair. The soil was soft, mostly red clay. Technically, each company held two hundred yards with two platoons in the front line and two more in reserve, though there were variations, depending on casualties and the weather.

The trenches were buttressed with timber and sandbags, and much of the day was spent bracing sagging walls, fire steps and parapets. There were also rotting duckboards to be replaced, stagnant water to be drained, and sanitation details. The wire, of course, could only be laid at night. Beyond the wire lay three hundred yards of open land gently rising to the German trenches. There were shell craters here and patches of scorched earth, but there were also some still-unbroken fields, actually beautiful at certain hours of the day.

Gray made sketches of this landscape, chiefly long views of poppies and skeletal trees. He would work at odd hours, usually between stand-to and breakfast, and tended to concentrate on the intricacies of light reflected off wire and scattered debris absorbed by charred stumps.

On the whole it was an insular war, medieval in certain respects. Many of the weapons—jam-pot bombs, gas-pipe mortars—were primitive, often constructed by the soldiers themselves. Tactics were still in a transitional phase, evolving on a trial-and-error basis. Eventually the British would pay for overmanning the firing lines, and everybody would pay for the frontal assault against machine-gun emplacements. As the accuracy of artillery improved there was greater emphasis on sapping and a subterranean existence.

In this war of attrition engagements were generally brief and conducted at night. The raiding parties were small, rarely more than a few dozen men. The objectives were intimidation and the mostly symbolic dominance of no-man's-land. As an officer of the line Gray was expected to lead three raids a month and any number of reconnaissance patrols.

Even during quiet interludes there were at least a dozen random fatalities a week, mostly from sporadic artillery, mortar, and machine-gun fire, but also from neglect and fatigue—pointless deaths from failing to clean a rifle, guard a light, observe the half-inch margin while moving along a communication trench.

Still, the most upsetting deaths were those inflicted by the German snipers. Unlike the British commanders, who tended to regard sniping as contemptible—not quite cricket—the Germans were enthusiastic, with elaborate training programs, camouflaging, and telescopic sights. Working in pairs behind concealed steel loopholes, the snipers always accounted for four or five casualties a day that tended to linger in everyone's mind . . .

Gray's first experience with a sniper came two days after his arrival in the line. It was a relatively quiet evening, with only intermittent fire to the south. Gray had spent the afternoon in a dugout with a friend from the depot, a quiet young lieutenant named Arthur Child. Toward dusk the two men had wandered out to a rear traverse for a breath of air and privacy. There were birds in the surrounding grass, sparrows and titmice. An easy breeze from the west brought odors of coffee and hawthorn, and there was a low bone-white moon above the ridge.

They talked about mutual acquaintances, popular novels, rumors of a spring offensive. Then, as if to seal the friendship, Child extracted two thin Dutch cigars he'd been saving. "My father sent them, although I can't imagine why, since I never used to smoke them."

"Maybe he thought it was time you started. Now that you're a warrior." A nice light moment. Then, offering the light cupped in his hands, Gray realized that Child's father had played a rather filthy joke, a ludicrous exploding cigar . . . except that it wasn't actually the cigar that exploded, but the top of Child's head—lifting almost gracefully high above the parapet.

Gray caught him as he fell, easing him to the duckboards, then cradling him in his arms. He shouted twice for a medical orderly but knew it was hopeless. All these years he had thought that brains were somehow a poetical figment, like broken hearts and cold blood, and yet here were bits of Child's brains splattered on the wall of the trench. On him.

He actually took a while to die: ten or fifteen minutes. He remained exceptionally still, breathing softly, his face pressed deep, deep into his friend Nicholas Gray's stomach.

After that, Gray began to fight the war in earnest. He would usually start at about midnight, with half a dozen men in a forward dugout off the firebay. There were nervous jokes as the raiding parties prepared themselves: shedding regimental patches, excess webbing, ration books, and shoulder flashes. Then silence as the weapons were distributed: truncheons and revolvers, knobkerries, bowie knives, and those jam-pot bombs.

From the dugout they would move along the firebay into a forward sap, then wait, listening for a moment before slipping through a gap in the wire. The first fifty yards were the most critical and had to be crossed quickly in order to minimize the risk of getting caught in a flare. Then came the high grass and a slow belly-crawl, with only brief pauses in shell craters.

There were corpses on the middle ground, casualties from a summer assault, and rats in the furrows. Even the night winds clattering over the brow of the ridge failed to carry off the stench. In the event of flares one could lie still among the bodies. Closer to the German lines the ground was usually moist, smelling of leaf mold and soaking their uniforms.

One usually saw the sentries first: heads and shoulders above the parapet, rifles resting in the crooks of the arm. Then there were odors of coffee and cheap tobacco, echoes of bootheels on the duckboards. Occasionally one did not see them until the last ten or fifteen yards, when they would appear suddenly, looming up like specters.

Which was how it happened the night of Child's death. Gray did not even see the sentry until he was nearly on top of him, a bulky silhouette swaying from left to right as he stamped his feet for warmth. The man's hands were enormous—he was always aware of a subject's hands, the challenge of them for a painter. Gray had to roll on his side, arching slightly to withdraw his serrated bayonet. It felt good, as natural as any palette knife.

The sentry was muscular under his greatcoat. Gray was surprised at the strength. It was like riding a bull to a sawdust floor, hand clamped around the snout. In death, however, the perspective somehow shifted again, so that the German finally looked a lot like Spangler.

Before moving off, Gray tossed four jam-pots into the adjoining trenches, two more into a dugout. Although primarily a fragmentation device, the concussion was devastating, rupturing lungs with overpressure, leaving hemorrhages along spinal cords. There appeared to be only a handful of survivors . . . a boy quite like that boy in Doberitz, three or four others also like Spangler. Gray killed them quickly, impatiently.

He took up sniping to help pass the slack hours, mostly working from the middle ground with an elephant gun and a Ross telescopic sight. He would start about an hour before dawn, slipping between the furrows and painting himself into the landscape. If his marksmanship was somewhat less than perfect, no one could fault his sense of perspective, or his skill at handling shadows.

There were afternoons in those fields, as satisfying in their fashion as any spent in front of an easel—the technique was very similar. As he gradually perfected his approach he tended to work the high ground at dawn because the German lines faced east and there were some fifteen minutes when his subjects were cleanly etched in black relief. In the evening he would slip into one of the shell craters to catch a stray runner along the footpath. On better nights he could sense them before he saw them, almost hear footsteps, a heartbeat, visualize breath on the air.

But the dawns, with bleak light absorbed, not refracted, by stones, and poppies asleep in the empty silence, were his favorites.

The War Years

If you didn't actually listen, he once said, you could sometimes hear a flute or a guitar . . . if you shut your eyes you might see another landscape someplace far away. And once or twice he even saw Zelle.

                                              He received a letter from her to-ward the end of December. She was in Paris, supposedly to collect her belongings from Neuilly-sur-Seine. She had met a marvelous man, a certain Marquis de Beaufort. There were occasional zeppelin raids, she wrote, but everyone took them in stride. She could be reached at the Grand Hotel, and naturally Gray was welcome to visit, assuming he could manage a pass.

In a more perfect world a bullet would have smashed his knee or a shell fragment lacerated his thigh. Fitting wounds for a true warrior. As it happened he only swallowed a bit of gas, giving him ten days' leave. He was supposed to spend the time in London under medical supervision. But he was convinced fate or some version of the inevitable was at work here, so naturally he went to her, arriving in Paris with a hacking cough and a mild but persistent fever. It was raining, and the war had left the back streets in an electrical black-out and uncollected refuse. The wealthier districts hadn't changed much, though—nor had Zelle.

He first saw her on the staircase descending to the lobby, where she had kept him waiting for more than an hour. Her hair was loosely pinned in a bun. Her dress was fairly modest, out of respect for the season. She greeted him with a perfunctory kiss but then gave his hand a secret squeeze as they moved into the cocktail lounge. After less than thirteen hours away from the front nothing looked real to him.

They took a table in the rear and he ordered cognac to deaden the pain in his throat. Strains of Debussy came from a tiny piano. She told him that he looked very handsome in his uniform, though his hair needed trimming.

Then, looking at him, for the first time really looking at him: "You've changed, Nicky. I'm not sure how, but you've definitely changed."

He tried to smile, couldn't seem to manage it. "Yes, I suppose I have."

She pressed her hand to his forehead. "And you're also ill, aren't you? That's why they gave you the pass, because you're ill."

He shook his head. "It's nothing really." He felt ridiculous trying to sound brave, to impress her.

"But surely it must have been terrible out there. I mean—" She broke off with a wry smile. "Sorry."

They sat in silence for a while, their eyes meeting briefly, their hands only inches apart. He felt exhausted.

"So what's this new man like?" he finally asked.

"New man?"

"The one in your letter."

She shrugged. "Very nice."

"A genuine marquis?"

"So he says."

"Rich?"

"Oh God, yes."

"Handsome?"

"In a way."

It went on like that until dusk. Small talk, tentative talk. She asked about de Massloff, and he told her he had only seen the man briefly. He asked about her life in Amsterdam, and she said that it was quiet, sometimes dull. She had made a few friends to help her through the worst of it, and setting up a new home kept her busy. There had also been a few tentative offers to dance again, and she had recently seen an attorney regarding custody of her daughter. As she spoke, he watched her eyes and her mouth, her profile whenever she turned her head.

By six—the hour when the day tended to dissolve quickly—they had run out of things to say. "I should go," she said. "Yes, I really must go."

"To see the marquis?"

She bit her lip. "He's not an unpleasant person, Nicky. In fact I think you might even like him."

"No, I'm sure I wouldn't."

She reached for his hand. "I suppose you're right. You probably wouldn't like him at all."

Her suite was what he had expected—extravagance at a man's expense. Her clothing lay on the floor and draped over the back of chairs. Her cosmetics were scattered everywhere. The maid had changed the sheets. There was a view of poplars on the boulevards below. What with the fever and exhaustion they did not make love, but she insisted that he take off his uniform, then slipped into bed beside him, and held him, just held him for a long while. When he woke up after dreaming about the front it took a moment before he remembered where he was.

"What time is it?" he asked.

"Late."

She was sitting in lamplight, drinking champagne, leafing through a magazine. Her dressing gown had fallen from her shoulders. Her hair hid her eyes. The sounds and smells were familiar—cigarettes and perfume, pigeons on the adjoining roof, distant traffic below.

"I ordered dinner," she said. "It's probably cold but if you're hungry . . ."

"What about the marquis?"

She tossed the magazine aside. "He'll understand . . . After all, this is a war." She smiled nicely.

He climbed out of bed, wrapping the sheet around his waist. The first few steps were unsteady, but he felt better. He moved to the window, unlatched it and took a breath of cold clean air . . . Yes, definitely better.

"There's beer," she said. "Probably warm by now."

He moved to her side, sank to his knees. "Margaretha, don't you think it's time to stop?"

"Stop? Stop what, Nicky?"

"You know. The marquis, that baron in Amsterdam . . . Isn't it just about time you *stopped?*"

She ran her fingers through his hair, then pressed his face to her breasts—against the cool silk, then to the bare skin. "That's something I've always loved about you, Nicky. You actually make me

211

feel as if I had some control over my life." This time she wasn't smiling . . .

He stayed five days, taking short walks in the mornings and evenings, resting in the afternoons or when she was off somewhere. As his health returned he gradually wandered afield, mostly across the river, where there were better memories.

On the whole she was very good to him during these days, very kind. Although she could not entirely neglect the marquis she never returned later than midnight. They shared the dawns, which were particularly beautiful, with a sculpture of leafless branches on the avenues, clear light on wet slate. Because they rarely discussed anything of importance—not the past, not the future, not even how they felt about themselves—Gray supposed that he would always remember this week as another timeless interlude between reality and escape from reality. They played Mah-Jongg without concentrating. They gave up champagne and drank diluted wine or beer. They spent an hour every morning in the lobby while a chambermaid cleaned their room.

The last day they hardly left the room, and Gray's unfinished pencil sketch more or less captures the mood: Zelle in profile at her dressing table, her eyes fixed on an empty glass, the cold light of evening, her hair still undone. Even an aerial bombardment couldn't seem to break the spell. They ate sandwiches, drank Burgundy, then lay down in the darkness and were very quiet, listening to each other's breathing.

There were a few parting words while waiting for a taxi in the morning. It was cold, with the promise of rain. Although he had told her to stay in bed, she insisted on accompanying him down to the carriage yard. The streets were deserted except for early delivery vans.

"I suppose we could write," she said.

"Yes, we could write." As if a letter from the warrior at the front would make the difference.

"Anyway, I'll need something to keep me occupied. I mean, while I'm in this . . . limbo."

He brushed her hair aside and bent to kiss her forehead. "I want you to stay in Amsterdam."

"Really, Nicky, I can't imagine—"

"No, listen to me. Go back to Amsterdam. Live with your daughter, live with that baron, but stay away from the war."

She broke away from him, jamming her hands in her coat pockets, staring out across the empty streets. "What are you trying to tell me?"

He moved to her side but didn't touch her. "There are people who might resent the way you live . . . who might distrust your motives."

"What people?"

"I don't know . . . Charles Dunbar."

She was smiling. It was a coy smile, like that of a child who has outsmarted her parents. "Oh, for Godsakes, Nicky. Charles doesn't matter anymore."

"Yes, he does. Look, the game is different now. The rules have been changed. All the idiots are in control."

"But Charles Dunbar? Really, Nicky."

"Just stay away from it, all right? *Just stay away.*"

Later, after the taxi had arrived, there was a more conventional farewell with a lingering kiss and a few whispered endearments. She told him to take care of himself and keep warm, to write and not be unhappy—all of which indicated she still had no conception of this war. None at all. And that worried him.

Less than two weeks after his return to the front he found himself in an assault on the north Cambrin salient. It was one of those early winter skirmishes that no one would remember. It began with a bombardment to soften the German trenches and cut the wire. Most of the shells were shrapnel and relatively ineffective. Following the bombardment the better part of two battalions left their trenches and proceeded into no man's land. The Germans responded with six surviving machine guns and cut them to shreds.

After an awful muddle at the wire Gray led two platoons across the sodden slopes before crossfire forced them into the shell craters. He spent the afternoon dispensing morphia and tossing an occasional grenade. Toward dusk the survivors returned, not in a panic but stolidly, benumbed, as if from a football match. Bursting shrapnel took a few more lives. There was some consolation when word reached the line that a particularly odious captain had died—apparently from heart failure after a shell fragment had grazed the back of his neck.

By the end of the year the war had degenerated into a stagnant slaughter, and frustration began mounting all along the Western Front. Commanding officers were continually leaving in disgrace as one offensive action after another failed to break the deadlock. For a while there was much talk about the crack Canadian units, and certain basic tactical changes. Then after still another stalled offensive, it seemed that everyone was talking about traitors and spies —the traditional excuse for military incompetence.

As for Gray, his thoughts were of Zelle, no matter the cold or the mudflats and shell craters, or the corpses and the blood.

Chapter Twenty

IF only she had stayed away from the war, if only she had stayed away and lived like other lonely women, collecting rags for the Red Cross, sewing bandages and knitting mittens. If only she could have kept herself out of it for a year or two, then possibly even the ones like Dunbar would have ignored her . . .

Dunbar. At the outset of the war his days were consumed with menial tasks. The nights were worse. For the first month he worked with an Admiralty cipher team, helping piece together a network of merchant seamen, drafting two or three estimates of German industrial capability and lunching foreign representatives that no one else would tolerate. On slack afternoons he kept himself occupied with the telegraph intercepts, and on solitary evenings he read or walked. Women continued to elude him.

It was not until late October that Dunbar returned to the question of Zelle. He and Southerland met in a Kensington chophouse, an inconspicuous place where no one of importance ate. It was raining,

215

and Dunbar had a cold. The tabloids carried headlines of a disaster at sea, but it was local events that especially troubled Southerland.

He talked about the case of an alleged German spy recently shot while attempting to escape from arresting officers. The suspect had been a woman and very young, but it was the waste that most disturbed Southerland—the waste of a tactical asset. He was also upset with Special Branch, calling their performance idiotic.

"Have you thought of taking the matter up with Cummings?" Dunbar asked.

Southerland shook his head. "You still don't get it, do you? We're not running an intelligence service. We're spy smashers. We're to provide the headlines to appease the home front. Let mum and dad know that it wasn't the general's fault that their kid was blown to bits . . . it was all because of a bloody spy."

"What about the Minister?"

"The Minister is a fool. Look, I don't know what they've told you, but it's not going at all well at the front. At best we're simply holding the line, and even then the casualties are atrocious. Meanwhile Walter Nicolai's people are running circles around us and no one's doing a damn thing about it."

"And that girl?"

Southerland shrugged. "Oh, the girl was a very small fish."

"Then what's the point?"

"The point is we could have used her. She could have told us something. Look, you've got to try and envision an octopus, one of those enormous tropical things. The brain is in Berlin. The tentacles extend everywhere, and the agents are those suction things. If we're to have any chance at all, we've got to follow one of those tentacles back. As it is now we've nothing, nothing at all."

The rain had stopped by this time and Southerland wanted to walk a bit, so they crossed Queensway to Bayswater and entered the gardens. "The fact of the matter," Southerland said, "is I don't think the Fourth Floor wholly trusts me anymore . . . not after Berlin and your bloody Mata Hari."

"Don't you think that's a bit harsh? I mean, there were indications—you know it as well as I."

"I only know what the Fourth Floor tells me, and they don't want to hear about Margaretha Zelle."

"What about Spangler?"

"He's in Madrid, not our province."

"That's absurd—"

"That's policy, Charles. Besides, we can't afford to waste the resources."

They had reached the broad lawns again, and a view of the pond, that same reassuring view from their first evening together when Zelle had also been discussed in these terms.

"She's connected, Martin. I'm certain she's connected to Berlin."

Southerland looked at him. "Then tell it to Special Branch. They'll be delighted to shoot her for you."

"Martin, I'm serious. The woman is a German resource."

"She's in Holland, Charles. Haven't you heard? She's living in Holland."

"Yes, but for how long? That's my point, don't you see? How long before they launch her again? Anyway, it shouldn't cost us much."

"To do what?"

". . . Watch her."

Southerland was actually smiling for the first time that evening. "Christ, she really took you for a ride, didn't she?"

"What do you mean by that?"

"Oh, I think you know."

Dunbar kept her very close to him after that, a secret in locked drawers and cabinets, a clandestine affair conducted at odd hours of the night. He began by reviewing past notes for something missed or forgotten. Then he submitted her name—merely one of a dozen others—to the foreign residencies. Finally (and a copy of the communique still exists in British archives) he discreetly altered the French, requesting surveillance should she happen to appear.

At first the response was disappointing, but if nothing else, as an observer-voyeur he was patient. Very patient. To help pass the nights he returned to the original files, scanning entries as if in an old photograph album. And indeed there were a few old photographs: a profile stolen from a distance, a close-up stirring memories, warring emotions. Eventually the strain began to show in a trace of red around the eyes, an occasionally dull and exhausted gaze. But given the season everyone was working pretty hard—if only to justify their existence, and keep themselves out of the bloody trenches.

It was toward the end of January when Dunbar's vigilance was rewarded, and this communique, too, may still be found in British archives. It bears the signature of Captain George Ladoux of the Deuxième Bureau, and so effectively marks his entrance into the story. The document comprises a chronicle of Zelle's mid-December stay in Paris, with annotated comments and a summary. Gray is mentioned; so are the Marquis de Beaufort and a nameless lieutenant she met on a train. There is nothing obviously compromising, but Dunbar was sure he would find his connections . . . one way or another.

Dunbar spent the better of part of two days drafting his proposal to the fourth floor, then spent another day waiting for an audience with Mansfield Cummings. By this time it was the first week in February, a dreary period for those attached to the British secret service. More than a dozen agents had already been lost between Zurich and the Balkans, while the Alsatian networks had been virtually blown to nothing. To a degree this was also a period of internal strife involving a particularly bitter feud with the Admiralty teams.

In any case, such was the climate in which Dunbar laid his first specific proposal concerning Mata Hari. It was a bleak day, and Cummings looked poorly. The windows were shut tight against drafts, the office was unbearably warm. When Dunbar entered he found Cummings bent over the grate, wearing a cardigan under his jacket, a shabby brown one that might have been knitted by his sister.

"I can offer you tea," he said, "but it's foul. Mandy's on leave and the new girl is hopeless." Then standing up from the grate with his milk-and-water smile: "I have, however, read your petition."

"Yes, sir."

"And so tell me about her, Charlie. Tell me about this Mata Hari."

"Well, sir, I hardly know what else to add . . . I think she's connected, and I'd simply like the opportunity to probe—"

"With five thousand pounds of my money, eh?"

"Yes, sir."

There were new maps on the wall: the North Atlantic, the Rhine valley, a series of photographs of the River Somme.

"Essentially I'm only asking for a little administrative lattitude . . . and a small staff."

Cummings smiled, moving from the mantle to his desk. "You know, I may have my limitations, Charles, but I know when someone is trying to twist my tail."

"Sir?"

"I'm referring to your little dance with the Frogs."

"Truly, sir, I was only attempting to—"

"Fan the fire a bit? Turn her into a real issue of the day?"

"I assure you that—"

"And next I suppose you'll be waltzing over to the navy with your Mata Hari campaign, right?" He moved to the window, brooding at the neighboring roofs. "I do not like this, Charles. I do not like it one bit. If you wanted to investigate her, then why didn't you simply ask—instead of trying to build a damn powerbase?"

"Really, sir, that wasn't my intention."

"No, of course not. You were merely trying to save me some time." Then sagging into the chair: "Look, if you want the woman that badly I certainly won't stand in your way. Only do try and maintain some degree of restraint. There's enough hysteria around here as it is."

Although he continued to keep her very close, he was obliged to share her with others. The next four weeks were a period of gestation—a gradual widening of Dunbar's influence as his Mata Hari became a recognized, and appreciated, issue. He met twice with the Admiralty, then again with Georges Ladoux in Paris. He also became rather popular with Special Branch, and others who had traditionally distrusted Cummings.

Yet it was not until the seventh week and a meeting with Martin Southerland that Dunbar once more became operational. By this time he had achieved no small degree of authority, and so there was an element of strain to his meeting with Southerland.

It took place along the Chelsea Embankment where Southerland had been conducting another of his unproductive surveillances. It was about one o'clock in the morning, and chilly to the bone.

"I suppose you've come to consult my technical brilliance," Southerland said.

He had been drinking whisky, and his eyes were very dark.

"Actually it's about Zelle."

"Of course it's about Zelle. Everything is about Zelle these days. You've made her the bloody talk of the town." He took another sip from his flask, and they began to walk, following a path past loading docks and vacant lots. Eventually they reached a footbridge and a view of shabby dwelling along the water.

"Nothing has really changed," Dunbar said. "I've only been given the authority to look into the matter."

"But will soon have a mandate from the Minister, no doubt. Look, Charles, I've heard what you've been doing—little chats in cocktail bars, drinks at the Admiralty. They also say you've made quite a hit at the Yard."

"There *is* evidence, Martin. . . the woman *does* seem connected."

"And so you've turned her into a bloody industry." He frowned at the rustle of rats below. "Look, what do you want?"

"She just spent six most curious weeks in Paris. Now she's back in Amsterdam. . ."

Southerland shrugged. "So?"

"So I'd like to speak to your man there. That Jewish chap."

"Emile Faust? He'll eat you alive."

"I don't want to run him. I merely want to talk to him, to enlist his help on a . . . minor point."

"He won't like you, Charles. He won't like you one bit. Besides, he doesn't have time."

"It will only take an hour, two at the most."

Southerland withdrew the flask again, found it empty. "You know, this is commencing to become quite crude. I really do hate to mention it, to offend delicate sensibilities, but it is indeed growing rather crude. . . . First she snubs you for Rudolph Spangler. Then there's that mess in Berlin, and now you seem to be waging your own private war against her—and all without a shred of hard evidence."

"Well, Martin, that's the whole point, don't you see? Faust is the only one who can get us that evidence."

"Us, Charles? *Us?* Talk to him if you like, but I'll have nothing to do with this . . . understand?"

And Dunbar did understand . . . especially the likes of Martin Southerland, chaps who wanted it both ways.

Given the caliber of spies during the First World War, Emile Faust was very much ahead of his time. Whereas most British agents were hastily trained amateurs primarily responsible for little more than the observation of troop movements and the like, Faust had actually obtained a position within the German intelligence apparatus in Holland. To this extent he was a "mole" long before the term had been coined. Specifically he served as an operational assistant to Karl H. Cramer, Berlin's resident spymaster and information service director. As a Dutchman with both British and German antecedents Faust was also afforded a great deal of freedom; hence his periodic appearances in London.

He was a thin man, handsome in an odd way, with dark features. He tended to dress like bohemian, and his voice was very soft. He was a fighter as well, and also an independent operative—consequently making him a challenge to even the most experienced case officers.

It was a Friday evening when Dunbar met Faust, another chilly evening with fog and suspended rain. Faust had landed the night before and was presumably to stay through the weekend. From the German's point of view he had come to brief an agent in Portsmouth. Dunbar, however, found him in a safe house off the Regent's Canal.

There was a housekeeper named Lilly, but Faust had found her annoying and sent her away. There was a fire in the grate but the walls seemed to absorb the heat. Faust was sitting at a table in the shadows when Dunbar entered.

There were none of the usual amenities between an agent and his case officer: no offers of a drink (although a bottle of Scotch lay on the sideboard), no inquiries about mutual acquaintances. Faust clearly resented Dunbar's intrusion and wanted him gone as quickly as possible.

He began by saying that Southerland had already explained what was needed, then launched into a general description of the German intelligence effort in Amsterdam. He was the perfect observer, putting nothing of himself into it, only describing what he had seen or heard. Although his voice never varied he could not help smiling when describing the heart attack of the German military attaché.

But for the most part, Faust talked about Cramer and the subordinate Dutch apparatus. He said that there were seventeen men and women attached to Cramer's staff with an operating budget for twenty-five agents. Cramer, however, had barely succeeded in recruiting half that number: pensioners paid a few guilders a month to watch the coast, the night clerk at L'Europe Hotel, one or two acquaintances from cabarets around the Thorbeckeplein. Apart from the maintenance of this rather paltry network Cramer's concern was his standing in Berlin. He was also continually pressing Faust to supply him with women.

When Faust had finished, he moved to the sideboard and the bottle of Scotch. He drank his first glass quickly, as if to kill a bad taste, then poured another and returned to the table.

"I wonder if you might tell me a little about Cramer's women?" Dunbar said. "I mean to say, is there any particular type he seems attracted to?"

"He'll take anything he can get."

"Prostitutes?"

"Anything."

"And are these relationships ever professionally based?"

"Do you mean, does he place them on the books? Occasionally."

"But primarily the interest is personal, is that it?"

Faust lit a cigarette. "Listen, Dunbar, there are no mysteries here. Karl Cramer is not a genius. You understand?"

Dunbar got up from his chair and moved to the window. A passing storm had swept the sky clean, and he could not recall ever having seen such a sky . . . except possibly with Zelle.

"I wonder if we might go over the recruitment process?" he said. "That is, how exactly does Cramer choose an agent?"

"Mostly with two left hands."

"Are you ever involved in the process?"

"Sometimes."

"In the actual selection?"

"Sometimes."

"So that if you were to recommend someone of potential value, Cramer would pursue it, proceed with an interview and so forth?"

Faust had finished his second whisky, but something stopped him from pouring a third. "I think we should clear a small misunderstanding right now. Just so we are both in full agreement. I don't smoke in bed, and I don't pave the way for agents I don't know. You follow me? I don't take those kind of chances, especially for you."

"But I'm not talking about one of *my* people, Emile. I'm talking about an actual asset of potential value, someone with clearcut German sympathies."

"What is this game we are playing now, Dunbar?"

"No game, Emile. I simply want you to whisper a name in Karl Cramer's ear, the name of someone who may be of use to him as a foreign representative."

"And who is this person? Who is this person with clearcut German sympathies?"

Dunbar turned from the window with his hands in his pockets. "Actually it's that dancer, Mata Hari."

There were sea shells on the mantle and an ivory cat, and especially a porcelain ballerina, lips slightly parted, body curved like a bow. Faust seemed to be studying her. "You know, Martin told me about you and that woman, Dunbar. He told me all about it."

"This isn't what you think—"

"And what do I think? That you are worried about her financial condition and want to arrange employment for her with the German secret service? Or perhaps you are concerned about my good friend and colleague Karl Cramer and are dying to help him fulfill his obligations to Berlin?"

Dunbar glanced at the clock above the mantle: half past midnight and still no end in sight. "Obviously I can't go into the details, but the operation is much bigger than you imagine."

"Oh, I don't think so. I think I can imagine it very easily. Having failed to discover firm evidence of that woman's complicity with Berlin, you are now about to manufacture this evidence. You are about to pass her in front of Karl's very sensitive nose, knowing full well from what I've told you that a man of his appetite will certainly take a bite. No, this isn't at all difficult for me to imagine."

Dunbar stood there, eyes fixed on the garish carpet, hands still jammed into the pockets of his trousers.

"I won't lie to you, Emile. I won't pretend that there's evidence when there isn't. The fact remains, however, that there are indications concerning that woman's link with Berlin, profound indications that simply can't be ignored—please, let me finish. All I'm proposing is that we give her the opportunity to renew old acquaintances. That's it. I merely want to give her that opportunity."

Faust was silent a moment, still examining that porcelain ballerina. "What would I say to him?"

"Tell him that she's just returned from Paris. I'm sure that will pique his interest. And show him a photograph of her."

"What about Martin?"

"Well, naturally I shall keep him informed, but I'd prefer if you reported only to me."

"In case it blows up in our faces, right?"

"Please listen to me. This is nothing, five minutes alone with Cramer. You simply tell him that there's a woman who may be of some interest, and suggest that he speak to her. That's the whole of it."

"And afterward?"

"Afterward you needn't even remember that we spoke." . . .

He saw her everywhere after that. He saw her in crowds along the strand, and watching him from passing limousines. He saw her beneath him on a twisted staircase, and above in tenement windows. She became the singular presence in every empty room. She became his world.

Although Dunbar's files contain only peripheral notes about the arrangement with Emile Faust, it is not difficult to reconstruct what occurred. It was a casual affair. Within a week of his return to Holland, Faust, the double agent and now in his guise as a German agent, simply approached Karl H. Cramer and suggested that he recruit a dancer named Margaretha Zelle on behalf of German intelligence. Naturally, Faust supplied Cramer with at least one photograph—including one of those early nude studies that had created such a stir before the war.

Chapter Twenty-One

IT was a Friday afternoon when Cramer appeared. He had written in advance, but Zelle had forgotten. Her home on The Hague's Nieuwe Uitleg was again under renovation; the fixtures not yet installed, the plumbing still unreliable. Nor had her furniture from Paris arrived, so that Cramer had to be received in a dining room.

He was admitted by the maid, Anna Lintjens. Zelle was upstairs quarreling with a carpenter and did not even hear the doorbell. Then, mistaking the man for a contractor, she nearly had Anna Lintjens show him to the basement, where the walls were crumbling from seepage.

He was a tall thin man with what women considered elegant features. He had first entered Holland on November 2, 1914, with the German Official Information Service. Originally from Bremen, he had formed his links with the secret world late in life, more or less as a stop-gap measure to counter Allied efforts in the Netherlands. He learned the ropes quickly, however, and his approach to Zelle was classic.

He began with flattery, saying he had once had the great pleasure of seeing her dance in Vienna. Next he talked a little about himself and his mission, describing his duties in public relations and the promotion of historic German ideals. Finally, he said that he would very much appreciate hearing about her experiences in Paris.

Tea—a fragrant Himalayan blend—was served before she could respond.

From this room there was a long view of the canal that she had always found reassuring, particularly in the afternoon, when children were on the white path returning from the convent.

He said, "You must find it very comforting to be home again after Paris?"

She snapped a biscuit in two but didn't eat it. "Comforting?"

"Away from the war."

She smiled, meeting his eyes. "But I wasn't involved in the war, Herr Cramer."

"No, of course not . . . "

There were heavy footsteps from the room above, then the rhythmic thud of a hammer. She shook her head. "I'm afraid that has become my war now, that and the plumbing."

He glanced at the bare whitewashed walls, the bay windows and the angular staircase. "Still, it's a lovely old house. Do you plan to stay long?"

She shrugged. "I suppose it all depends on you."

"Me?"

"Well, it's you and your people that are making this war . . . and consequently spoiling my career."

"But that's unfair, madame. We are not the only ones responsible. There's England, too, you know."

She looked suddenly serious. "Your people took my luggage, which I would very much liked returned."

He put his teacup down. "Ah, so now we get to the heart of the matter. I came here today anticipating a pleasant discussion about Paris, while you were intending to file a complaint."

"The luggage was confiscated last August by agents of your government. Repeated letters have produced nothing."

He smiled. "I'm afraid this is not exactly my province."

227

"Then I suggest you make it your province, because my furs alone are worth at least fifty thousand francs. And there was jewelry."

Cramer's hands were long and slender, the nails immaculate. "I will see what I can do," he said. "The war does tend to complicate such matters—"

"Well, you know, the French would have never allowed anything like this to happen."

"Ah, but the French know how to treat a beautiful lady. I doubt, however, that they are treating the British officers with outstanding kindness."

"The British that I saw were treated very well."

"Even by their colleagues in the French military?" He realized he was being unsubtle, but he had limited time and if there was any future in the woman he needed to know as quickly as possible.

She began toying with crumbs on the tablecloth, wedging them into tiny fortifications. "I think there is something you don't understand, Herr Cramer. I went to Paris for six weeks to collect my possessions. Naturally I met a few people, old friends, maybe a new friend. But mainly I went to collect my things."

"But surely you must have observed something of the local situation, something, for example, of the morale."

She smiled again. "Actually I was really much too concerned about my luggage to observe much of anything. I am, you see, a practical person. Possessions are important to me . . . of course there are bad feelings. War brings out bad feelings, doesn't it?"

"Even among the Allies?"

She nodded, watching for those children on the white path. "I suppose so."

"And the civilians, how are they holding up?"

"How do you think? Look, Herr Cramer, why don't you forget about my luggage and just tell them to stop the war. I think maybe that would be most useful in the long run. Certainly for my career. Anyway, I need to work again . . . you have no idea what this house is costing me."

He took a sip of tea. "Cold."

She sighed. "I can ring Anna."

"No, please don't bother." Then leaning forward as if to take her hand: "You know, I think you are a very intelligent woman, Madame Zelle. I think that possibly under different circumstances we could have been great friends. As it is, I think we can at least be of use to one another, of benefit to one another."

She drew her hand back. "And what benefit would that be?"

"Did you know that Dutch merchants are no longer able to do business in France? Now, of course, this is agreeable to the British, but very disagreeable for me. The problem, you see, is that occasionally I require the services of traveling merchants in order to obtain a certain commodity, a certain commodity that my government is willing to pay a great deal of money to obtain."

She was toying with the crumbs again. "I'm not a merchant, Herr Cramer."

"No, you're not a merchant. You're a very great dancer, an artist. Still, I think you might be in a position to help me obtain this particular commodity."

"And exactly what is this commodity?"

"Information."

She swept the crumbs away and got up from the table. The canal was deserted, the carpenters had left for the day. He was behind her when he spoke. "The information we seek is not of an unduly sensitive nature. I mean to say, there's no danger of any kind."

"Of course, no danger." Turning to face him again: "You know, I'm really not certain whether to be angry or amused, Herr Cramer. Really, should I be angry or amused?"

"I had hoped that you might be interested."

"Oh, but I am interested. I'm outrageously interested in why anyone would possibly think I would agree to become a spy. And that is what this is all about, isn't it? You want me to become your spy?"

"Technically, no."

"Then what? Secret agent, perhaps?"

"I think correspondent is the better term."

"Correspondent then. Yes, foreign correspondent . . . which I'm afraid is equally absurd."

"There is also compensation. Say, ten thousand francs?"

She moved back to the table, posing with a hand on her hip. "Actually, Herr Cramer, ten thousand francs wouldn't cover my expenses. Besides, I have no intention of returning to Paris. This is my home now, or will be if they ever send my furniture."

She accompanied him as far as the garden, her conventional garden with ranks of perfect daffodils and tulips. There was a waiting limousine in the street, which she pretended not to notice, just as she pretended not to notice how he squeezed her hand when offering his calling card. "Just in case you should ever change your mind."

And that was the whole of her aborted recruitment on a Friday afternoon in Holland, late February of 1915. After Cramer's departure she returned to her home—rented from another local merchant, paid for by the Baron Edouard van der Capellen, half furnished by an earlier lover she had all but forgotten—and slept. Toward nightfall, a particularly blue twilight, she moved back to the garden with a cocktail and a copy of *The Brothers Karamazov*. Cramer's tastefully embossed calling card would mark the unread portion.

She would always be remembered here, often seen walking by the outer canals or sipping morning coffee on a terrace. Children would catch a glimpses of her watching from the edge of playgrounds, and of course they knew her in the shops. With the newspaper articles and the promotion of a Mata Hari biscuit in a decorative tin, it seemed that everyone had heard of her. There had even been a few who had seen her dance.

"The Hague is my purgatory," she would write to Gray. "They tolerate me here but I do not think they accept me." She also wrote that the women were the worst of it, but that was to be expected, given what had been printed in the newspapers. Still, there were pleasant afternoons in the Mauritshuis and the smaller museums where the students tended to congregate. Socially her life revolved around the baron, but since he was not a particularly demanding lover, many of her evenings were spent alone.

She read a lot at night, reviving old passions with a battered translation of the Upanishads and tales from the Pandava cycle. She also attended to her correspondence, including references to a possible performance in the spring. The piano offered some solace on otherwise too-quiet evenings, and occasionally she danced to selections of Mozart on the gramophone. On the whole, though, it seemed that memories sustained her through these days—memories, and a photograph of her daughter, Jeanne-Louise.

She wrote more than a dozen letters before receiving a reply from the child's father, Rudolph John MacLeod. Although his note was terse and apparently written with possible litigation in mind, he did agree that she should at least be allowed to see the girl . . . if only for an afternoon. He also enclosed another photograph: Jeanne-Louise at about fifteen, along the seashore in a white dress; his own face in the background, stirring still more memories of the East.

They met in Rotterdam on the first of June. Zelle had hardly slept the night before. She had also had difficulty securing a room, and sudden rain had all but ruined her hat. Still, the hyacinths were in bloom and reflections of shifting clouds tended to break the monotony of water.

Rudolph MacLeod was nearly sixty by now, his daughter—Margaretha's daughter—had just turned sixteen. Her eyes and hair were dark, like her mother's, but she seemed to have her father's gaze and that hint of strength in the jaw. Her one painfully formal letter had essentially described a life that Zelle had left some fifteen years earlier. She was studying to be a teacher, with the hope of securing a position in one of the secondary institutions. She was very fond of horses, and believed that with faith and determination a person could accomplish anything.

It was about noon. Jeanne-Louise and her father were making their way along the quay, she in white, he in drab blue. Margaretha saw them first from the window of a small cafe adjacent to her hotel, then briefly lost them against a darker stretch of wharf. Closer, she saw that MacLeod had hardly changed—no doubt a consequence of a rigidly disciplined life. He took the child aside before entering the cafe, then sent her across the promenade to wait while he tested the water.

His eyes had never been particularly good, and he hesitated in the doorway, scanning every face before approaching. He moved awkwardly at first, stiff from boots to collar. He did not smile a welcome, and looked only at the waiting chair. Even after he sat down he hardly looked at her.

"How are you, Margaretha?"

"Well enough. And you?"

"The same."

A waitress brought him a *café crème,* laid it on the table beside his folded hands.

"I thought it best that I spoke to you alone first," he said.

"All right."

"Because there are certain things you should understand about Jeanne-Louise . . . about her life."

She glanced out the window. Her daughter was sitting on a bench in a treeless park.

"She's very beautiful, isn't she?" Zelle said at last.

He smiled, briefly. "She looks like her mother."

"But has her father's temperament?" Then carefully sliding her hand to his wrist: "Rudy, I'm not here to make trouble. I just want to be part of her life for a while. I want to help."

"She has a stepmother, I married again."

She nodded. "I heard."

"And they're very close—Jeanne-Louise and Elisabeth."

"Yes, that's very nice . . . but *I'm* the mother, Rudy."

She saw his hand closing to a fist, then gradually relaxing again. "Tell me what you propose."

"Let her live with me for a while."

"Where?"

"In The Hague. I have a house. She can enroll in the conservatory—"

"She wants to be a schoolteacher."

"All right, then she can attend the teacher's college. I'll pay the tuition. Rudy, please. Give us a chance together. *Please.*"

He turned his head to the window. The girl still had not moved from the bench. "Do you ever think about us?" he asked. "Do you ever think about how it was on those islands?"

She touched his wrist. "Sometimes."

"Because recently I've been thinking about it a good deal. I think about that little house in Toempoeng, and that other shack in the village. I also think about the night the baby died, and how things might have been different . . ."

"Rudy, listen to me—"

"And do you remember when they had to kill all the dogs because of rabies. Seven hundred and thirty-nine dogs. Do you remember? Seven hundred and thirty-nine dogs shot in one day. And then you cried, because you thought they were also going to shoot that little terrier."

"Rudy, let her come and live with me, at least for a while."

His eyes were moist as he said, "It's too late, Margaretha. She's not your daughter anymore. She doesn't know you, and she doesn't love you."

"It's because of what you've told her about me, isn't it?"

He shook his head. "It's because of what the world has told her about you. Maybe you've finally made something of your life, maybe you're a great figure, a celebrated dancer. But you're not her mother any longer—"

"But that's only because I haven't had the chance to show her . . . Rudy, it's time she got to know me."

He shook his head. "No, the time for that is over. Now she merely wants to read about you, to tell her friends. Do you understand what I'm saying? You can't cry over those dead dogs, and you can't turn the clock backward. She has her own life, she doesn't need you anymore."

There was nothing left to say. Later, in the park, a mild breeze had risen, smelling of the sea. The promenade was all but deserted. Jeanne-Louise was still on the bench with her hands folded in her lap. She got up as her mother approached, but her arms stayed at her side.

"Darling?"

"Hello, mother."

"How are you?"

"Fine."

They walked for a while, Zelle trying a speech she had prepared, an apology for having stayed away so long. There was nothing, however, close to her dream of how it would be, not even a tearful embrace. The journey back was in an overcrowded railway carriage, with a number of women sitting together who might have been mothers and daughters.

She lived erratically after that day in Rotterdam, rising either very early or very late, wasting the afternoon with mindless pursuits. Her little house on the Nieuwe Uitleg would never be completed—the rooms only half furnished, walls unpainted, windows without curtains. There were, however, four memorable performances with the Royal Theater in Arnhem and an abbreviated ballet in The Hague. She also received some critical acclaim for a series of eight "mood" pieces in yellow veils.

But eventually it was clear. There was nothing for her here, nothing to hold her through the restless hours, nothing to grip through the bad hours—including the baron, although he remained kind and generous. So she drifted again, sometimes literally along familiar canals into neighborhoods she remembered from her youth; sometimes only in daydreams while resting in a cane chair among the garden ferns. On rainy afternoons she often found herself at that piano again; not actually playing, just tapping out notes as they came. On warmer afternoons she often browsed through the local shops but rarely stopped to buy. On slower nights she continued to read or leaf through old photograph albums from Paris, where she decided she'd been happy.

It was early October when she seriously began to consider returning to Paris, late April when she finally received her passport. Contrary to later allegations, the decision had not been prompted by a scandal or some indiscreet affair. Merely, there was no one who cared enough to keep her from staying away from it, and she lacked the foresight to keep herself away. Even after the obvious signs, even after Karl Cramer . . . she still couldn't see it.

Unused furniture was draped with dust clothes, the valuables locked away, the garden, as if sensing her imminent departure, had withered with a late frost.

Cramer arrived at about ten in the evening. Zelle had dismissed the maid an hour before, then retired to her bedroom. The house had been fixed in slatted moonlight since dusk. The neighborhood was still again. She heard the limousine, then saw him from the window as he moved up the path. His tuxedo seemed incongruous with the briefcase tucked under the arm.

"Hello. Do you remember me?"

"What do you want, Herr Cramer?"

"May I come in?"

"It's rather late, isn't it?"

"It's rather important."

She led him to a library off the entrance hall, a cold room, now even colder with bare shelves and sheets draped over the furniture. She supposed that he expected her to offer him a drink, but she remained watching from the mantle.

"Do you always pay unannounced visits to women at this hour?"

He laid his briefcase on the coffeetable. "This is not a social call."

She ran a hand along the plaster. "No, I don't imagine it is."

"We know that you are leaving for France and we—"

"Paris, Herr Cramer. I'm leaving for Paris."

"Very well, you are leaving for Paris, and we should like you to render us some service."

She smiled, couldn't help it. "Oh, I see. We are back to your spy service."

"I am prepared to offer twenty thousand francs. Twenty thousand francs as an initial retainer, more upon the delivery of acceptable material."

She turned to the mantle, to the blank wall. "How did you know that I applied for a passport?"

"It's our business to track such matters. Now please understand that I am not suggesting you do anything improper. It is just that you are a woman with access to certain people that—"

"That also demand privacy. No, I really think all this is out of the question."

He sat down on the arm of the sofa as if to collect his thoughts. "It is a small thing, actually, a matter of keeping one's ear to the ground."

"But the ground, Herr Cramer, could cover a good deal of territory. Besides . . . you never recovered my luggage."

"Luggage?"

"My furs. You were to secure the release of my furs from your government. I really don't know what we have to talk about."

She was, he realized, quite serious. He moved to her side, risked a hand on her shoulder. "Won't you at least consider my proposal . . . as one professional to another?"

She hesitated, watching his hand slide from her throat to trace the neckline of her gown. "Very well, Herr Cramer, I shall consider it."

And in a sense she kept her word, later explaining how she spent the night with a bottle of sweet sherry and the useless correspondence from Berlin concerning her furs: ". . . furs which cost me at least twenty thousand francs, so that I finally decided that it would be fair exchange to get as much money out of those Germans as possible." Also from this night there is a copy of the note she sent Cramer instructing him to bring the money, and an unusually candid letter to her daughter concerning "men who believe they understand woman but in fact understand nothing . . . men who will never give anything of value, except what you learn how to take."

Chapter Twenty-Two

SO she left for Paris with twenty thousand francs and three bottles of secret ink that Cramer had insisted she use when corresponding with him. Once past the harbor, she tossed the bottles into the sea with a flourish, and returned to her still-unfinished copy of *The Brothers Karamazov*— still using Cramer's old calling card as a bookmark. Although several French and British agents awaited her arrival, at least for the moment she felt quite happy and free . . .

A blown leaf now, Gray reported later. A swimmer drawn into a riptide. She tended to live only for immediate pleasures . . . after all, she had lost the love of her life, her daughter. Among those awaiting her arrival were a number of young French and British officers recruited on an informal basis by either Dunbar or Ladoux. Some had been instructed to watch her, while others had been told to become part of her life.

The first to approach her was a young English captain named Tom Merrick. Tall, graceful, with dark hair and gray-blue eyes, he met her in the bar of the Grand Hotel.

By this time she had laid Dostoevsky aside and returned to the darker tales from her youth in the East . . . specifically the legend of Durga—the Black One, the Hag of Lust. Feeling restless at about ten o'clock, she put the book down and wandered into a bar adjacent to the dining room. Merrick was waiting at a table in the rear, watching the doorway in a mirror.

He began by introducing himself as a friend of Vadime de Massloff's, then told her he had seen her dance once in Madrid. He moved with a slight limp, a trophy from Rheims, but his eyes remained steady, warm.

They talked about de Massloff at first because he was all they had in common. Then they went on to the war and Merrick's wound. Merrick had actually never met the Russian photographer, having received all his information about the man from Dunbar. But the wound was real. Through it all they continued drinking champagne until the closing hour, then returned to her room with a bottle of white wine.

He did not sleep with her that first night, or the second, or the third. But he continued to return every evening with gifts—paid for by British Intelligence. He was kind in a way that reminded her of Gray. Besides, given the war and her personal anxieties, she was glad simply to have another man in her life.

On the fourth night he appeared a little later than usual, explaining that he had just come from one of the medical centers. His knee, he said, was going to require more treatment, and even then the prognosis was uncertain. In response she kissed him lightly on the lips and told him that it was going to be all right. Then, moving to the lamp, she extinguished the lights and slipped off her dress.

Afterward they lay in the darkness, except for three candles she had placed on the mantle, free of the brighter light that had attracted moths, enormous ones that kept battering themselves against the walls.

After a while he said, "I realize that this is probably premature for you—probably ridiculously premature—but I want to marry you. Yes, I definitely want to marry you, Margaretha."

She rolled on her side, smoothing her negligee over her hip. "I'm not certain this is the best year for marriage, darling."

"Which means what? No?"

She reached across the bed, sliding her hand along the base of his spine. "Which means that there's a war."

"Oh to hell with the war."

"You may not feel that way in a week or two."

He turned to face her, tracing her jaw with his finger. "Listen to me, Margaretha. I think we should get married. Yes, married."

She rolled on her back, watching a circling moth. (It was said, she recalled, that Durga also sometimes appeared as a bug, but usually a beetle or a wasp.) "Why don't we sleep on it? Yes, sleep on it."

"I realize you probably don't love me—"

"I didn't say that."

"Is there someone else?"

She overlooked the banality, hesitated, then said, "I don't know."

"Who is he? De Massloff?"

"No."

"Then who?"

"Someone."

"What's his name?"

"Nicholas."

"Nicholas what?"

"Just Nicholas."

"And he's asked you to marry him?"

She hesitated again. "No, he hasn't asked me to marry him."

Merrick slid across the bed, his lips close to her ear. "Well, in that case I shouldn't imagine that he really will have much to say one way or another."

Later, Gray would say that we should view her at this point as a romantic, an absurdly hopeless romantic that almost any man who was reasonably attractive could take advantage of if he knew what buttons to push. And Merrick had been briefed on these.

239

After the seventh day he returned to a hospital in Vittel, for conventional treatment or an operation, to be determined by the doctors. Either way, Merrick's case officer, Dunbar, wanted Zelle in the area as well: she mustn't cool on Merrick, and Dunbar knew too well how she could cool. So after another evening in her room Merrick began insisting that she accompany him. She told him that Vittel was in the military zone and off limits to foreign residents. Oh, but obtaining a pass wasn't a problem, he countered. Indeed, thinking but not yet saying it, he even had an acquaintance within the French government who could arrange it—a certain Georges Ladoux.

It was a Thursday when she appeared at Ladoux's office at 283, boulevard Saint-Germain, to apply for a visitor's pass to Vittel. Earlier she had seen Merrick off at the station and then breakfasted with an old friend from the theater. A number of clerks would later recall her that morning: first rather breezy in a blue skirt and blouse, then rather irritated after being shuttled from room to room until she reached the heart of French Intelligence.

Captain Ladoux would later write an account of his first meeting with Mata Hari in his memoris, *Le Chasseur d'Espions.* There is much in it that is false, but the general feeling of their encounter seems accurate enough. It was a warm day, and he saw her first in the corridor. He offered her a chair in his office, which was small and shabby, with ranks of green cabinets against one wall. The light was poor and the window looked out to a barren street.

Ladoux, a thin man with a narrow face and hollow eyes, initially struck her as an inconsequential clerk. Later she would remember him as a fox or some other thoroughly distasteful creature.

"Tell me, madame, he said, "do you have any idea why you are here?"

She laid the application on the desk. "To process this shred of inconvenience, monsieur."

He lit a cigarette, a foul North African blend. "Actually, I'm afraid it's a bit more complex than all that. You see, Vittel is clearly out of bounds for enemies of the Republic."

She shifted her gaze to the one window. "I'm afraid I fail to see the point, captain."

"The point is, are you an enemy of the Republic?"

"I shouldn't think so."

"Ah, but the British seem to think so."

"What are you talking about?"

There were one or two stray papers on his desk: visible fragments of telegrams, a typewritten list of names.

"Tell me about your relationship with Jean Hallaure," he said.

She shrugged. "He's a friend, and I really don't see what—"

"And Thomas Merrick?"

She had been watching his hands: the cigarette in his left like a peashooter, a fountain pen in his right like a tiny rifle.

"Who are you, captain?"

"A soldier."

"Then, soldier, why aren't you fighting the war?"

"Oh, but I am. Every minute of the day."

"And am I truly one of your enemies?"

He smiled, revealing a speck of tobacco on a tooth. "I don't think so, no."

"Then why won't you allow me to visit my fiancé?"

"Ah, so Merrick is your fiancé?"

"Well, we've discussed marriage."

"And may I ask when the wedding is to be held?"

"We haven't set a date."

"But it won't be long, yes? Perhaps just as soon as he recovers from his wounds?" He got up from his desk, moving to the window. "I shall be candid with you, madame. My British colleagues seem to feel that you're a potentially dangerous woman—please, let me finish. Now I don't actually hold that opinion, but it's necessary to at least investigate their claims. Hence you are here. Hence we are talking."

She continued to watch his hands for a moment, then withdrew

241

a handkerchief to absorb the perspiration on her own. "Yes, but what are we really talking about?"

"Loyalty. We are talking about loyalty to France. Tell me, how long have you lived in Paris?"

"A long time."

"And how do you feel about it? Do you love it?"

"I love people, not places."

"Then let me put it another way. What would it cost me to hire your services on behalf of the French people?"

"And what sort of services would you have me perform?"

"Oh, I think you know."

She was watching the back of his head, those deceptive scarecrow shoulders. "Do I really, monsieur?"

"Yes, definitely, I think you know." Then suddenly turning from the window to face her again: "Give me a price, madame. Purely for the sake of argument, give me a price."

She sighed, thinking that it was a dream, the worst kind of repetitious dream. "A million francs."

"Excellent. A million francs."

"And my pass to Vittel."

He moved back to his desk, and scrawled a signature on her application. "There, you are free to join your gallantly wounded fiancé in Vittel. The million francs, however, will require somewhat more discussion."

She slipped the application into her pocket, said nothing.

"I should like to see you when you return from Vittel."

"Is that an order, captain?"

"I think so, yes."

In fact, she spent eight days in Vittel, visiting the spa in the mornings, returning to Merrick in the afternoons and evenings. It would be said that she made a brief side trip to Contrexeville, to inspect a new French airstrip for her German masters, which was untrue. Nor did she attempt to recruit a young corporal, or glean information from Thomas Merrick regarding British troop strength at the Somme. Indeed, after the fifth or sixth day she was mostly concerned about how she would tell him that she did not love him after all . . . not compared to her feelings for Nicholas Gray. It was also Gray who would have us see her as a rather foolish opportunist without any notion of how the world really worked. It seemed he was right, but also wrong—an opportunist out of necessity as she saw it; a steadfast romantic for whom the world had little room or time.

It was a Friday morning when she returned to Paris and Georges Ladoux. By this time Ladoux had exchanged several cables with Charles Dunbar to finalize a plan designed to bring her closer to the British net. The city was in the grip of an early summer heat wave and the streets were virtually empty. On her way to Ladoux's office a man trailed her on bicycle. If she had been aware of it she probably would have made a joke of it.

"Perhaps if you had stayed another week," Ladoux told her, "you might have escaped the heat."

"I suppose so. But I thought it was important to see you, to have our further discussion, or whatever."

Her smile irritated him. He leaned forward. "We know all about your relationship with Karl H. Cramer."

She remained composed, mainly gazing at the photograph on his wall and a map of Europe studded with pins. Then, still with her smile: "Well, if you really know all about it, captain, then you know that I actually have no relationship with the man."

"No? I was under the impression—a twenty-thousand-franc impression—that there was a definitely a relationship."

"Well, as a matter of fact, that money was accepted in payment for valuables confiscated at the German border. I have no idea what your agents may or may not have discovered, but that money was simply in payment for my furs."

"But not necessarily intended by Cramer to be payment for your furs, correct?"

"What Cramer intended is irrelevant. I am not a German spy."

"No, madame, I believe you're not. However, the Germans don't know that." He paused to light a cigarette, leaving another pungent stench in the air. "This is my offer, madame. Return to Amsterdam. Develop a relationship with Karl Cramer. Find out one or two small things for me, and I will pay you fifty thousand francs. Now, what do you say to that?"

"I say that having taken Cramer's money and given him nothing in return, he would hardly trust—"

"Ah, but I can make him trust you. I can make him believe that his twenty thousand francs was the best investment he has made all year. And once you have gained his trust, we can work wonders together."

She picked up a fountain pen from the desk, that same pen Ladoux had toyed with the day before. "I'm not at all certain that I'm ready to go back to Amsterdam, captain. I'm just beginning to enjoy Paris."

"There may not be a Paris much longer, madame, unless lovely and talented young women like yourself help us defeat the Karl Cramers of this world. In any case I don't imagine it will take more than a month or two . . . surely you can give a month or so of your time to the survival of France, especially the Paris you so favor."

"I'll have to think about it."

"Of course."

Her tragedy, Gray would tell us, was that she still believed all men took her seriously. At her word. By the time she returned to her suite at the Grand Hotel (one more room she couldn't afford) Ladoux had already sent a cable to Dunbar informing him that the German agent Mata Hari would soon be in his control. And by the time she had returned to his office on the boulevard Saint-Germain, several agents had been told to prepare for her arrival.

Yet for Margaretha these were still days of faith, faith in herself, but also faith in France, which she did love. In all she spent three weeks preparing for her "mission abroad." She dined with a few old friends from the artistic community. She dined with Jules Cambon. She wired her once and former lover in The Hague, and eventually separated him from another five thousand francs.

Then she was gone, leisurely traipsing back to Spain with a mountain of luggage and a ticket to the Netherlands . . . in Madrid they would later say that she sent at least two Allied ships to the bottom, while in Vigo they would say that she had hopelessly compromised the British offensive on the Somme. In truth, she spent her time much as she had always spent it. She dined with available gentlemen. She danced at the home of a Spanish industrialist. She posed for a local photographer, leaving us three more nude studies that show her off as she so badly needed and wanted to be seen: an exquisite, to be adored, desired, and thereby finally accepted.

PART IV

The Last Year

Chapter Twenty-Three

THE Somme is a quiet river. It winds along ill-defined banks choked with brush and clumps of grass. The valley is shallow and wide among the chalk downs. The soil is soft and uncertain. The pace of life has always been slow here, with routine harvests of sugar beet and potatoes. The countryside is also slow under the gaze of a traveler or soldier who takes the old Roman road above the trench-lines.

There are more than fifty cemeteries here to commemorate the British dead. Most are kept immaculate by the Imperial War Graves Commission, and have been arranged geographically according to where the battalions fell. Opposite Beaumont Hamel, for example, there is a circular garden dedicated to the 1st Newfoundlanders, slaughtered within minutes of leaving the trenches. Above the Ancre Valley there are several commemorative monuments for the Ulster divisions cut down in successive waves along the marshland. Of particular interest is a bronze memorial near La Boiselle, where

Nicholas Gray advanced with four battalions of Tyneside Irish into a bizarre and, as it turned out, pointless massacre.

Although there were eight phases to the fighting here, when Gray would later speak of the Somme he would mostly refer to that first morning in July—sixty thousand British casualties, the flower of an empire. His account of it is as pointed as any. After a visually impressive but useless bombardment (owing to the shells having been fused to burst on impact rather than underground, where the Germans were waiting), he had led two platoons onto the grassy slopes. They walked because they had been told to walk. They carried their rifles to the left because they had been ordered to do so. Although occasionally forced to circumvent shell craters, the ranks remained nearly symmetrical in long waves across the fifteen-mile front. The first signs of resistance almost seemed innocuous: a gentle tac-tac-tac from a thousand yards away. Soldiers seen slipping to their knees were thought to be picking up souvenirs. (Nose-caps were especially popular). But the German machine-gun tactics were surprisingly sophisticated by this time. Their teams were like skilled technicians operating high-precision lathes; not so much disciplined as mechanized. Working with predetermined accuracy set by the traversing screws, they mowed down the British lines like rows of corn.

Young men in docile lines, bent and silent, plodding to their deaths. Gray would never speak of this day except in terms of the larger Mata Hari story, and even then he would only note that nations faced with military disaster often turned to secret schemes.

There were three days following the assault before Gray returned to Mata Hari's world. For the most part he spent these days recovering wounded from the field. (The forgotten ones would simply crawl into shell craters and die). He had lost all hope of survival, and supposed that if he did not fall in the next assault there would always be another. He had also lost all sense of time, so it was either dawn or dusk when the orders came recalling him from the front, either the butt end of Tuesday or the crack of Wednesday. The orders were delivered by a messenger on bicycle, and within a matter of hours Gray found himself on his way back to England.

His escort was a stiff young captain named Hooper who seemed to think that Gray should have been ecstatic at the prospect of leaving the front. Gray met him in the courtyard of a ruined hotel on the edge of a rear village. It was a warm day, with a wind raising dust from abandoned fields. A black Renault and driver waited under the withering poplars to take them to the railhead.

"I don't suppose you're going to tell me what this is all about," Gray said.

Hooper grinned. "Afraid not."

"Why not at least tell me who sent you?"

"Sorry."

"What if I refuse to go?"

"Then I'll have to arrest you."

"What if I kick your stupid face in?"

They spent the night in an inn just east of Saint Omér. There were only inconspicuous signs of war here: a hospital for the shell shocked, abandoned trucks, an occasional cripple. There were also no lights and the landscape was pitch dark. The food, however, seemed reassuring: sausages, beer, and a beet stew.

At first they dined in silence, their eyes fixed on their plates. Earlier that evening it had occurred to Gray that the farther he moved away from the front the less substantial he became. After a while war was the only reality. Fifty, sixty miles from the trenches and one hardly existed at all.

Hooper said something, a feeble attempt at conversation because he obviously couldn't handle Gray's hostile silence: "I understand that you lived in Paris before the war."

Several beats before Gray even looked at him. "Yes, I was in Paris."

"Painter, wasn't it?"

"Yes, painter."

"Well, it must have been lovely."

"Huh?"

"To have been an artist in Paris—what a life, eh?"

Gray laid down his knife and fork. Hooper's eyes were like the button eyes on a stuffed bear—virtually shining with enthusiasm.

Finally Gray said, "You're from the back room, aren't you?"

"Back room?"

"You're one of those idiots from the M.I. group."

The button eyes grew slightly duller, the mouth a little pinched. "Look, we're only going to be together another day. Can't you at least make an effort to be civil?"

They left shortly after dawn. The sky remained flat blue until the coast, where the fogbanks lay. They boarded one of the commercial steamers, a gray thing from another era. The decks were jammed with frightened women scanning the water for torpedoes.

After two or three whiskys in a second-class bar, Gray also moved up to the deck. Although most faces seemed pinched and drawn, there was one rather beautiful girl. She stood at the stern, watching the widening furrow for a while, then left him with a profile . . . almost as perfect as Zelle's. Zelle. He felt her presence in the water, felt it descending with the wheeling gulls, all confirming what he had suspected for years: Zelle was like a tropical storm—there were always small signs in the stillness preceding her arrival.

They landed at Dover, where another car and driver were waiting beyond the customs house. The driver was a lean sergeant with a chipped face, reminiscent of Sykes. He spoke softly to Hooper, said nothing to Gray. The fog had gathered all along the waterfront, slowing the trucks from the factories.

It was nearly dusk by the time they reached the edge of the city, early evening when they arrived at their final destination. The house stood in a wooded vale off the main road. Oaks lined the half-paved lane, willows grew along the grassy slopes above a stream. Leaves were still ticking after an earlier rain. The driver stopped in a circular motor court between the tangled garden and the entrance. There were one or two lights in upper windows.

"We call it the Bentley House," Hooper said in reverent tones.

Inside were vast shadowy rooms, smelling of mildew and wet stone. An oar hung above the mantle, a dark pastoral landscape above the staircase. Beyond double glass doors was a conservatory with the silhouette of an enormous fern, an empty bird cage, wastes of black furniture: the place from which he would start the road back to Zelle.

It was near-midnight when Southerland showed up. Gray had been resting in a bedroom at the top of the stair, a long narrow room with stylized daffodils on the walls. There were four more rooms waiting for guests, but Southerland was the first. Gray heard him on the staircase with the driver, then questioning Hooper in the corridor:

"Did you discuss anything in particular with him?" Southerland asked.

"No, sir," Hooper replied, "nothing at all."

"Did he mention anyone of interest?"

"No, sir."

"Then what the hell *did* you talk about?"

"Very little. He was uncommonly rude."

"Rude? You're lucky he didn't take your head off."

The dialogue began in the morning. Gray had gotten up early, and after a breakfast of coffee and cigarettes found Southerland waiting for him in the garden, a haphazard place, a remnant of someone's earlier enthusiasm; weeds had begun to invade the neglected lawn, the hedgerows had lost definition. An ornamental fountain was caked with moss, which lay so thick on the flagstones that one might have been walking on flesh.

Southerland was sitting on a white wrought-iron bench underneath a stunted oak. There was a newspaper on his knee, the remains of a biscuit at his feet. He stood up as Gray approached but kept his hands in his pockets.

"Hello, Nicky. How are you?" Receiving no reply, he inquired if Gray had slept well. "Because frankly I've always found this place

253

unbearably damp, must have something to do with the vegetation or perhaps it's in the fabric of the walls . . . Incidentally you must inform us if there's anything special you'd like in the way of meals, our cook isn't the best but if there's something you'd particularly like—"

"Tell them to bring me rat meat," Gray snapped, "and stop flirting around. I'm through with your kind. I've had it with the whole circus."

Southerland sank back to the bench with a deep sigh. "And how about the dancer, Nicky? Are you through with her as well?"

"Piss off."

Then they sat in silence for a while, watching a spider between the tendrils of fern. It was a clear, classically beautiful summer day. But since returning from the front Gray had found that he did not like open spaces. He liked small rooms with thick walls.

"For whatever it's worth, Nicky, I wasn't the one who brought you here. It came from the top."

"The top of what? Your fop organization?"

"As a matter of fact the Admiralty is involved."

"Oh for Godsakes, what did she do? Sleep with the Kaiser?"

Southerland laid the newspaper aside and stood up. "Actually it has something to do with what happened the other day on the Somme."

There were two paths extending through the garden, and they now took the darker one between shaggy hedgerows and tangled vines. Past a rotting pergola lay skeletons of lawn chairs and an overgrown tennis court—reminders that there hadn't always been a war.

"The tally still isn't in," Southerland said blandly, "but as far as we can tell the count is up to fifty thousand dead and wounded. Now obviously one mustn't jump to conclusions, but clearly *something* went wrong."

Gray smirked, then, just as blandly, "Oh I can tell you what went wrong, old man. The whole affair was a stinking mess from the start. First they laid the shells on the surface, then they tried to cut the wire with shrapnel. Beyond that no one had the faintest idea what they were doing."

"Still, there's a notion about that if the element of secrecy had been preserved. . . ."

Gray stopped, turning with an odd smile. "Oh, I get it. Oh, this is really too marvelous. You're going to pin it on a bloody spy. You're going to lay it on *Zelle.*"

"There are indications, Nicky—"

"Oh, I'm sure. I'm sure you've got a whole truck of filthy indications."

"She specifically mentioned the event in conversation with one of our people last June. That is, she made a specific reference to an offensive over the river three weeks before the attack."

"So? Everybody knew it was coming. Even the Huns knew it was coming."

"Yes, that's precisely the point."

They had reached the paddock, and here too were vague testaments of better English days: a tennis ball rotting in the grass, a rope dangling from a laurel, a disintegrating handkerchief.

"It's the little things that concern us, Nicky. The pattern of small events over the years."

Gray tossed a burning cigarette into the grass. With any luck the whole world would catch fire. *"What* are you talking about?"

Southerland stepped closer, speaking quietly. "Why do you suppose Spangler bought that portrait of her . . . your famous portrait of her?"

Gray scowled. "How the hell should I know?"

"A memento? A small reminder of the woman who destroyed his best agent?"

"Maybe."

"Or was it simply that he was also fascinated by her? Refresh my memory. How exactly did they meet?"

Gray had coiled a vine around his wrist, and the skin was still laced with red welts. "They met through Michard."

"A chance encounter?"

"More or less."

"So then it was love at first sight. The dashing German officer meets an exotic Eastern dancer. Sudden infatuation turns to lingering desire, and the next thing we know he buys her portrait from the colonel's estate. Now, is that our story, Nicky? Is it?"

Gray faced him. "Look, you can't judge Zelle from the men in her life. You simply can't do it."

"Oh, really?"

"She has . . . different standards. She has affairs. She gets involved in things, but for Godsake, it doesn't mean she's a *spy.*"

Southerland had moved to Gray's side again, both staring at a foot of stagnant water filled with weeds and rotting tubers. "Listen to me, Nicky. The Germans have her on their books in Amsterdam."

"Go away, Martin."

"Nicky, I'm not lying to you. They bought her for twenty thousand frances."

"Leave me alone—"

"Her case officer is an old hand named Karl Cramer. He pays her on a submission basis."

"I said leave me *alone.*"

They came together again in the afternoon, first in a latticed summer house, then along a less devious path through wasted shrubbery and high grass. Someone had planted a vegetable garden between the laurels and the far wall, but a late chill had left the stalks black.

"I shall be candid with you," Southerland began. "Were this my case, I probably would have dropped it. All right, so she's been dancing with the Germans—it hardly seems to represent a *tangible* threat. That's the way I tend to see it. There are those, however, who tend to see it otherwise."

Gray looked at him. "Are you talking about Charles Dunbar, Martin? Is that what this is all about?"

Southerland sighed. "I suppose it's embarrassing, really. I mean, I recruited the man and now he's virtually running the show with his Mata Hari campaign. Rather clever, though, how he seized the reins. More or less circumvented the Fourth Floor by enlisting the French. And once the French became involved . . . well, it just snowballed, rather."

"What in hell makes you think I'll go along with this . . . this whatever it is you spooks have in mind?"

"Look, Nicky, it's already set in place. If not you, then, I'm afraid, it's somebody else. Don't you think she has a better chance with you? And remember, hard as it may be for you to conceive of it, she just may be guilty . . . and even you, with your feelings, couldn't abide that . . ."

Gray ran his hand across his mouth—still the smell of cordite. "All right, Martin, what's on?"

"You're to watch her. You're to gain her trust in whatever manner you see fit, and then watch her until you've found out precisely who she's running with. If she is, of course."

"And what do I tell her?"

"Oh, I think that's really up to you . . ."

"How do I explain the fact that I'm off the front?"

"Tell her you swallowed a bit of gas or something."

"And if she smells a rat?"

Southerland hesitated, examining a twig he had snapped off at random. "Well, that's the point really. I mean she does believe in you, doesn't she? You above all people have always been a friend."

"Yes, and now I'm—"

"Turn her around, Nicky, convince her to work for our side and I'll make sure she slips out the back door. Fair enough?"

They began to walk again, skirting a reflecting pond and beds of untended roses. Ahead lay a shadowy glade filled with shepherd's weatherglass and pimpernel. In another life—that's what it seemed now—Gray might have spent hours sketching these slow-withering flowers to capture the timelessness.

"When would I go?"

Southerland shook his head. "I'm not entirely sure. You see, she believes she's on her way to Holland on behalf of the French, and we still have to pull her off the ship."

"What are you talking about, Martin?"

"We simply felt that your placement would be easier if she were under stress and on unfamiliar ground. I mean, she'd have no one else to turn to."

"So you had the French send her on some sort of trumped-up errand, is that it?"

"She thinks she's en route to Holland, but we'll take her off the vessel in Falmouth. The difficulties of placing you next to her in Paris were unacceptable. You know how she is there . . . besieged by old friends. This way it will be just the two of you."

"Not to mention the fact that now you've got additional proof she's a German spy, correct? I mean, obviously she wouldn't have agreed to help France in the first place if she wasn't some sort of double agent, right?"

"I don't believe that, no."

"But Dunbar does, doesn't he?"

"I suppose. Yes."

There were lawn chairs at the edge of the glade; a collapsed table, and the remains of an umbrella. Gray sat down and put a cigarette between his lips, didn't bother to light it.

"What else haven't you told me, Martin?"

Southerland had also found a chair, sagging into it as if exhausted.

"That you're not the first one we've tried to place."

"What are you talking about?"

"One of Dunbar's people. Someone named Merrick. He was used to watch her in Paris."

"Christ."

"It was a temporary solution. She arrived in Paris suddenly from Holland. We needed someone next to her and Merrick happened to be in the area."

Gray got up from the chair, walked a few steps, then suddenly stopped and turned. "Did he sleep with her?"

"Nicky, you've got to realize that—"

"Did he sleep with her?"

"Yes."

Gray tossed the unlit cigarette away. "When does Dunbar get here?"

"Tomorrow."

"I'll want to talk to him alone."

"Of course."

"I won't work with him but I want to talk to him."

"I understand."

"And if either of you hurt Margaretha, no matter what, I'll kill you. Do you understand me?"

There was rain all through the night, and still more when Dunbar arrived the following morning. As before, Gray's first glimpse of the man was from an upstairs window, a fleeting impression, as Dunbar moved from a limousine across the wet flagstones. Then, even through tangled ivy, it would have been a clean shot, the bullet tumbling on impact and shattering the skull.

They met in the library, a room filled with broad Regency stripes and the heavy smell of leather. There were more landscapes on the wall and etchings of military campaigns: Trafalgar, Crimea, a stirrup charge on the African veldt. Dunbar was seated at a table when Gray entered, but immediately rose and extended his hand.

"It's good to see you, Nicky. It's really terribly good to see you."

Except that he kept avoiding a direct gaze and fixed his eyes on objects around him: a fountain pen with a gold nib, a sheaf of papers bound in red ribbon, a bottle of Scotch on the sideboard.

"I suppose we might as well clear the air first," he said. "So if there's anything you wish to say about what happened in Berlin, please feel free."

"No, Charles, there's nothing I want to say about Berlin."

"Very well, how about the current round? Any problems? Any particular question?"

"Yes, I suppose there is one."

"And what's that, Nicky?"

"Who the hell do you think you're fooling?"

The Scotch was poured, and they drank in silence while Gray examined a watery oil of ponies under dark skies.

"Incidentally, I believe I saw one of your drypoints in the Tate," Dunbar said.

"I doubt it was mine."

"Ah, well, then perhaps it was the National." He put a pack of cigarettes on the table, lit one, and moved to the window. "Nicky, I don't mean to be polemic but I honestly think you're misjudging our intentions."

"That so?"

"I also rather think you're misjudging the woman."

"Her name is Margaretha. You used to be in love with her, Charles, remember? So let's stop playing games. Her name is Margaretha."

"Very well, her name is Margaretha. The fact remains, however, that I still think you're severely misjudging her. For example, do you recall those stories she used to tell? I'm referring to the ones about how her husband beat her and so forth, actually tie her to the bedpost and beat her."

"What about it?"

"Then there were stories, equally absurd, about how the temple priests used to flog her, chain her to a wall and flog her thighs with willow sticks."

"Look, just get to the point."

"Well, don't you think it's interesting that she was always talking about how men mistreated her? I mean, let's assume for the moment that subconsciously she resents men. Let's further assume that this resentment comes from a deepseated fear of them, a fear of their power over her, their sheer physical dominance. Now of course it's only speculation, but don't you think it's possible that I'm right, that in fact she's always despised men? Especially the ones she could manipulate, and betray . . .?"

"Christ," Gray said, "no wonder she left you."

The rain had stopped, drawing them into the garden again—Dunbar in a classic greatcoat, Gray in a borrowed mackintosh. The wind had also subsided, leaving the rainwater ditches like mirrors. They followed the same path Gray had taken the day before, but only as far as the summerhouse. There were birds, mostly sparrows and titmice all along the hedgerows.

"I'm not going to try to convince you of her guilt," Dunbar said. "But I think you should at least entertain the notion for a moment."

Gray took a deep breath. "What are you talking about?"

"Let's assume for the moment that you're a soldier back from the front. You've come to Margaretha's suite for an entertaining evening. Now what do you suppose she's wearing? Something oriental perhaps?"

"Sod off."

"She pours you a drink, probably champagne. You chat for a while. She tells you that she's been terribly worried about your safety. Indeed, maybe she's even had a disturbing dream. In an effort to console her, you start telling her about the conditions out there. At first it's all rather meaningless. You talk about the food, your mates. But after a few more drinks you find yourself talking about the terrain, the unit strength, the battalion—"

"Oh for Christsakes, piss *off.*"

Dunbar shrugged and picked up a rusting teaspoon, another sign that this place had been abandoned very suddenly.

"Very well, Nicky, let's try another route. Let's just say that we're extremely interested in her current associations."

"Like her association with Merrick?"

"Merrick, as you've been told, was a temporary solution. We needed someone in Paris to keep an eye on her while I coordinated the larger effort."

"And who represents the larger effort? Me?"

"Nicky, you've got to realize that Margaretha is only a step on the ladder. We're not so much interested in her as the people around her, people she may not even be aware of."

"People like Spangler?"

"Actually we believe this is much bigger than Spangler. This is an entire German network aimed right at our heart." He didn't smile when he said it.

Gray sank down to the chair. "Look, cut all this. Where and when am I supposed to meet her?"

Dunbar had also found a place to sit. "I'm afraid it's not that simple. There are other factors to consider—"

"Like the Frogs?"

"The French have been assisting us, yes."

"Meaning what? They also want to put her head on the pike?"

Dunbar tossed the spoon away, his first frustrated gesture. "Despite what you think, Nicholas, I'm actually conducting this investigation with, well, a tilt in her favor. Indeed, there are those in the department who feel I'm completely off my trunk for even suggesting that the woman can be turned around . . . much less trusted."

Gray shook his head. "I'm sure she'll be eternally grateful for all you've done, Charles."

"Very well, Nicky, see it as you like. The fact remains, however, that I'm probably saving her life . . . and yours . . ."

Gray stood up, tapped one finger to his temple. "Oh, I get it. This is the little game we play to keep ourselves out of the trenches."

"Please sit down, Nicholas."

"Of course. Catch a spy and save our bloody necks."

"Sit down."

"And the funny part is she never even loved you, Charlie. She just felt sorry for you, because she thought you were stupid. But she underestimated you, Charlie. We all did. Who would believe just how vindictive you could be . . ."

Dunbar merely waved him off, as one might dismiss the ravings of a soldier too long at the front.

There was a lavish meal that evening, presumably, despite earlier heat, in the interest of fellowship. Then, retiring to a drawing room with Southerland, Gray was presented with a typewritten copy of the case notes . . . another display of trust. The papers were loosely bound in cardboard and secured with string. But even without touching the notes, he could see that there were more photographs.

"You needn't study everything," Southerland told him. "Merely familiarize yourself with the basic pattern of her involvement."

Gray picked the thing up. "Her involvement?"

"With the Germans, of course."

Next, there was the money, two hundred pounds in a pale blue envelope with his majesty's crest.

"Obviously this is just to see you through the slack period," Southerland said. "I'll see that you get more once the operation starts."

"And when is that supposed to occur?"

Southerland crossed the room to pour a second brandy. "We've received word that she's on board a ship en route from Vigo to Amsterdam. We have tentative plans to pull her in at Falmouth and hold her for a few days for questioning at Scotland Yard."

"On what charge?"

"Suspicion of one sort or another, mistaken identity . . . The point is to get her off that ship, detain her until it sails again, then slip you into the scheme of things."

"And then?"

"Send her back to the continent and watch."

"And if I don't see anything?"

There were books along the wall, superbly bound in lambskin. Southerland withdrew one at random, glanced at the flyleaf, and put it aside.

"Look, Nicky, I shall be painfully honest with you. It's quite likely that this entire Mata Hari business is merely Charles Dunbar's circus. Nonetheless the case has caught the attention of some very influential people. As a result you and I are to play spycatcher for a while. If in fact she's actually connected then we'll do our best to entice her back to our team. If on the other hand, she's innocent, then we've both had a lovely time wasting the taxpayer's money. Now frankly I can't think of a more agreeable way to fight this war, can you?"

He smiled, clearly pleased with himself.

There were at least some six hours when they left him alone with her: cigarettes on the nightstand, Scotch on a table, rain mixing with the blackness to form a solid wall so that no one could touch them. For a long time he simply lay very still, gazing at a patch of sky through the curtains. Then at last he turned to the file. There were two classic nude studies from her stay in Madrid—the first, a full-length back view so that he could not see her face, but the slender hips, the slight buttocks, and the mane of dark hair were unmistakable; the second, a seated frontal view with her hands laced behind her head to reveal the smooth hollows of her arms. She seemed to be smiling at something beyond the camera; her eyes were alight with a dazed tenderness.

Zelle. Oh Lord, Zelle.

Chapter Twenty-Four

SHE was arrested at Falmouth on the twelfth of November, allegedly mistaken for a notorious German agent by the name of Clara Benedix. The presiding officer was a George Reid Grant, assisted by his wife Janet. In a 1965 interview Grant would say, "A message came down from Scotland Yard instructing me to detain a certain woman if she happened to pass through Falmouth, and to bring her to headquarters for interrogation." In order to facilitate identification, a photograph of Zelle had been attached to the order: a 1913 publicity shot of her dressed as a Spanish dancer. Reid, however, had been told only that the suspect's name was Clara Benedix, and was advised to disregard all evidence to the contrary.

Although an intensive search of the suspect's belongings—and a strip search of her person—revealed nothing incriminating, Grant and his wife nonetheless escorted Margaretha off the ship and took her to their lodgings in the village. There, according to Grant, she spent a despondent afternoon, "drinking an awful lot of coffee, but refusing all food." At about six o'clock in the evening the party then boarded a train for London, where Margaretha was finally turned over to Chief Inspector Edward Parker.

As a footnote to the story, Janet Grant would always maintain that she and Zelle had actually become quite close, considering the circumstances—and some forty years later she would still cherish a tiny glass dog given to her by the extraordinary Mata Hari as a token of her affection.

She was locked up for thirteen hours before the first round of questioning began. The interrogating officer was the celebrated Sir Basil Thomson, of later "Zimmermann Telegram" fame. Educated at Eton and New College, Oxford, Sir Basil had been governor of British prisons before heading Scotland Yard. He was fifty-five years old at the time of Zelle's arrest, at the height of his power.

They met on the morning of November thirteen in a windowless concrete room adjacent to the cells. Zelle wore what she had been wearing at the time of her arrest: a green blouse and a sober blue skirt with a jacket. Sir Basil was accompanied by a young officer with a stenographer's pad. She had breakfasted on an overdone egg, bread, and coffee.

It began in formal fashion. Sir Basil explained the charges, while Zelle calmly maintained that she had never even heard of Clara Benedix. Next there was a series of questions concering Zelle's movements between Paris and the Netherlands, as well as an attempt to find out whether or not she had been in South America, where Benedix was known to have operated. Zelle, by this time clearly frightened and exhausted, continued to maintain her innocence but did not have the strength to fight back effectively.

That first day, following the first round of questioning, she drafted a letter in her cell. It was addressed to the Dutch Legation in London, and was written in that bold, extravagant hand of hers, so at odds with what she often felt.

The Last Year

. . . I am at my wits end, am imprisoned here since this morning at Scotland Yard and I pray you, come and help me. I live in The Hague at 16 Nieuwe Uitleg, and am well known there as well as in Paris, where I have lived for years. I am all alone here and swear that everything is absolutely in order. It is only a misunderstanding, but I pray you, help me.

Sincerely

M.G. Zelle

The nights were bad, with echoes of dripping water and turning locks, but the mornings were the worst, with that waking glimpse of the bars. Afternoons they allowed her twenty minutes in a caged yard between the brickwork. She slept as much as possible. She lay on her cot and toyed with a bit of string. She ate very little. Now and again she thought about Gray, directing her mind briefly, like the shutter of a camera, to recall some comforting gesture or remark, but he was dim . . .

Sir Basil returned on the second morning, and announced that his office was now satisfied that she was not Clara Benedix. There were, however, still indications that something was amiss, and he proceeded to question her about her movements between Paris and the Netherlands. She parried his questions for about twenty minutes before finally admitting: "To be quite frank, sir, I am not traveling for myself. I am traveling on an assignment for the French government."

"And who advised you to take this assignment?"

"Ladoux," she replied. "Captain Ladoux of the Second Bureau."

"And what is the nature of this assignment?"

"I don't think I'm . . . well, I'm not at liberty to say." She was beginning to feel her role.

"But, madame, you are currently not at liberty period." He smiled briefly in apology for his very small, and tasteless, joke.

There followed an exchange of cables: Sir Basil to Ladoux, Ladoux to Sir Basil, Dunbar to all concerned. The record, however, has very likely been sanitized, leaving only Ladoux's denial of ever having recruited her in the first place. DO NOT UNDERSTAND, he replied to Sir Basil's query. Then, in accordance with Dunbar's plan: SEND HER BACK TO SPAIN.

Sir Basil waited only three or four hours after receiving Ladoux's cable before returning to Zelle. By now it was the fourth day, and she was definitely showing the strain. Her eyes were red from weeping, and she had developed a hacking cough. She had also complained of stomach cramps, which she said were from the poor quality of the food. When Sir Basil told her she was free to leave England, providng she returned to Spain, she responded with only a nod and a half-whispered thank you.

They released her that same afternoon, returning her jewelry and luggage, then turning her out on the streets. And for as much as Scotland Yard wanted to tail her, Dunbar insisted that their agents stay away, out of concern that they might spoil Nicky Gray's approach.

So, in a way, she was his again: Sunday afternoon, November seventeen, at least for the moment, she was his again. He approached her in the foyer of the Savoy with a bouquet of roses and a story about how a friend in Special Branch had told him of her arrest. As he spoke she continued to stare at him, one hand still clutching the roses, the other limp at her side.

Try to instill an element of good cheer, Southerland had told him. *Let her know that the worst is over now.*

From the foyer they went to her room, an oblong suite done in soft pastels against cream gilded walls. There was a lovely view of the river through a mesh of elms along the grassy embankment. Beside the bed lay two or three novels she would never read, and that dog-eared copy of the *Mahabharata.* On a tiny lacquered chest were a bottle of sherry and a bottle of gin that she had purchased en route from the prison.

Order champagne. Let her know that your reunion is a wholly celebratory event.

Their first moments together were strained, even awkward—she had for example, poured three glasses of sherry, and did not know what to do with the third. At the window she pulled at the curtains, and bits of lace came off in her hand. And then she began to cry, but silently, and still facing the window.

Remember, it's to be a party. Let her know that this is only the start of very good times to come.

". . . What can I do for you, Margaretha?"

"Nothing."

"Would you rather be alone?"

"What? Oh . . . no . . . no . . ."

"Do you want something to eat?"

"No."

"Does it make any difference that I still love you?"

She fell into his arms then, still crying.

He had thought she was asleep when she finally whispered his name. "Nicky?" Then again, so softly that it might have come from another room: "Nicky? We have to talk."

He kissed her on the forehead—a regression. "No, we don't—"

"But you don't understand."

He kissed her again, properly this time, catching a scent of falling perfume. "Yes, I do."

She drew away from him, becoming a silhouette. "Nicky, listen to me. I've been involved in things, dangerous things . . . in fact, that's part of the reason I was going to Amsterdam . . . to become a spy. It sounds ridiculous, but—"

"I know."

"You know? How? Who told you?"

He continued to watch her for at least another minute, suddenly conscious of that same perfect calm that one felt before lying down beside her, picking up a paintbrush, or squeezing a trigger.

"Nicky, who told you?"

And if she starts getting close to the truth, then for Godsakes change the subject.

269

"Nicky, I want to know who told you."

"The same people who sent you to Ladoux in the first place also sent me."

He had expected her to cry, and somehow felt proud when she didn't. She drank, however—first another glass of sherry, then gin. The light had now faded from gray to blue. The corridors were filled with sounds of carefree guests descending to the dining room for supper.

"How long have you been waiting for me?" she asked.

"A few weeks."

"And what did they tell you to do? Did they want you to spy on me?"

"More or less."

"To sleep with me?"

"If necessary."

"To marry me?"

He stood and filled her glass with more gin, then filled one for himself. Once more there were river sounds: a clanging barge, waterfowls, faintly beating oars.

"Everything was arranged," he said. "From the moment you left Amsterdam nothing was left to chance."

"And who did they think I'm working for?"

"Spangler . . . Cramer . . ."

"But I haven't even seen Spangler. And Cramer . . . I think he mostly wanted to sleep with me."

She had slipped off her bracelet, and began spinning it on the table. They had still not turned on the light, but he sensed her exhaustion in the darkness.

"If they think I'm working for the Germans, then why did Ladoux want to send me to Amsterdam?"

The bracelet was like a top, a gold blue.

"Ladoux was just trying to get you here."

"And why did they want me here?"

"So I could move in. Keep you under surveillance."

"But why you?"

"Because, I'm your closest friend."

The Last Year

She slept for a while and he watched her from an armchair, alternately smoking and drinking. Once or twice he heard her whisper something—a name, a phrase—but he couldn't make it out. When she finally woke he was standing at the window. She didn't speak but he felt her eyes.

"You've never seen the Thames, have you?" he said.

"No."

"It's not a bad river, but it's not like the Seine. It's best at twilight or dawn, not at night."

She slipped off the bed, and drew an old coat around her shoulders. There had been a peal of distant bells, then the throb of another barge.

"Why are they sending me back to Spain?" she asked.

"Because they think you'll lead them to people there that they're interested in."

"Are you supposed to go with me?"

"Yes."

"To spy on me?"

"That's right."

"To make love to me?"

"Margaretha, listen to me. We'll go to Spain, we'll spend a few weeks in a room, I'll make my reports, and eventually they'll realize that you're innocent. That's why I took this assignment, to help you prove that . . ."

She let her coat slip off her shoulders. Even her unconscious gestures were perfect. Even alone and in the darkness, she moved like a dancer.

"But, Nicky, how can you be sure I didn't agree to work for Ladoux because I'm a German spy? How can you be sure that once we reach Spain I won't betray *everyone?*"

"Oh, for Godsake, Zelle, grow up. This isn't a game. It's foolish, but it's also dangerous. These people, I assure you, take themselves seriously—they're deadly serious. It's their life. Now please—"

She waved her hand at him, smiled. "Nicky, Nicky . . . I've had to play life like a game for as long as I can remember. It's how *I* live, how I survive. Surely you can understand that . . ."

271

He waited until she was asleep again before going down to the lobby. Apart from the night porters there was no one about. He placed the telephone call to Southerland from the desk, visualized him half asleep on a cot in his office, surrounded by empty coffee cups and scraps of paper relating to Zelle.

"It's me."

"Yes, where are you?"

"Where do you think?"

He imagined Southerland sitting up now, a thin figure in underwear with sleepless bruises under his eyes.

"How did it go?"

Gray hesitated a moment. "Fine."

"No unforeseen difficulties?"

"Everything went fine."

"Is there anything you'd like to tell me now?"

"No."

"Did she discuss her plans for Spain?"

"She intends to go, if that's what you mean."

"And you will be accompanying her?"

Gray hesitated again, and imagined Southerland groping for a light switch with the telephone still pressed to his ear. "Yes. "I'll be going with her."

"Then listen to me, Nicky. We need to see her in Madrid. Do you understand? If she's going to be any use to us at all it's going to be in Madrid. After all, that's where the Germans are so active."

"Yes, I understand. Madrid."

He had to keep reminding himself . . . if not him it would be someone else. And of course, it did give him a chance to be next to her.

She was still asleep when he returned to her room: her hair like a shadow on the pillow, one hand dangling off the edge of the mattress. The perspective seemed obvious, but after hours of working with charcoal and a pencil he still couldn't duplicate the perfection.

Damn her.

Chapter Twenty-Five

I T was the winter of 1916. They boarded the *Araguya* on the first of December, sailing from Liverpool to the coast of Spain. The ship was old, soon to be refitted strictly for cargo. The cabins, however, were reasonably clean, and the porters seemed attentive.

On departure, she and Gray remained below drinking whisky at a zinc bar. Once past the harbor they moved out on deck, where it was cold but deserted.

"We have to put the past behind us now," she told him. "Do you understand what I'm saying?"

He had been trying to light a cigarette, but the wind kept snuffing out the matches. "I think so."

"We're not the same people we were yesterday, and we'll probably be different again tomorrow. We've only just met, and everyone we once knew has been killed in the war."

As she spoke, she had been prying a ring off her finger, slowly working it past the joint. Finally free of the thing, she pressed it into Gray's palm. "There. Throw it into the water."

He turned it over in his hand. It was a simple gold band with a large diamond. "What is this, Margaretha?"

"A gift from that boy. Now throw it overboard."

"Are you sure?"

"Yes."

"But it's got to be worth at least—"

"Do it."

What with the low mist and the spray, they never actually saw the ring hit the water. Rather, it seemed to vanish in the air moments after leaving Gray's hand.

"Now come with me," she told him.

"Where?"

"Just come with me."

When they reached her cabin she told him to sit on the bed. The curtains drawn across the portholes, the light was soft like evening light. The sounds, too, were comforting: the throb of turbines below, faint Spanish voices from above.

"Remember, now," she told him. "We've only just met. We know nothing about one another, not even last names."

She undressed slowly, methodically, standing in front of him just out of arm's reach. She was thinner than he remembered but otherwise the same.

"We're also a little afraid," she whispered. "You see, the German submarines are everywhere. At any moment a torpedo could strike, and the sea could come crashing through the wall."

She reached for his hand, pressing it hard against her left breast. She had always loved the contrast of their skin. "And neither of us has made love in a long time, so we're a little unsure how to proceed."

She knelt at his feet, put her head in his lap. He ran his fingers through her hair, and shut his eyes. She trembled as his lips slid down her spine, then lower to the smooth hip. Then, although she continued to lie very still, he felt her breasts rising and falling against his chest with each breath. Her cool thighs also began stirring as she guided his hand across her belly.

"And we're lost," she whispered. "That's another thing. We're completely lost."

The Last Year

Afterward they rested, ignoring the cocktail bell and laughter from the passageway. It was dark, and once again she was like a shadow beside him. He couldn't even hear her breathe.

Then suddenly out of nowhere: "Tell me about Charles. What's he like now?"

Gray turned on his side. Her nipples were stiff, prominent in the weak light from the porthole. "I thought he no longer existed, I thought he was killed in the war with the rest of them—"

"Just tell me about him, Nicky."

"He hasn't changed all that much."

"Did he ever find a wife?"

"No."

"A lover?"

"No, I don't think so."

"A mistress?"

"I don't think so."

"Then he still hates me for leaving him, doesn't he?"

"Probably."

He had lit a cigarette, she was staring at the ceiling. The voices from the passageway had faded, but the throb of the turbines seemed louder.

"And now I want you to tell me about what happened at that battle," she said.

From the corner of his eye he actually thought he saw her breasts trembling with the heartbeat. "What battle?"

"You know. The one at the river Somme."

He took a while to answer, then said briefly, "Mostly it was machine guns."

"How many were shot?"

He shook his head, still looking at the breasts. He had never known a woman with nipples like hers. "I'm not sure."

"Ten thousand?"

"More."

"Twenty?"

"About sixty, so they say."

He heard her whisper something, then louder. *"Sixty thousand in one day?"*

"Yes."

She drew the sheet over her shoulders and turned on her side away from him. "Sixty thousand in one day?"

"Margaretha."

"And now they're trying to say it was all my fault, aren't they? I tipped off the Hun."

"Not really."

"Yes they are. Sixty thousand soldiers shot in one day, and it's all my fault."

"Margaretha, I really don't believe that anyone is seriously—"

"Oh, but you told me they were serious. And I'm sure Charles Dunbar is serious. He's very serious, and what's more, he's very pleased that he finally has something to be serious about."

A storm broke that night, a black gale that rose to a furious pitch within the space of a few hours and brought still more memories of the war. By morning half the passengers were too seasick to leave their cabins, and there were a number of nasty accidents in the passageways. Gray awoke to a messy breakfast of coffee and a melon. Later he found Zelle in the lounge, wedged into an armchair with her collection of Indonesian fables.

"I had no idea that a ship this size could pitch like this," she said.

"At least you're not ill."

Chandeliers were swaying above stained tablecloths.

"And what about you?" she said. "I heard you prowling around like a cat in the night. You couldn't have slept more than an hour."

"I read, from that book of yours. Who's Durga?"

A porter appeared, bracing himself in the doorway for a moment, then lurching down the corridor.

"It's just an old myth, Nicky. Durga was the wife of Siva."

"And not a particularly pleasant sort, I take it."

"She drank blood and ate flesh." She said it with only the hint of a smile. "I thought she might make a useful guardian angel."

"Margaretha, there's nothing to be worried about. Dunbar hasn't got a real case against you—"

"Does he need a case? With all the stupid rumors." Her eyes were on those swinging chandeliers. "I've been sensing her presence, you know. That's why I can tell this is going to turn out badly . . . because I've been sensing her presence more and more as the days go by."

"Margaretha, listen to me."

"You think I'm joking, don't you? Well, it's true. I feel her all around me—Durga. We Easterners are psychic, didn't you know that? Anyway, nothing can be the same again. The war has seen to that. I mean, look at you . . . you're not the same at all. You're lean and grim. Tell me, Nicky, did you kill a lot of men?"

"Come on, let me take you up on deck."

"You did, didn't you? You killed dozens of men, and now you're a ghost, you're one of those living ghosts I keep hearing about." And she squeezed his hand, as if trying to deny it, to find something palpable in him . . . in her life.

The storm gave way to a fog-bound stillness. Mornings blurred into afternoons, nights were very black. One hardly felt time passing.

"How would you like to travel once we get to Spain?" he asked her. "I could take you to all those out-of-the-way places one never gets an opportunity to visit."

It was the third day of the voyage. Gray had returned from the ship's library with an old guidebook to Spain. He had also found a map of the provinces and a bottle of sherry.

"We could go to the south coast," he said, "I bet you've never been to the south coast."

She seemed to want to smile, but it wouldn't come. "No, never."

"Or Segovia. We could go to Segovia, and see the castles."

She got up from the chair, crossed the room and kneeled beside him on the bed. "What are you trying to tell me, Nicky?"

"They want me to try to get you to Madrid. I told you . . . that's the center of the German espionage effort, and they want you there."

She sighed, collapsing to her elbows. "I despise this, Nicky. I really do."

"So then let me take you away from it. We'll go to the coast and sit on the beach for a month. I know places where they'll never even find us."

She slid off the bed and moved to a view through the porthole. "It's too late for that. Don't you see? Once you've been accused of these things it just never leaves you. People are always talking behind your back, doors are always closing in your face. You might as well retire to a monastery. Or nunnery." She shivered at that last.

He tried to reassure her, not believing his own words. Later that evening she even pointed out the spot on his map: Montserrat, above the river Llobregat, just the place to end a life that seemed not for this world.

Although they were all but inseperable, and continued to sleep in the same bed, by the fourth day he felt she was slipping away again. The pretend game of a new life was over. On occasion she would speak almost enthusiastically about Spain, describing certain restaurants she had known from before, then without warning she would lapse back into depression, with a bottle of sherry or gin, and those stories of the bloody Durga, bitch of schemes.

They landed at Vigo just after daybreak and secured a room in a small hotel on a rise above the harbor. It was the sort of place that Gray had always imagined they would find in Spain: a white room with tiled floor, a view of the sea through blue-shuttered windows. Below were hanging gardens and a patio with terra cotta urns. They lunched on soup, bread, and wine. It was a brisk day, and the wind had brought out the color in her cheeks. Her eyes, too, were clear again.

After lunch she left him on a terrace for a couple of hours to browse, she said, through the local shops. Then they returned to their room and dozed together on the narrow bed. What had begun as a drab day with yellow mist along the shore ended magnificently with contrasting shades of pink and green.

"You know, we could always just stay here," he told her. "We could stay here for a month."

There was a bottle of Burgundy at her elbow, a plate of dried fish and grapes. Since her return from the shops, however, she had apparently lost her appetite.

"What would we do when the money runs out?"

He reached for her hand. "I'll paint, and you'll dance. We'll become a famous couple.

"I'm tired of fame, Nicky. If that's what it is."

He moved behind her, put his hand on her bare shoulder, then let it fall away. "Are you also tired of me, Margaretha. Is that really what's happening now?"

She grabbed his wrist with something in her eyes that he'd never seen before. Quite apart from the tears, there was definitely something that he had never seen before.

"No, I'm *not* tired of you. I never will be."

Her other hand clamped to his arm and drew him closer. "Do you understand that, Nicky? I will never grow tired of you."

"Darling, what's wrong?"

"Just tell me that you understand it. Tell me."

"All right. I understand."

The kiss, too, was like nothing before it. A painful, almost desperate kiss that tasted of Burgundy and salt. Then she couldn't seem to get rid of her clothing fast enough, and actually tore her dress before moving into his arms. She had to feel his hands all over her body, lips to her breast, heart to her heart.

An hour later she was unusually quiet, lying on her belly and toying with a trinket she had picked up along the quay. She kept gazing through a bit of polished glass, sighting the moon above the palms. It was a white disk of a moon, perfect as any in Paris. When his hand finally slipped back across the sheets to her thigh, she stirred but still said nothing.

Then from the very heart of her silence: "Nicky, I lied to you. I didn't go to the shops this afternoon. I went to see the French consul, Martial Cazeaux."

He shifted slightly so that he could watch her eyes. "Why?"

"Because I wanted to talk to him."

"About what?"

"My status. I believe that's what they call it."

"Margaretha, a man like Cazeaux isn't in a position to tell you anything."

"But he is. He was able to tell me a great deal—"

"Such as?"

She shook her head. "It's too late to explain, Nicky. It's already started. They've already begun spreading the word about me. I told you about the rumors. Now it's worse. I'm not to be trusted. I'm a dangerous spy . . . a spy and a whore."

In a way, the worst of it was that she wasn't even crying. Her voice was strained but her eyes were dry and still on that disk of a moon.

"Margaretha, *listen* to me. You haven't done a damn thing. What's more, they haven't got a case and they know it. So all you have to do is stay away from trouble for a while, and it's all going to pass—"

"No, you listen, Nicky. I'm marked. It won't just go away. Somehow I've got to wash it off. It seems the burden of proof is on me, and I've got to show them where I stand with some kind of positive action. Nicky, I've got to *do* something."

Two trains departed daily from Vigo, one to Madrid and points east in the morning, another along the coast in the evening. Obviously she had checked the schedule that first afternoon because her timing was very good. She had sent him out to fetch breakfast and a newspaper at about half past nine. When he returned he realized that everything must have been arranged in advance with that consul—the ticket, the taxi, the boy to collect her luggage. She had probably even prepared the note beforehand:

"It's not because I've grown tired of you."

Chapter Twenty-Six

T was four o'clock in the afternoon when Gray finally
succeeded in locating the
French consul in Vigo. A warm, dry wind had risen from the south.
The shops were on the verge of closing. The consul was sitting on
the terrace of an old cafe above the bay: a heavy man in a tropical
suit. There was a bottle of rum on the table and newspapers on his
lap. Although he appeared to be reading, his eyes kept following a
slender waitress.

"You're Martial Cazeaux?"

He had the typical thin moustache that drooped at the corners of
his mouth. His fingers were stained with nicotine.

"I'm Cazeaux, yes. Who are you?"

"The one who came with Mata Hari."

"The English painter? Too bad."

A waitress brought Gray a clean glass, and Cazeaux filled it with
rum. His hands looked like white animals, hairless mice that moved
independently of the rest of him. Gray wished he had brought a
knife, something with a serrated edge.

He said, "I understand you saw Margaretha Zelle yesterday."

Cazeaux nodded. "Yes, that's correct."

"What did you tell her?"

"What do you think?" He took out a thin cigar from his coat: rodents toying with a snake. "I shall be frank with you, monsieur. Margaretha Zelle is a very lovely woman. I'm sure she is also very accomodating. At the moment, however, she is in a great deal of trouble."

"And is that what you told her? That she's in a great deal of trouble?"

Cazeaux had bit off the end of the cigar. "Personally I think all this espionage business is farfetched. Your Mata Hari strikes me as a bit obvious to be a German spy. Although I suppose that could be a tactic. Still, as you people say, it seems too clever by half. In any case, it seems that our respective governments feel differently."

"So what did you tell her, Cazeaux?"

"I told her what I am telling you now. She is under grave suspicion and is not to be trusted until such time as she demonstrates her loyalty."

"By doing what?"

"An errand in Madrid. Monsieur, let us be honest with one another. Your government has ideas about how this woman should be investigated. My government felt that these methods were too slow . . . too passive. Consequently I was instructed to—how do you say? —raise the temperature a little."

"What did you tell her to do?"

"The German spymaster of Berlin, Rudolph Spangler, has a man in Madrid. Name is von Kalle. I've never actually met the fellow but apparently he is like his chief in certain respects. That is to say, von Kalle is also very fond of beautiful women. Now we thought it would be very interesting to see what happens if your Mata Hari and this von Kalle were to meet . . ."

"So you sent her to sleep with him, is that it?"

"Please, monsieur, I merely suggested that if she were to gain his confidence based on her earlier friendship with Herr Spangler, and then to exploit that confidence on behalf of the French government

. . . well, obviously, we—my superiors—would see her in a more favorable light."

"Who told you to do this?"

"I can't say."

Gray had taken a mouthful of rum without realizing it. His hand had simply slid to the glass, then the glass to his lips—rum, which it seemed they always doled out before a bad show. He hated the stuff.

"Listen to me, monsieur, I am merely a go-between in this matter. However, it is my strong recommendation that you stay out of it. Yes, I think this would be my advice to you—stay out of it."

"Cazeaux, I think you're lying. I think you've been lying to me, and you lied to Zelle. You sent her to von Kalle because your fop organization doesn't have enough rope to hang her."

"This is very thin ice you are now walking on, monsieur."

"You told her to go out and prove her innocence but in fact you're just trying to prove she's guilty by identifying her with a German espionage base in Madrid."

"You have no idea just how thin the ice is, nor how deep the water is below it—"

"Too *bloody* fancy, monsieur, I also think you lied about your own supposedly minor part in it. I think you're up to your filthy neck in all this, and I think I should probably kill you for it."

After that, he was ushered to the door and told to sleep it off. And thereafter a cable was sent to London.

She saw herself now as a figure in one of her own fantasies, a desperate woman with a mission. Yet as Gray would say, a scheme was not a mission, and the secret world, often indulgent of its own, was vicious to those it used.

She had become a rumor again by the time he reached Madrid. Although she had booked a suite in the Palace Hotel she had mainly been seen at the Ritz. A porter would remember her requesting a copy of the diplomatic yearbook, while a doorman would recall her asking directions to the German embassy—23 Calle Castellan. And an old friend and journalist would admit that she spent at least two hours on Friday afternoon questioning him about a certain Major von Kalle of the German legation.

It was the following Monday when Gray caught up with her again. The backdrop was typically Zelle: a cluttered suite at midnight, champagne in a bucket of lukewarm water, a mess of correspondence on the writing table. She looked lovely in white chiffon, her cheeks flushed from either an excess of rouge or a mild fever.

"You shouldn't have come," she told him. "You shouldn't have followed me."

He was exhausted. Perspiration had ruined his shirt, and too many cigarettes had given him a headache. "I spoke to your Martial Cazeaux," he said.

"Fine. Then you know what I'm doing here."

"I also did some checking on your Major von Kalle."

"Then you know why the French instructed me to meet him."

"For Godsakes, Margaretha, he's a German military attaché."

"But that is the idea. By the way, did you know that he and Rudolph were in school together?"

"How nice for them. But not for you."

There were photographs on the desk, a stack of old publicity shots she must have been carrying for years. "When did you see him? Rudy's boyhood chum?"

"The major? Saturday."

"What did you tell him?"

She had picked up a feather boa, a prop from the make-believe that was her life. "I told him that I was an old friend of Rudy's and I wanted to talk to him about my arrest in London. That I wanted to find out who Clara Benedix is."

"And what did he say?"

"Not much. Anyway, that was only how I managed to get in to see him. After that we talked about . . . a good many things."

"Such as?"

She had draped the boa over her shoulders, and was posing in front of the mirror again. "Rudolph Spangler, submarines, other matters that might save French lives . . . and British." Then, suddenly tossing the boa away and turning: "That's correct, Nicky. I may have obtained information to save—"

"Did you sleep with him?"

"Really, Nicky."

"Did you sleep with von Kalle?"

"Not yet." Once again the coquette in spite of herself.

She had picked up a negligee, held it to her shoulders, then frowned and let it drop away. "Nicky, you don't seem to understand. My entire status has changed. Everything I'm doing now has been sanctioned by the French. As a matter of fact I even sent off my first report today."

"Sent it to whom?"

"Captain Ladoux. I was told to report to him."

He dropped a cigarette in the champagne bucket.

"You're quite right, Margaretha. Your entire status has changed. You see, originally they intended to use you to catch a big fish, possibly even Spangler. Ladoux changed all that. Instead of using you as the bait, they're simply going to serve you up as the main dish. It's all being arranged now. You're to be their real catch of the day—Mata Hari, the spy bitch of Berlin."

She was watching him closely again. "I haven't the faintest idea what you're talking about, Nicky." But she did, she simply couldn't accept it.

"It's simple. The war has been going poorly for our side. The commands have been coming in for criticism. Now the slaughter at the Somme has demanded that heads roll. Better yet, that *a* head rolls. Sixty thousand sods took it at the Somme, twenty thousand dead. Now obviously one can't blame something like that on the generals—bad for morale, worse for the generals. No, you've got to get yourself a bloody scapegoat, someone you can point the finger at and say, 'Look, it wasn't our fault. We were stabbed in the back by a spy.' And everyone knows that the Huns have been using beautiful women to seduce our lads . . . beautiful, scandal-ridden women like yourself."

She was facing the mirror again, but watching her own reflection, not his.

"I know you're only trying to help, Nicky. I know I shouldn't really be angry. But Martial Cazeaux has assured me that—"

"Don't be bloody stupid. Every man doesn't jump through hoops for you. Cazeaux won't even remember talking to you. When the time comes, he won't even remember it—"

"And that's another thing, Nicky. You've always underestimated me. You really have."

"No, I just don't underestimate them. Listen to me. First they send you to Cramer to set the price. Remember his money offer, and you even negotiated it, thinking how you were finally being repaid for your bloody *furs*. Then they send you to Merrick to size you up, and he pronounces you fit and ready. Then it's on to Ladoux to prepare you for the slaughter, and then they send you to me, promising to let me save you if you're innocent. Only they get impatient, annoyed that I'm not producing. And of course they don't trust me. So they gave you to Spangler's man here."

She was half smiling, a smile he was sure she had used in the presence of hopeless lovers.

"The French are giving me an opportunity to clear myself, Nicky, an opportunity that I wanted and intend to take."

"Oh Christ, open your eyes. They're fattening you up for the kill. They don't want you to spy on von Kalle. They just want you to be *seen* with him—the Madrid arm of the spymaster Spangler. Can't you understand that?"

But her eyes were on his in the mirror, while her hands were locked into fists. "I'll tell you what I begin to understand, Nicky. That you've been saying anything to keep me for yourself, in *your* bed. You've tried to turn me against every man I've ever been with, every man with the . . . the means to give me a life— Rolland, Rudolph, Vadime, even Charles—all so you could have me for yourself. I see that you tried to smother me from the first moment we met, from the first time you painted me, *captured* me on your precious canvas." Her voice rose to a shout. "Well, you never just wanted to paint me. You wanted to possess me."

And of course he had to acknowledge to himself that she was

more than a little right. But she was also so wrong, so tragically wrong, not to believe him now . . .

It was about a mile from the Palace to the Bristol, a twisted mile through a warren of half-lit streets. He knew he was feeling ill, with a fever, as he stumbled along, but he did not know how ill he was until he reached his room. Then he lay down on the bed without undressing, and waited for the howitzers to open a barrage in his head. Once again he realized she had been right about him, which made her unable to believe him when her life depended on it.

He shut his eyes, abruptly saw her at her worst, as he detested seeing her: an amateur whore with an excess of rouge. He drew the blankets up to his shivering neck and remembered her at her best: inspired by more than a wealthy man, a woman-child unable to resist taking, and leaving, what she wanted at will. All promiscuity was a search, he supposed, even, perhaps for some sort of martyrdom. Well, love, God help us, you're about to find it. After a lifetime of affairs on your terms you're involved in one with no pity, no bleeding heart. Zelle . . . Zelle . . .

He dozed, with half-formed images of that first afternoon they had met. He slept, then woke again at dawn, to find that nothing had changed.

He stayed in bed for five days. After a physician had been called to give him an injection, he slept through most of it.

Of course Zelle was gone by the time he was well enough to leave his bed . . . presumably waltzing back to Paris in order to collect her reward for having outsmarted German Intelligence. (There was a story told to Gray by a certain Senator Junoy, who had dined with Zelle just before her departure. According to Junoy, Zelle had returned to Paris in a rage after learning that French agents were still spreading the word that she wasn't to be trusted. And as for von

Kalle, he, too, it seemed, no longer was entranced by her after she had refused to undress in his office.)

At any rate she had gone back to Paris, leaving Gray in the midst of another cold spell with nothing except a lingering fever and three or four sketches from their first night together. It also occurred to him that the physician with the sleep-inducing injections might well have been provided by . . . Southerland? Dunbar? Cazeaux? Good fellows all, all patriots in the service of their countries.

After cabling London with a brief description of his circumstances, he waited another whole week before receiving a reply. Then it seemed that they only wanted him back in England . . . presumably to ruin someone else's life.

Chapter Twenty-Seven

T HEY came for her on the morning of February 13, 1917—five inspectors under the command of Police Chief Priolet. Having only just gotten up after a night at the Opera, she received them in her dressing gown. The formal accusation read:

> The woman Zelle, Margaretha, otherwise known as Mata Hari, residing at the Palace Hotel, of Protestant faith and Dutch nationality, five feet eight inches tall, being able to read and write, is accused of espionage, tentative complicity and intelligence with the enemy, in an effort to assist them with their operations.

A photograph was taken shortly after her arrival at La Prison Saint-Lazare, but by then she was scarcely recognizable. Her first cell was padded and very small, hardly more than a closet fitted with stuffed canvas panels. There were no facilities, no furniture, and poor light. Her first visitor was a physician, a Dr. Leon Bizard. (An unusually sympathetic figure, his later memoirs would contain the only factual account of her stay at St. Lazare. All other stories—her insistence upon a daily bath of milk, her attempts to seduce a guard, her outlandish nude ballet—were lies.) Her initial demands were entirely reasonable; she wanted a blanket, the use of a telephone, and a basin of warm water.

The first round of questioning commenced at about one o'clock in the afternoon. She was escorted through a maze of corridors to a third floor room in the chancellery, where she met a lean officer with a large head, arched eyebrows, and a thin mustache. Privately she would call him the "egg man," and compare him to a character from a political cartoon. In fact he was the formidable Captain Pierre Bouchardon, the chief investigating officer. Forty-six years old, he had earned a reputation as a dogged prosecuting attorney in Rouen before accepting the post of *rapporteur militaire*. He was a fiercely conservative, self-denying man with a firm commitment to that element of French society that had always distrusted those from the artistic community.

His office was small, and he complained that with ten or twelve officers meeting to discuss the case, "it felt like the Métro at rush hour." There were two chairs, a desk, and a bookshelf with glass doors. The one window looked out onto the river and a lovely stretch of the Quai de l'Horloge. From the prisoner's chair, however, one saw nothing.

She was tired, exhausted really, and desperately wished they had permitted her to wash. Bouchardon reported that she had entered his office with a "haggard look in her eyes, and bits of hair sticking to her temples." She was not, however, unduly frightened, not in the beginning.

It started on a fairly conversational note:

"Please tell me the story of your life," Bouchardon said. Zelle fumbled with a handkerchief she had found in the sleeve of her dress, Bouchardon with a fountain pen and the ledger that would form the backbone of his case.

She began tentatively, focusing on what she assumed Bouchardon wanted to hear—her relationship with Germans. She said that as an international woman she had never been conscious of political barriers. Naturally the Germans were somewhat gauche, but one could say the same of the Austrians and the Turks.

"And the French?" Bouchardon asked. "How do you like the French?"

She gave him a sigh and said that she liked them less today than usual . . . Politically, she said that she had never given much thought to the Germans until the spring of 1914. Then, and of her own free will, she wrote a lengthy letter to Adolphe Messimy, the French war minister, advising him of certain disturbing rumors she had heard while in Berlin.

"And exactly what was the nature of those rumors?" Bouchardon asked.

"War," she replied. "The nature of those rumors was war . . ."

"So you were acting as a spy on behalf of France even before the outbreak of hostilities. Is that correct?"

"I wouldn't say that I was acting as a spy, captain. Rather I would simply say that Monsieur Messimy is an old friend, and I was acting as a concerned citizen of the Republic."

"But you are not a citizen of the Republic, madame. You are the citizen of a neutral country that has been profitably selling bullets to the belligerents."

"Very well, then, I was acting as a woman who preferred peace to war, who cared about peace . . ."

Describing her later adventures with the Germans in Madrid, it seemed she had come to believe her early fantasies. She said that she had had to use all her wits to outsmart her opponents, as well as a bit of feminine cunning. Despite an apparently simple demeanor, Major von Kalle had actually proved to be a very clever sparring partner. Twice in conversation he had nearly tripped her up . . . all while her hand lay only inches away from a pistol in his desk.

"And precisely how did you know that the major kept a weapon in his desk, madame?"

"From the look in his eyes, captain. I sensed it from the look in his eyes."

"Remarkable. And you still continued to engage him in a danger-ous game of cat and mouse, with a pistol so close."

"My reputation depended on it. My mission. I also knew he possessed important information about the German submarine offensive and I was determined to get that information—"

"And did you?"

"I believe if you read the report that I sent to Captain Ladoux the answer to that question would be apparent."

"Oh, but I have read the report, madame, and I must tell you that your information was worthless—nothing that couldn't have been fabricated from any German newspaper."

"Well, perhaps you should read it again, captain."

"No, I really don't think so."

That afternoon she was trans-ferred to a cell in another section of the prison, at the corner of the rue du Faubourg Saint-Denis and the boulevard Magenta. Locally known as the *ménagérie,* the whole cellblock had been specifically allocated to spies. Conditions were abysmal. The corridors were infested with rats, the pallets with lice. The cell was bitterly cold, with drafts through the apertures. The food was bearable, but she was actually expected to pay for it.

She had two visitors during the first three days: the physician, Bizard, and a Protestant clergyman. Bizard had little to say, while the minister talked about salvation. She had also been given a Bible, a mildewed volume with hundreds of notations in the margins. She read it haphazardly, leafing through pages until she found some psalm or passage familiar from her childhood. She could rarely take it for more than an hour, except late at night when she found herself drawn to Genesis and certain later chapters from Revelations.

Nights were the worst. There was an Alsatian girl, half mad, who sobbed and sang hymns. There were two or three Germans, who also seemed to be out of their minds. There was someone with a mouth organ, and a woman with an incessant cough. Occasionally there were screams.

She returned to Bouchardon on the morning of the fourth day. A cold front the night before had sent the temperature well below freezing, and her fingers were still a little numb. She had also found that her gums had been bleeding, from an absence of fresh fruit, she thought. Bouchardon only noted that she had seemed uneasy on entering the office and seeing a young stenographer, Manuel Baudouin.

Bouchardon had compiled a list of questions from the previous day's testimony, and Zelle soon found herself returning to the middle years and that dismal season in Berlin. The tone, however, was slightly different from that of the previous session. She no longer made an attempt to embellish the insignificant or minimize the rest. Her voice was flat. She kept drawing the handkerchief through her thumb and forefinger.

"At what point did you become aware of Rudolph Spangler's real profession?" Bouchardon asked.

She shook her head. There were also traces of dried blood on the handkerchief that seemed to have no source. "One doesn't become aware of something like that all at once."

"All right, then approximately when did you become aware of his real profession?"

"I suppose it was in Madrid."

"Before you agreed to accompany him to Germany?"

"Yes."

"So then why did you continue the relationship?"

She shook her head again. "Please?"

"If you knew that the man was a German spy, why did you continue to see him. Indeed, why did you agree to accompany him to Berlin?"

She heard herself say, "I must have thought I was in love. I tend to do that . . ."

"You must have thought you were in love? Very well, then at what point were you not in love with him?"

"I don't know."

"Was it after he had arrested your Englishman, the painter Nicholas Gray?"

She shrugged, still looking down at that handkerchief in her hands . . . Nicky had said that white was really the most deceptive color—

"Was it after he had arrested your English—"

"*Yes.*"

"But if your relationship with Rudolph Spangler had ended with the arrest of Nicholas Gray, then how were you later able to persuade Herr Spangler to release Mr. Gray? Please, tell me how this was achieved."

She stared at them for a moment . . . Bouchardon, so apparently relaxed behind deepset eyes, the young stenographer with his fountain pen poised above the ledger. "I'm afraid . . . I'm afraid that I don't . . . I don't understand."

"But the question is simple enough, madame. If you had severed your relationship with Spangler on the arrest of Gray, then how were you able to later revive that relationship and obtain the prisoner's freedom?"

"I don't know, I'm not sure . . ."

Money seemed to be the next topic of interest. Bouchardon began by explaining, "We know that you accepted twenty thousand francs from the German spymaster Karl Cramer. Now perhaps you can tell us a little about that arrangement."

"I accepted the money because the Germans had taken my furs."

"Your furs?"

"When I left Berlin in the summer of 1914 my furs had been confiscated at the German border. I felt it was only fair that I take Herr Cramer's money as a reimbursement."

"But surely Herr Cramer had not given you the money as a reimbursement."

"No."

"He gave you the money as an advance payment for services rendered in Paris . . . services rendered as an intelligence agent for the German war machine. Isn't *that* correct?"

She nodded, watching the stenographer's fountain pen jumping to the paper again. "Yes, the money was to have been an advance."

"But you only took it for your furs, is that correct?"

"Yes, my furs."

"Then why did you also accept three bottles of professional ink?"

For a moment she couldn't seem to form the words. "Professional ink?"

"Secret ink. Invisible ink. You know what I'm talking about, madame."

"But I threw it overboard." As though her former private act of defiance was universally known.

Bouchardon had removed a pale-gray envelope from his desk. She supposed that it must have been waiting for her from the start . . . a pale-gray envelope and three or four typewritten pages.

"We have done a detailed chemical analysis of certain personal possessions found in your room. Among these items was a small vial containing oxycyanide of mercury. Further experiments revealed that this substance can be quite successfully used for the transcription of—"

She shut her eyes. "It's a disinfectant, monsieur."

"A what?"

"A *disinfectant.*"

"Ah, a disinfectant. And you purchased this disinfectant for what purpose? You were a little careless perhaps in the bathroom? There had been a small accident with a razor perhaps?"

Eyes still shut tight: "To prevent pregnancy."

"To prevent pregnancy? Is that what you said, madame?" Then turning to the stenographer, "Is that what she said? To prevent pregnancy? This vial of oxycyanide of mercury is a substance to prevent—"

"To be applied after . . . after, to prevent pregnancy."

"Ah, I see. Well, that certainly explains everything, doesn't it?"

And finally the theme became suspicion. Bouchardon had gotten up from his chair and moved to the window. For a moment he appeared to be watching something below—a passing barge? A tree in the breeze? Wind breaking on water?

Then, rather dramatically—he was French, after all—spinning around to face her again: "Tell me how you felt when you first became aware that you were under suspicion of being a German spy?"

She felt her shoulders rising for another shrug, lips parting to say that she didn't understand. "How I felt?"

"Yes. How did you *feel* when you first learned that you were suspected of collaborating with the enemy?"

"I suppose I . . ." She shook her head.

"Well, come now. What was it? Anger? Fear? Anxiety? What?"

"Anxiety . . . ?"

"I'm sorry, I didn't hear that."

"I said anxiety."

"About what people would say? Friends and so forth?"

"Yes, I suppose so."

"So you were anxious about your *social* standing. You have just learned that you are suspected of being a spy, and you're anxious about your *social* standing." He turned back to the window, tapped a nail against the glass. "Be honest with me, madame. Wouldn't you agree that our river is far more beautiful than the Rhine?"

She looked at her hands. Somehow that handkerchief had knotted itself around her fingers like a tourniquet, leaving the joints white. "Please?"

"The river, madame. The Seine. Wouldn't you agree that it's far more beautiful than the Rhine?"

"Yes, oh yes . . ."

"Even at its worst, far more beautiful?"

"Yes."

Then suddenly turning again, voice rising: "Where do you think you are, madame? Just where in the world do you think you are?"

She watched his face blur through tears. "Here."

"That's right. You are *here*. Now, you say you were worried about your precious reputation when you realized that they thought you were a spy. And is that why you went to see von Kalle in Madrid? In order to save your reputation?"

She had managed to loosen the handkerchief from her fingers . . . a small victory. "I had been advised that if I were to secure information on von Kalle it would end all the suspicion against me."

"And who exactly advised you of this? Martial Cazeaux?"

"Yes."

"So the consul in Vigo advised you that if you were to spy successfully on von Kalle, all official doubts concerning your loyalty to France would end. Now is that correct?"

"Yes."

"And you believed this man?"

"I had no reason not to . . ."

"What about your companion, Nicholas Gray? Did you not admit just the other day that he had had doubts about the consul's advice? Indeed, he had even tried to keep you from seeing von Kalle."

"I thought at the time that Nicholas had other reasons for wanting me to stay away from Madrid."

"So you ignored your companion Nicholas Gray, and proceeded to von Kalle on the consul's advice, correct?"

"Yes."

"You proceeded to spy on von Kalle because Martial Cazeaux had told you that that was the way to clear your name, correct?"

She took a deep breath, tasting more blood in her mouth. I need citrus, she thought, I must have citrus . . .

"You proceeded to spy on von Kalle because Martial Cazeaux had told you that—"

"Yes."

He returned to the chair, leaning forward across the desk. The egg man.

"Well, listen to this, madame. I have received a complete report from Martial Cazeaux, and he does not so much as recall seeing you in Vigo. In fact he recalls only meeting you once, and that was in Paris a long, long time ago."

Shortly after this interrogation she wrote a letter in pencil, addressed to Bouchardon:

> My suffering is too terrible. My head cannot bear it any longer. Let me go back to my country. I know nothing about your war, and have never known anything more

than was written in the newspapers. I have asked no one and gone nowhere for information. What more do you want me to say?

The letter was signed, "Respectfully yours, M. Zelle", and included her prisoner's identification number: 721 44625. It was routed by hand to Bouchardon and routinely placed in her file.

She heard nothing for two days. Then, on a Thursday, she was awakened at dawn and led to a courtyard behind the rear entrance. Although she had heard that executions were occasionally held here, she had also heard that prisoners were sometimes released from this point. The walls were twenty feet high, but one could clearly see a portion of the back street through the bars of the gate: the ranks of blackened tenements, the balconies and fire escapes.

She had been escorted from her cell by one of the younger guards, a quiet fellow who was said to have lost part of his stomach at Verdun. Although he hadn't spoken to her, she was almost certain that she had seen the suggestion of a smile on his lips. She had also heard voices from beyond the wall, then footsteps on the outer staircase. Finally she even thought she caught a glimpse of freedom . . . with Nicky and a car to take her far away.

But it was not Nicky. It was Tommy Merrick, and he had obviously come on foot.

He faced her through the bars of the gate, a small brown parcel under his arm, a little paler than she remembered. The guard approached first, but only to accept a bribe, not to unlock the gate. Then he stepped back and motioned her forward. Merrick had extended his arm through the bars, presumably to take her hand. Somehow she couldn't bring herself to touch him.

"I can only stay a few minutes," he said.

"Then why did you take the trouble at all?"

All his weight was on his left leg, presumably because they had failed with that right knee.

"Margaretha, I swear I never knew this would happen. They just wanted me to get to know you."

"And to make love to me? To ask me to marry you?"

"Margaretha, I swear . . ."

She glanced back at the far wall, and the first patch of sunlight in days. There was a scent of rain on the breeze, a deeper scent of the river.

"Who hired you, Tommy?"

"It doesn't matter."

"Who?"

"Charles Dunbar."

"And what did he tell you to do?"

"He wanted me to find out who you were spying for. Look, I'm sorry, I really didn't know this would happen."

She glanced at his hands tightening on the bar, then at the parcel under his arm. "What's that?"

"A gift. I mean a real gift. They didn't tell me to bring it." Then, thrusting the parcel through the bars: "I know it's not much, but you said you liked this sort of thing."

She took it without looking. "Thank you."

"And if there's anything else I can do. Anything at all . . ."

She glanced back over her shoulder again, then took a step closer. "There's someone I want you to find for me."

"Anything."

"I told you about him before. Nicholas Gray. I think he's in London."

"London?"

"Find him. Find him and write to him for me. Tell him what's happened."

"But I'm still—"

"Please. Just do it."

The parcel that Merrick had given her contained a thin volume of Indian verse from the *Bhagavad-Gita*, the Song of God. An English translation by Sir Edwin Arnold, the work was actually quite far from the original Sanskrit. There were, however, several lovely illustrations and a number of passages relating to a subject that had always intrigued her—reincarnation. At first she concealed the book beneath her cot; then, fearing a search of her cell, she finally opened an end of the pallet and stuffed it deep inside the infested straw.

Chapter Twenty-Eight

T was the sort of place that one would never have frequented before the war: checked tablecloths, candlesticks stuck in wine bottles, crossed oars above the bar. The waiter was a dull fellow, possibly another shell-shock case. The only other patrons were prostitutes and soldiers. Through torn curtains lay a view of a boulevard and a platoon of clerks and typists waiting for a tram.

Gray arrived at five. A half-hour later Southerland joined him— looking very pale in a black overcoat and homburg, left eye slightly inflamed. Merrick's letter lay between them on the table. They had ordered beer but it was flat and warm, so they turned back to brandy.

"She hasn't been abused," Southerland said. "That's all I can tell you at this point. They haven't physically abused her—"

"What provoked the arrest?"

"I don't know . . . everything, I suppose."

"Her visit to Spangler's man in Madrid?"

"Seems likely."

"The money she took from Cramer?"

"That too."

"The Somme? That *especially?*"

Southerland signaled the waiter for another glass. "Look, it's not my show. In fact I only just heard about the arrest myself, and frankly I'm as disgusted with the whole affair as you. That may be hard for you to believe, but—"

Gray waved him off. This was their first real conversation since Gray's return from Madrid: this Tuesday afternoon, this London bar along the riverfront, this last movement of Margaretha's story.

"You must try to understand the situation," Southerland went on. "She's precisely the sort of woman that the public *wants* to see as a German spy. She's beautiful in a too obvious way. She spends a lot of time in bed with various men. She takes off her clothing in public and receives a lot of money for it. She thumbs her nose at society and calls herself an artist. That sort of behavior might have been acceptable before the war, but not now. People are too serious now . . ."

"So what exactly are the charges?" Gray wasn't interested in what he considered Southerland's self-serving exegesis.

Southerland shrugged. "Sinking ships, poisoning wells . . . it's really immaterial. The fact is we took a terrible beating at the Somme, the command look like blundering fools. They need a head for the pike."

"Whose idea was it to send her to von Kalle?"

"Ladoux's."

"And who fixed her up with Cramer?"

"Dunbar."

"Then if it was all set up from the start, why the bloody hell did you even bother sending me to Spain with her?"

"Because I was bloody stupid." Then, signaling to the waiter again, "Look, in the beginning I actually thought it was a legitimate investigation. Dunbar, however, had a different viewpoint, Ladoux still another, though for both she was the target."

"And now?"

"Now it seems they've managed to coordinate their plans, and I'm afraid there's nothing you and I can do . . ."

They paid the bill and began to walk. "For whatever it's worth," Southerland said, "I believe the evidence is still only circumstantial. They have her taking money from people with the wrong bankers, and they have her meeting with von Kalle. They don't actually have anything concrete, not so far as I can tell—"

"Does it make a difference?"

"I think so. After all, one still must convince a judge."

"When does she go to trial?"

"I'm not sure. Two or three months, perhaps four."

"Then we still have time."

"Time for what?"

"To prove she's innocent, of course."

They had come to a window display of ornamental dolls, some porcelain, some wooden. One was armless, another had lost the glass eyes.

"Honestly, Nicky, it's out of our hands now. I don't even think you could get in to see her—"

"I don't *want* to see her, Martin. I want to prove her *innocence.*"

"Well, I'm afraid that you're not in a position to do that."

"No? What sort of files does Dunbar have on her? His Mata Hari file. What's it like?"

"Massive."

"Where does he keep it?"

Southerland shook his head.

"Where does he keep the file, Martin?"

"In his office . . . and locked up."

"Do you have a key?"

"No."

"Can you get one?"

Southerland was watching with the sympathetic look one might have used to deal with the wounded or dying. "Nicky, I'm telling you the truth. There's nothing anyone can do."

"How can we possibly know that until we've seen Dunbar's files? How can we possibly know anything until we've seen his files and determined what sort of case he's built?"

"Nicky, please—"

"You owe this to me, Martin. You owe this to me for what happened in Berlin."

"Nicky, for Godsakes."

"And if nothing else, I owe it to her for getting me out of Berlin. Out of that damn prison . . ." And for more, much more. For being Margaretha . . .

It would all be in Dunbar's files, he told himself. Every myth that would later condemn her, every rumor that she would never outlive: her "insidious" relationship with Spangler, her "treachery" at the Somme and Verdun, her role in the failure of Ypres, her convoluted, "immoral" life as a spy— all methodically noted in the files.

"Charles is quite mad. I never actually realized," Gray said.

It was dawn the following day. Gray had spent nearly six unbroken hours in Dunbar's office, while Southerland had waited in the adjoining room. To avoid the morning security check they had hurried from the Richmond annex and returned to the streets.

"And if I'm not mistaken," Gray went on, "he's still obsessed with her. What's in those files tells his story more than hers."

Southerland remained unmoved, very tired again. "As long as you realize that I can't let you use anything that you saw last night, we shouldn't—"

"No point in using it, Martin. Not in a court. Belongs in a clinic. Dunbar hasn't chronicled a conspiracy. He's chronicled an illness. His illness. In addition to his real grievances against her, he's convinced himself that she's out to destroy him . . . personally destroy him. So what more reasonable, to him, that he get her first . . ."

"Nor can you ever discuss the content of that file with anyone other than—"

"No point in that either. The 'case' is pretty damn thorough. Might even hold up in court."

"Well, I'm certain that given an equally thorough defense—"

"Ah, but that's where Charles has been especially clever. You see, he's already begun cutting off her means of defense. Already begun covering the trail."

They began to walk, moving past another rank of vacant shops. Street cries came up through the cold air: old clothes, apples, a man who wanted chairs to mend.

"Tell me something," Gray said abruptly, "what do you know about the telegraphic intercepts between Berlin and Madrid?"

Southerland had paused to turn up the collar of his overcoat— "I don't follow."

"Apparently a major part of Dunbar's case against her now rests on a series of intercepted telegrams between von Kalle in Madrid and Spangler in Berlin. He mentions them twice in memos to Ladoux, and makes a great to-do of them in a note to the Admiralty."

"What's the context?"

Gray shook his head. "I only know that he seems to feel that they're somehow conclusive."

"He could of course be lying—advertising a minor piece of evidence to keep the case moving."

"He could also be measuring her for the stake. Martin, I need a few more weeks. I need a pass, and a few weeks abroad."

Southerland was gazing out across the empty road and shaking his head. "You don't seem to understand, do you? Even if they permitted you to see her—"

"Not to see Zelle, Martin. I want to talk to Rudolph Spangler."

Southerland was glancing at the tenements around him—rows of windows shattered in a zeppelin raid, a dozen yards of scorched pavement. "For Godsake, Nicky, try to face it—"

"And see if you can't get me a copy of those telegrams."

Gray spent the rest of that afternoon getting ready. He destroyed compromising notes and drawings. He emptied drawers and packed a suitcase. He withdrew the bulk of his savings. He kept himself from drinking. Although there may have been no need to shed shoulder flashes, he could not keep himself from habitually cleaning the weapons—an American .45 automatic, and that serrated bayonet.

When he was done he sat down at a table and wrote to her.

Dear Margaretha, after all the things that we have done . . .

He included a drawing of a cat on a chair in a sunlit room. He supposed that they would never let her have the letter, but at least they might let her have the drawing. After all, what would be the point of denying her a harmless sketch from a harmless English lover?

Chapter Twenty-Nine

THE telegrams alluded to in Dunbar's file were not actually entered as evidence until the fourth week of March. Bouchardon has left the most detailed account of the day in his 1954 memoirs, *Souvenirs.* The investigation, he wrote, had more or less stalled when the War Ministry propitiously submitted the text of several cables obtained and decoded with the help of a British liaison team and facilities on top of the Eiffel Tower. The telegrams purported to constitute an exchange between von Kalle in Madrid and Rudolph Spangler in Berlin. Although Mata Hari was not specifically mentioned by name, her alleged German identity code appears: H–21. There were also a number of obvious references to information she had supposedly passed to von Kalle, as well as a direct reference to her "infiltration" of the French intelligence service.

It was about ten in the morning when Bouchardon confronted Zelle with the text of the first two telegrams. Recalling the day, he would note, "Since I had to play a careful game, I closed my door to everyone, spreading the news that I had gone to a prison in

Fresnes for some hearing. Thus while the press was looking for me elsewhere, I prepared myself to meet Mata Hari with the convicting evidence of the Third War Council."

It was a warm day, a premature taste of June in the depths of March. Bouchardon's office was dark: the blinds lowered, the lamp light trained on the prisoner's chair. On entering the room she also noticed that his desk had been cleared of everything except a plain brown folder.

Bouchardon began on a seemingly minor point: "You mentioned in a previous session that you were not able to tell the German military attaché von Kalle anything because you knew nothing of importance. Is that correct?"

She nodded. "I don't recall specifically having said that, captain, but it is correct."

"And is it also correct that you approached von Kalle under the pretense of clearing up a misunderstanding that led to your detention in London?"

"Yes."

Bouchardon then laid a sheet of blank stationery and a pencil on the desk in front of her. He had still not touched the folder.

"Let me offer you some advice, madame. A full confession at this point would save us both a great deal of time and trouble."

"I'm afraid I don't know what you're talking about, captain."

Then, finally—and rather melodramatically—opening that brown folder: "I am talking about material evidence of your guilt, madame. I'm talking about this."

There were three typewritten pages in the folder, but Bouchardon removed only one. He would later refer to this page as his "trump card," then still later as the "death warrant." He would also note that he had deliberately memorized the text in order to watch the small changes in her facial expression as he spoke.

"December thirteenth. von Kalle to Spangler. 'Agent H–21 of Central Information has arrived here requesting funds and instructions. She has feigned to accept services of French Espionage Bureau and to carry out trial mission on their account. She intended to travel from Spain to Holland aboard the *Hollandia*, but was arrested in Falmouth when mistaken for another. Once error was recognized, she returned to Spain because of continued British mistrust. Now requests advice and operational assistance.' "

She remained still, betraying not the slightest emotion. "I believe that there has been an error, captain. Yes, there must have been an error."

"I hardly think so, madame."

"Then a joke. Someone is playing a dreadful joke."

"No joke either."

"Then someone is lying. Yes, someone is maliciously lying."

"No, madame. You are the only one who is lying. Yes, you."

Next Bouchardon proceeded to read the text of the second cable: "December fourteenth, 1916. Spangler's response to von Kalle. 'Agent H–21 to proceed to Paris and continue assignment. Will receive five thousand francs from Cramer on Comptoir d'Escompte.' "

She remained silent, unmoving. Bouchardon would later note that she had been weeping, but actually the tears did not come until later. Indeed, at this point she could not have appeared more in control.

"As I told you before, captain. The five thousand francs I received upon returning from Madrid was a loan from a friend in The Hague."

"A loan, madame?"

"A gift, then."

"And precisely who is this friend in The Hague?"

"The Baron Edouard van der Capellen."

"Ah, so the Baron Edouard van der Capellen sent you five thousand francs despite the fact that you had previously left him for the arms of another man."

"He has always been very kind and understanding."

"Yes, obviously very kind and understanding. What a pity that we all can't be so kind and understanding of traitors and whores."

"I have wounded her," Bouchardon told a colleague. "I have not succeeded in bringing her down, but I have drawn the first blood."

And he was right.

She tended to live deep within herself after that critical morning in March. She lay on her cot for hours on end. She moved and spoke as if in a disconnected trance. She ate very little, slept only in short restless fits. She tended to weep without provocation and be inordinately concerned with otherwise meaningless details. Dr. Bizard noted that she seemed to have almost lost the will to survive, and prescribed a daily ration of wine coupled with twenty-five minutes of exercise in the compound. It did not seem to help.

Throughout the long afternoons and endless nights it appeared that her only comfort was that slender translation from the *Bhagavad-Gita*. She may not have understood such things in it as curious references to eternity as a circle, existence as an extinguished flame, time as a myth, but the essential message seemed pretty clear—they could break her legs, but they could not keep her from dancing.

Also from this same week in March was a second letter to Bouchardon, an at once penetrating and poignant letter:

> I realize that your new evidence seems to resolve this case for you. But if I could examine the date and text of these telegrams I feel that I might be able to satisfy your doubts about me. I look forward to your reply, and hope to see you very soon.

Once again, however, there was no reply, and more than seven days passed before she was again brought to Bouchardon. Then it seemed that all he wanted to discuss was her systematic betrayal of British Intelligence, and her insidious affair with Rudolph Spangler.

Chapter Thirty

AMONG the questions submitted to Zelle were the matters of Rudolph Spangler's secret espionage center in Berlin and of the secret identity he used in Paris when briefing and debriefing his French agents. In fact, the German intelligence effort was at this time still headed by Walter Nicolai, and as for Spangler's secret French identity—he was actually living quite openly in Geneva as an art dealer named Otto Broome . . .

He generally began his days early here, rising at about seven for a brisk morning walk along the quai des Bergues. After a light breakfast in his hotel he would walk again, weather permitting, to a cramped gallery south of the canal. There he would conduct his ostensible business until five or six in the evening. The only women in his life were an occasional prostitute or a chance encounter from the cafes. His agents—and there were about thirty at this point— were mainly serviced at night in a nondescript house off the Grand-Rue.

The Last Year

Like any spy in a foreign city, Spangler depended for his survival here largely on a strict adherence to dozens of small precautionary measures. He always made a point, for example, of comparing faces in crowds to his memory of faces in restaurants where he dined. He made a point of noting the faces of guests in the hotel where he lived, and of the neighbors surrounding the house where he conducted his secret life. He never left that house without wedging matchsticks above and below the lock, just as he never entered without pausing a moment to listen at the door. Although he rarely carried a pistol, he did carry a deceptively heavy stick—not unlike the stick he had once used on Gray.

The stick was ebony, and weighted with a lead rod. The ferrule was steel, tapered to a point. The handle was brass and detached to reveal an eight-inch dagger. In moments of stress Spangler maintained a low grip so as to wield the thing like a club . . .

He held it in this fashion now as he approached the house off the Grand-Rue to draft a report about an agent in Milan. Although nothing specifically had alarmed him, the approach to this house had always left him uneasy, particularly at night when the darkness collected in the back streets. He also disliked the garden entrance with its two flights of unlit stairs to the gate. Yet he felt most vulnerable along the last passage to the door—a twisted flagstone walk beneath shadowy junipers.

So he held the stick low in his right hand, watching for a sign in the blackness . . . the branch that became an arm, the clustered vines that became a face.

Gray, however, remained as still, as faceless as any fallen tree until Spangler was all but on top of him. Then, stepping out like any shadow from the trenches, he brought up his knee into Spangler's groin.

Spangler was able to sit, but only if he leaned forward. He held both hands in front of him, his forearms jammed into his lap. Gray watched him from across the room, the .45 automatic leveled at the chest. The house was dark and cold, clearly no one's home. The furniture consisted of a circular dining table, four chairs, a decaying sofa, and a wall of empty shelves. There was whisky and soda on a sideboard, which Gray eventually poured for the two of them.

Gray began with a catechism. Was Spangler meeting an agent tonight? Had he brought a boy to watch the streets? Was there a second entrance and if so where did it lead? What were the safety signals?

Through it all Spangler remained motionless. His face was pale and studded with perspiration.

"I suppose it was stupid of me not to have expected you," he said. "When I began to realize that someone was tracking me down I should have expected it was you—still carrying what I believe is called the torch for your Mata Hari."

Gray lowered his automatic. "She's been arrested. They're holding her at Saint-Lazare."

"But of course she's been arrested. What did you expect?"

"The case is based on some telegrams . . . telegrams between you and one of your idiots in Madrid."

"Yes, Major von Kalle. Actually a fine gentleman. And very competent."

"I want to know the truth, Spangler. Right now."

Spangler took a deep breath and pointed to a pack of cigarettes on the sideboard—another exotic Turkish blend. "May I? thank you . . . I believe it probably dates back—oh, I don't know—thousands of years. When the kingdom has been afflicted, a scapegoat must be found. I seem to recall reading that the practice was quite common during the great plagues. The land was overrun with death, and consequently scapegoats were sacrificed—generally women were burned as witches to rid the land of evil. Now, of course, it's somewhat more complex, but the theory is the same. As well, in this instance, as the practice. England and France have been afflicted by disaster, and now your Mata Hari must be burned at the stake."

Gray moved to the sofa but kept the automatic on his knee. "Tell me about von Kalle."

"The major was a political appointment, but capable, as I said.

Yes, capable but not especially subtle. Frankly I prefer dealing with his junior."

"What about the telegram you sent him?"

Spangler grinned, shaking his head. "You still fail to grasp it. The abstract painter still fails to grasp the obvious symbolism. These details are meaningless. The case against Mata Hari doesn't rest on evidence. It's a matter of *convenience.* A miscalculation was made by your generals at the Somme, and now Mata Hari is to be the ready-made scapegoat. The convenience."

"And Rudolph Spangler? How does Rudolph Spangler feel about that?"

"Ambivalent. Distressed for Margaretha. But, after all, they might well have arrested one of my valuable agents instead of an exotic dancer. That would not be a good tradeoff."

Gray had moved to the window, drawing back the edge of the curtain. The street below was like a black river between cliffs of tenements. Behind him Spangler was still smoking, elbows resting easily on the arm of his chair.

"Despite your memories of that prison," he now said, "I am not actually a callous man. Indeed, there are those who find me positively sentimental. Look here, what can I possibly do for the woman? Offer them my word as a German officer and gentleman that she was never my spy? Petition Charles Dunbar or Georges Ladoux? I think there would be a slight problem of credibility, don't you?"

Gray had crossed the room again to the sideboard, poured another two fingers of whiskey and tossed it down. His right hand still held the automatic, but the hand felt numb, useless.

Then, turning and raising the weapon again: "Tell me about the telegrams. Tell me about what you cabled to von Kalle."

Spangler braced himself against the table to rise to his feet. "Come into the bedroom, Nicholas. I want to show you something."

"The telegrams—"

"No, first let me show you. Otherwise you'll never believe me. Come into the bedroom, please."

The bedroom lay in darkness off the sitting room. It was a long and narrow plaster cell with only the barest necessities: bed, dresser, reading lamp.

"Of course I'm basically a German monster," Spangler was saying as he groped for the light. "And of course I took advantage of the woman. But that doesn't mean I never cared for her, or continue to care in my own peculiar fashion—as you can plainly see."

Except that the light was so feeble Gray saw only a hint of something, a thin memory of a haunting face on the wall.

"There." Spangler's voice was a whisper. "There, you see? I still have it. Purchased more than a decade ago from poor Rolland Michard's estate, and I still have it—your very first portrait of our dancer."

He had even hung the thing opposite the bed, no doubt to inspire dreams.

"And as for your telegrams, Nicky, I suggest you look elsewhere, because I never sent a telegram regarding Mata Hari. I may be a German beast, but even German beasts have certain sentimental feelings when it comes to a woman like Zelle."

He left Geneva in the morning, after cabling Southerland to meet him in Paris, and collecting a copy of those Mata Hari telegrams from the hotel safe. At first the train was crowded, and he found himself sharing a compartment with a salesman from Berne. Closer to the border, however, he found himself alone. For a time he dozed, lulled by more whisky and the clatter of wheels. Then, finally laying the flask aside, he withdrew those telegrams and a cheap canvas notebook he had purchased for a penny at the station.

It is possible that this penny notebook still exists somewhere in British archives: blue with an embossed silhouette of a scribe on the cover. It is also possible that Gray's supplementary tools still exist: his transcript of the telegrams, an old schedule of trains, his magnifying glass, and a pocket calendar for 1916. The true meaning of these items has been lost—at least until now.

Chapter Thirty-One

GRAY'S notebook contained a chronology, an unflinching look at Zelle's last eight weeks of freedom. The first entry concerned London and that tentative reunion on the seventeenth of November. The last concerned her arrest on the thirteenth of February. In between lay dozens of notations concerning what Gray would describe as Dunbar's parting kiss—those controversial Mata Hari telegrams.

There were six telegrams to cement the case against Zelle, but Gray talked mostly about the first. He and Southerland had reached Paris within a day of one another, and met in the Tuileries. It was a beautiful morning. The air was fresh after the night's warm wind. The trees were filled with new buds. Gray was back in uniform, Southerland wore his April tweeds. The surrounding gardens were empty except for the elderly attendants.

"So, how is Herr Rudy?" Southerland asked as they sank to a bench beneath the poplars.

"Useless, I'm afraid."

317

"You should have killed him anyway. You should have put a bullet right between his eyes."

Gray ignored it. "Martin . . . I'll want to see her when we're through here. Even if it's only for a few minutes, I want to see her."

"I don't know if that's possible, Nicky. I told you before, she's not—"

"Just arrange it." Then, withdrawing the blue canvas notebook again, "Not that she's going to be in there much longer. I can promise you that."

Gray had filled thirty pages in that notebook with assorted observations and conclusions. There were also two or three crude maps of Spain and a few idle sketches of trees that he had made while his mind had been elsewhere.

"We might as well start with Spangler," Gray said. "For whatever it's worth to you, we might as well start with what he said."

"Oh, I can tell you what it's worth to me, Nicky."

But Gray again ignored him. "I've also made some notes about von Kalle. The fact is, Spangler never sent a telegram to Von Kalle, and von Kalle never sent one to Spangler. There may have been a few routine inquiries between Berlin and von Kalle, but Spangler wasn't involved."

Southerland took a deep breath. He was bent over, elbows resting on his knees. "I suppose you realize that the second-hand testimony of Rudolph Spangler, German spy, is hardly admissible evidence."

"He wasn't lying, Martin. He may have used Margaretha against us at one time, but he wasn't lying to me."

"Even if so, how can you possibly expect a court to believe—"

"There's also the matter of von Kalle's status. Spangler said he doesn't even deal with the man unless it's unavoidable."

"Nicky, listen to me. Spangler has made a career of lying, and those telegrams are—"

"Fakes, Martin. *The telegrams are fakes.*"

Gray turned to the last of those thirty pages. The page had been divided into two columns—days of the week recorded on the left, notations on Zelle's movements recorded on the right. There were also supplementary notations about the departure of trains from Vigo.

"I was baffled at first," Gray said. "True, the text seemed a little obvious, but there it was just the same . . . agent H–21 and all the rest of it . . . they'd even gotten the name of the bloody ship right, and the five thousand she'd collected in Paris—"

"Which is an incontestable fact," Southerland put in. "You realize that, don't you? She definitely picked up a check for five thousand."

"Right. It was from her Amsterdam baron." Gray quickly turned to an earlier page. "She also borrowed a few pesetas in Madrid, but none of that matters. What matters are the *dates.*"

Southerland pressed his palms to his eyes. "It's a long road now, Nicky. What happens if you don't reach the end?"

"Already reached it, Martin. That's why we're sitting here." Then, suddenly shutting the notebook again . . . "Listen to me very carefully. It's the end of the first week in December. Zelle and I have just landed in Vigo. Without warning Cazeaux turns up and gives her some story about how she has to turn von Kalle inside out in order to clear her name. The next day she's on her way to Madrid, and arrives on a Friday—Friday morning to be exact. That afternoon she sends a note to von Kalle, and by Saturday they're actually meeting. Now, of course—"

"Nicky, I realize that you've been—"

"Saturday was the sixteenth, Martin. December sixteenth. Even if she had seen von Kalle on a Friday, that's still only the fifteenth."

Southerland shook his head. "I fail to see how—"

"Martin, the first telegram is dated December *thirteenth. Wednesday, December thirteenth.* Von Kalle supposedly informed Spangler of her arrival in Madrid on December thirteenth, but she didn't actually arrive until the fifteenth, and von Kalle didn't know it until the sixteenth."

"Well, perhaps she wired in advance from Vigo."

" 'Agent H–21 has arrived . . .' "

"Then perhaps von Kalle simply got the dates wrong."

"Martin, it was fixed, manufactured, and you know it. They

couldn't build a legitimate case against her, so they forged the evidence. Only they mucked up the dates. They mucked it up by forty-eight hours."

They began to walk now—without even discussing it. They simply started following one of those shadowy paths that Gray could never disassociate from Zelle. She was also part of the shuttered stillness, and of the breeze that rose up suddenly from nowhere.

"Why do you suppose that none of this occurred to her when she was questioned by Bouchardon?" Southerland asked him.

"Do *you* recall how you spent last December thirteenth?"

They had entered one of the floral groves filled with tulips and spidery ferns. She also might have been waiting here, peering out of the ivy or sculptured hedgerows.

"If you're right," Southerland said, "and I'm not saying you are or aren't . . . but if you are, how would you . . . we . . . proceed?"

"Look, I know it's still equivocal at this point. We've got enough to raise questions, but a biased court still might not believe us. We need more proof—irrefutable proof."

"A witness?"

"If possible. Where is Dunbar holding court these days?"

"They've given him a suite of rooms on the Saint-Germain, but he also works out of his hotel room at the Continental."

"And what exactly does he do?"

"Technical liaison."

"With Ladoux?"

"For the most part, yes."

"Who processes the intercepts?"

"It's a joint effort. Ladoux's people handle the practical end. Dunbar's people do the decoding."

"Roughly how many people are we talking about? I mean on Dunbar's end."

"Ten, maybe twelve."

"Anyone you can trust?"

"I'm not sure."

They had reached a second grove, darker than the first. There were toadstools among the shadows and long fingers of fresh moss.

"There have to be others who know," Gray said. "Someone in the coding room, a translator, even a bloody typist . . . If Dunbar forged a cable then there *must* be someone else who knows about it."

Southerland sighed. "I suppose I could check the duty roster. Might give us a clue as to who was manning the desk. I also imagine there must be some sort of record, even if only to keep the sequence straight."

"And see if you can't find out about Bouchardon. He's obviously lying too."

Now they had drawn up to the edge of a lily-clotted pond where tadpoles were breaking the surface.

"You've really come to hate him, haven't you?" Southerland said.

"Dunbar? It's not as simple as hate."

"Well, by God I hate him. I think I have for years. My excuse, I suppose, is that one isn't *supposed* to hate one's colleagues . . . particularly in time of war. That's what's so bloody upsetting about this Mata Hari business. She's turned everything upside down. You're meeting with Spangler for cocktails, and I'm pulling the rug out from under the Paris liaison—upside down."

"I wouldn't let it bother you, Martin. Dunbar started this game, not us."

"Yes . . . so it seems . . . Look, if you still insist on seeing the woman, we should probably get a move on."

It was not until five in the afternoon that Southerland succeeded in arranging a meeting between Gray and Mata Hari—and then they were only given fifteen minutes. It took place in the same disused courtyard where Zelle had met with Merrick. It was the cooling end of an unusually warm day, and the pavement was cleanly divided into sections of blue and black shadows.

There were four flights of stairs from the street, then another narrow staircase to the courtyard gate. Zelle was standing in the last patch of sunlight between the walls. A guard was smoking behind her in the shadow. She wore a plain cotton dress and wool stockings, and was holding a blanket tight around her. Her hair had been tied with a bit of string, but several stray locks still fell free.

The gate remained locked. There was nothing anyone could do about the gate, but by reaching through the bars he was still able to embrace her.

"How are you?"

She forced a smile. "I got your drawing."

"What about the letter?"

She shook her head. "They just gave me the drawing of the cat." Then, reaching through the bars again, and brushing away her tears, "Well, the cat was all that mattered anyway."

She let her head fall against the bars, and he caught the scent from her hair, smelling of that cheap disinfectant they used to inhibit lice.

"Nicky, I want you to know that I'm sorry for what happened between us in Madrid. I'm sorry for what I said, and I want you to know that—"

He cut her off with a finger to her lips. "Don't even think about it now. Besides, you were right."

A gust of wind rose, tugging at her hair. There was also a rattle of blown paper, and something snapping back and forth on the rooftop.

"I'm going to get you out of here," he whispered. And when she did not respond: "Margaretha, do you understand? I'm going to get you out of here."

She let her eyes close. "I appreciate what you're trying to do, Nicky, but I think maybe you should stay away from it. I think maybe there's no point in letting them shoot us both."

He reached for her hand through the bars, lacing his fingers through hers. "Margaretha, listen to me. They're not going to shoot you. They lied about the evidence and I can prove it."

She seemed to be smiling. Her eyes were still closed, but her lips seemed to be parted in a faint smile. "I love you, Nicky. I always have, but I don't think I really knew it, or accepted it, until right now."

"Margaretha, please. The telegrams were—"

"And I know you love me too, but I'm afraid we simply don't have much luck together."

It went on like that for a little while longer . . . a few more disconnected sentences, a few more dreadful moments of silence as they clung to one another through the gate. When he tried to tell her that she mustn't lose hope, she merely shut her eyes again and smiled. When he tried to explain about the telegrams again, she shook her head and said that he shouldn't make himself a target, too.

Then their time was up—fifteen minutes past the hour, and the guard had finished his cigarette. As she moved away, she mumbled something else about that Spanish monastery—a last try at a private joke. She was trying to make *him* feel better? Or was it that she clung to the hope that in the end they would not condemn her? As she vanished down the rear staircase, it occurred to him that he had actually brought her nothing except promises—not chocolate, not orchids, not even another bloody drawing.

The night collapsed rapidly after that; first with three or four drinks in cafes that had lost their appeal, then with Southerland in a cheap hotel not far from the prison at Saint-Lazare. It was nearly midnight, always one of Zelle's better hours. The streets were still wet from an hour of rain, and, Gray thought, she might have been part of the reflection in every pool of water below . . .

"Nicky . . . I think I have found our witness," Southerland had said when Gray had met him earlier. "Used to be one of my people, but Dunbar has him working with his coding team now."

Then, in a taxi before the rain had stopped: "He's convinced that someone fiddled with those Mata Hari cables, possibly inserted at least three forgeries into the sequence. And he's willing to talk to us. That much is certain . . ."

Except that once they had reached the hotel room, nothing seemed very certain. The room had been done in shades of brown: a frayed carpet, a table with a peeling varnish, tattered curtains, and the ruins of wallpaper—all brown to one degree or another.

"I took it just for the occasion." Southerland smiled. He struck Gray as inordinately apologetic.

There was whisky and three glasses. After a long silence Southerland poured two and handed one to Gray.

"When does he arrive?" Gray asked impatiently.

"Soon . . ."

"And you said that you knew him before?"

Southerland nodded.

"What's his name?"

A slight hesitation. ". . . Piper. His name is Piper."

"And why is he doing it?"

"Mmm?" Southerland shrugged. "Well . . . it could be he believes
that Charlie is about to be exposed and he doesn't want to fall with
him."

"Is that what he told you?"

"Well, yes. More or less . . ."

The eyes and the voice now seemed as equivocal as the words.
Gray had moved to the windows—classic French windows that led
to a balcony and a fire escape. The street below was black, and led
nowhere except to the mouth of an alley.

Finally, without turning around: "What in bloody hell is going
on, Martin?" No answer. "What's going *on?* Who are we really
waiting for?"

"Nicky, I want you to know that I honestly did make inquiries.
I honestly tried—"

"Who?"

Southerland wet his lips, glancing from a chair to the floor to a
lamp on the table—an ugly porcelain thing with a flowered shade.

"It's just that it's all much bigger than we thought. It's not only
Dunbar any more. It's the whole Fourth Floor. They all want her
now . . . and I simply wasn't in a position to oppose them. Nor are
you, Nicky."

"Which means exactly what, Martin?"

"Which means that Zelle has become a political entity—everybody's favorite spy. Everybody who counts, that is."

Gray turned, putting down his glass. "I see. Then who are we
waiting for?"

"Nicky, please try to understand, they just want to talk to you—"

"*Who?*"

The Last Year

Gray heard them before he saw them, at least a dozen footsteps on the steps below, then the sound of revolvers being cocked. Southerland had also drawn a pistol, but hardly had a chance to cock it before Gray was on him.

He went for Southerland's wrist, jamming it back until the pistol fell . . . then farther until the bone snapped. Southerland sank to his knees, screaming, and Gray brought his elbow across the man's jaw. But there wasn't time to kill him, not even time to drive a heel into his ribcage before the door burst open.

There were five: four French officers and an Englishman in a bowler and overcoat. Gray heard the first shot as he slipped over the railing to the fire escape, then another as he landed on the pavement. He didn't feel it, however, until he reached the mouth of that alley. Then it was like the impact of a club, or scalding water against his back.

A flesh wound, he told himself. Keep moving, just a flesh wound. He got up, stumbling for the deeper blackness between the tenements. He knew he could never outdistance them, not with a bullet in the shoulder. His only hope was the sniper's solution—to lie silent and motionless in the shadows.

In all, he waited an hour before they gave up searching for him, a full hour bleeding beneath a tenement staircase. There were rats, but not nearly as aggressive as those monsters in the trenches. He also took a little comfort from the fact that he knew the terrain.

Chapter Thirty-Two

THE room was large and bare with yellowing plaster and a skylight. The bed had been placed by the stove, a faulty leg secured with bricks. There was a window that provided only a restricted view of the cobbled street. There were several sketches along the wall but nothing recognizable.

From Gray's first moments here he had the thought that it had all begun in a room just like this: a narrow mattress beside a wrought-iron stove, bare floorboards, and rainclouds through a skylight. Even the weather seemed the same—a late winter chill well into May.

His Good Samaritan was an aging model he'd once used and befriended, Marie Leclerc. She'd never much cared for Zelle, but she'd never forgotten Gray's kindnesses. A physician was summoned. The bullet was found embedded in the bone. Then followed eight more days fighting infection and fever. A small quantity of morphine had been left for the physical pain, but there was nothing anyone could do about the danger.

And that was it—an empty room, a bed by the stove, rows of bloody bandages on a table. After ten days he finally was able to sit, but still not to walk. After another week he could walk, but only as far as the window. More than once an unexpected knock at the door had sent him into the closet to crouch behind old clothes, forgotten canvases and boxes of yellowing letters. Twice he reopened his wound reaching for objects on the nightstand.

He had been bedridden about three weeks when Vadime de Massloff showed up—more or less like the shaggy dog he had always been—apparently in response to a letter from Marie Leclerc. He arrived in the rain with a black patch over his left eye—another souvenir from Verdun. Gray had been dozing, still weak with a fever. The rain, the physical surroundings were all reminiscent of their first days together.

"How are you, Nicky?"

Gray managed a smile, but the rest remained immobile: the numb left arm, the tired right, the infected shoulder.

"I heard about her," de Massloff said.

Gray nodded. "Yes, I imagine everyone's heard by now."

"And I'm sorry, Nicky. I'm honestly sorry, but I hardly think—"

"She's innocent, Vadime. She's innocent and I can prove it."

De Massloff got up from the chair opposite the bed, searching for something to use as an ashtray. There were still traces of blood on the floor, still odors of sulphur and disinfectant.

"You didn't ask what happened to my eye," he said at last.

Gray took a deep breath. "All right, Vadime, what happened to your eye?"

De Massloff shrugged. "Gas. And I didn't even see a bloody German. Didn't even get a photograph." Then, suddenly turning: "Nicky, listen to me. You can't go on like this. They've already begun searching the quarter for you, and if nothing else you should be in a hospital."

Gray simply continued watching from the bed, his eyes following every movement, restless fingers toying with a bottle cap. "You were never particularly fond of her, were you?"

"Nicky, for Godsakes."

"Not that I blame you . . . she's not the sort of woman one can

appreciate merely as a friend. Maybe if you had slept with her
. . . or spent a few days—"

"Nicky, stop it."

Marie Leclerc appeared briefly in the doorway, exchanged glances
with de Massloff, then left. Soon there were sounds of boiling
water, presumably to sterilize another dressing.

"The trial is to be held next week," de Massloff finally said.
"They say that she's got a very good attorney. Name is Clunet."

Gray lightly touched his fingers to his shoulder. At least the blood
was dry. "The trial will be a joke, Vadime."

"But you can't know that. You can't possibly know that." Then,
glancing at Gray's shoulder: "Besides, there certainly doesn't seem
to be much you can do at the moment anyway."

As soon as Gray was able, he
moved to more secure lodgings that de Massloff had found through
friends. It lay on the edge of the city—another narrow room above
a tiny garden court. Most of his time was spent compiling a detailed
account of his findings about those telegrams. When he was finished
there were more than fifty pages—handwritten on sheets of white
foolscap, secured with tape torn from a bandage. In better moments
he imagined delivering these pages to one of Zelle's more influential
friends, possibly Jules Cambon or even the duke of Cumberland.
Then again, he also could see them lying beneath the floorboards
until discovered by some future tenant years after her death. He
tried to put that last thought out of his mind.

Chapter Thirty-Three

THE trial of Mata Hari began on the afternoon of July 24, 1917. The evening before she had been transferred from Saint-Lazare to the depot at the Conciergérie adjacent to the Palace of Justice. Here, after bathing and washing her hair, she was permitted to select a dress for the following day. She chose blue.

It was a warm day, sticky and warm in those sealed chambers. Edouard Clunet, Zelle's seventy-four-year-old attorney, was particularly affected, and actually suffered from heart palpitations. There were also complaints from the jury. Eventually an hour or two of rain would bring a little relief, but in the beginning it was very hot.

She had roughly three solitary hours before the trial, and she spent them dressing slowly in the corner of her cell, brushing her hair while seated on the edge of the cot, then trying to rest. Although she had been denied mascara, one of the attendants had brought her a little rouge. She had also been given pins for her hair, and the dress had been pressed.

After dressing she was led to another sealed room adjacent to the court. Here she was given coffee and a slice of buttered bread. After another half hour her attorney entered—the distinguished Clunet, a gaunt white figure in striped trousers. There were rumors that he had been a secret lover—of course he hadn't—but in fact they were simply friends. On entering the room he took her hand, pushed away the remains of her breakfast, and sat down. His upper lip was already beaded with perspiration, his face flushed.

"How are you feeling?" he asked.

She managed a weak smile. "Better than I thought I would."

"Well, you look absolutely marvelous."

She smiled again. "Is that to our advantage?"

"Oh, I think so. You see, the jury is entirely composed of soldiers."

A woman appeared briefly in the doorway. There were also footsteps from the corridor, and someone was complaining about the heat.

"I imagine they'll begin with the obvious questions," he told her. "The point is to remain calm, and try to answer without hesitating."

"What if I can't answer at all?"

"Don't worry. Just tell the truth. And look beautiful."

The woman appeared again, exchanging another glance with Clunet. Moments later a young uniformed clerk came in. Apparently it was time. "Yes," Clunet said quietly, "I think they're ready now."

For a moment she couldn't seem to move, except to slide a hand across the table to his. "Are we afraid, Edouard?"

The presiding judge was fifty-four year old Lieutenant Colonel Albert Ernest Somprou of the Republican Guard. The seven-member jury had been chosen from the Third Permanent Council of War. The prosecuting attorney was the skeletal Jean Mornet (who would eventually serve as Marshal Pétain's prosecutor following the next war). They had all more or less assembled by the time the prisoner entered, some speaking softly among themselves, others merely watching.

She entered slowly, a step behind Clunet. Her arms hung loosely at her side, her eyes remained fixed on the floor. In dreams she had imagined a larger room in marble, not these cloistered chambers with a single row of windows on the northern wall. She had also imagined a younger jury, and a gallery filled with friends from the better salons. It was also much warmer than she had expected.

It began with a series of innocent questions, just as Clunet had predicted. Her inquisitor was the lean Mornet, whose style reminded her of Bouchardon. He tended to speak very slowly while pacing back and forth. His eyes, too, seemed in motion except when meeting hers.

These first questions were broad, plainly intended only to define her character. He asked about her political beliefs and why she had so often been seen in the company of soldiers. Next he asked about her movements since the outbreak of the war, and her apparent fascination with young officers. Then, without changing the pace, he asked about money.

"Tell me, madame, if it is a well-known fact that the Germans generally pay their spies poorly, how do you account for the twenty thousand francs that you collected from Herr Cramer?"

She brushed a stray lock of hair from her eyes, the first of several casual gestures she had actually practiced the evening before. Then, as if the entire subject were beneath her: "Actually I have always been under the impression that Herr Cramer had more in mind than a business relationship."

"Meaning precisely what, madame? That Herr Cramer had hoped the money would cement a romantic relationship?"

"I might have phrased it differently, but essentially that is correct."

"And are you normally in the habit of forming romantic relationships with men who give you money?"

She wanted to smile, but supposed that it might be inappropriate. "No, I wouldn't say that's the only basis—"

"Very well, then why do you suppose that Herr Cramer believed that he could win your affection with twenty thousand francs?"

"I suppose you'll have to ask Herr Cramer that question."

331

"But I am asking you, madame."

"Well, I am afraid I can't help you."

There was a brief respite while Mornet conferred with an associate and Clunet exchanged encouraging glances with his client. Then without warning it started again: questions concerning the prisoner's career as a dancer—and suddenly Mornet had withdrawn those telegrams.

He faced her now from the prosecutor's bench, leaning on his knuckles. It was said that he never touched spirits, not even wine. He also did not smoke and did not eat meat. There was nothing particularly healthy about his eyes, however, and the skin seemed much too tight around the skull.

As before, the initial questions seemed relatively harmless. He wanted to know why she had chosen to stay at the Palace Hotel in Madrid rather than the Ritz. This was followed by a series of questions concerning her financial status, and specifically her lifestyle in Spain.

She answered cautiously, watching him toy with a pencil. "Actually Madrid is a rather inexpensive city," she said. "One can live very well for next to nothing."

"But you hardly lived for nothing, madame. Your accommodations alone totaled fifteen hundred pesetas. And surely there must have been other expenses. Clothing, perhaps? Jewelry?"

She held his gaze for another moment, then glanced to the jury. "A woman is not expected to buy her own jewelry, monsieur."

"Of course, not. "Only to pawn it." Smiles. "Now tell me, madame. How did you manage financially in Madrid?"

"I had previously received money from a friend in Holland."

"The Baron van der Capellen?"

"Yes."

"And this money sustained you from the time you left England until your arrest in Paris?"

"The baron has always been a generous man."

"Then why did you find it necessary to request an additional five thousand francs from the German espionage center in Berlin?"

Her answer satisfied no one. "As I have said before, monsieur, all money received from abroad came only from the baron."

"Except, of course, for the five thousand francs mentioned in this telegram . . . correct?"

"No, monsieur, that is not correct."

"Then how do you account for these telegrams?"

"I do not account for them, sir. I deny them."

"Deny them, madame? How can you deny them? I am holding an exact transcription of the text in my hand at this very moment. How can you possibly deny them? Please, I am certain that the court would be most interested to know . . . how can you possibly deny them?"

And so it went for another thirty to forty minutes: a series of damaging questions about the documents, and answers that were only denials. Through it all she once more found herself compulsively knotting a handkerchief around her fingers.

It was seven o'clock when the court recessed. The anticipated thundershower had passed, and the evening remained hot and windless. After a meal of shredded pork and potatoes, she was again locked in her temporary cell in the depot. A female guard, posted just in sight of the bars, ensured that there would be no suicides.

The cell lay at the end of a long and narrow corridor. There were no windows, and no real ventilation. The light was also bad. On entering, she undressed to a brief slip, then lay down on the cot. At first there were continual voices and echoes from above. Then it gradually grew quiet. By the time that Charles Dunbar appeared, there were virtually no sounds at all.

He must have been watching her sleep for a long time before she awoke. He sat in the guard's chair, facing her through the bars. There was a cigarette between his fingers, and several butts on the floor. There also seemed to be a bottle of whisky or brandy on the ledge. The eyes, too, looked bad with dark circles and dull whites.

"Hello, Margaretha."

She sat up, reaching for something to cover her bare thighs, but the sheets and blankets had vanished. "What do you want, Charles?"

"To talk. After all, it's been a long time."

She clutched her hands to her shoulders as if cold. "Yes, it's been a long time."

"And I don't suppose you've given me much thought, have you?"

She sighed. Her hair was still damp from perspiration, and formed dark ringlets around her face. "No, Charles. I suppose I never gave you much thought. Apparently that was a mistake."

He got up, unlocked the door, and stepped inside. He was a good deal heavier than she remembered, the hands seeming especially fleshy.

"I want you to know that I'm sorry for the way that things turned out. I'm truly sorry, and if there's anything I can do, in a meaningful sense . . ."

She shut her eyes, breathing deeply again. "Thank you, Charles. But I really think you've done enough already."

He lit another cigarette and sat down beside her on the cot. She had drawn her knees up to her chest, her bare thighs and shoulders seeming even more pronounced against this overweight man in his shirtsleeves.

"By the way," he said suddenly, "your painter friend Gray has been causing us no end of trouble, and now it seems he's disappeared. Run off, no doubt, with his artist friends . . ."

She let her head fall to her knees. "Why are you doing this, Charles? Why are you trying to hurt me?"

She heard him exhaling more cigarette smoke, then felt his finger toying with her hair. "I'm not trying to hurt you, Margaretha. I'm simply trying to keep you from hurting others. I think you can understand that."

She wanted to push his hand away, but couldn't seem to lift her arm. It must have been the heat.

"I also want you to know that I'm not personally angry with you," he said. "Actually, I don't believe I could ever be angry with you. Of course, I can't expect you to feel the same way . . . but

perhaps you'll come to see the truth. I do still love you very much."
His hand slid from her hair to the nape of her neck, clinging for a
moment like a crab before she finally was able to remove it.

Now he was running it across his eyes. Possibly he was crying?
Or then again it might just have been the perspiration. After a while
she said, "Nicky was right. You're mad." And, to herself, pathetic,
which was even worse. He did not, however, appear to have heard.

"Well, I should be going now, Margaretha. It was awfully good
talking to you. Perhaps I'll come again before the trial ends."

There was very little left of her
trial now, hardly more than five hours of a sweltering Wednesday.
It began again in the morning with a few remarks from Somprou,
then proceeded with a reading of statements from absent witnesses.
In all, more than half of those called did not appear—some actually
restrained, most simply unwilling to become involved. Of those
who remained there were only a manicurist, a fortune-teller, and a
casual lover from better days.

The closing statements began immediately following the noon
recess: first Mornet with a tidy and predictable summary of the
government's case, then the defense with an elegant but slightly
garbled plea for acquittal. Put aside the prejudice of the day, Clunet
admonished the jury; examine only what has been said, not what
has been implied. Remember that one life is no less meaningful than
a hundred lives, and that if we condemn an innocent then ultimately we are all condemned. Through all this she remained largely
stiff, with her eyes fixed on any empty frame that had once enclosed
a picture of Christ.

There were approximately forty-five minutes between these closing statements and the verdict, and once more she spent the time
alone in a room at the top of the staircase. There were two oval
windows here, providing a rather stunning view of the city. The sky
was white, except to the north, where the last of the rainclouds lay.
The only immediate sound was from a solitary typewriter.

She remained quite still, with both hands pressed against the bars.

Then it seemed that she had to sit; even if it meant withdrawing from the window, and the fine view, she had to sit down. In an earlier fantasy, she had seen this moment as becoming intensely meaningful, with some sort of last-minute revelation and a sense of peace. She would have settled for a little mascara and a glass of white wine to help her face the jury.

It was four o'clock in the afternoon when they led her back to the courtroom. The temperature was eighty-two degrees Fahrenheit with no relief in sight. The earlier rain had hardly dampened the streets, and the subsequent humidity had left everyone drained. The prisoner, observers were later to say, appeared listless. Her attorney was drenched in perspiration. Even the court clerk had difficulty rising to the occasion as he read the verdict: death.

Chapter Thirty-Four

THERE were three sweltering days after the trial, then—following an odd wind and distant thunder—more rain. Gray had been on a narrow bed, examining his shoulder. At the sound of the rain he put on his shirt and moved to the balcony. Then, although no one had specifically told him, he knew. He knew.

De Massloff came at about four o'clock, and once again Gray first saw his friend from a distance, at least fifty yards along the lane. In spite of the rain, the man was walking very slowly. His good eye was fixed on the pavement. He did not even attempt to avoid the puddles.

They met on a small terrace above the garden. There were azaleas here, and classic long-stemmed roses. There was also, of course, a clear-cut sense of Zelle.

"They say that there's still a very good chance for an appeal," de Massloff was saying. "And of course one can't rule out the possibility of a pardon."

Gray had still not been able to light a cigarette or even move his arm. "Why don't you just say it, Vadime."

"Nicky, listen. There are always options in situations like this. Dutch intercession. A presidential review—"

"Just *say* it, Vadime. They're going to kill her . . ."

His friend's silence was loud confirmation. He got up from his chair and moved to the edge of the terrace. After another moment he began to work the shoulder, began to work it up and down, back and forth. It was still stiff but he could handle the pain.

"Where is she?"

"Nicky, don't do it."

"Where?"

"Saint-Lazare. Nicky, for Christsakes listen to me—"

"And where's Dunbar?"

"Nicky, please."

"Where?"

"Fourth floor at the Continental. Nicky, don't do this."

Gray turned and looked at him, watching that good eye as it shut to avoid the issue. "I'm not asking you to help. I just don't want you to try and stop me."

"Nicky, if you could only see yourself for a moment, just one moment—"

"I will, however, need that revolver you're carrying. And a few rounds of ammunition."

"Nicky, how can you possibly think that she's worth this? How can you possibly think that anyone is worth this?"

Gray began working the shoulder again—up and down, back and forth. "You never did like her much, did you Vadime? I mean you never *really* liked her, did you?"

Again, his friend's silence was loud confirmation.

Gray left just after dark, moving on foot through the back streets, de Massloff's revolver in the waistband of his trousers. A warm breeze had temporarily replaced the rain, filling the air with the familiar scents of charcoal and refuse, vegetables and oil, damp leaves from surrounding gardens.

After the first mile on foot he realized that his shoulder was hurting again, so he sat for a while until the pain subsided. Then he pushed on, because, after all, she had been waiting a long time too. There were military caravans everywhere, but only the boulevards were still alive. There were a number of prostitutes along the side streets, but no one perfect enough to kill for.

It was close on to ten when he reached the Continental. The doorman had retired and the night clerk seemed half asleep. Like all of Dunbar's favorite hotels, the ambiance was definitely English. There were odors of boiled meat and bay rum, potted rubber plants in the tearoom. There was even a portrait of the King—who according to some had also once made love to Zelle.

As de Massloff had said, Dunbar's room was on the fourth floor —his precious *fourth floor*. Earlier Gray had worried that he might not be in, but now it seemed that he could even sense him from the stairwell: brooding by lamplight with a bottle of gin and one more Mata Hari photograph. "Charles is actually a wonderfully emotional and complex man," she had told him not long after they had met. How would she describe him now?

The last corridor was silent and empty. There were also no sounds from neighboring rooms, and not even the whine of elevators. As Gray approached the door he withdrew the revolver, removed his coat, and laid it beside him on the carpet. He had already decided that if Charles demanded to know who was knocking, he would answer in slurred French: *télégramme*—it seemed cruelly appropriate.

Dunbar responded to Gray's knock without speaking, drawing back the door like any gentleman with nothing to fear. Gray hit him twice as he lunged inside; first in the mouth with the muzzle of the revolver, then with a knee to the groin.

Dunbar stayed on the floor for several minutes. His hands were clamped to his testicles, and there was a fair amount of blood from his mouth. Gray had locked the door, drawn the shades, poured himself a glass of gin. The leg of a table had been shattered, and the carpet was littered with papers: letters on beige stationery with his majesty's crest, typewritten sheets of onionskin, handwritten notes on yellow foolscap, and a dozen photographs of Zelle.

The photographs were old, from her first tour abroad. Gray could see that Dunbar had scribbled something on the back of one but could not make it out.

"You never actually saw an early performance, did you?" Gray said.

Dunbar's eyes kept following him across the room. "I won't be able to protect you, Nicky, not after this."

"Personally I've always felt she was better in those days. Not as technically accomplished perhaps but wonderfully spontaneous."

"I'm warning you. There are going to be very serious repercussions—"

"You really should have seen her perform at the Olympia, Charles. Believe me, she danced spectacularly that evening."

"Look, Nicky, I don't want to see you hurt . . ."

Gray crossed the room and swung the heel of his shoe into the base of Dunbar's spine. "I don't want to see you get hurt either, Charlie."

Dunbar's eyes remained open. Traces of vomit had mixed with the blood on the carpet.

"I don't know what you expected to gain from this but you can't possibly—"

"Oh shut up."

He poured a second glass of gin and placed it on the window ledge alongside Dunbar's head.

"Tell me about her, Charles. How's she holding up in there?"

"It isn't too late to stop this, Nicky. I can still look the other way."

There was a fountain pen on the writing desk. Gray picked it up and tossed it at Dunbar's chest. "Here, draw us a little diagram. I want to know where her cell is. Exactly where it is."

"Nicky, this is starting to become—"

"And show me where the guards are posted. We'll need to know that, won't we?"

"Nicky, for Godsakes. What can you hope to accomplish?"

Then, yanking the telephone from the wall: "It's like this, Charlie. You put her in there, and now you're going to get her out."

It was a slow two miles from the Continental to Saint-Lazare, even slower if one avoided the boulevards. Then too, Dunbar drove badly, stalling twice on the rue de Caire and once more below the Ménagérie. It was also raining again.

Dunbar was to stop the car at the edge of the prison walls, Gray said. From there they would walk to the main gate. Once they met the guards he was to identify himself and demand to see the prisoner. A wrong word or gesture would end his life.

"Nicky, let me just say one thing."

"As soon as she's out of there, we'll walk back to the car. Do you understand?"

"Look, I don't even have the authority to do this."

Gray laid the revolver's muzzle against Dunbar ribs. "Then you had better get the authority."

The rain had subsided to a drizzle by the time they were in sight of the prison walls. As they stepped out of the car Gray put his raincoat over his arm to conceal the revolver, then moved to Dunbar's side and they continued on foot toward the main gates.

The approach to the gate was long and narrow, a cobbled stretch of road between the high walls. Except for the gatehouse and the towers above, nothing was lighted. As Gray moved to Dunbar's side he again shifted the revolver to Dunbar's ribcage, proding him forward. It was quiet again, with only the sound of their heels on the cobbles, and possibly her heartbeat synchronizing with his step . . .

He supposed that this was the war that he had always been fighting: this concrete in no-man's-land, this slow walk to the enemy trench, this borrowed revolver and ridiculous yet vicious hostage. If the tactics were a bit unorthodox, it was only because the odds were so outrageous—an army of one against the world. Their world.

He walked a little stiffly because his shoulder had begun to hurt again, keeping his eyes fixed on the gate ahead, which was the first objective. He kept the revolver leveled at Dunbar's ribs—that was the form. He tried to keep himself from thinking about Margaretha. At sixty feet he was able to make out the first guards: two wavering figures against the tower. Still closer, a third and a fourth appeared by the gatehouse. Although suspicious, they could hardly have a clue to what this was was all about . . . All lovers are at war with the world, she had once smilingly said to him, but of course never realized the truth of it until now—clinging to the bars of her cell, tapping a finger in time with his footsteps. Yes, he thought, she definitely senses that I'm close . . .

The last fifty feet were particularly dark, with meshed shadows from the walls to the towers and only a hint of light from the streets. Still, it seemed that he could hear her now, actually whispering his name. *Nic-ky.* And again, like the sound of a shutting door or even a cocking rifle . . . *Nic-ky, Nic-ky* . . .

He turned, glancing back at tributary streets, then to the walls above. Although there was nothing apparently wrong, she was obviously trying to tell him something . . . *Nic-ky.* Even Dunbar must have heard it now, also hesitating as she continued . . . *Nic-ky*— exactly like the gentle click of a cartridge slipping into a chamber.

A rush of impressions came to mind before he actually saw the soldiers: the rifles were French judging from the sound of the sliding bolts, the officers were only waiting for Dunbar to stand clear before giving the order to fire, de Massloff would have never betrayed him if only he'd taken the time to get to know her . . .

He became aware of the voices, English and French, Vadime shouting from close by: "Don't shoot. For Godsakes don't shoot him."

And then came the lights, long arc-lights converging on him from the towers, defining every cobblestone.

He heard Dunbar shouting something in his ear and tried to club him across the mouth, but the man had already dropped to the cobbles.

Shots—two, maybe three rounds at his feet, and a fourth to his left thigh. But he didn't go down, not with Zelle so close. He simply stumbled, glaring around him like a wounded bull, then slowly continued walking.

They seemed to hesitate before firing again. Someone had even shouted an order, but still nothing . . . then another weak step forward, and then a last shot to stop him.

He lay very still now, conscious of the moisture seeping through his clothing, the dull pain spreading from his legs. Although there seemed to be a lot of blood, he supposed that it wasn't really all that bad—more the sort of wound that one prayed for at the front. After a while he heard their footsteps approaching—at least a dozen of her jealous lovers . . . Dunbar, Michard, Spangler . . . united at last to keep him from taking her away.

And their spokesman, his old friend, de Massloff . . . "Christ, Nicky. Christ, I swear I never meant this—"

"Why did you tell them, Vadime?" As if the answer weren't written in that eye of his.

"Nicky, you've got to understand, I was concerned. I didn't have a choice—"

"Why?" As if it wasn't written in all their eyes.

"Because, damn it, she's just not worth it."

He refused to listen, as he always had.

After that he only saw her from distances. He spent four days in a sealed ward; then they brought him to a clinic on the edge of Taverny—one more white room with barred windows. There, amid regular doses of morphine and a series of medical complications, she mostly appeared in dreams. Some were quite vivid, others prosaic . . . the sort of passing visions that had haunted him for years. Best of all, though, was the one of her in the night sky, pulling him up to her a thousand feet above the city she loved.

Chapter Thirty-Five

THERE were two small ventilation slits cut into Margaretha's cell, two rectangular
vents just below the ceiling. Although it was possible to peer out
of these slits, the view was severely restricted. She could see a slice
of the sky and a portion of the marshaling yard . . . but certainly
she could not have been able to see Gray.

Still, on hearing those shots, she lapsed into a despair from which
no one could recall her. The devoted Sister Leonide spent more than
three hours trying, but Zelle would not say what was troubling her.
The physician Bizard was called in, but he, too, failed. Then, as
suddenly as it had begun, the weeping stopped, and she grew quiet
again, and although she stayed a little distant through the days that
followed, it seemed that she had definitely found some peace to
sustain her.

It is tempting to imagine Mar-
garetha Zelle with Nicholas Gray locked in some psychic embrace,

344

but perhaps it is best to say goodbye and to stop pretending that we can listen to her thoughts. Bizard has left us with enough in his memoirs to give us a feel of her last weeks. There are also statements from Sister Leonide, and the record of her attorney's attempt to save her.

It appears that hope sustained her through these last days—hope and a poignant . . . perverse? . . . belief in French justice. Correspondence helped keep her busy: petitions for a pardon, pleas for Dutch intervention. She also spent a good deal of time with the Scriptures, and chatting with the attendant Sisters of Mercy. Although her health remained stable, she did continue to suffer from insomnia and spells of nausea. Her spirits, though, did not seem to decline, and several witnesses would later recall that she actually laughed on occasion. In response to Sister Leonide's curiosity about the kind of dances she used to perform, Zelle even managed a few innocent steps . . . which over the years, in various accounts, became nude ballet.

After three weeks of rejected appeals and ignored petitions, they entered her cell on a Monday morning. She was sleeping. Bizard had given her a double dose of chloral, and Sister Leonide had to shake her awake. She rose to her elbows, and her eyes moved slowly past the kneeling sister to the faces of the four convening officers: Bouchardon, Albert Somprou, Dr. Soquet, and an Emile Massard of the Parisian Military Authority. It was at this point that she was heard to whisper, "But it's impossible . . . impossible . . ."

They left her with Sister Leonide to dress, but for several minutes she simply remained seated on the edge of the cot. It was still quite cold, and the light was feeble. Finally the sister laid a hand on her shoulder and whispered, "I think it's time now."

Zelle shook her head and smiled. "Don't worry, sister. I can't imagine that they'll start without me."

She was given a choice of two dresses, and first held up a simple one in white. "What do you think? Too sacrificial?"

345

But by now the sister was on the edge of tears and could not respond.

"Yes, much too sacrificial," and she chose the pearl-gray with a blue cloak, straw hat, and veil.

She grew silent again while dressing, grateful to the sister for the hand mirror propped against the wall. Her public expected due attention to the details: hair, makeup, jewelry. Unfortunately they still hadn't brought her mascara.

There were approximately seven minutes between the time that she finished dressing and her descent to the main floor. Bizard had returned with a colleague for an obligatory formality—an official declaration that she was not pregnant. Meanwhile a few young Republican Guards had assembled to control the crowd below. The temperature remained at thirty-five degrees Fahrenheit, with a mist all about.

From the cell she was escorted to a first floor office known as the Pont d'Avignon. It was here that she left the custody of Saint-Lazare and officially became a military concern. It was also here that three last letters were written and later passed to her attorney. There were no last embraces, and only Sister Leonide had begun to cry.

Seven vehicles waited in the rain-swept courtyard below, including the prisoner's black Renault. The Reverend Arboux had already settled into the back seat, while Sister Leonide waited on the curb. Although the streets were still deserted except for predawn delivery vans, one still couldn't help imagining hundreds of eyes peering from darkened windows.

She was silent for the first few miles, eyes straight ahead. The trees had been shedding their leaves for at least ten days, gradually exposing more and more of her city. Even from the rim of Vincennes she was able to see the crowd—more than a hundred who had come to watch her die.

"Who are they?" she asked. "What do they want?"

No one responded, and Reverend Arboux continued reading from his Bible.

The Last Year

There were also spectators lining the road from the château gates, and still more along the rim of the polygone. But if she had hoped to see a familiar face, she was to be disappointed. None of those responsible was waiting: not Georges Ladoux, not Bouchardon, not even Charles Dunbar. For the most part there were only curiosity seekers, and those journalists who had always followed her trail.

The motorcade stopped at the edge of the field. A Captain Thibaud and a Captain Robillard approached first, but the Reverend insisted on finishing the Twenty-third Psalm before allowing them to take her. The wooden stake—six feet high and ten inches around—had been erected on a grassy rise below the poplars. The two rows of twelve riflemen had assembled at twenty paces. Still clutching Sister Leonide's hand, Zelle hesitated only a moment before stepping onto the field. No one spoke as she walked to the stake.

There were only minutes left now, scarcely time for the traditional ration of rum or a formal reading of the sentence. Sister Leonide and the Reverend Arboux had already left the field. Two attending officers secured her to the stake. A third withdrew his sword. Then, despite the overall quality of French marksmanship, only four bullets actually struck her—one in the left shoulder, one below the right breast, and two more in the heart.

Montserrat

THOSE in search of the site where Margaretha Zelle is buried are usually directed to an unmarked grave at Père Lachaise in Paris. In fact, her body was taken to the dissecting room of a local municipal hospital. The remains were apparently burned, and there is no record of what happened to the ashes.

Still, there was an aftermath. There was a last letter to her daughter, and a brief note of thanks to her attorney. A later rumor would have it that she even wrote to Rudolph Spangler, but in fact she remembered none of her former lovers except for Nicholas Gray.

The letter reached him about one month after the execution, delivered by a circuitous route to the hospital in Taverny. It arrived on a Wednesday, and by the following Tuesday Gray had slipped over the walls and disappeared.

At first there were a few half-hearted attempts to find him, and the British expressed a passing interest in reports that he had gone to Spain. It was not until years later, however, that journalists began to search for him on the heights of Montserrat.

There were nearly as many rumors about Nicholas Gray as there were about Mata Hari. Some claimed that he finally went mad with grief, while others said that the grief turned to rage and he died attempting to kill Charles Dunbar in London. Only rumors.

But what of those rumors of Zelle?

All through the 1920s and 1930s there were those who claimed that she had somehow survived to join her English painter on a windswept Spanish plateau. A few even claimed to have seen her dance in some nameless Castilian cafe.

Finally, it seems that there is little we can really know for certain: except that if one man honestly loved her, then she probably lived forever.

Author's Afterword

The Man Who Loved Mata Hari is fiction extending from a core of truth. Mata Hari was, of course, executed at dawn, on October 15, 1917, for crimes against France. The remains were lost in a municipal dissecting room, and her personal effects were sold in order to cover the court costs. More importantly, however, the whole affair did in fact rest upon a handful of telegrams, which the author firmly believes were forged.

In short, Nicholas Gray's revelations concerning those telegrams are correct: the dates were wrong. That is, the woman was convicted on the basis of a cable that could not have been written simply because it described an event that did not take place until after it was sent. There were other subtler discrepancies involving money, and no case officer would ever include—then or now—such a detailed description of an agent in a message of this kind.

Also essentially accurate are the portrayals of Georges Ladoux, Bouchardon, Cramer, Sir Basil Thomson, and most of the other "minor" characters. There was a man named Vadime de Massloff, though his betrayal of Zelle was less obvious.

On the whole the greatest departures from fact involve the basic plot-line. Charles Dunbar, Martin Southerland, and Rudolph Spangler were invented. I believe, though, that a man like Dunbar may very well have existed, but his story is pure fiction. The dancer's early involvement with Rolland Michard is likewise a fiction, as are the events that took place at Fontainebleau.

And finally—as much as I hate to admit it—there was, to my knowledge, no man who ever loved her quite so selflessly as the painter Nicholas Gray.

—D.S.

Montreal, 1985